He started along the wharf. A newly arrived woman caught his eye, for she seemed more hesitant than the others who disembarked with her. Even from a distance he could see that she bore herself with inborn grace. Her slim body was encased in a simple black dress, her net coif and veil neatly in place. She had the delicadeza of high nobility, yet no servants hovered around her as they would around a lady of rank. She stood at the edge of a bulkhead and gazed around the area, seeming to focus on the crudely ostentatious viceroy's mansion and the squat town church. Lifting a hand, she drew the veiled coif from her head.

Armando stopped dead in his tracks, momentarily dazzled by the sunlight glinting off her glossy curls, and by the shock of recognition. Then he was moving—running—calling her name, brushing past faceless strangers as he made his way to her.

"Gabriella!"

She turned and spied him. Her smile brought back every bittersweet moment of love he had ever felt for her. She came into his arms. Her feet flew out as he spun her around. Joy felt like a sickness, a fever that made him giddy.

Then he was kissing her, hard and fervently, filling his senses with flavors and scents and textures that were uniquely hers. He had forgotten—or perhaps had never appreciated—how soft and womanly she was, how full her breasts were.

After an endless moment, she pulled back.

"Gabriella!" he shouted. "Christ Jesus, it's a miracle!"

Tor Books by Susan Wiggs

October Wind
Jewel of the Sea

JEWEL OF THE SEA

SUSAN WIGGS

TOR

A TOM DOHERTY ASSOCIATES BOOK
NEW YORK

This is a work of fiction. All the characters and events portrayed in this book are fictitious, and any resemblance to real people or events is purely coincidental.

JEWEL OF THE SEA

Copyright © 1993 by Susan Wiggs

Cover art by George Bush

A Tor Book
Published by Tom Doherty Associates, Inc.
175 Fifth Avenue
New York, N.Y. 10010

Tor ® is a registered trademark of Tom Doherty Associates, Inc.

ISBN: 0-812-52160-9

First edition: April 1993

Printed in the United States of America

0 9 8 7 6 5 4 3 2 1

DEDICATION

In memory of Lucy, who was my friend.

ACKNOWLEDGMENTS

Heartfelt thanks to fellow writers Joyce Bell, Arnette Lamb, Barbara Dawson Smith, and Alice Borchardt; to my favorite librarians Pat Jones, Suzanne Rickles, and Pat Lester of the Houston Public Library, and to the Friends of Fondren Library, Rice University.

Special thanks to Marie Orozco for her proofreading skills, and all the Spanish words, and to the world's best computer jockey, Roger Bell.

HISTORICAL NOTE

The first battles for freedom on this continent were fought by the natives of Florida. History leaves no definitive evidence of an alliance between the Calusa tribe of Florida and the Tainos of the Caribbean. However, the tribes of Florida made such a fierce and effective stand against the conquistadors that some experts suspect that the Florida natives must have been warned by, prepared by, and possibly allied with itinerant Caribbean tribes.

Catherine of Aragon's companion, Doña Elvira Manuel, was actually banished from England in 1505, somewhat earlier than the event occurs in this story.

Although best known for his voyages in the service of England, Sebastian Cabot did indeed visit the West Indies. Records show he was in the service of King Ferdinand and attained the post of pilot major under Ferdinand's grandson, Emperor Charles V.

The mysterious green pool with its magical properties has never been rediscovered.

PROLOGUE

Cayo Moa
February 1505

The stranger came ashore, stumbled onto the sand, and fell before the horrified dwellers of the cay. One of his hands had been severed, the wrist bound with cotton cloth and rope. His flesh was torn and punctured by the teeth of dogs.

"They're coming," he gasped out. The color drained from his face and lips. The clan rushed to gather round the dying youth. He was a native of the islands; he had spoken in the Arawak tongue. The people stood in stunned silence and watched the boy breathe his last.

"They're coming," someone repeated, and no one questioned the words, for the meaning rang clear to the dwellers of the cay. The bearded conquerors. The slave hunters. The murderers of children. The rumors had started quietly, like the first mild rains of autumn. Now, with the dead island youth, the storm had arrived.

A sound of pain keened from the throat of a tall, thin man. Whiteness streaked his long hair and beard, and an air of melancholy hung over him. His name was Joseph, and he was not born of the blood of the clan. He was a Spaniard.

The dwellers of the cay had renamed him Guahiro—one of us—and respected him as the mate of the powerful medicine woman, Anacaona. Many rains ago, he had come across the great water with the conquerors. But he himself bore the scars of torture meted out by the Spaniards; now his loyalty belonged to the clan.

Anacaona took his hand. "We're not safe here anymore. We must leave as soon as we bury this child."

Heads nodded in grim accord. In the manner of the ancients, the grieving clan laid the youth to rest, placing cassava bread and sweet water at the head of the grave. Anacaona stepped forward to sing up the boy's spirit. Her voice had the sharp edge of sadness mixed with good magic. Rattling snail shells on strings, the people brushed their hands on the ground and then lifted them to the sky to ask the four brother gods to bring the spirit of the unknown youth into the light.

The celebration ended abruptly, for the clan had work to do.

Runners went to scan the coast for the sinister ships of the slave hunters. Children gathered storax wood, which burned hot and fragrant, the flames hardening the tips of spears and arrows. Women teased venom from centipedes for poisoning the arrowheads. Men felled three huge ceiba trees for making dugout canoes.

Joseph rushed into the *bohía* he shared with his family. Lines of strain pulled at his gaunt features.

"Anacaona, where is our daughter? Where is Paloma?"

On the other side of the island, Paloma walked to the water's edge. It had taken her since sunrise to reach this place. She hoped her parents would not scold her for leaving without telling them where she had gone. But the village had lain sleeping, and the promise of a brilliant new day had lured her away from the chores of weaving and baking.

Coral and underwater weeds made the sea sparkle in hues of green and blue and purple. Yellow and pink clusters of *poui* blossoms fringed the beach, and blue tanagers trilled amid the branches.

Cayo Moa had been her home for all of her eleven rains. She had grown tall and strong on its bounteous fruits.

She turned and ran away from the beach and into the forest, her bare feet silent on the pad of fallen leaves, the wind a cool stream over the tiny buds of her breasts. She burst from beneath a canopy of leaves and emerged at the top of a limestone bluff. Carefully she picked her way down to the water, clear as air and fringed by a broad curve of blinding white sand.

There she paused, cocking her head as she heard the snap of a twig trodden underfoot. Her skin prickled. She looked around, fearful that a wild peccary stalked her. But she saw only the green darkness of the forest, moss and vines hanging thick and impenetrable from the *carbana* trees.

She ran down to the water and knifed into the blue depths. Like all her people, she swam fast and strong. Paddling out to the first coral reef, she found a deliciously cool current.

She dove deep, watching the blur of rainbow color as a school of fish flashed past. Beyond the reef, she found a bed of red mussels and wrenched one free. Pushing off from the bottom, she shot to the surface, kicking to keep herself afloat while she took the onyx knife from its strap at her ankle.

She opened the shell, and a sound of triumph burst from her. There, nestled in the flesh of the mussel, lay a pearl as large as a parrot's eye. A prize to add to her amulet of feathers and shells, and the flat silver badge her father had given her long ago. She ate the mussel, then drew the pearl into her mouth and held it there while she swam for shore.

Wind and current had swept her in the direction of the setting sun. She walked ashore at a lonely stretch of beach, humming to herself, feeling the smooth shape of the pearl tucked into her cheek. Her hand stole up to touch the silver ornament hidden among the damp feathers and shells of her amulet. Her finger traced the strange animal depicted on the pendant.

A lion, her father called it. The silver lion of Ribera, with symbols etched beneath it: D-E-O-G-R-A-T-I-A-S. The device was the only token her father had kept from the land of his birth. She considered it her special totem, the only one of its kind among the clan.

A wide track scored the sand from the surf to a fringe of brush and trees. Probably the path of a turtle that had struggled to shore during the night to lay her eggs.

But this track lacked the regular winglike indentations a turtle made with her flippers. Curious, Paloma followed the path and saw where it entered the woods. Close by, she heard the brush of a leaf, and then a hiss: alien, frightening, the sound of a snake about to strike.

She turned to race back to the settlement, far on the other side of the cay.

From out of the darkness came a strong arm, wrapping around her waist and slamming her backward against something hard. Paloma opened her mouth to scream. Only the pearl came out.

"Be still, little pretty," said a quiet voice in her ear.

She froze in terror. Her captor spoke the sharp, rapid Castilian her father had taught her. Men from the sky. In the early days, the people had believed it. But in time, they had seen the strangers bleed and die, fight and conquer with fire and sword. The men came from another world. But not a better world.

The man had a horrible smell of sweat and iron from the strange headpiece he wore. "Here's another one, Panfilio," he called. His breastplate, heated by the sun, burned her back. "A wench this time. A bit young, but prettier than most."

A second Spaniard emerged from the woods. His long sword slapped against his thigh. Like the other, he wore a crested iron helm, a pointed black beard, and a wide smile of delight.

"Excellent, Silvio," he said. "She'll more than replace that young buck who jumped overboard."

Keeping one arm firmly around Paloma, Silvio bent and retrieved the pearl. "Better than that, Panfilio!"

"A pearl diver!" Panfilio regarded Paloma speculatively, his eyes as small and cold as a wild pig's. "D'you think there's time to send her down for more?"

Paloma started to tremble. She had heard rumors of islanders forced to dive for pearls until they drowned.

Silvio tucked the pearl into his belt. "We'd best get back to the ship. Captain Ponce de León will wonder what's keeping us."

Panfilio put his fingers to his lips and emitted a long, high-pitched whistle. Paloma heard a snuffling sound, then a crashing in the underbrush. Out of the woods came a huge, furred creature, its black lips rolled back in a snarl.

Paloma gasped. She had heard of such creatures. Dogs, they were called, or mastiffs or hounds; slave hunters used them to track and torment their prey.

Panfilio snapped an order. The dog sat on its haunches.

"Let's go," said Silvio, yanking Paloma's arm.

How dare they? The thought whispered to her in the hush of the surf on the sand. Her fear burgeoned into rage. *How dare they?*

He pulled at her hair. Paloma dug her feet into the sand. Panfilio dangled a cluster of bells in front of her. "Look, girl,'' he cajoled. "*Chuque, chuque!* Don't you want this?''

Her mind burned with the rebellious anger she had inherited from her father. She kicked sand in his face.

Silvio bellowed with laughter. Panfilio coughed up the sand. "Witch!'' He drew back his hand and struck her. The stinging blow snapped her head to one side.

"Easy now,'' said Silvio, snatching her out of Panfilio's reach. "We can't afford to mark her.'' He swung Paloma up and over his shoulder like a sack of beans.

She screamed, high and shrill. She called for her parents, called for the brother gods' protection. She pounded her fists on the ironclad back. Spitting an oath about the Christ god, Silvio set her on the ground. Apparently forgetting his caution about marking her, he backhanded her cheek. The blow numbed her face briefly, then caught fire with pain. Silvio hooked his arm beneath her chin, squeezing until the screaming stopped.

Moments later Paloma lay, collared in the same manner as the dog, in a ship's boat. She raised her head and looked back. Cayo Moa glittered like a jewel in the sea, distant and unreachable.

The deck of the caravel swarmed with soldiers, Spanish sailing men, and a group of islanders who clung to one another and shrieked in terror. Silvio hobbled Paloma's feet and shoved her toward the women and girls.

Ropes whined through pulleys, and sails snapped taut. The wooden deck moved, and Paloma clung fearfully to the rail. She squeezed her eyes shut, trying to deny what was happening to her.

Father, she thought. Her father was brave and strong. He would rescue her. She opened her eyes to gaze at the island, a hazy rise on the darkening horizon. Unless . . . She forced herself to finish the thought. Unless the invaders had slain her father, her mother, and the rest of the clan.

"Did they take others from Cayo Moa?" Her voice rasped with fear.

A woman pressed her hand to Paloma's bruised cheek. "No, they found nothing but an abandoned village. Most of us were seized from Guayabo."

"Where are they taking us?"

"Some will go to Española to work in the fields and mines. Others"—she shivered—"will go across the big water to the place called Castile."

Paloma clung to the rail to keep from trembling. The iron rings on her ankles chilled her flesh. Being aboard a ship was a horror, yet a wonderment.

A man in gleaming armor and a plumed helm strode up and down the deck. More iron, thought Paloma. Clad in iron, a face like iron. In his iron hand he held a tarred whip, which he slapped rhythmically over his palm. "Bercerillo!" he called.

A mastiff or hound, larger than the first one Paloma had seen, loped across the deck. The dog had powerful jaws, watchful eyes, and muscles that knotted with each stride. A native woman screamed; someone silenced her with a blow.

"Read the Requisition," said the armored man.

"Yes, Captain." With the breeze blowing the hem of his long gown, another man read from a sheet of paper. The Spaniards used symbols to code their words, as if they did not trust their memories to save them. Paloma had seen her father use a turkey quill and berry juice to write codes on bark.

"We shall take you and your wives and your children," the robed man read, "and shall make slaves of them."

The threatening words pricked like cold rain on Paloma's scalp. The thought of never seeing her family again caused the words to blur in her mind.

"We shall take away your goods, and shall do all the harm and damage that we can, as to vassals who do not obey. . . . And those who are present should be witnesses to this Requisition."

The recitation ended, and more Spaniards gathered round to write on the document. The islanders continued to wail and strain at their bonds. Paloma sank to the hard wooden surface of the deck and drew her knees up to her chest.

A movement erupted among the men. A youth leaped over the rail. But no splash sounded. Collared at the neck, the young man choked to death.

"At least he's free," one of the island women muttered.

Paloma watched, dull inside, as the corpse was cut loose and dropped into the sea.

Puffing on a roll of *jouli* leaves, a tall man strode over to the captain. He had beautiful hair, night-dark waves that flowed to his waist. Streaks of pure white showed at the temples. He had sharp, clean features, a full mouth, and snapping black eyes.

"Just a minute, Captain," he said to the leader. "They don't understand the Requisition."

Annoyance scored the captain's brow. "Calm down, Don Santiago. I've followed the letter of the law."

"The damned law is wrong." Flipping his cigar over the side, the man called Santiago addressed the islanders. "Do any of you understand Castilian?"

The natives—all except Paloma—regarded him blankly. She huddled against the rail, too frightened to respond.

The man rubbed his brow in frustration and spoke slowly. "What this means is if you show submission, you will be granted the rights of Spanish subjects. But if you resist, if you fight us, then you are the enemies of Spain and we can enslave you."

In a rapid whisper, Paloma related the speech to the

woman beside her. The woman's eyebrows lifted. "You understand?"

Paloma nodded. "What they ask is wrong."

Captain Ponce de León flung up his bearded chin in contempt. "Save your wind, Santiago. They're treacherous heathens."

"You'd know about treachery, wouldn't you, Juan?"

Juan Ponce de León's nostrils thinned; his voice lashed like a whip. "Shut up, you gypsy bastard. Colón made you a grandee, but I'm in command of this expedition."

Colón. Paloma mouthed the name. Her father had spoken of Cristóbal Colón, the first bearded *cacique* of the islands. They had been friends once, long ago.

"Tell them," the woman beside Paloma said. "Tell them we submit. Tell them to set us free."

Paloma bridled with angry hesitation, her pride battling the idea of bowing down before her captors. Prodded by the woman, she stood. The ship lurched, and she braced herself to keep from stumbling. Silvio eyed her curiously, his hand at the hilt of his sword.

"We submit," she said in the scholarly Castilian her father had taught her. The wailing of the islanders drowned her statement, so she raised her voice. "We submit to Spain and to the Church," she shouted. "We are subjects of—"

Silvio's hand shot out and clubbed her temple. White flashes of agony obliterated her vision. Paloma felt herself sinking, heard the faint hollow echoes of voices.

"Was that wench speaking Castilian?" someone asked.

"No," said Silvio hastily. "Just babbling. They're great mimickers."

We submit . . . Paloma tried to force the words out, but the pain pressed at her head, driving her deeper and deeper into blackness.

CHAPTER 1

Seville, Spain
May 1505

"Stop her! Stop the wench!"

The hoarse cry rang through the crowded river wharves, but was nearly drowned by the hubbub around the fleet newly arrived from the West Indies. The hulls of the battered ships bristled with the long ash sweeps that had propelled them up the river from Sanlucár.

"Stop the wench!" More voices took up the call. A clutch of pikemen in green tabards flurried into motion, their crested helms flashing in the late afternoon sun as they dispersed along the riverfront.

Armando Viscaino de Hernández went to investigate the disturbance. Probably a *ladrona*, he decided, who had picked the wrong pocket. Still, even a common chase held more appeal than an afternoon working as a scribe in the *Casa de Contratacíon*.

Armando's father, *contador* of the *Casa*, had given the youths the afternoon free to witness the off-loading of the fleet.

But the greatest treasure Armando anticipated was not a mask of gold or a cache of pearls. It was a person.

Sweating beneath his cloak, he hurried through the press of women and children who had come to welcome their loved ones home. His gaze followed the progress of pikes as the soldiers fanned out after the unseen thief. Armando passed royal treasury officials come to claim the King's Fifth, shoved aside bawdy women who gathered to entertain the adventurers, slipped by soldiers and clerics craning their necks for a glimpse of the treasures from the paradise Colón had discovered.

"She's getting away!" someone shouted. "Grab the heathen!"

Armando's gaze probed the crowd for the fugitive, but he left off his searching when he spotted the familiar red shirt and black mane of his godfather.

The tall man wore tight leather breeches, cuffed boots, a ring of Indies gold in one ear, and held a cigar between his lips. He had always been Armando's pirate king.

Forever linked with the fabled first voyage, he had left Spain a gypsy outlaw, and returned an envied hero. His easy, rolling gait carried him past women who sighed and threw flowers at his feet. His grin made the carnations seem bland.

"Santiago!" Armando waved his arms above the crowd. His amulet, an agnus dei wrought of Indies gold, slapped against his chest. The ornament had been a gift from his godfather.

In seconds, Santiago appeared, hugging him, placing loud kisses on the youth's cheeks. He smelled of sweat and brine and sunshine. "Look at you, *hombre!*" Santiago held him at arm's length. His black eyes shone with affection. "Christ above, you've grown a full hand since I left."

"I missed you, Santiago! Did you find the passage to the east?" Armando asked.

Quick as heat lightning, humor turned to fury. "We

made no explorations. Juan Ponce de León turned the damned enterprise into a slave hunt.'' He blew out a sigh. ''Queen Isabel's barely cold in her grave, and already we defy her wishes.''

Colón himself had once brought back a shipment of six hundred islanders to sell as slaves. Appalled, Queen Isabel had sent them back, laden with gifts and apologies.

But now she lay entombed at Granada, the city she had reclaimed from the Moors. And her husband Ferdinand, less scrupulous, less intelligent, and more crafty, more ruthless, had opened the trade again for human cattle.

''Could I . . . see them?'' Armando asked, hating himself for his curiosity.

Santiago twisted the ring in his ear. ''Perhaps you should see them, *hombre*. Or what's left of them.''

They shouldered a path to a large fenced area. Baggage tumbrils rigged to draft horses stood waiting. Santiago brushed past a robed Franciscan who swung a smoking censer in small arcs over the area to prepare the captives for a mass baptism.

''Look your fill,'' said Santiago.

Armando gawked. Penned like livestock, the Indians wore rough brown tunics. Their filthy, matted hair, bluntly cut over the brow, hung in hanks about flat, bewildered faces. He had a swift impression of wide noses, coppery skin, eyes tilted up at the corners, and thick lips set in stoic lines. Painfully thin shoulders hunched as the sailors drove them into the carts.

''Grab her! The wench is getting away!'' The hoarse call came again.

''Here, I've got her,'' a man called. ''I've got—'' He gave a roar of pain. Armando and Santiago hastened past the tumbrils. A soldier lay on the ground, his face pale as parchment, his hands cupping his groin. A brown-clad figure streaked past and darted between a ship's hull and a wooden railing.

"Mother of God, it's an Indian wench." Santiago flung down the stub of his cigar. "Come on, *hombre!*"

Exhilaration shot through Armando. He raced after the girl. Her black hair streamed in a wild tangle behind her; her bare feet skimmed over the boardwalk along the wharves. Twisting away from the hands that grabbed at her, she headed toward the *Torre de Oro*, the round riverside tower just south of the fleet.

Armando ran like a mountain deer, his movements swift and sure despite the cloak swirling around his thighs. Drawing closer, he could hear the short, quick gasps of her breath.

The sound had a curious effect on him. He had started the chase like a farmhand after a runaway pig. But her ragged, desperate breathing reminded him that she was human. And very frightened.

And what, he wondered with a jolt of confusion, would he do when he caught her?

She disappeared around the rear of the Gold Tower. Armando put on a burst of speed. Rafael Viscaino, his father, wouldn't recognize him. Look at me now, he wanted to say. I may be a laggard in the House of Trade, but in footraces I have no equal.

He was right behind her now, an arm's length away. He reached for her. She threw one glance over her shoulder, then lifted her arms and knifed into the water, cutting the surface so smoothly that she barely made a splash.

Armando skidded to a stop at the cut-stone bulkhead. "She'll drown!"

Panting, Santiago leaned against the tower and shook his head. "Islanders never drown. They swim like dolphins."

Awestruck by the girl's grace and power, Armando

stared at the line of bubbles trailing toward the middle of the broad river. "Mother of God! She's swimming away!"

A clatter of boots drew his attention back to the wharf. "Did you see her?" the captain of the pikemen demanded. "Which way did she go?"

Santiago took a step forward and opened his mouth to speak. Armando didn't think. He planted himself in front of his godfather and pointed in the direction of the Giralda bell tower to the east. "That way!" he cried, gesturing wildly. "I almost had her, but she slipped up that alley."

The pikeman gave him an offhand salute and motioned his troop toward the heart of the city.

Armando stared, shamefaced, at the ground. "Sorry," he mumbled, then forced himself to face Santiago's wrath.

To his amazement, Santiago grinned, his eyes shining like dark stars. "Good for you, *hombre*. But we'd best get across the river. The girl won't be much better off on the other side."

Armando started to bolt; Santiago pulled him back. "Easy now. We're just taking a casual stroll."

Two *compadres* arm in arm, they left the wharf area, their pace slow until they reached the bridge of Saint Telmo. Then they started to run. The girl swam downriver, sleek and swift as an otter. Armando felt a spurt of anticipation. This was no game, but an earnest chase. She was running for her life.

No, a rescue, he corrected himself. Surely Santiago would not drag the poor girl back to the slave pens.

They reached the other side of the river and ran toward a clump of trees. The girl stood uncertainly on the bank amid tall marsh grasses that swayed in the spring wind.

"Slowly," Santiago cautioned. "Don't spook her, now."

She spied them and froze like a cornered rabbit. Locking eyes with her, Armando caught his breath. *Madre de Dios,* she was just a girl, probably no older than he. Her black hair, streaming with river water, hung dead straight over her shoulders. Her face, flushed and swollen, seemed finer boned than the faces of the other Indians.

It was her eyes that tugged at the free spirit deep inside him. How light they were, the color of amber glass with a candle burning behind it. They shone with a radiance of their own. Pride and courage, Armando thought. And fear.

The girl blinked. Her legs wobbled. Then she sprinted up the bank, heading for a narrow, shadowy alley off Zorilla Street.

"Damn!" Santiago burst out, starting after her. The long alley stank of refuse and brackish water. At the end loomed a high wall, the top spiked with iron finials.

The girl sprang upward, grasping at one of the finials. She struggled to get over, her bare feet scrabbling on the wall.

Santiago called out in an unfamiliar tongue. She threw a desperate glance over her shoulder and renewed her efforts.

"What did you say?" asked Armando.

Santiago wheezed with exertion. "I told her she'd die if she didn't stop. But I'm not sure that matters to her now."

"Tell her we won't harm her. Give her your word of honor."

Santiago snorted. "How much do you think a Spaniard's word means to her?" He went down on one knee. "Here, get on my shoulders. You'll have to help her down."

Armando planted his feet and braced his legs as Santiago stood. They edged toward the girl. She gave a low scream and tried to squirm away.

He grasped her wrist. Her skin felt damp and hot, her bones fragile beneath tense muscles. She made a growling sound in her throat. Armando resisted the urge to let go.

"Please," he said. "Please. We want to help."

The girl stared at him for a moment, her unusual eyes

flicking rapidly. Then she let go of the finial. Her drop
sent her, Armando, and Santiago tumbling in a heap.

Armando felt a sharp pain in his hand. Yelping, he drew
it back to see the imprint of the girl's teeth. She tried to
run away, but Santiago held her fast around the waist. She
fell still, panting, regarding them with helpless rage.

Santiago drew a knife from his boot.

"No!" Armando lunged for his godfather's arm.

A humorless grin curved Santiago's mouth. "Give me
a little credit, *hombre*." He used the knife to cut the rope
from around her neck. The tension in her thin body seemed
to ease slightly.

"Give her your cloak," Santiago ordered.

Armando readily relinquished the red-and-black garment. Santiago draped it around the girl's shoulders. She
seemed startled by the feel of silk and velvet against her
skin.

"Damn. She's got the smallpox," said Santiago, fasten-
ing the cloak and eyeing the pustules that dotted her throat.
"The islanders have no resistance to the disease."

Armando put out his hand and smoothed the rich fabric
over the bony shoulder. Santiago gripped his arm. "Don't.
She's infectious."

"Mama says you can only get smallpox by way of saliva
and nasal secretions." Armando gazed at the girl, touched
by her pain. "What are we going to do?"

"We wait until dark." He said something soothing to
the girl. She clutched at her necklace of shells and sodden
feathers.

"You speak her tongue, then?"

"Very little. Enough to do business with them." He
leaned back against the dank wall. The girl's eyes closed.
Her grip slackened on the necklace. She shivered, and
seemed to relax. Her eyes hazed with fever; then she closed
them and sagged against Armando's shoulder. His first
instinct was to draw away, but he held himself still.

Santiago tucked the cloak protectively around her. "Maybe she'll keep quiet a while. We'd best stay put until dark."

Armando stared at the small, frail form slumped against him. "And then what?"

Santiago shrugged. "We'll think about that later. So. I've been gone almost eighteen months. Tell me, how is your *mamacita*?"

Armando grinned. Their reunions were always the same. A burst of unabashed affection followed by the customary query about Catalina. As usual, Armando was struck by the tenderness in Santiago's voice. He seemed to have a special affection for Catalina, the bold, blonde lady who had survived the Moorish wars to become one of the most prominent physicians in Andalucía.

"Mama's fine. She had another baby."

Santiago slapped his forehead. "*Dios!* Another!"

Armando nodded. "A girl this time. Clara." With each baby, Armando felt himself draw further away from his mother. That's as it should be, he thought. He was growing up. Fast.

"Tell me about the slaves," he said, eyeing the girl.

"The mission was the idea of Juan Ponce de León." Santiago groped in the pouch tied around his waist and drew out a cigar, flint, and steel. Sparking the cigar, he inhaled deeply and let out a stream of bluish smoke.

Armando's eyes smarted. "Don Juan's cousin, Baltasar, works in the *Casa de Contratacíon* with me." He grimaced as he said the name. "He's a bootlicker and a bully."

"Much like his kinsman." Santiago dropped a cylinder of ashes on the ground. "Anyway, revenues from the Indies haven't been what they should. Juan decided a slaving mission would be a way to turn a quick profit." He hammered his fist against the wall. "I spoke against it. A planter from Española, Bartolome de las Casas, joined my protest, but Juan was captain general of the fleet. Bastard

overrode me. Me! I was marshal of the Second Voyage
while he was still a seaman serving under me."

"How did you . . ." Armando glanced at the fitfully
sleeping girl and then at the sky. To his relief, the sun had
begun to set. "How were the slaves taken?"

"By every dishonorable means you can imagine, *hombre*. Bribery, trickery, abduction. Some were incited to
rebel, and then taken prisoner. That way it's all perfectly
legal." Santiago ground his teeth in distaste. "About half
of them died on the voyage, mostly from disease. Others
starved themselves or committed suicide." He drew a deep
breath. "Some, we murdered."

Armando shuddered. "You?"

Santiago coughed up a mouthful of smoke. "Not me
personally."

"What will happen to the survivors?"

"They'll be sold on the block like prize sheep. This
one's a *mestiza*, probably fathered by a marauding sailor.
Her eyes and skin are light, her nose narrow and lips . . .
different. Quite beautiful, don't you think?"

Armando studied the long sweep of her lashes, the high
cheekbones, the broad brow. Deepening shadows sculpted
her finely made features. "We've got to get her away from
here."

"Christ, I have no idea where to take her. Maybe the
charity hospital."

"If she doesn't die there, the soldiers will find her. She
needs a doctor, Santiago. Let's take her to my mother."

The gypsy's cigar glowed in the gloom. "No. Catalina
just had a baby. We're not going to bring her a wench with
the smallpox. What about that Moorish physick, Hamet?"

A strange darkness rushed over Armando's heart. "He's
gone, Santiago."

"Damn it. God damn it! Was it the Holy Office?"

"Yes. They're not burning the Moors yet, but they've
made life difficult for them."

"Christ. First the Jews, and now the Moors. We're becoming a nation of idle nobles and superstitious peasants."

"The Church likes it that way. It makes people easy to manage."

Santiago looked at him over the girl's head. "Mind your tongue. Such talk could earn you a visit to a Holy House."

Armando shrugged, hiding his fear. The girl sagged against his chest, her weight a fragile pressure. "What about her?"

"Let's see. There's Señora Adora's—"

"*Not* a brothel," Armando snapped.

"Other than your mama, I don't know any other kind of woman."

"Señora Adora wouldn't welcome a girl with the smallpox. Can't you think of anyplace else?"

"I'm thinking, I'm thinking."

Armando plowed his fingers through his curly black hair. "This is bad. I feel like we're harboring a *Marrana*."

Santiago snapped his fingers. "That's it!"

Startled, the girl awakened and cowered against Armando's chest. His hand cupped her shoulder. "What is it?" he asked.

"I know someone who can help her, someone who has devoted her life to sheltering Jews from the Inquisition. But I'm counting on you, *hombre*. You've got to keep a big secret."

Armando thrust up his chin. "Have I ever betrayed you?"

Santiago regarded him intently, his look unreadable. "No, you haven't. You make me proud."

Armando glanced away to underplay his pleasure in his godfather's remark. "Where are we going?"

"To the Triana district. Help her up."

Armando drew the girl to her feet. She swayed, and he

tightened his grip around her shoulders. A wild animal smell mingled with the water scent in her hair. He hesitated, his hands trembling slightly. There was something precious about her that awakened a feeling of protectiveness.

Santiago went to her other side. "It's a long walk," he warned. With the girl supported between them, they moved quietly through the dark streets of Seville, ducking down alleys when they spied the mounted members of the *Santa Hermandad*, the dread police force of Castile. The girl made no sound, nor tried to flee. In the street of Saint George, a group of young noblemen left a tavern and mounted their horses. Santiago pulled Armando and the girl into the recess of the doorway, and they waited for the men to pass.

After a few moments of slurred goodnights and clopping hooves, quiet settled again over the street. They stepped out to find one rider waiting in the middle of the roadway. Armando recognized the three long feathers in his hat. "Shit," he said.

"Watch your language, *hombre*."

"That's Baltasar de León," Armando explained.

"Shit," said Santiago. "Just keep your head down. We'll walk past."

Armando had little hope of avoiding recognition. The scribe had long ago singled him out as a rival in the *Casa de Contratación*. Several paces away from the brawny youth, Armando turned his head toward the girl. He hoped the breeze stirring her hair would conceal his face.

Baltasar came out of the saddle and landed with catlike grace in front of them. "Why, it's my good friend Armando," said the older boy. He carried himself with the arrogance of a young man who had been told from the cradle—not incorrectly—that he was astonishingly handsome. "And who's this? Ah, your gypsy godfather. I wonder, Don Santiago, why you aren't at my cousin's residence tonight celebrating the return of the fleet.''

"I've better things to do than celebrate the arrival of a load of human livestock," Santiago snapped.

Baltasar's gaze probed the twilight. "Who's that with—" His sharp eyes traveled downward to the ragged hem of the tunic and the girl's bare feet. "Bravo, *compadre*," he cried, clapping Armando on the shoulder. "You've caught the runaway slave girl!" Leering, he rubbed his crotch. "How is she?"

Armando's gaze flashed to Santiago, then to the yellow squares of the tavern window. The street was deserted.

Clenched like a rock, his fist sped out and smashed into Baltasar's face. Baltasar stumbled back, blood spewing from his nose. He gave a strangled cry and lurched forward, arms swinging wildly. Armando aimed a flurry of punches at his face, then kneed him in the gut. Baltasar gasped out a curse and pitched forward into the street.

"Jesus," Santiago whispered. "Where did you learn to fight like that, *hombre*?"

Armando flexed his hands, wincing at the stinging pain in his split knuckles. "From you."

Silence and pain had filled every one of Antonia's days for the past thirteen years. Loneliness was a familiar acquaintance now, like the brown lizard that sunned itself on her patio wall.

She watched the world from behind a veil of sheer black lace and seldom ventured from her house in the quiet Triana district of Seville. Her neighbors thought her odd, reclusive. Their children chanted that she was a witch.

They couldn't know she was Antonia de Urtubia, once a sought-after court beauty. Later she was sought just as avidly, but for a different reason.

For heresy.

She sighed and went back to sorting the dried herbs in

her pantry. Sweet marjoram for perseverance, sage and fennel to calm the nerves. Rosemary for remembrance.

Remembrance. She wished to remember nothing—not the giddy joy of loving a wonderful man, not the horror of having him torn from her by the long arm of the Holy Office, not the wild terror of nearly dying in a fire with a madman.

The unscarred side of her mouth slid up in a grimace. Only a handful of people knew her identity. The rest believed the beauteous Doña Antonia had perished with her monster of a husband.

She worked in silence for a time, enjoying the scent of sweet and bitter herbs in the air. Outside in the darkened patio, swallows chittered, darting in and out of the masonry.

The circle of her world was so small, so tight. She would keep it that way until she died.

Mateo, her one servant, banged around in the kitchen. He alone was allowed to enter her house, to be part of her life.

Mateo was totally blind. He could not see the scars, could not see what she had become.

The riders of the *Santa Hermandad* had chased him down for stealing. They had caught him, put out his eyes with hot irons, and left him for dead. Antonia had nursed him back to health.

A tapping sound came from the door to the street. She fell still, wondering. Seldom did anyone come to see her; her only visitors were fugitive Jews with nowhere else to turn. She stood and brushed leaves and dust from her skirt, and went to the main door. It was no fugitive whose face she saw framed in the small, square grille in the door, but a friend from her past.

"Santiago!"

"Hello, Antonia. Look, I need a favor."

She unlatched the heavy gate and pushed it open. "But

it's been years. What can I—'' She broke off as he waved his arm. Two others entered the dim passage with him.

Instinctively she lowered her head. The veil obscured her face, but she never quite trusted it. "Santiago," she said furiously, "I've told you never to bring anyone here."

"It's an emergency. The girl's sick."

Antonia's gaze leaped to the two youngsters. She went to the girl's side and took her hand. "Why, you're burning up with fever."

"It's smallpox," said Santiago. "I'm sorry. I just didn't know what else to do."

"She needs to be in a hospital, not here."

"I can't take her to a hospital. She's, er, a fugitive."

Antonia peered at the girl. In the folds of the concealing cloak, she could discern only a patch of feverish skin, the glint of wary eyes. "Is she a *conversa*?" she asked softly. Over the years, she had helped many converted Jews escape questioning and torture by the Holy Office.

"No, just a heathen like me," Santiago said with a half-smile. "She's from the West Indies. Caught on a slave-hunting mission."

Antonia gasped. Everything about the New World fascinated her. It was to the wild, distant islands that her lover, Joseph, had fled. It was there, too, that he had died.

The girl seemed to shrink into the folds of the cloak. Sensitive to her mood, Antonia regarded the other youngster with Santiago. The tall, handsome youth had a familiar and engaging look about him. Glancing from the boy to Santiago, she said, "And this must be your—"

"—godson," Santiago filled in quickly, darting a meaningful glance at her. "This is Armando, eldest son of Rafael and Catalina."

Antonia paused, assimilating the information. In a matter of seconds, she understood. The younger man was unaware of his true relationship with Santiago. She extended her gloved hand. "Armando. I knew Rafael—years ago."

Memories washed over her—a naive young man, a disturbed young woman impregnated by her own father, a plot Antonia had been compelled to foil. It was the event that had ended her life as Doña Antonia, Lady of the Queen's Bedchamber and wife of the cruel and twisted Bernal de Montana. "Rafael and I did each other a kindness, once."

Armando's smile made Antonia think of smitten girls sighing behind their fans. "Everyone speaks well of my father," he said, and she detected a hint of resentment in his voice.

The West Indian girl swayed where she stood. Antonia reached for her arm. The wary eyes peered at her veil. Antonia knew the mysterious black lace must frighten the child, but her naked face was worse. "Come," she said in her kindest voice. "You need to lie down."

They passed through the dark, cool *zaguán* where Antonia paused to hand Armando a lighted candle. In the open patio, a fountain burbled into the silence. Antonia led the way to a small guest chamber with lime-washed walls and a scrubbed tile floor. Later she would move the girl into the secret room reserved for fugitives. "I want to help you." She reached for the laces of the cloak. "I'm a friend. You can trust me."

The child made no protest as Antonia removed the cloak. She took in her breath with a hiss. Small pustules covered the girl's neck and downward, into the vee of her cheap brown smock.

"Lie down, child." Antonia gestured at the bedstead. She drew back the coverlet of boiled wool and patted the crisp linen sheets. "Please, lie down."

Santiago said something in a halting, strange tongue.

The girl hesitated. Her eyes darted from the bed to the high, recessed window, to the plaster Christ hanging on the wall. Then she lowered herself to the bed. When her back touched the fluffy feather mattress, she gave a start of surprise.

"There now," Antonia soothed. "Just lie down." She made a smoothing motion with her hands.

The girl drew up her skinny legs and lay down, her bare feet on the pillow.

"Her head's at the wrong end," Armando pointed out.

"Leave her be," said Santiago. "It's the first time she's ever seen a bed."

"Can you heal her, señora?" Armando asked.

"I shall try." She went to the door and called for Mateo, asking him to bring bread and herb tea.

"Would it help to pray?" Armando asked.

Antonia and Santiago exchanged a glance. "Some people think prayer helps," Santiago said.

Candle in hand, Armando stepped toward the bed. The light slanted across the girl's face, gilding her high cheekbones and full lips. Antonia felt a flash of something, a subtle tug of memory. But the feeling vanished; she dismissed it as merely another of her strange, lonely visions. "I wonder what we should call her. It's awkward not knowing."

"We could give her a name," Armando suggested.

"I have a name." The small, weary voice came from the figure on the bed.

"My God." Santiago dropped to his knees beside her. Antonia and Armando joined him. "You speak Castilian."

The girl's eyelids drooped in fatigue. "Yes. I speak the tongue of your clan."

"What's your name?" Armando's candle wavered. Melted beeswax dripped onto his hand, but he continued to gape at the girl.

"It's . . . Paloma."

CHAPTER 2

Santiago rapped on the door to the small house in the Santa María parish near Seville. A servant, unkempt and smelling of *aguardiente*, peered through a barred opening in the door.

"Yes?"

"I'm here to see Admiral Colón."

The red-rimmed eyes narrowed. "Are you a royal courier?"

"Yes," Santiago lied. The state of the servant boded ill. Wondering if he had been wrong to come to Colón for help, he gestured at the badge of castles and crowns that fastened his cloak. "My credential."

The servant drew back the door. "The admiral's in his study."

As Santiago went through a low-arched passageway, he nearly stumbled over the buckling tile floor. The door to the study stood ajar. Inside, a man with a froth of hair the color of sea foam bent over a small desk. His fingers clutched a quill pen, and the feather quivered as the nib scratched over the page.

My God, he's old. The thought struck Santiago in the chest. The wizened man bore little resemblance to the strapping Lord High Admiral of the Ocean Sea who had challenged the western horizon—and won.

"It's me, *viejo*," Santiago said softly.

The years had not dimmed Colón's hearing, for his head snapped up. Weary lines scored his face. But his eyes still burned with the lively light of a man of action.

He rose from the desk. "Damn. A heathen gypsy." His gaze darted to Santiago's stolen badge. "By God, they're letting anyone wear the office of royal courier these days." He held out his arms. The two men embraced fiercely, holding each other for a long moment. Long enough for Santiago to feel the thinness and sense the aching in the admiral's bones.

Angry, he broke away. "Cristóbal, you don't have to live like this." He moved about the room in agitation, touching the rickety desk, drawing a line in the dust on the window sill. "Look at this place! The ceiling's crumbling, the walls are damp. . . ." He brushed his neck. "There's a draft coming from somewhere. You have your own apartments in the alcázar, Cristóbal. You're still Admiral of the Ocean Sea. You should live in a way befitting your rank."

"Too many hangers-on at the palace. Everyone from sailors to glassblowers wants something from me. Usually things—patents, indulgences, land grants, back pay—I can't give."

"Other than that, how are you, *viejo*?"

"Sick as a dog. Mad as a cornered peccary. And you?"

"I just got back from an expedition with Juan Ponce de León."

The blue eyes kindled. "I remember him from the second voyage. A typical blue blood, but he had ambitions. Well?''

''We found no passage across Tierra Firme to Cathay. Only a load of slaves.'' Fighting to contain his anger, Santiago shuffled over to a brazier and stirred the olive pits that gave off a faint heat. ''That's what I'm here to talk about.''

''The slaving?''

Santiago closed his eyes, seeing the girl he had left at Antonia's the night before. He pounded his fist on the desk. ''Cristóbal, it's got to stop. We're killing those people.''

Colón stared at the floor. It had been he who had first suggested slaving. But like many of his other plans, the traffic of natives had burgeoned out of control, become an obscene corruption.

''And you think I'm the one to stop it?'' he asked.

Santiago spread his hands, palms up. ''You're Admiral of the Ocean Sea. One of the highest grandees in Spain. You could petition King Ferdinand or Cardinal Cisneros.''

Colón snorted. ''Ferdinand never liked me. He only tolerated me because Isabel believed in my cause. Now that she's gone, I have no one's ear. Besides, you know what Ferdinand's response will be. A healthy West Indian—like a good horse—is worth its weight in gold. The king likes gold. He likes it a lot. He likes slaves, too. Gives them away as novelty gifts to the members of the Council of the Indies.''

''What about Cisneros?''

''The Grand Cardinal sees nothing wrong with slavery.'' His voice quavered with regrets. ''All those souls, just waiting to be converted.''

''Damn it.'' Santiago made a fist. ''Just try, will you?''

Colón drew his hands over his long, stark cheeks. ''The royal court's in Segovia. I'll send a letter tomorrow.''

Santiago knew better than to feel relieved. ''Do that.''

"Will you stay a bit?" Colón lifted a napkin from a plate on the sideboard. He scowled at the uneaten meat and cheese. "I have a terrible cook, but the *aguardiente*'s excellent."

Santiago considered his plans for the day. He saw an image of a pretty house with geraniums on the wall. He thought of a blond-haired woman with a smell like sunshine. The only woman he had ever loved.

She was married to his best friend.

"I have to go, Cristóbal. Rafael and Catalina are expecting me for supper."

"Give them my regards." Colón walked to the window and paused, a pain that was deeper than physical flashing in his eyes. "Will you see her, Santiago? Will you see Beatriz?"

"Probably. I'll go to Córdoba soon."

"Tell her . . . tell her I—"

"Damn it, Cristóbal. *You* go to her. *You* tell her!" Santiago gripped the older man's shoulders. "For God's sake, you were her only lover. She gave birth to your younger son. And Fernando's a sight better than your firstborn, Diego. Fernando's loyal as his mother, Cristóbal. See her. She loves you."

Colón's face closed. "No. I can't go to Beatriz."

"For Christ's sake. You crossed the Ocean Sea when all the scholars of Europe swore it couldn't be done. How can you be afraid to face a woman who loves you?"

Colón smiled sadly, giving Santiago a glimpse of the handsome man who had once enthralled a nation. "My friend, the human heart is far more mysterious and infinitely more treacherous than a mere thousand leagues of uncharted ocean."

Santiago thought of the evening ahead. "I'm afraid I agree. But go to Beatriz before it's too late."

"It was too late the day we set sail on that first voyage. Beatriz knew I'd either perish or become a nobleman—

either way, she'd lose me. I refused to believe it. She was right about a lot of things.''

Santiago glanced one last time at the letters scattered on the desk. An old man's scribblings, destined to be read and discarded by a lowly *alguazil* without ever reaching the king. A pity, for the writings of so great a man should be preserved.

He eyed Colón at the window and suppressed a sigh. He had been wrong to come here. Despite his lofty titles, Cristóbal could do nothing to stop men like Juan Ponce de León from dealing in the trading of humans.

Santiago bade the admiral good-bye and made his way through the darkening streets of Seville. Soldiers and men of the *Hermandad* swaggered through the byways, and Santiago wondered which of them might be searching for the girl called Paloma.

He yanked off the badge. He had to believe she was safe for the time being.

The last of the day's light glanced off the minarets and arches of the alcazar, and the smells of onion and herbs wafted on the air, mingling with wood smoke from the forges where Indies gold was melted down to make coins and holy reliquaries. Thanks to trade with the West Indies, the ancient city had prospered. Wealth flowed upstream against the currents of the Guadalquivir. Nobles and merchants alike lavished their fortunes on palaces, churches, convents, parks, and public buildings. Like soldiers of fortune, men of lowly birth had prospered. Santiago himself, a half-breed gypsy, had escaped the hangman to become a landholder, a leader of expeditions.

He was thirty-six years old. He had an estate near Jerez, houses in Córdoba and Cádiz, mistresses of all colors in many ports, and a life of unending adventure.

And yet, as he paused in the dooryard of Rafael's house, he felt the ache of emptiness in his chest. Through the patio he could see the children holding hands and skipping in a circle. Near a trickling fountain, Rafael and Armando spoke together, laughing from time to time. Catalina sat with her back turned, elbows cocked to form a cradle for her newest child.

The picture of familial contentment slammed home the source of Santiago's restlessness. He was adrift like a ship with no one at the helm. He saw himself years from now, mirrored in Colón's eyes. Like Colón, he had given too much of himself to exploring the earth and taken too little time to understand the vagaries of the human heart. He would live alone, like Colón, friendless and frustrated. An object of pity.

Angry at the maudlin thoughts, Santiago squared his shoulders, set his panached hat at a rakish angle, and strode into the patio. *"Amigos!"* He spread his arms and went down on one knee.

"Santiago!" The four younger children flung themselves into his arms. They covered his face with kisses and squirmed like a litter of puppies. The smell of them filled his senses with a mixture of soap, sugar, and fresh air.

"What did you bring me?" demanded nine-year-old Isabel.

Santiago slapped his forehead. *"Ay de mi, muchacha.* I forgot." Familiar with the game, Isabel dove for his purse and tugged at the strings. With teasing affection, he doled out the treasures: a conch-shell trumpet, a handful of parrot feathers, a dried gourd rattle, a sack of polished rocks.

While the little ones exclaimed over their prizes from the Indies, Santiago went to greet the others. With Armando he shared a brief and seemly handclasp. *Dios,* but the boy had grown into a handsome young man. Santiago struggled to conceal his fierce, secret pride. Then he turned to Rafael.

Twenty years of friendship lent strength to their embrace. Then Santiago held Rafael at arms' length. "Look at you, *hombre!* You're getting some meat on your bones at last.''

Although nearly the same age as Santiago, Rafael had never lost the look of boyish wonder in his wide eyes. "Come," he said. "Meet my new daughter." He took the baby from Catalina's arms and brushed back the woven blanket. "This is Clara."

Santiago made a sound of admiration, but his gaze strayed to Catalina. Like dessert, he had saved the sight of her for last.

She stood, swaying slightly as she stepped into his embrace. Covering his alarm at her weakness, he caught her against him and buried his face in her hair, inhaling its familiar citrus scent and another mysterious smell he could not place.

"Easy there, *mi corazón,*" he cautioned.

She laughed. "I'm just four days out of childbed. Did you expect me to dance the flamenco?"

He forced himself to laugh, too. What he had expected—what he always expected—was the girl he had known twenty years before, the girl with gawky long legs, a quick mind, and a yearning heart.

The girl he had—for one magical summer—loved more than life itself.

The thoughts passed in a flash of regrets, and once again she became a woman. Thinner than ever, smiling as always, oddly beautiful despite the plainness of her features. He hugged her a second time, able now to identify the strange perfume that clung to her. It was the birth smell, blood and earth and musky sweetness.

"You should slow down, *madrecita,*" he cautioned. "You of all people should know how to keep from having so many babies."

The old secret passed between them. Santiago had once told her—a good Catholic girl—a gypsy way to prevent conception.

God, would that she had employed it that long-ago summer!

He crushed the thought. No! That summer had given them a treasure he would never wish away.

Supper was a frantic affair, with five hungry children all vying for the attention of Santiago. Barely tasting the food and wine, he denied the envy and the longing that rose in him.

"When do you sail next?" asked Armando, selecting a dried fig from a bowl. At last the younger children had been bundled off to bed, and the four of them sat in the *sala*, listening to the nightingales in the arbor outside and sipping honeyed lemon juice with ice from the high Sierras.

Santiago considered for a moment. There was never any question that he would go; the only question was when. "That depends," he said. "I won't take part in another slave hunt. When I go, it'll be as captain general of a voyage of discovery. God, there's so much to see. Islands beyond counting, and then Tierra Firme to the west of the Indies. It's like a gift just waiting to be opened. Rafael, you ought to come back."

Grinning, Rafael reached across the table and squeezed his wife's hand. "And leave this wild brood? No thanks. One voyage was enough for me."

"We want to hear more about the girl," Catalina prompted and gazed fondly at her son. "Armando can't stop talking about her."

Armando blushed to the tips of his ears. "You said it was all right for me to tell them."

Santiago sent him a sympathetic smile. "Of course." He looked at Rafael and Catalina. "It's lucky for her that Armando acted so quickly, or she'd be back in Ponce de León's hands. Intriguing wench. She has the look of a half-breed. Still, I was surprised to hear her speak Spanish."

"Don't many of the islanders learn Castilian?"

"Yes, but she was taken from a tribe of Lucayans who had never had any truck with the Spaniards—or so we thought. And yet she knows the language. A curious thing, no? Perhaps a renegade Spaniard lives among them. I wanted to ask her, but she's ill and needs her rest."

"Does she have a chance of surviving the smallpox?"

Santiago heard the worry beneath Armando's question. "If she were full Indian, I'd say no. But her Castilian blood might give her some resistance. At any rate, she's in good hands."

Rafael and Catalina exchanged a glance. The pain and understanding that passed between them reminded Santiago of that summer long past, the summer that had changed so many lives.

"How is Doña Antonia?" Rafael asked.

"The same. A recluse behind a veil. But her heart's as soft as ever. I'll check on the girl tomorrow." He turned to Armando. "You'll come with me, *hombre*?"

Dark fire shone in the youth's eyes. "Of course, I—"

"He'll come," Rafael interrupted, "after he finishes his work at the House of Trade."

"But Papa, Santiago said—"

"No, *hombre*." Santiago held up his hand. Privately he sympathized with the boy's aversion to sitting for hours, bent over a desk, recording figures in registers. But years ago he had relinquished any right to object. "Work first, then we go to see Paloma."

Catalina excused herself. In a short time, she returned with several jars. "I want you to take these to Antonia. Here's some chamomile to soothe the itch of the pustules. And an unguent to prevent scarring." She lined up the corked jars in front of Santiago. "Herb tea for the fever, and some sleeping powder. I've written it all down."

Santiago ignored the squiggly lines. Reading was one

skill he had never bothered to master. "Antonia will appreciate that."

"Will there be trouble?" asked Rafael. "The girl's a fugitive. I won't have my son running afoul of the law."

Armando's hand, the knuckles split in his fight with Baltasar, dove out of sight beneath the table. In that instant, Santiago realized Armando had not told his parents everything about the encounter.

"There's a search going on right now," Santiago explained. "But Antonia's prepared for searches." From time to time, whole families of Jews hid with her while she falsified *limpiezas de sangre*, certificates that proved the purity of their blood, and arranged transportation, usually to Venice or Persia.

"If the girl survives," he added, "we might have a problem on our hands."

The low roar of a signal horn penetrated the silence of the opulent accounting room. The familiar sound released the laborers from the fields of Triana across the river. To Armando, the signal was a siren's call, luring him from the stultifying chores spread out before him.

Viciously suppressing the urge to jump up from his tasseled seat and race down to the street, he dipped his quill and applied it to the parchment document he was copying. The boring list of supplies for a colonizing venture to the Indies blurred before his eyes. All around him, the other *escribanos* worked with a diligence that was deaf to the calls of the horn.

A drop of ink fell from the nib of his pen. Gritting his teeth, he blotted the stain with a small square of cloth, now black from his repeated mistakes.

Work first, then we go to see Paloma. Armando stared in frustration at the smudge. A breeze, fragrant with the scent of almond blossoms, wafted through the narrow, unglazed windows. As though of its own accord, the pen came down and embellished the smudge. He transformed the mark into a sea eagle, its wings spread to embrace a vast, limitless space. The crude but vital drawing expressed the yearning that boiled in his heart.

A snigger sounded from the next writing desk. He glanced up to see Baltasar de León, who managed to look haughty despite his massive, swollen nose and the dark purple bruises beneath his eyes. "Such artistry," Baltasar hissed, fingering the wiry sprouts of his first beard.

Armando's hand closed into a fist. "Shut up, Baltasar." He kept his voice low so that his father would not hear. "Unless you want me to break your nose for you again."

Baltasar flushed crimson. Out of pride, he had told everyone his injury was the result of a fall from a horse. "You'll die for what you did, *pendejo*. I've made sure of that."

Armando formed his fingers into a cross. "I quake in fear, O great warrior."

Baltasar craned his neck toward the door as if expecting someone. Seeing only Rafael at his ornate raised desk and the *escribanos* bent diligently over their work, he announced, "My work is done. You'll probably be here all night scribbling pictures." With that, he penned the customary *Deo Gratias* at the bottom of his document, dried the ink with sand, and swaggered to the front of the office to present his work to Armando's father.

Armando watched the exchange. As *contador* of the House of Trade, Rafael supervised the control and recording of all trade with the Indies. At thirty-five, Armando's father still seemed youthful. Some men commanded attention by their handsomeness or pride. But with Rafael, a gentler quality arrested the eye.

Always, even when considering the most pressing trade problem, he wore a look of such blissful contentment that people often stared. His rarefied delight in his quiet life endeared him to all, and sometimes made Armando feel detached and lost.

How could he be so different from his own father? The written word came as naturally as speech to Rafael, while Armando struggled to write the simplest phrase. Rafael satisfied every curiosity by burying himself in books, while Armando longed to poke his nose into the very essence of life itself, to see into the center and touch its core.

Blowing out a sigh, he shaded his drawing and imagined the girl at Antonia's house, lying ill in a strange bed. She had eluded a clutch of pikemen, had swum the Guadalquivir, and yet she seemed as vulnerable as a blossom in a breeze.

A shadow fell over Armando's paper. He glanced up to see his father standing over him. Any of his younger brothers would have blushed and stammered excuses. Armando merely sat, helpless and unapologetic, awaiting Rafael's reaction.

Instead of a scolding, he got a smile. "I used to draw when I was young. Sea monsters and clouds with angry faces."

Armando almost wished his father would yell at him, give him a shake, demand that he rewrite the ruined document. But Rafael showed endless tolerance for Armando's deficiencies.

And so the two merely eyed each other, thinking private thoughts that would never be spoken.

We don't *fit*, thought Armando. Though father and son, an unnatural strangeness hung between them. Affection abounded, to be sure, but it lacked the easy unity he had observed in other fathers and sons.

The horn sounded again, three short blasts. Longing swept over Armando. Rafael must have sensed it, for he addressed all the scribes in the room. "We'll say the *Ave María*, and then you're all excused for the day."

Armando couldn't utter the prayer fast enough. Though

clumsy with the pen, he had a facile tongue and an ear for imitation. He could converse competently in French, Italian, English, and Latin.

With the collective "Amen" still ringing in his ears, he raced from the chamber, through an open gallery, and across the patio of the alcázar. The sunburst pattern of the flagstones passed in a blur. He expected to find Santiago waiting for him. Instead, he ran straight into a hornet's nest of blue-liveried officials of the *Santa Hermandad*.

"Not so fast, there." A large hand grabbed Armando's arm.

He struggled, slamming his elbow into the man's ribs. With a grunt, the man twisted Armando's arm high behind his back. Armando gritted his teeth as his muscles and tendons caught fire with pain. "What do you want?" he gasped.

"Answers. What do you know about that slave girl who escaped?"

Baltasar! The name blazed in Armando's mind. Baltasar de León had informed on him. "What?" he asked stupidly. "I don't know what you're talking about."

"Look, we have it on good authority that—"

"Captain Montoya!" Welcome as springtime, Santiago's voice called across the patio. "I see you've found my godson."

Montoya dropped Armando's arm. "Don Santiago. We were just asking him if he might know anything about the runaway slave."

Santiago cuffed Armando on the side of the head. "This heathen? Hardly. He was with me that day, cadging souvenirs from the Indies." Santiago flipped a silver *dinero* to Montoya. "Good luck with your search, *amigo*!"

As he hauled Armando away, he leaned over to hiss in his ear. "Close one. We'll take the long route to Doña Antonia's."

As they ambled along the narrow, cobbled Street of the

Serpent and headed for the bridge to Triana, neither noticed a cloaked horseman turn his mount toward them.

Paloma caught at the dream like a monkey reaching for a vine. She clung to sleep-blurred images of a white island rising from an emerald sea, a bearded man singing songs to her beside a roaring fire, the brush of her mother's hand over her brow.

But all too soon, wakefulness crashed over her with the force of a storm-driven wave. Her eyes flew open.

The room lay in darkness. The scent of oil told Paloma the lamp had been burning recently. The lingering perfume of flowers meant that the woman called Doña Antonia had been here, too.

Paloma did not know how much time had passed since the black-haired boy had fought the bigger youth in order to save her. She felt weak and shivery hot. Days and nights clouded together like a dream of dark and light.

She reached for the pottery jar on the table. Vaguely she remembered Doña Antonia placing it beneath her to catch her urine. Pulling up her white garment, Paloma clumsily used the jar and set it on the floor. Then she reached for the water bottle beside the bed. Her hand shook with weakness as she put the drinking vessel to her lips. Footsteps tapped somewhere, muffled by thick walls. The sound pounded strangely in her ears. The Spaniards wore shoes on their feet.

Muffled voices—men's voices—joined the tramp of the footsteps. Paloma shivered in fear. During the long nightmare voyage across the big water, she had learned to cringe at the guttural sound of male voices. She had seen desire in the eyes of the Spaniards when they looked at her. They might have mated with her, but the man called Santiago, who seemed to hold some power, had forbidden mating between the sailors and the captive women. Then the fever had come on her, and she had been isolated with the other sick islanders. There had been some talk of throwing the infected people overboard, but the greedy Spaniards were loath to part with the goods they had captured to trade.

The male voices rose in volume, followed by a soft murmur from the woman. Paloma recognized that voice. In the dazed half-sleep of fever, she had heard the woman speaking, sometimes crooning a song of gentle sweetness.

Swaying with dizziness, Paloma reached over to set the drinking vessel aside. The crockery bottle slipped from her fingers and shattered with a loud crash.

Paloma froze. The voices fell silent; then the woman spoke again, a note of strain raising the pitch. Other noises drifted into the darkness. Thumping sounds, the shuffle of feet on the cool, slick tile floor that Paloma found so fascinating.

Light-headed with fear and sickness, she drew her knees up to her chest. The crusty pustules itched, but she dared not move. The woman spoke rapidly for several more minutes. Finally the footsteps grew softer, as if retreating.

Paloma stretched out on her cot. The leather straps creaked, and she could not get comfortable. She longed for the swinging cradle of her hammock, but quickly crushed the yearning. She could not let herself think of home, of her parents. She was like a creature in a fragile shell. One errant thought and her cocoon would shatter.

Antonia felt brittle as she bade the soldiers good luck on their quest to find the runaway slave. The tension of pretense stretched her nerves. Her fingers ached with an icy chill.

All had gone smoothly at first. Her appropriately befuddled reaction to the news: ''A slave girl from the Indies. My, but I should like to see that! Is she dangerous? Ah, you gentlemen certainly put a widow's mind at ease, you with your sharp swords and pikes.'' She wondered now if the horse-faced sergeant had caught her irony. His search had been particularly thorough. He seemed acquainted with the customary *converso* hiding places: cellars, false walls, lofts above the rafters.

Fortunately, the bookcase—filled solely with volumes that would never appear on the Index of forbidden books— had been constructed so seamlessly that even a practiced eye could not discern the hidden hinges.

She leaned out the window and gazed at the empty street. Certain the *Hermandades* had gone for good, Antonia hurried to the library. The books lay scattered on the floor, some open with pages crinkled from the searchers' ill handling. She sank to her knees and started to move the books aside. The crash of crockery had alarmed her and alerted the police. But Mateo had come bumbling in, blaming his blindness, saying he had dropped a bowl.

She picked up a slim volume of poetry. A pressed rose, colorless with age, fell from the pages. Antonia fell still, the child, the brush with discovery, forgotten. Even now, twenty years later, the faint smell of the rose clung to the pages.

Remembrance of a night long past came rushing back, a night of magic and splendor, when her life had glowed with golden promise. She and Joseph had been at court then, celebrating a victory in the Moorish wars.

Sweet Mary, how happy she had been, breathless as a girl and so deeply in love with the young count of Ribera that she had been blind to the evil that stalked her lover.

He had given her the rose and the book of poetry that night, mere tokens of a love so great that its loss had hurt worse than the inferno that had scarred her.

She glanced down at the page, which was oily from the rose. Her sadness ran deep and hot. With a shudder, she replaced the rose and set the book on the shelf. Gulping air to compose herself, she took a lamp from a wall bracket. She shied away from looking at the flame, for it reminded her of the fire.

Very carefully, she slid back the panel of the bookshelf. One of the first persons she had sheltered here had been a *converso* carpenter who had remade the shelves to be almost undetectable. Ducking through the low opening, she stepped into the small, windowless room. The figure on the bed stirred, drawing into a tight ball.

"It's all right," Antonia whispered. "You're safe. The men are gone." She approached slowly, carefully, for she detected the smell of fear mingling with the sickness, sharp as damp iron. "Are you hungry, Paloma? Thirsty?"

"No." The girl's voice was gravelly with disuse.

Antonia knelt beside the bed and brushed aside shards of the crockery bottle. "I mean to keep you safe." She spoke slowly and distinctly. "Do you understand, Paloma?"

"Yes."

"I'm glad you're awake. Santiago, the man who brought you here, came with his godson to see you earlier today. I sent them away, for you were still asleep." Antonia hoped Paloma could hear the smile in her voice. "I want to know about you. But first, I should explain something." Her gloved hand touched the black lace that obscured her face. "Some children are frightened of this veil. My face is scarred, Paloma. I was in a terrible fire. It's not pretty to look at."

The girl unwound her arms from her knees. Encouraged, Antonia said, "Paloma is a Spanish name. Santiago thinks your father must have been Spanish, and your mother is Indian. Is that correct?"

The girl moistened her lips. "My father is Spanish, yes. But he's also *guahiro*, one of us, one of the people of the cay. The Spaniards call my mother Indian. This is not what she would call herself."

Hearing the wry humor in the girl's voice, Antonia smiled in delight. Like all children, Paloma was resilient, quick to heal so long as she was not wounded too deeply.

"I don't suppose she would." Antonia smoothed the sheet over Paloma's legs. "Tell me about your home. Your family."

Once again, the knees drew up and the skinny arms encircled them. Paloma's mouth flattened into a taut, obstinate line. Her eyes filled with pain, and the look touched off something unexpected and hurtful inside Antonia. Recognition. Somehow, she *knew* that look. That stubborn fatalism.

"Paloma. I intend to shelter you here until you are well. And then I'll find a way to send you home."

"Home?" echoed Paloma. "Back to the cay?"

Antonia nodded. "Fleets sail from here every few weeks." Her mind galloped ahead. Santiago was rich and influential. He could pass Paloma off as his servant, carry her back to her people. Yes. Santiago was one of the few men of honor left in the caldron of greed and intolerance Castile had become since the Inquisition had taken over. "I'll find a way, I promise."

Looking wary, the girl leaned back against the bedstead. "My mother came from an island called Guanahaní. That means iguana in your language. The *cacique* Colón named it San Salvador." Her lips pressed together. "Holy Savior, their name for the Christ god. When the Spaniards came, my mother's clan moved on."

"And your father?"

"He came with the *cacique* Colón. But he was not like the other Spaniards. He didn't seek gold and spices."

Antonia guessed the girl's age to be around ten, perhaps eleven. "Then that was the first voyage." The voyage that had taken Joseph from her forever. "What was he seeking, if not treasure?"

Paloma rubbed her forehead, disrupting a scab there. Antonia took a handkerchief from her sleeve and gently daubed it. "Try not to disturb the healing. I don't want you to scar."

A corner of Paloma's mouth lifted in the beginnings of a smile. "You have words in your language, words that stand for ideas. My father was teaching me, for they are not the ideas of my people. He was looking for . . . peace. Solitude. To be away from the other Spaniards."

"I understand. Some men—and some women—don't fit in here. Your father was lucky to escape. He must love you very much."

Bland indifference came over Paloma's face, giving her an uncannily adult look. "Love is a Spanish idea."

"Your people don't feel love?"

"We love the earth and the sea and the brother gods and our ancestors who walk in the Spirit World."

Antonia was fascinated by the girl. She spoke in tones more cultured, more refined than those of most convent-educated gentlewomen. "I want to know all about your life. Will you tell me?"

The girl poked a finger at her lower lip, and Antonia found the gesture endearing. She saw with relief that Paloma's cheeks had faded to the natural color of rich doeskin rather than the angry red of fever.

"My mother is called Anacaona. The word means gold-flower. I have a brother, Malak, who is much older than I. He traveled with the *cacique* Colón, and we have not seen him in many rains. The Caribs killed his father." The child's speech had a distinctive rhythm, as if she recited from rote. It must be, Antonia thought, the way of her people to memorize their history.

"I've heard of the Caribs. They make war on the other people of the Indies."

The girl's fingers twisted together in some cryptic sign. "My mother is a wise woman. She sees things in her dreams."

Antonia hesitated. Dare she ask? "And your father? You called him Guahiro."

Paloma's hand came up to loosen the braided string

around her neck. She removed the cluster of feathers and shells that hung from the string.

Antonia held herself very still. The girl could not see through the veil, but Antonia shot her a penetrating stare that burned with expectancy. The urge to hope pounded in her head. She felt fragile, as if she would shatter with the answer.

The girl held out a small silver object that had been buried among the feathers. It felt warm in Antonia's hand. She stared down at the medallion. A lion device. The lion of Rivera.

Antonia's heart took fire. "Where did you get this?" she whispered, not daring to believe. "Surely you found it on the beach or—or traded for it—"

"It is from my father." Paloma raised her face, and suddenly her features looked as familiar and beautiful to Antonia as a long-cherished dream.

"Paloma, I must know. Did he tell you his Spanish name?"

"My father's name is Joseph. Joseph Sarmiento of Ribera."

CHAPTER 3

Armando and Santiago walked through the shadow of the ancient Gold Tower overlooking the Guadalquivir. Three weeks had passed since the men of the *Santa Hermandad* had tried to seize Armando. The incident had fueled his imagination. He had bested Baltasar de León; he had outwitted the police. He longed to share the adventure with Rafael, but knew he would earn only disapproval and admonitions. He had to content himself with swaggering along the docks with Santiago after work each day, wishing for a life that could never be his.

Santiago eyed the broadside of a ponderous *nao* of about a hundred tons. A ship's carpenter, in leather apron and cap, bent to examine a worm-eaten section of the hull.

Santiago halted and turned to Armando. "So, how was your day at your father's offices?"

Armando pulled a face and spread his ink-stained hands. "The House of Trade has an official form for everything from sail plans to fireboxes. All those words on paper, and for what? No one'll ever read them. I'd rather have your job.''

Santiago's black eyes flickered. ''A gypsy's job is not fit for a dog.''

''It's good enough for you.''

Clapping Armando on the shoulder, Santiago bent close. Armando saw the golden glint of his godfather's earring.

''Listen, *hombre*. Your father is a very important man. Very smart. You're to do exactly as he says.''

''But you get to sail the world, see new places—''

''Understand?'' Santiago's grip tightened on his shoulder.

Armando stared at the yellow stone pathway along the dock. ''I suppose so.''

''Good. Any more trouble with Baltasar de León?''

''No.'' Armando tried to keep the relief from his voice. ''He hasn't been in since the day the *Hermandad* came.''

''I have someone for you to meet.'' Santiago drew him over to the ship's carpenter. ''This is Master John Longwood of England.''

''My pleasure.'' Longwood's Castilian had the harsh, flat accent of his native England. Armando was not surprised to encounter the foreigner. Since the Jews had been exiled from Spain, they had left great gaps in many trades. The Castilians who remained fell into four groups: men who labored, men who fought, men who ruled, men who prayed. Not men who built ships or ran banks or debated great issues in the universities.

The presence of Catherine of Aragon in England had forged a link between the two countries. Englishmen were as common as Italians in Seville.

''It's an honor to meet you, sir,'' Armando said in English.

The wide-eyed reaction of Santiago pleased him. ''*Demonios!* You speak English like a native!''

Armando smiled. ''Not quite as well. Master Winningham at the House of Trade swears I have a gift for languages.''

'' 'Deed you do,'' Longwood agreed, impressed. He had blunt Saxon features, strong hands, and bad teeth. ''Might serve you well one day.'' Shading his pale eyes, he gazed down at the long, lazy stretch of the river. ''I'd like to see the New World myself, and I shall, once the restrictions against foreigners in the Indies are lifted.''

''Don't haul your spars yet,'' said Santiago in his own heavily accented English. ''The papal bull made King Ferdinand absolute master over all the Indies.''

Longwood nodded glumly, his broad, swarthy face creased in chagrin. ''He'll not part with a single tobacco leaf or stalk of sugarcane for a foreigner—not if he can help it.''

Santiago shook hands with Longwood. ''I'm off, then, taking my godson to get his supper. You'll manage the repairs?''

Longwood stirred his bucket of pitch. '' 'Course, sir.''

They walked away down the wharf. ''Supper?'' asked Santiago.

''There's something I'd rather do.''

Santiago lifted an eyebrow. ''So long as it doesn't involve strong drink or naked women, I'll grant you your wish.''

Armando ducked his head to hide a blush. ''I want to see the Indian girl. Doña Antonia turned us away last time because Paloma was too ill, but surely she's recovered by now.''

Santiago quickened his step. ''Best you stay away from contagion, *hombre*.''

''Smallpox is not that contagious.''

''Your mother'd not like you to consort with fugitives. You'd run afoul of the law, and I'd run afoul with Catalina.''

''She never gets mad at you, Santiago.''

"Not true. But she always forgives me. Almost always." The gypsy's voice sounded tight. "You understand you may speak of this to no one. Not your parents, not the other scribes in the *Casa*, not even the priest in confession. Can I trust you?"

Armando nodded, swaggering a little. "Of course. I'd not want to lose her after all we risked to save her. You don't think she"—he swallowed—"don't think it's too late?"

Santiago shook his head. "Antonia would have found a way to tell me if the girl hadn't survived." He wiggled his eyebrows. "This is the first time I've seen you interested in a female."

Armando's ears heated. "Sure I'm interested," he mumbled. "We rescued her, didn't we?" He lengthened his strides to match Santiago's. He shot sideways glances at the earring. Perhaps he, too, would wear a golden hoop one day and grow his hair to his waist. The thought of the horrified reactions of his parents made him grin.

The day felt new and clean, the shadows of the orange trees along the streets dappling the stone walkways. A housewife hurried past on an errand, and a group of fishermen walked by, heading home with their catches in wicker baskets. When by chance Armando glanced back at the river and saw a flicker of movement near the corner of a building, he shrugged off the sight as a trick of the sunlight through the trees.

Fifteen minutes later, the blind houseboy Mateo ushered them into the *zaguán* of Antonia's house. Waiting on a carved wooden bench, Armando toyed with the frogs of his doublet. He looked up to see Santiago's knowing grin. Flushing, he folded his hands and forced himself to sit still. He wouldn't preen for any girl, least of all an Indian slave.

Doña Antonia entered through the patio door, her head

held high and her gait brisk. The black veil obscured her features. The two visitors rose. Armando made his best bow.

"You're certain it's safe for you to be here?" asked Antonia. "You weren't followed?"

Armando remembered the shadow near the building, but he said nothing. Just a trick of the light.

"No," said Santiago. "How is Paloma?"

Armando mouthed the name as he had done secretly many times. Paloma. He had an image of a smooth-breasted brown dove rising on a whir of wings into the sky. Paloma. The name suited her.

"She's getting well." Excitement thrummed in the mysterious woman's voice. Armando wished he could see the face behind the veil. Her hands clasped Santiago's. "It's a miracle," she continued in that excited voice. "Paloma is Joseph's daughter."

Santiago's body snapped like a whip. "It's impossible."

Antonia handed him a circle of silver. Armando leaned forward to peer at the etchings on the surface.

"The lion of Ribera," Santiago breathed.

Armando searched his memory. Ribera. The title had been attainted, he recalled, and the lands seized by the Holy Office. Apprehension squirmed through him, for he knew it meant that this Joseph, Paloma's father, was a Jew.

His heart sank. It was dangerous enough that she was a runaway slave. But half Jewish, too?

"It's a miracle," Antonia said again.

"But how?" Santiago handed back the medallion. "All the men left at La Navidad were slain by natives." His face darkened. "I know. I was there. I saw the burned-out fort. The"—he ran his fingers around the inside of his collar—"the body parts."

"A woman named Anacaona took Joseph away with her." Hope rang clear in Antonia's voice.

"*Dios*. Joseph. Alive. It's amazing!" Cautious joy shone

on Santiago's face. "I must see the girl—speak to her. Find out what's become of a man I'd thought long dead. I'll take her back with me. We'll find Joseph." He pulled Antonia into his arms. "And then I'll bring him back to you."

She stiffened and drew back. "No. You must never do that."

Santiago shot a glare at Armando, who read the message clearly. "Excuse me," he said. "I'll wait out in the patio."

Fat bees hummed amid tall stalks of borage and daisies. The clay pots were painstakingly aligned in rows. Probably for Mateo's sake, thought Armando, trying to ignore the murmur of voices from the *zaguán*. A blind boy would need everything precisely in its place.

Armando scowled. At the moment, he could summon no interest in the servant, not when he kept hearing snatches of the conversation within. His father had taught him manners; the Church had taught him guilt. But his training weakened beneath an onslaught of curiosity. Overcome, he moved to the window.

"Antonia," Santiago was saying, "Joseph thinks you died in that fire. He—"

"—has a new life in the islands." Armando heard the sounds of her footsteps pacing the tiled floor. "Anacaona has obviously been a wife to him. She saved him from the massacre, gave him a daughter." Her voice rose in pitch. "For the love of God, Santiago, you can't ask him to leave the life he's built."

"He'd do so for you, Antonia. My God, how he loved you."

"He loved a beautiful, selfish, foolish young woman."

"And he loves you still. I'm bringing him home, Antonia. I'm bringing him back to you."

Santiago sounded desperate. Why? Why was it so important to bring two lost lovers together? Because Santiago himself had never settled down with a woman?

"No," said Antonia. "Damn you, Santiago. He's a Jew and not welcome in Spain. Besides, what would he want with *this*?"

"Antonia, don't—"

Unable to resist his fascination, Armando edged closer to the open window and looked inside. He froze.

Doña Antonia tugged off her black gloves and flung them to the floor. Her hands, silvery with scars, tore at her veil. "Can he love this, Santiago?" She pulled the wisp of lace free.

Armando clapped his hand over his mouth to stifle a gasp. The left side of her face was a mass of scars, pulling her eye down and her mouth up, making a slick hairless furrow into her scalp. She had no ear. And yet the right side of her face was perfection, beautiful creamy skin and lovely sculpted features. The flawlessness only served to make the disfigurement more obscene. Armando stood fascinated by the grotesque spectacle.

Her shoulders shook, and tears ran from her good eye down her cheek. What a beauty she must have been when the man called Joseph of Ribera had loved her.

Santiago's throat worked as he swallowed hard. With the tenderness of a man handling an infant, he pulled out a handkerchief and dried Doña Antonia's face. Then he replaced the veil, securing it with a hair comb and the rolled coif of black velvet. Armando's eyes stung suddenly. Doña Antonia's pain and Santiago's compassion made him ashamed of his own petty complaints about his life in Seville.

"You insult him, Antonia," said Santiago. "To think a few scars would keep him from loving you."

"He must never know I survived the fire," she vowed. "I won't do that to him. I won't force him to make that choice. I won't have him come back out of pity or a sense of duty. Swear that you'll say nothing, Santiago, if you find him. Swear it."

"I—damn it, Antonia, that's not fair. He deserves to—"

"—to live his life in peace!" She clutched his red shirt. "Swear it!"

"As you wish, but you're cheating both Joseph and yourself. . . ."

"You shouldn't spy on people," a voice whispered in Armando's ear.

Cheeks flaming, he swung around to see a dark-haired girl standing behind him. Her approach had been silent as cats' paws.

Bare feet peeked from beneath a crimson gown cut in the old style with a stiff bodice and split overskirt that revealed an embroidered petticoat. His gaze traveled upward over her slim torso. Bareheaded, she had the most unusual hair he had ever seen. Straight and unstyled, it was the color of moonless midnight. The dark strands framed a face that caused an unfamiliar stirring inside him. "Wh-what?" he heard himself ask.

"I said," she repeated in a voice that sounded too low, too rich for a mere child, "you shouldn't spy on people."

He planted his hands on his hips and swung fully around. "Who says I'm spying?"

"I say so."

"Well, who're you?"

Her eyes widened; then she grinned broadly. "You truly don't know, *hombre*?"

Armando held himself very still. His gaze picked out the high cheekbones, the exotic tilt of her eyes, the lilting curve of her mouth . . . and the few faint healing pox scabs on her neck.

He took a step back, his shoulders pressing against the plastered wall. "Paloma?"

Her smile disappeared, the sun tucking itself behind a

cloud. "Yes. I remember you, too. Your name's Hombre."

He frowned. "That's not my name. It's just what Santiago calls me sometimes. I am Armando Viscaino de Hernández." He started to bow, then hesitated with his chin out and his torso angled forward. His father had taught him courtly etiquette, but he could think of no rule to govern the greeting of an Indian girl whom he'd rescued from slavery. Like his awkward stance, the world seemed suddenly off-balance. He could not fathom the status of such a girl. She was a Spanish nobleman's daughter; her Jewish ancestors had held royal courts of their own in times past. And yet she was a savage who—if the stories at the *Casa* were reliable—went about stark naked and ate raw human flesh.

Chagrined, he pulled himself straight and tall. Even barefoot, she equaled his height. To his shame, he realized he was more comfortable knowing her as a sick, frightened slave than a wildly attractive and maddeningly poised girl.

In unfocused annoyance, he turned his back on her and stomped across the patio. He passed a tiled fountain with a stone gargoyle in its center that sprouted a stream into the basin below. The spicy perfume of bloodred geraniums filled the air.

Paloma approached with a smooth, gliding step. She paused at the fountain, studying the stone figure. "Is it a god, or a demon?" She reached a finger toward the stream of water.

"What?"

She pointed at the gargoyle. "God or demon?"

Laughter burst from him. "It's neither, you goose. Just a fountain, run by a pump that is powered by the river current." He studied her blank expression and realized with a start that despite her cultured speech, words like *fountain* and *pump* were alien to her.

"What's a goose?" she asked after a moment.

"It's a sort of bird."

"Like a dove?"

He started to laugh again, but the innocence in her face stopped him. For all her stunning beauty, she was still a child torn from a far-off land, a fugitive with a thousand leagues of angry Ocean Sea between her and home. Abashed by his own callousness, he dropped his voice. "Yes. It's something like a dove. Paloma?"

"Yes?"

"I'm glad you're better. Most Ind-er, most people from across the sea die if they get smallpox."

"I know." She spoke softly. He could tell that she had seen the effects of the disease firsthand, probably on the ship that had brought her here.

He propped his hip on the rim of the basin and waited.

"I'm going home," Paloma stated, staring into the spray. The sunlight through the water made a rainbow against the *azulejo* tiles. "Doña Antonia will find a way to get me to Cayo Moa."

Armando nodded. "It sounds like Santiago will be the one to take you—" Catching her bemused expression, he stopped himself.

A smile of sly sweetness curved her mouth. "So you were listening to them."

He shrugged and spread his hands. Somehow her tone put him more at ease. She was just a girl, after all, with a girl's mischief shining in her eyes. Little different from the young ladies at the convent of San Leandro, who draped their arms over the balconies and pretended not to notice the boys from the *Casa de la Contratacíon* as they walked home each evening.

Still, he had to acknowledge that she was different. More forthright, more . . . beautiful, in a wild, pagan fashion.

"You're not afraid to make the crossing?" he asked.

"I am very afraid, Armando Viscaino de Hernández."

"I'd find it exciting," he stated.

Her gaze cooled. "No doubt you would. I am afraid of the things I don't understand. But I will go to find my parents and my clan again." She paced in a circle around the fountain. "I hate this place."

His pride injured, Armando demanded, "Is your home any better? Santiago says the Indians go about naked. You have no books and no religion. You use tools of stone and wood."

"Yes," she agreed readily.

"Then why wouldn't you want to stay here? You could pass for a Spanish girl." The fantasy appealed to him. "My parents could take you in. You could have fine clothes and a servant, learn to read books and give your soul to the Church."

Her eyes widened in bafflement. "That's not the way I wish to live my life." She seemed remote once again, exotic and incomprehensible as the parrots the explorers brought from the Indies.

Santiago and Doña Antonia came out into the patio. Santiago supported her arm as if she were an old lady. Having seen the unflawed side of her face, Armando knew she could be little older than his parents.

Santiago spied Paloma and drew up short, a stallion scenting something strange. *"Qué preciosidad,"* he said under his breath. "Antonia, she's amazing."

Antonia held out her gloved hands to Paloma, and the girl stepped willingly into her embrace.

"Do you remember Santiago?" Antonia asked.

Paloma's eyes gleamed dark with wariness.

Santiago's handsome mouth twisted in self-disgust. "You're afraid of me, *muchacha*. I don't blame you. But I didn't approve of the slave-hunting expedition. I'm ashamed of what happened, and I want to take you back."

Paloma moved away from Antonia. "When?"

He grinned at her eagerness. "Soon, *preciosa*." She

smiled, and he caught his breath. "By God, Antonia, she is as lovely as the moon."

A foreign heat prickled over Armando's skin. Santiago was always so smooth, so easy with females.

"I know," said Doña Antonia. "Paloma has her father's eyes." Her voice was strained, wistful, and Armando was amazed that she could love a man she had not seen in years. She put her hand on Santiago's arm, leaned to murmur something in his ear.

"Of course he's trustworthy," Santiago assured her. "He's my godson, and a scribe of the *Casa de Contratación*."

Antonia seemed to relax, and Santiago went on. "The next fleet sails in August. Use the time well. She's got to pass for a Castilian servant through and through, because I'll give out that she's my new maid, or"—he slid a speculative gaze over the girl—"perhaps my mistress. That would be more in character."

Armando's back stiffened and a protest leaped to his lips. Even before he could speak, Antonia tugged smartly on Santiago's arm. "No! You're not to compromise this child."

He shrank back in mock fear. "It's just a story," he assured her. "To avoid uncomfortable questions."

Armando released a sigh of relief. "She learns quickly," Antonia declared, and her voice rang with maternal pride. "She has the mind of a scholar—like her father."

"Tell me about Joseph," Santiago said to Paloma. "We were great friends, once. My heart soars now that I know he didn't perish with the others of La Navidad."

"He told me of the colony. As soon as the *cacique* Colón left in his ships, the white-eyes who stayed behind made . . ." She paused, searching for the right word. "They made havoc on the islanders. That is when my mother and father left. My father is now *guatiao*, a blood brother. He is a very great man."

Armando thought of his own struggles in the scriptorium and felt a pang of resentment. Why couldn't he be more like his father, who was sought out by sages from many nations for his ideas on cosmography?

That's not the way I want to live my life. Paloma's words whispered in his mind, and he understood better now.

"Good." Santiago slapped his hands together. "I'm leaving for Jerez in the morning, and Armando's coming with me."

"I am?" Armando's voice broke, and he blushed.

Santiago grinned. "Your parents gave you permission to travel with me." He turned to address Antonia. "Since I have no heir, my godson will inherit my estates, and it's time he saw his inheritance. Would you like that, *hombre*?"

Armando thought of traveling with his roguish godfather, escaping the tedium of the *Casa*, the baths his mother insisted he take, the books his father insisted he read. With Santiago, he would be able to ride and fight and swear, to drink *aguardiente* for breakfast and skip mass.

Though he tried to feign nonchalance, he could not stop the wide, slow smile of delight that spread across his face. "That would be fine, Santiago."

Antonia and Paloma walked with them to the patio gate. They stood under an arch that opened out to the deserted street.

Santiago faced Armando, serious now. "Listen, *ahijado*. No matter how you're tempted to talk, you're to say nothing of our plan. Do you understand?"

Armando bristled. "I already told you I'd keep quiet."

"Word of honor?"

"Word of honor."

"Good." Santiago embraced Antonia with careless ease. "We'll be back within a month." He hesitated, then pulled Paloma into his arms. "Work hard, *preciosa*," he whispered, his brown hand stealing up to touch the silk of her hair. "Learn our ways. The knowledge will protect you until I take you home."

Armando's world tilted off center once again. He envied Santiago's effortless charm. He envied the adventure that awaited Paloma.

Her cheeks glowed pink as she stepped away from Santiago and looked expectantly at Armando. His ears went hot as his tongue froze. He made a stiff bow and retreated to the street.

Santiago closed the thick wooden door, chuckling. "It's about time you had an outing with your godfather. Córdoba wasn't enough. You're as awkward as a yearling with the ladies." He ruffled Armando's hair. "Just like your f—just like Rafael."

Armando stared at the ground. He was nothing like his father. Couldn't Santiago see that? Idly, he noticed footprints on the dusty stoop and thought it odd the way they pointed in different directions, as if someone had been loitering there. He touched the back of his neck.

"Santiago, look at—"

"Enough looking. Let's go, *hombre*. You've got packing to do." Santiago clapped him on the back in manly fashion. "I've bought a new horse for you to ride."

Armando gave a whoop of delight. "A new horse? Really?"

"A sleek mare with a mouth as soft as a convent virgin's. She's tall, but you'll grow into her."

Armando's sense of foreboding burned away on the high fires of anticipation, and he ran all the way home.

Groggy with sleep, Antonia blinked into the predawn darkness. She could not place the sound that had awakened her; then she heard it again. Knocking.

Shivering with apprehension, she draped a veil over her head and pulled a shawl over her shoulders. She paused by Mateo's room off the kitchen. His snores came from the small chamber. Then, to assure herself that nothing was amiss, she went to the bookshelf that hid the entrance to Paloma's secret room. Although the child took her meals with Antonia, she slept in the hidden chamber, and did so without complaint. She understood that she was a fugitive, sought after like a stolen racehorse.

Yawning, Antonia shuffled to the front door and threw back the opening of the peephole. Three men stood in shadow, their forms indistinct. One of them held a small, flickering brass lamp with a glass chimney.

"Yes?"

"Might we have a word with you, *doña*?"

"It's the middle of the night."

"The Trade Constables never sleep."

"Private citizens do. Good night, sir—"

"I'm afraid I must insist."

One of the figures behind the speaker moved to the side. Antonia saw a gleam in the lantern light. He wore a silver badge with islands and anchors like the one Armando had worn the day before. Damn the boy! For all his assurances, he must have boasted about the slave girl he'd rescued. She shouldn't have trusted Armando. He was only a boy. The tale of how he had saved a beautiful Indian captive was simply too delicious to keep to himself. No doubt he had blurted his tale to the scribes of the House of Trade.

"This is a private home," she snapped. "I have a right—"

The constable shoved against the door. The latch came away with a metallic wrenching sound. The three men pushed past her and stepped inside. "Señora, you gave up any rights when you offered haven to a fugitive slave."

She planted herself in front of him. "I order you to leave my house, señor."

"Restrain her," the constable commanded. "Baltasar, come with me." The youth from the *Casa* followed him through an olive-bead curtain into the main part of the house.

Antonia started after them, but strong hands gripped her upper arms. She did not bother to struggle, for their physical strength exceeded hers. As the constable and Baltasar began a slow, methodical search, she tried to think, to plan.

Mateo was a light sleeper. No doubt he had heard the commotion. Would he know to go for help? She couldn't count on him; he knew no one. Santiago had already left for Cádiz.

A scuffle sounded from the kitchen. Moments later, Baltasar and the constable dragged Mateo into the room.

"Leave him alone!" Antonia pleaded. "The boy's blind and helpless!"

"You must be very loyal to your mistress," the constable said to Mateo. "Very few ladies would employ a blind and helpless servant."

The youth stiffened, his empty eye sockets boring into the darkness. "Doña Antonia?" His face turned toward the sound of her breathing.

"I'm fine, Mateo. You need not answer—" One of her captors clamped a sweaty hand over her mouth. She nearly gagged on her veil.

Mateo made a whimpering sound in his throat.

"We haven't hurt her . . . yet," said the constable. "It would be a pity if we had to."

"*Cochino!* I won't let you hurt her!" Mateo stumbled forward, his hands outstretched toward Antonia.

She grabbed her captor's arm. With a surge of strength, she shoved him away. She braced herself, expecting him to lunge. Instead, he and the others stood frozen. A light breeze caressed her face. Her veil hung from the constable's hand.

Antonia loosed a scream of terror and humiliation. She covered her face with her hands. The constables bolted into action, one of them grabbing her from behind. Baltasar's mouth moved in soundless horror as he stared at her.

Mateo seemed to sense that Baltasar had lowered his guard. With a growl, he leaped for the youth. At the last instant, Baltasar recovered, spinning around and pulling himself into a crouch. "Don't come any closer," he warned. A knife blade glittered in the dim light.

"He has a knife!" Antonia screamed to Mateo. But the blind servant was already hurling himself at Baltasar. Almost instantly Mateo sprang back. The dagger was buried to the hilt in his chest.

Antonia slid to her knees beside him. Baltasar began to sob. "*Madre de Dios*, I didn't mean to kill him!"

"Pull yourself together, boy," snapped the constable.

Antonia wept in silence, cradling Mateo to her breast, heedless now of her disfigurement, heedless of the hot blood that stained her bosom. Her grief felt like the dagger itself.

"But I've done murder," Baltasar wailed.

"Your cousin's well connected, and both of you are kin to the Marquis of Cádiz. He'll protect you," the constable said. He jerked Antonia to her feet. "Where is the girl?"

She lifted her chin and fixed him with a stone-cold stare that made him flinch. "I don't know what you're talking about."

"You swear there's no one else in the house?"

"I swear it." Her voice was hoarse with loathing.

"Fine. Then if by some unfortunate accident, this place burns to the ground, no lives will be lost. You're afraid of fire, aren't you? Very understandable, my lady."

His lackey lifted the chimney of the lamp and let the flames lick the books on the shelf.

"No!" Antonia cried. "I beg of you, don't burn my books."

"Are they so precious, then?" His hand squeezed

tighter. "Or are you worried about something more than the books?"

The choice was clear. She could either let Paloma perish in a fire, or betray her to these callous hunters.

"Curses on you," she hissed, jerking her arm away. Part of her began to die as she removed a stack of books and reached for the hidden latch.

"Ah." The constable gave a quiet exclamation. "So that's how it's done." A click sounded; then the panel glided smoothly in its track, revealing a black emptiness. Sick with dread, Antonia held her breath and prayed wordlessly.

With a trembling arm, Baltasar held a lamp high. Yellow light streamed into the chamber with its low bedstead. A white shape rushed toward the opening. The constable started; then he snatched the girl and brought her, struggling, into the room.

"Qué milagro," the constable breathed, his hands clamped on Paloma's shoulders to imprison her while he stared.

She wore a long white shift. Her black hair streamed over her shoulders and down her back. High color flagged her cheeks, and the whiteness of fear rimmed her eyes. She struggled in silence, pushing at the constable's chest and kicking wildly.

"Be still, wench!" He plunged his hand into her hair and jerked her head back so that her tender neck lay bare and taut.

"Stop it!" Antonia shouted. "You're hurting her!"

Paloma's eyes widened at the sight of Antonia's unveiled face, but she showed no disgust or horror.

The constable's lackey restrained Antonia. "By God," he exclaimed, low in his throat. "The wench is a beauty."

Baltasar edged closer to peer at the girl. "She's different from the other savages, in looks at least."

The constable nodded. "She'll do for a grandee's court,

no less. I hear the Duke of Albuquerque is seeking retainers for a voyage to Naples.''

Antonia's heart pounded. King Ferdinand's courtiers would eat the child alive! She gazed helplessly across the room at Paloma. Antonia herself had lived through enough brutality to want to see human decency served.

Now that she knew Paloma was Joseph's daughter, more than human decency gave her a cold, fierce sense of protectiveness.

In the years since she had lost Joseph—lost everything—she had drifted, aimless as a cloud on a spring wind, on the fringes of life. Occasionally she would shelter a family of Jews, and for a time she would sparkle with purpose, but once they left, the spark faded, and the fugitives were probably glad to be away from the strange woman in her black veil.

It was as if she had been waiting all her life for this moment, when she must choose between the sterile security of her empty life and opening herself once again to heartbreak.

Antonia looked at the beautiful child and thought of Joseph. Her choices dwindled to one.

Swiftly, violently, she wrenched herself from her captor. Bending, she jerked the dagger from Mateo's chest and threw herself at the constable.

''Bitch!'' he said, releasing Paloma to push Antonia away and clutch his upper arm. Blood seeped from between his fingers. ''You'll rot in prison for this!''

''Paloma, run!'' Antonia screamed, but the girl got no farther than the door.

''I'm sorry, Joseph,'' Antonia whispered. Defeat tasted like gall in her throat.

CHAPTER 4

Valladolid, Spain
20 May 1506

The admiral lay dying.

Armando sat on the stoop outside Colón's house in the north of Castile. Valladolid was a city of washed-out colors, shades of clay and bone and ochre bleached by the strong, early summer sun. Isabel and Ferdinand had married here, uniting all the provinces of Spain; and here they had set in motion the machinery of the Inquisition.

Inside the house, the murmurs of scribes and notaries mingled with the whispers of Admiral Colón's sons and friends.

A week earlier, Don Fernando, Colón's seventeen-year-old younger son, had sent an urgent message to Rafael and Santiago in Seville. Colón was failing and had asked for them. There had been no question. They had come immediately.

Armando had been pleased for the excuse to escape the *Casa de Contratación*. Even waiting for a crazy old man to die was preferable to copying trading certificates. The absence of Baltasar de León magnified Armando's boredom. A year earlier, his old rival had joined the household of the Duke of Albuquerque and gone off to Naples. The vicious jibes and backstreet brawls of the past had yielded to safe, suffocating tedium.

Armando pitched his dress dagger into the dust of the dooryard. With an idle eye, he watched a white stork nesting in the bell tower of *La Magdalena* church down the street.

The wild jangle of clinking brass pots and harness bells drew his attention to the roadway. Rising to his feet, Armando went to the gate to see a gypsy train heading north. Their painted wagons were ornate as oversized toys, the gay decor at odds with their sharp, hungry faces and watchful eyes. How strange to think that Santiago—a respected *hidalgo*—had grown up with the gypsies.

The fountain burbling atop the boundary wall of Colón's rented house awakened a familiar memory. For a moment, he fancied himself back in Doña Antonia's garden, telling a strange, bright-eyed girl about gargoyles and water pumps. The past year came rolling back at him like a wave stirred by a distant storm. Had it only been a year ago that he had gone chasing after a runaway slave? It seemed so much longer.

He thought often of the girl who had so briefly touched his life. Even now he could picture her face, arresting in its uniqueness—the tilted eyes, the high, sculpted cheekbones, the fall of startlingly black hair. Even now he could see her mouth curved into a shy, almost-smile, could hear her speaking the words of an innocent with the precision of a scholar.

He felt again the slow burn of helpless rage. He and Santiago had returned to Seville to find Antonia's house deserted, rank with the smell of rotting food. Their anxious queries around the neighborhood had yielded only baffled shrugs about the veiled woman, and superstitious signs against hexes.

Armando had joined his father and godfather in scouring every back alley from Seville to Cádiz. Santiago had, by means he refused to disclose, acquired records from the Holy Office. Rafael and Armando had pored over the documents, but found no mention of Antonia, Paloma, or the blind servant Mateo. Rafael had gone to the court of King Ferdinand, but not even the most loose-tongued gossips had ever heard of the two women. It was as if Antonia and Paloma had been sucked from the face of the earth.

Defeated in his quest, Armando had grown more discontented with his life as a scribe. Paloma's words haunted him: *That is not the way I want to live my life.* Sensing this restlessness, his father had assured him that in another year he would be ready to matriculate at the University of Salamanca.

Salamanca! Rafael spoke the word with a hushed reverence reserved only for miracles. To Rafael, who had in his youth borne the stigma of charity student, there could be no finer place for a young gentleman to start his life as a scholar.

But Armando knew Salamanca would feel like another prison.

Huffing out his despondency, he pushed away from the low plaster wall and stomped back into the house. Christ Jesus, he was acting like the spoiled son of a *hildalgo*. He had come to bid farewell to the Admiral of the Ocean Sea, not to wring his hands about his own predicament.

The house smelled of sickness and incense. In the outer chamber, two Franciscan brothers knelt and murmured prayers in Latin, their tonsured heads bent over their rosaries and their fingers urgent as they handled the beads.

Armando paused outside the bedchamber, reluctant to enter a place of death. Then, steeling his nerves, he stepped through the door.

Inside the admiral's room, the musty curtains were drawn against the white sunlight. A notary's pen scratched into the uncomfortable silence. Rafael and Santiago stood at the foot of the bed. Diego and Fernando Colón stood at the head. At twenty-six, Diego stood tall and handsome, flame-haired as Santiago had sworn Colón had been in his youth. Armando couldn't be certain in the dim light of a wick lamp, but he thought he detected a faint sulkiness in Diego's lips.

Fernando, in contrast, was swarthy and serious, his hands twisting together as he gazed lovingly at the figure on the bed.

Armando regarded the object of Don Fernando's despairing adoration. Colón didn't fit on the bed; his big bare feet stuck off the end. He lay still, his lined face drawn with pain and his eyes closed. The sallow coloring gave his skin the waxen look of an effigy. Armando fought the urge to shrink away. The men in this room revered Colón like a saint. Peering through the shadows of age and illness, Armando tried to see the strapping hero who had once defied man and nature, who had won a queen's favor and planted the standard of Spain in a strange new world. He saw only a tired old man, inches from death.

Colón's cloud of mist-colored hair shifted on the pillow. His eyes crinkled at the corners; then he opened them. As if aware of Armando's thoughts, Colón looked directly at him.

Armando caught his breath. Now he saw it. Now he saw the quality that had given Colón the courage and the lunacy to cross the Ocean Sea. It was all there in the eyes, the sea-blue eyes. The lightning bolt of pure, wild genius. Comets and storm winds, dreams and miracles, raw courage and implacable determination. But most of all those eyes burned with a savage mystery that was frightening in its intensity.

Pushing back his mortal pain, Colón saw the expression

on the youth's face change from impatience to awe. Somewhere in the swirling depths of his dying mind, he recognized the look, for he had seen his effect on people a thousand times. With his commanding stare he had beguiled the Queen of Spain. He had intimidated prelates and princes, had captivated island natives, had overpowered sour-mouthed scholars.

The youth's look pleased Colón. He still had the power to move a man who was too young to have shared in the brief flash of glory that had belonged to Colón in the gilt-edged months following his return from the first voyage.

Colón frowned into the lamp-lit face. Someone put a flask to his lips; with a feeble hand he brushed it away. He tried to place the young man in his mind. Santiago's son, no doubt, but Santiago had never married and acknowledged no children.

Rafael, the steadfast scholar, had married well.

While he, Colón, had managed to surge through life on a storm of raw ambition. Like a ship without a home port, he was never caught in the moorings of emotional commitment. Ah, he had loved and loved deeply, but always with the cold certainty that he was destined to die alone.

The thought buried a dagger of pain in his head. He turned slowly to look at the sons he would leave behind.

"Diego." He breathed his elder son's name, and Diego knelt, bending forward to hear. "I leave you with my title. The status I built with my own stinking sweat and my own aching flesh."

Diego nodded, his mane of red hair falling forward. Colón took pride in his son's handsomeness, but something about Diego troubled him. Perhaps Colón had been wrong to hand over his achievements like a bequest of gold coin. The boy had done nothing to earn the honors and titles. He might do nothing to preserve them. Colón let out a sigh. It was too late now. "Live your life well, son," he concluded. "Do yourself honor."

"Of course, Father."

Colón's gaze wandered to Fernando, his other son. The hot blade of agony twisted in his gut. He would leave the world with many regrets, but the most wrenching of all was Beatriz, Fernando's mother.

Colón studied the broad peasant's face of Fernando, the shining dark eyes and the wealth of coarse dark hair. Even through closed eyes he could see her features, only now they belonged to Beatriz as she had looked many years before.

Beatriz! She had been but twenty, and a virgin when he had met her. Her faith in him had been the guiding hand on the tiller of his life. Through the years of struggle before the first voyage, she had stood as strong and unwavering as the Pillars of Hercules. And yet in his arms she had been willing, pliant, delighting in his flights of passion and imagination.

A fresh wave of torment broke over him, like the night sweats that had plagued his sleep for years. Sucking in his cheeks, Colón dragged his eyes open again. He must do one more thing for Beatriz, paltry as it was.

"Hinojedo."

Pen in hand, the notary Pedro de Hinojedo moved in close.

"Add this to my bequests: 'Watch over the welfare of Beatriz Enriquez de Harana, and see that she is in a position to live as befits a person to whom I owe so great a debt. And let this be done as a relief to my conscience for it weighs much on my soul. The reason for this is not licit for me to speak of here.' " Colón wet his lips and tried to smile at the sea of inquisitive faces. Ah, they would puzzle for years over that one. No one would ever guess the reason for his gut-tearing guilt. No one would ever know that Cristóbal Colón had once lost all faith in his own enterprise, had nearly given up his quest. No one would ever know that it was a common peasant woman who had restored his confidence in himself.

"You'll carry out my wishes?" he asked Fernando.

Fernando gripped his hand. Like his mother, he thrived on physical contact. Colón felt the pressure of his son's strong handclasp. Would to God he had clasped Beatriz with that strength. And then Fernando let go, and Colón's world listed. Eyes closing, he spun, directionless and out of control, across a black, fathomless void. The mysteries there beckoned to him just as the mysteries of the Ocean Sea had once done.

He knew again all the anger and frustration that had darkened the last years of his life. Outlawed in his own viceroyalty, forsaken by his king, scoffed at by the haughty adventurers who had come after he had cut the first wake, he was but a bridge spanning the Sea of Darkness.

He grasped at the freedom offered by the fathomless void. But against his will, his eyes opened again. With sudden, blinding clarity he saw them all, hovering, hungry, still wanting something from him.

He had given the world all he had. He'd flung continents at their feet, poured riches into their coffers, brought savage souls to the True Faith. How could they demand more from his broken body, his fevered mind? He had nothing left but words.

"Rafael."

With tears coursing down his ascetic face, the slim, green-eyed scholar stepped forward. "Yes?"

"You were the first man I met when I came to Spain."

A familiar half-shy grin broke through the tears. "I was hardly a man at the time, Cristóbal. Just a snot-nosed charity student afraid of my own shadow."

"Ah, but you weren't afraid to dream, Rafael."

"Your plan was worth dreaming about, *compadre*."

"My dream," Colón said bitterly, "is but a pile of rubble sifted through by greedy adventurers. I should have fought harder, sailed farther, pushed on—''

"Forgive yourself, Cristóbal," said a smooth voice. "You did your best. We gypsies have a saying: A tree cannot catch birds beyond its top.''

Colón shifted his gaze and focused on a dark, handsome man. Damn! Was the gypsy Santiago enchanted in some way? He looked as young as he had the day they first set sail. Comely, arrogant, rakishly engaging. "Santiago." He clasped the slim brown hand. "Still looking for the Isle of Women, eh?''

"Er, Admiral, I'm Armando, not Santiago.''

Colón realized his error as the boy named Armando stepped back to give way to Santiago. The figures in the room moved soundlessly; a dreamlike quality blurred the moment. The real Santiago had streaks of white in his long hair, scars on his face, even a rope burn around his neck. But the charming insolence of his smile remained the same. He pressed his hand firmly to Colón's shoulder.

"Always, Cristóbal. I won't rest until I find it.''

Muttering prayers, a priest came forward to administer the viaticum. The host of the Eucharist felt dry as old timber on his tongue, and he swallowed it with difficulty.

Vaguely Colón noticed that Armando withdrew, slipping away like a candle blown out by the wind. One by one, the other faces in the room went out, each a tiny flame smothered by a brass cup. First went the clerics and notaries, the men who had taught him to pray like a Christian, and those who had chronicled his words and his deeds.

Then his friends left him: Mendez and Fieschi, both heroes from the Jamaican ordeal that had launched him into his long descent toward defeat. Then Rafael and Santiago, men who had believed in him from the time he had been a penniless weaver's son fresh off the boat from Portugal. Finally his sons, Diego and Fernando, whom he loved as much as it was in his capacity to love, flickered away.

When he could see no more, Colón's vision turned inward, and he saw those who were present in spirit if not in fact: Fray Juan Pérez, the humble friar who had cleared Colón's path to the royal court. Queen Isabel, a woman strong and brilliant enough to share his vision. He saw Joseph Sarmiento, running for his life and then finally finding safe haven among the savages in the Indies. He remembered the islander he'd dubbed Diego, a man he had come to love, a man murdered by Colón's detractors.

Last of all there was Beatriz, round faced, with a compelling earthy beauty, holding out her arms for him.

Colón reached, but the distance gaped too wide. And then, like the last candle in a dark room, the light went out.

Alone in the black final moments, Colón felt his essence skimming like a seabird over the endless smooth nothingness that had been his life. All the pain and joy and horror and ecstasy washed beneath him, no longer touching him. He saw the men he had been—the dreamer, the schemer, the admiral and the viceroy. Those men were nothing now, brief and brilliant flashes as quickly gone as a streak of lightning.

What endured was the wind and the waves, and the night sky a spinning bowl over the pitching deck of a ship. What endured was the sailor who had thrown himself into adventure, the man who had always seen more clearly, heard more keenly, and felt more deeply than other men, the man who had launched himself like an eagle from a cliff, heart and soul, without looking back.

From his last clinging awareness he conjured his final words, mumbling them into an ear pressed close. "In manus tuas, Domine, commendo spiritum meum." And from his last shred of strength he managed an admiral's smile for the unseen, weeping men standing around him.

"By God, lads, don't grieve! It's been a high adventure, has it not?"

Darkness closed over the city of Valladolid, throwing steeples and wall towers into sharp, black relief. Armando walked aimlessly through the twisting narrow streets near the river Pisuerga. He heard raucous songs from a tavern; he heard the bell of the college of San Gregorio toll nine times. The windows of the church of San Francisco blazed with light as the faithful celebrated the Feast of the Ascension. The smell of onions sizzling in olive oil wafted from a nearby house, but Armando felt no pang of hunger.

He supposed the admiral must have died by now.

Yet Colón's words stuck like a burr in his mind. Santiago. The admiral had taken his hand and called him Santiago.

Armando kicked at a loose cobblestone in the street. Surely it was the honest mistake of a feverish man on his deathbed.

But he worried the problem like a cat toying with a cockroach. The admiral had taken his hand and called him Santiago.

Although a balmy breeze off the river warmed the night, Armando shivered. In a field just north of the city he saw a series of flickering camp fires. The gypsies had circled their wagons for the night. Seeing them crouched and laughing around their fires—mothers crooning to infants and the men strumming guitars and singing softly—reminded him anew of Santiago.

Santiago, his godfather. In his mind's eye Armando saw his life spread out before him. His father, so pale and scholarly. Santiago, earthy and laughing, swearing that Armando must one day inherit his estate near Jerez. He thought of his brothers and sisters, fair-haired while he was dark—his hair, his skin, most especially his eyes. As dark as sin they were. As dark as . . . Santiago's.

A cry of pain broke from him, and he started to run. Back to Colón's house, back to confront the two men who had hidden a terrible secret from him.

Torches lit the central patio, and a black cloth draped the heavy wooden door. The chant of vigil prayers drifted from the opened windows.

Colón was dead.

Without breaking his stride, Armando swiftly made the sign of the cross. In the patio, he saw a faint orange glow and recognized the scent of Santiago's tobacco. He and Rafael stood leaning against the wall, heads bent in conversation. They were alone, but Armando would not have cared if the entire population of the city were present.

He pounded toward them over the tiles, then came up short. Rafael's face, orange in the torchlight, was creased with worry. "Where have you been? We were just about to go looking for you."

On a rush of fury and fear, Armando blurted, "You're not my real father, are you?"

Rafael blinked; then he and Santiago exchanged a glance. "Armando, I don't understand why you'd ask such a—"

"Because I deserve to know!" Heat pressed at the backs of his eyes. He rounded on Santiago. "Colón mistook me for you."

"*Hombre,* the poor man was breathing his last. Is it any wonder his eyes were dim?"

"He saw me clearly!" Armando's voice broke, but he didn't care. "He thought I was you. I want to know why." He faced Rafael again, peered into the gentle, quiet face that had always regarded him with a mixture of unreserved love and frank bewilderment. "I want to know why I'm dark as a gypsy while you and Mama and the younger ones are fair. I want to know why you have a talent for writing while I struggle just to hold a pen in my hand. And why I can ride and fight when you have no talent for either!"

Tears splashed down his cheeks, hot with the sting of betrayal.

"Armando," said Rafael, "these questions you ask—"

"It's not natural," Armando broke in. "I don't belong to you." His voice dropped to a hoarse, aching whisper. "I think I always knew it. But it took Colón to open my eyes."

Rafael reached for him. Armando stepped back, his head flung up and his fists on his hips.

Rafael lowered his hand slowly. "Armando, I can explain—"

"Then damn you, I wish you would." He saw Santiago's eyes narrow, but he would not acknowledge the gypsy.

"Come here." Rafael gestured at a stone bench. "We'll talk." He put his hand on Armando's shoulder.

Stung by the gentle touch, Armando shoved him back. Terror and rage and confusion gave force to the motion. Rafael stumbled and fell, his face striking the tiled surface of the patio.

He looked up, and the three froze in a tableau of disbelief. Then Rafael put up his hand, touching the trickle of blood at the corner of his mouth.

Armando was mortified by the sight of the man he called father sprawled on the ground and bleeding. "Oh, God," he began, dropping to his knees. "I didn't mean to hurt you."

Santiago's arm lashed out and seized him by the collar, choking him and hauling him to his feet. "God damn you," he spat, glaring into Armando's defiant eyes. "You God damned little ingrate, you—"

"Stop." Rafael's low order cut off the tirade. "Let him go, Santiago."

"The whelp hit you!"

Rafael got to his feet, working his jaw. "Yes. You used to hit me often. We'd best tell him, Santiago." He lowered himself wearily to the stone bench and drew a deep breath.

Chanted prayers and ragged male weeping drifted from the chamber where the dead admiral lay.

Rafael looked up at Armando. "You were born the year we returned from the first voyage." He spoke in a dull flat tone.

Something in his expression made Armando feel cold and brittle, a chunk of ice about to shatter. He fought the impulse to clap his hands over his ears.

"I know," he said. "You married my mother after I was born, but I felt no shame in that." His eyes cut to Santiago. "Until now. Until I realized I'm a gypsy's bastard." Rage and fear exploded in his head. "You both had her, didn't you? You had my mother like a cheap whore passed around the camp fire—"

Like a bolt of lightning, Santiago's arm shot out. Armando felt the back of a sinewy hand against his cheek, felt his head snap to one side, tasted blood in his mouth. Strangely, he felt no pain. Shock had drained all sensation from him.

"Santiago," said Rafael. "Don't touch him again."

Armando recognized a quiet command in his voice, pure steel veiled by innate civility. He looked from one man to the other. From the dark gypsy who had given him life to the gentle scholar who had raised him. Santiago had always been there, roughly affectionate, laughing, never acknowledging that he had once fornicated with an innocent woman. Rafael had been the one who had read him stories at bedtime, bandaged his hurts, and with infinite patience had taught and guided him.

Armando stared at them both and felt nothing but betrayal. His tongue poked into the torn flesh inside his cheek. Grasping the chain around his neck, he tugged smartly. For years he had worn the agnus dei of Indies gold, his present from Santiago. Now he flung it as far as he could throw.

Then he took a deep breath and strode past them both, out of the house that grieved for the admiral's passing.

"Armando," Rafael called. "Don't go."

Armando kept walking. He did not look back.

The darkness of the city, the air heavy and sweet with myrtle blossoms, passed unacknowledged as Armando wandered the streets once again. The smells of refuse and river water wafted on the breeze. He had come to the rough wharf-side district along the banks of the Pisuerga. The calm water reflected wavering squares of lights that burned in a few windows, but the street seemed deserted. The windows, he realized, belonged to the residence of the Marquess of Valverde. Rafael had told him that a troop of soldiers was stationed there.

He avoided the inn where he and his fath—he and Rafael had been staying. No doubt they expected him to appear there, broken and full of remorse, eager to accept their flimsy explanations.

He would prove them wrong. He did not need them, did not need men who lied and deceived. He turned blindly into a narrow alley filled with the watery light of the rising moon.

Two shadows, sleek as hunting cats, poured over a high plaster wall and landed in front of Armando. He stopped, staring at the threatening snarls on a pair of grimy gypsy faces.

He felt no fear. The duplicity of two men he had loved and trusted all his life had scoured his heart of emotion.

"Out of my way," he grumbled, moving to stride past them.

A wiry arm snaked out, gripping his shoulder. "Not so fast, little *hombre rico*." The voice was sharp with a Romany accent. "Just give us your valuables, and pray we let you live."

Armando furtively studied his surroundings. Damn! His

aimless path had brought him to a deserted warehouse district on the riverfront north of town. The street lay in shadow, a high wall behind him and two hungry gypsies in front of him.

He hooked his thumbs into his stomacher. The fingers of his right hand tickled the hilt of his dagger, while his other hand felt the strings of a purse, heavy with the gold Rafael had given him earlier to make an offering for the soul of Colón.

A few hours before, he would have handed over the gold, the dagger, and his beautiful brocaded doublet. He would have been grateful to escape unharmed. But the revelation had given him a new ferocity, a sense that all of life was a fight.

He forced a cold little smile. "All right. You have me." He shrugged out of his doublet.

The gypsies exchanged a glance and a few words in their Romany tongue. "These stupid rich boys," said one. "Cowardly as women, eh, Miguel? They take the sport out of stealing." Armando gave no sign that he understood the language. Santiago had taught him Romany songs and stories and proverbs. Armando had not known it then, but now he realized his gypsy blood must have absorbed the language thoroughly.

"Here." He opened the quilted doublet. "Hold this while I untie my purse."

"Will you listen to that, Constantin? Must be used to having a valet." Miguel, whose lopped-off ear marked him as a horse thief, reached for the thick padded garment.

Driven by the strength of his fury, Armando jammed the doublet down on the youth's head. At the same moment, he brought his knee up, thumping it into the gypsy's groin.

Even as Miguel fell, silent and gasping in agony, Armando whipped out his dagger and crouched low, facing

the boy called Constantin. Armando's speed and instinct
sprang from an untapped source deep inside him, and in
a cold rational corner of his mind he realized it was his
own gypsy blood coming to life with an exultant surge of
power.

"Come on, you cowardly scum," he said in the ancient
clicking tongue of Rom.

Caught off guard, Constantin fumbled with his own
knife. Armando lunged. The point of his dagger caught
the youth's thin shirt. Blood welled from the wound. It
was Santiago's training that sent Armando leaping forward, toppling his adversary and landing with a thud on
his chest. It was Rafael's ingrained sense of decency that
made Armando look into the boy's terrified face and hesitate.

"You're not worth the trouble," he muttered, levering
himself up and retrieving his doublet. "Go back to the
cess pond you crawled from."

It was Armando's own foolishness that made him turn
his back on the gypsies.

He felt the wind at the back of his neck a split second
before a solid blow landed on the top of his head.

His vision wavered, but he spun around and brought his
foot up, clipping the gypsy beneath the chin.

Constantin fell backward with a howl of pain. Miguel
swore and dragged himself up.

Armando lunged to meet the attack. He jammed his
elbow into Miguel's ribs. The youth's breath, foul with
aguardiente, rushed from him. Then, with a guttural oath,
he twisted free, lowered his head, and butted Armando
against a crumbling wall.

A bony knee came up and crushed him in the groin.
The pain took his breath away, speeding up through his
body like a forest fire. His eyes and nostrils streamed.

Clublike fists battered his face, his stomach, his groin

again. He sagged against the wall. Only the flurry of punches held him upright.

Through a haze of agony, Armando knew he would die tonight, a gypsy's bastard too stupid to see the truth until a dying mystic had revealed it.

A well-aimed blow flung his head back against the wall. He sank, with a curse on his lips, into blackness.

CHAPTER 5

His head had swelled to twice its normal size, he was certain. He could not lift it. Every hair had become a chain binding him to the strange, bristly pad beneath him.

The pain surrounded him like the glow of a fire. His body throbbed with a hot ache. He forced his eyes open. Still dark. The moon had set. Where the hell was he? Apparently the gypsies had stripped him to his small-clothes and left him for dead.

Uncomfortably aware of his state of undress, Armando pondered his choices. His first impulse was to find his way back to the inn, to the comfortable room he shared with Rafael.

But the memory of his own words stopped him. *You both had her, didn't you? You had my mother like a cheap whore passed around the camp fire—*

God. They would never forgive him for his remark. Nor, he decided mutinously, did he crave their forgiveness. As for his mother . . . Armando shuddered. His outburst proved he was no worthy son for her.

With that thought, the pain came up and engulfed him again, and he sank into sleep.

He tried to lie still, but a jostling motion kept jarring him. A harsh herbal smell, reminiscent of his mother's surgery, hung in the air. His head pounded abominably.

Jangling, creaking noises stabbed into his brain. A horse whinnied. With a grimace, he dragged his eyes open and found himself staring at a brightly painted wood beam above his face. A rough horsehair pallet scratched his back. He turned his head to see a tiny, shuttered window shaped like a fan, the frame painted with strange, serpentine hex signs.

Mother of God! This was no ordinary horse litter. It was a gypsy caravan! The heathens were carrying him off, the same as they did in the nursery tales spun by superstitious old women.

Springs groaning, the wagon sank to one side. A heavy tread thumped on the floorboards. "Is he awake?" asked a man's voice.

Armando closed his eyes and strained to hear. The voice came from the cramped depths below the bunk where he lay.

"Not yet, Gregorio."

Armando recognized the voice of Miguel. He felt a thumb pry up one eyelid, then let go. "Well, you should have left him in the alley instead of dragging him back here."

"He's a rich *hidalgo*'s son. He'll wake up so scared that he'll promise us a fortune to take him back to his family."

Fat chance, Armando thought grimly. Memories of the previous night rushed back at him, infinitely more painful than the bumps and bruises dealt by the gypsies. The issue was not how to get back to his family, but how to stay away—forever.

"Fortune, ha!" said the deep voice of Gregorio. "You'll have the *Hermandad* breathing down our backs."

Lulled by the rocking motion of the wagon, Armando slipped into a heavy sleep. When he awoke, he lay under the stars, a camp fire crackling at his feet and a smelly blanket draped over him. He still wore only his small-clothes. He heaved a sigh of disgust and blinked up at the sharp white stars.

"I see you're awake." The girl's voice was soft, intimate.

He turned his head, forcing himself to ignore a bolt of pain. "Yes." His mouth felt dry as sand.

She leaned down and her face came into focus. The firelight outlined the plump curve of her cheek and the sweep of her black eyelashes. Two thick black braids twined with beads and bells hung down over the lush swell of her breasts. She wore a loose blouse and red embroidered vest, and layers of skirts.

"My name is Lara."

Habit gave him the urge to bow, but his supine position and state of undress rendered the courtesy impossible. "Armando," he said, deliberately leaving off his family names. They expected him to pledge a fortune to be reunited with his parents. He had no intention of revealing who he was. "You know . . ." He frowned. "You live with Constantin and Miguel?"

She nodded, setting her braids to swinging. "They're my stepbrothers, the swine. They're Gregorio's sons. He was married to my mother. After she died, Gregorio kept me on because he didn't want to have to train up another woman to serve him." Her teeth worried her ripe lower lip. "Are you hungry?"

"Yes."

One of her eyelids drooped slightly, giving a lazy quality to her smile. She rose with a languid ripple of motion and strolled over to a larger fire where cook pots bubbled over the coals. A few minutes later she returned with a mug of wine and a clay bowl filled with something hot and fragrant.

"Here, I'll help you sit up." Her arm slid beneath his shoulders. The musky female scent of her surrounded him. Bracing his arms behind him, he sat up. The blanket pooled around his waist, but since she seemed unoffended by his bare chest, he began eating. In a vague way, she reminded him of Paloma, eschewing the prudishness of proper Spanish girls. Yet Lara was coarser, more guileful. Untrustworthy.

An older man with a sun-browned face and hard, calculating eyes joined them. He pushed Lara aside in an offhand way. "You should know better than to turn your back on a gypsy," he said, combing his fingers through a thick, graying mustache.

Armando recognized Gregorio's voice from the wagon. "True." He ate a spoonful of the soup. The meat had a gamy quality that roused his suspicions, but he was too hungry to question the contents of his meal.

Five painted wagons and a dozen tethered horses circled the camp. In a trampled grassy area, Constantin and Miguel were abusing a piebald stallion. With a singular lack of skill, they tried to force the half-wild horse to accept a bridle and bit.

The other gypsies sat on the ground, sharing wine and laughter and talk with an easy familiarity alien to Armando. Schooled from the cradle to courtly formality, he found himself enjoying the unself-conscious ease of the Romany people. Young ladies of quality barely saw a man before their wedding day. The women here joked and drank and swore as heartily as the men. Armando caught himself remembering Santiago's breezy personality; then he scowled the thought away.

"I expect you'll want to be getting back to your family," Gregorio suggested.

Armando set his spoon in the bowl. "For a price, of course."

"Of course."

"Your sons have already taken my dagger, my purse, and my clothes."

Gregorio spread his hands. "It's a living. Your family will offer more to gain your freedom."

"I don't think so, sir. You'll make no coin on me."

"Ah, but that doublet is the garment of a well-bred young man. You were a happy find indeed."

Armando tried to grin, but the bruises on his face stopped him. "Your mistake. My family will be glad to be rid of me. In fact, they paid me that purse of coins just to stay away."

Gregorio seemed used to getting his own way. "I don't believe you. Tell me your name."

Lara giggled into the hem of her skirt. Spitting a Romany oath, Gregorio backhanded her across the face. "Pipe down, slut, or you'll find yourself sold to a full regiment of lusty Turks. Nobody makes sport of Gregorio of the Road."

Armando drew a sharp breath; his instincts told him to defend Lara. The pain and guilt of his failure to protect Paloma from bondage lent strength to his grip on Gregorio's arm, raised for a second blow.

Yet Lara seemed more annoyed than hurt by the beating. "Let's keep him," she suggested, speaking in the ancient tongue.

Muttering another oath, Gregorio twisted his wrist out of Armando's grip, but made no move to hit the girl again.

"There cannot be a prettier young man in all of Castile," Lara added.

Armando lifted his mug to hide his flush. Apparently

Constantin and Miguel had neglected to tell the others that their captive understood Rom.

"Don't think you'll be ransomed, eh?" Gregorio reverted to Spanish. "Then what are your plans?"

Armando shrugged, then winced at the pain in his shoulder. "Just traveling."

"Traveling where?"

He shrugged again. "I expect I'll know when I get there."

"Bah! You're no man of the road. Your hands are soft, your body is clean and well fed. You'll run back to your family."

Armando banished a fleeting image of Rafael and Catalina sitting in the garden in Seville, the little ones cavorting at their feet. He gazed at the moonlit field. The piebald had thrown each of the brothers several times; now the horse stood with its sides bellowing and its head lowered in suspicion.

"I have no family."

"Then why should we keep you?" Gregorio took out a broad-bladed knife, spat on a whetstone, and began sharpening the blade with long, rhythmic strokes. "Feed you from our kettle, let you ride in our wagon? Why should we do that for a *gorgio*?"

Armando refused to be intimidated. "I'll work for my keep. Besides, my purse ought to feed you for a year."

The gypsy snorted. "Work! Rich *gorgios* never work."

Armando pointed at the piebald, the two youths squatting out of range of its snapping teeth. "You wish to sell that horse?"

"Yes." The knife rasped against the whetstone.

"You'll get a poor price for him. He's a pretty animal and appears healthy, but he's mean." The piebald's ears flattened, and his skin flinched each time one of the brothers sidled close.

"Any fool can see that."

"Even the fool you expect to buy him."

"I'll give him some of Old Zannah's nerveroot to calm him. He'll be tractable enough."

"Let me lunge him for you. He's been poorly broken, but I can make him behave."

Gregorio snorted again. "Big words, *gorgio*."

"Let him try, Gregorio," said Lara. "What can it cost you?"

Gregorio tested his blade with the pad of his thumb. "Done. Have him ready by morning."

Despite his aching head and tired muscles, Armando welcomed the challenge. He waved away Lara's extended hand and rose to his feet. His vision swam; then he steadied himself, quickly donning an old tunic Gregorio handed him.

"Can you get me something to feed the horse?" Armando asked Lara. "Something sweet, maybe?"

She gave him another of her slow, lazy smiles. "I have something sweet." She sauntered off, the bangles around her ankles jingling. A few minutes later she returned with a scarf full of sugared orange rinds.

"Those will do." Armando took the scarf, along with a saddle blanket and lunge bridle. Constantin and Miguel made a great show of bowing to him as if he were a matador, then jabbing each other in the ribs as they stepped back to watch the *gorgio* being trampled to death.

Moonlight silvered the field, and rooks croaked in a stand of alder trees. The scent of night-blooming primroses spiced the air. Armando walked slowly toward the piebald.

The horse's nostrils dilated and his ears went back.

"Come there, *amigo*," Armando whispered under his breath. "It's all right . . . all right."

The stallion bit at him, a vicious snapping of healthy teeth. Armando forced himself to stay still and hold out the food. The piebald exhaled through its lips. Armando dropped the candied orange. The animal snatched it up as it hit the ground.

"Gracias al cielo," Armando muttered to himself. He felt the eyes of the gypsies on him, heard the derisive murmurs of Gregorio's sons. He held out another piece of orange, dropped it, and repeated the gesture, edging closer with each offering. Finally, when his nerves were strung taut and even Constantin and Miguel had fallen silent, the piebald ate from his hand.

Armando's low murmurs of persuasion filled the night. He spoke to the horse like a poet, touched the animal like a lover, caressed its neck, its cheek, its flank. Santiago had made Armando a bastard, but he had also taught him a beguiling skill with horses. Before long he had the lunge bridle over its head and was leading it around the make-shift paddock.

Armando shed the trappings of the past like a suit of outgrown clothes. He let his hair grow long and wore loose trousers, a blousy shirt, and a gaudy embroidered vest. Throughout the summer he traveled with the caravan, learning the Romany ways and perfecting his command of the Romany tongue.

Gregorio's eye for good horseflesh, coupled with Armando's talent for training, made their trade a lucrative enterprise. Near the bigger cities, the troupe performed acrobatics, juggling, and riding tricks, and while the crowd threw coppers to the performers, the other gypsies picked pockets and cut purses. Gregorio performed astride one excellent horse with Arab blood, and he would accept no price for the mare. Her name was Amadora.

By autumn's end, as the troupe began to work its way south to spend the winter in the caves outside of Guadix, Armando had learned to ride for show. He owed his talent to constant practice, for working with the horses was his only escape from the past. The numbness of sheer physical exhaustion kept the nightmare memories at bay. Thanks to his diligence, he could leap astride the mare from a run. He could stand on Amadora's back while she cantered in a circle. He could bend down while riding at a gallop and snatch a flaming torch from the ground.

But Gregorio never let Armando perform in public. In his gruff way, the gypsy man was devoted to his sons, and would not humiliate them by letting a *gorgio* on horseback outshine their juggling act.

Until one night when the troupe camped on the outskirts of Valencia. Lara and some of the others had gone into town to cry up the gypsy show. Gregorio and Armando readied Amadora, slipping on her red bridle with plumes and brass bells, and braiding her tail and mane with ribbon streamers.

Lara and the others returned at dusk, a large crowd of curious townspeople in their wake. The women lit torches in a large oval bordering a sandy field. Armando smoothed his hand down Amadora's gleaming neck. "Ready, Gregorio?" he asked.

When he heard no response, he looked over the horse's back to find Gregorio slumped in a pile of hay. He rushed to the man's side. "Gregorio? What's wrong?"

"Short of breath." Gregorio waved his hand. An unhealthy blue outlined Gregorio's lips. Armando caught himself wishing for his mother, for her knowledge of healing. He forced the wish away. That part of his life was over now.

"I'll get Old Zannah to bring you some medicine."

"Bother Old Zannah," Gregorio said. "Big crowd tonight. Expecting a show."

"You can't ride. You're too sick."

"You ride her, *gorgio*. I'll be all right."

Excitement surged through Armando. The tumblers and jugglers had whetted the crowd's appetite, and they were calling for more. Taking hold of Amadora's bridle, he studied the sea of torch-lit faces, the bright eyes eager for a spectacle.

Armando knew he had the power to thrill them or frighten them, to make them laugh or gasp or sigh with relief.

"Yes, you're ready," Gregorio said as if he had read Armando's thoughts. "Go on."

Armando slapped the mare on the rump to send her trotting out into the ring. He followed at a run, placing his hands above her tail and vaulting onto her back. A ripple of admiration swept the audience.

The months of training made each movement fluid and effortless. Drunk on the calls of encouragement, Armando went through the routine like a kestrel sailing through the clouds. He leaped and cavorted, his grin gleaming in the torchlight, his loose shirt billowing around him, and the calls of the crowd as sweet as a *cante jondo* in his ears.

He finished by standing erect with the mare's back warm beneath his bare feet. In one hand, he held the reins. His other arm was flung out as if to embrace the crowd. He noticed the furious glares of Constantin and Miguel, who looked like poor jesters in their jugglers' costumes, but found himself laughing in the face of their open hostility.

Coppers dropped like rain at the mare's feet. A sense of triumph filled his throat. It was as close to happiness he had felt since the night he had last seen Rafael and Santiago.

After the show, he rubbed down the mare and gave her a bucket of water and some sweetened oats. Lara sat waiting for him on the stoop of the wagon. Her skirts were hiked above her knees, and her bare toes traced random patterns in the dust.

"How's Gregorio?" he asked, lowering himself beside her.

"Sleeping. Zannah gave him a draught of hippocras."

"Is his illness serious?"

"He gets these spells of breathlessness sometimes. Usually when we get into the mountains. They pass in a day or two." She handed him a cup of honeyed wine. "You were wonderful tonight. Everyone—except my stepbrothers—is saying so."

Still flushed and sweaty, Armando grinned. He took a swig of the wine, savoring the honey flavor on his tongue.

When he lowered the bottle, Lara's lips were there, pressing hard to his, the taste of her sweeter than the wine. His eyes widened in surprise. She held him by the shoulders, drawing closer, fitting her tongue between his lips.

White heat bolted through him. His loins jerked painfully, and he heard a sound like a torrent in his ears. The pressure inside him built until he thought he would explode. He tried to bring his hands up to push her away, but only succeeded in brushing her breasts, the nipples straining against her blouse.

At last he managed to draw back. "Christ Jesus!" The cry burst from him as if he had been holding his breath.

She curled her hand around his thigh. "You liked that, eh?"

"Gregorio would kill me if he knew." But even that truth failed to cool the fire in his loins.

"Zannah gave him enough hippocras to keep him dead asleep for hours." Lara stood, pulling him up against her and kissing him again. He felt the curves of her plump body, cushiony and yielding. In some part of his brain he acknowledged her coarseness, the oniony smell of her, and the softness that would one day run to fat. But his ungovernable body knew only the billowy femininity, the slickness of her lips, and the feel of her little pointed tongue jabbing inside his mouth.

"I know a place where we can be alone," she suggested.

Armando forced his hands to his sides. "I'd not dishonor you, Lara."

She laughed with ill-bred harshness. "Still the courtly gentleman."

"You're not thinking. One night with me—with any boy—before you're wed would ruin you."

She caught at his hands. "I am thinking, Armando. Gregorio has already accepted a bride price for me."

Armando didn't know which surprised him more, the news that Lara was to become a wife or her matter-of-fact way of disclosing the news. "He has? From whom, Lara?"

She curled her lip in disgust. "From Raoul, the tinsmith. He's *old*, Armando. Older than Gregorio." She moved even closer to him, her hand brushing against the front of his trousers. He nearly came out of his skin at her touch. "Why shouldn't I have a man I want before I pledge myself to a sour old tinsmith?"

He found his arms overflowing with her, his senses filled with the musky scent of her and his mouth flooded with the taste of her. His every nerve and muscle burned with vivid desire.

"Just this once, Armando." She rose to bite at his ear. "You looked so handsome tonight, out riding in the ring. Gregorio saw, you know, before the drug made him too sleepy." As she spoke, she drew him deeper and deeper into the shadows, toward the night woods. "Aye, he saw you, and he couldn't have been prouder if you'd been his own son."

His own son. The words sluiced over Armando like a bucket of ice water. He wrenched free of Lara and stepped back. "No." His voice rang with hard-won conviction. "We won't do this. Not now, not ever."

"Armando, what's wrong?" Her fingers trailed over his chest, his stomach, and his groin. "Don't you want it, too?"

Frustration fueled his temper. "Of course I do, you stupid wench. But it's wrong. What if we make a baby?"

She laughed. "Then my new husband would have a

wonderful surprise, and one he'll be too proud to deny as his own." She lifted his hand to her breast. "I hope it's a boy."

A coldness spread through him, freezing his passion. He could never risk bringing a child into the world, foisting a babe on a man who had not fathered it. He could not condemn a child to the shame and confusion he himself had suffered.

Wrenching his hand free, he took another step back. Resolution sat like a stone in his gut. "No, Lara. It's not right. You'll go pure to your husband."

And I, he thought, shuddering with thwarted passion as he walked back to the open cart where he made his bed, will be as celibate as a devout monk.

The next spring, as they forded the Río Odra near Burgos, Armando dropped his comb into the shallows. As he dismounted to retrieve it, he caught a glimpse of his reflection in the still, flat water.

He froze, staring at a strong-featured sun-browned face, the stubble of a beard shading his cheeks. His long hair fell forward in dark waves. Christ Jesus, he thought, is that me?

The changes had been gradual, unnoticed until this moment. Now he realized how much he had changed in the past year, from a spoiled *hidalgo*'s son to a young man of strength and skill. Perhaps that was one reason his vow grew more and more difficult to keep. Lara had dutifully and sulkily married, and gone off to live with her husband. But in her place came other gypsy girls. They lifted their skirts and danced for him. They laughed into his eyes and kissed him on the mouth. But their efforts to entice him further met with failure.

He did most of the riding himself now. He and Miguel had come to blows more than once. Gregorio, ever ready to capitalize on a skill, saw a channel for the enmity. Miguel and Armando staged mock sword fights to thrill the crowds. After each performance, town girls would flirt with them, and Miguel enjoyed their favors indiscriminately. On fire with frustration, Armando discovered ways to pleasure them without compromising their honor. Such carryings-on always left him panting and dissatisfied, but he had only to remember his vow and the reason behind it, and his ardor cooled.

Ironically, he gained the reputation of a ladies' man, for the gypsies drew their own conclusions from the wet-mouthed, satisfied girls returning from their assignations.

In the winter of 1508 the tribe stopped in Santander on the north coast of Galicia. Normally they went south to balmy Andalucía for the winter, but not this year. The elders of the tribe, disturbed by the specter of the Inquisition, had decided to seek more hospitable crowds in France.

Gregorio had acquired a string of light Moorish ponies, which he sent to market with Armando. With uncanny luck, Armando, Constantin, and Miguel found a grandee who had seven spoiled daughters. Armando's easy conversation enchanted the young ladies, and he soon had them convinced that their lives would not be complete without the dainty animals. An hour later, his purse heavy with the grandee's gold, he started back to the camp. Constantin and Miguel were nowhere to be found; he decided they were probably off picking pockets or cadging for coppers.

He barely acknowledged the gang of wharf-side ruffians coming toward him. Wearing red sailors' caps and cheap homespun clothing, they excited no more than a passing interest in him.

Too late, he realized that the six men had joined him on his walk. The law forbade common seamen to carry swords, but their long knives were just as formidable. Casually reaching up, Armando tugged the brim of his hat down to shadow his face.

"Look at that, *caballeros*." Sticking out the tip of his knife, one of the men prodded the leather coin purse tied at Armando's waist. "A gypsy man, probably fresh from bilking honest folk."

The blade came up and knocked the hat from Armando's head. "Hey! He's the pretty boy who rode in the show last night. I lost fifty *maravedís* betting he couldn't keep his seat."

"I'm not looking for trouble, *amigo*," Armando muttered. He tried to brush past.

"A gypsy doesn't have to look for trouble. A gypsy *is* trouble." The man nudged his companions. "You know, this one looks as if his soul needs saving. Perhaps a session at the Holy Office would—"

Armando bolted across the cobblestones. No gypsy interviewed by the Holy Office had ever emerged alive.

"After him!" The shout rang through the crowded plaza. "Stop, thief!" Heavy boots thundered in his wake.

Armando careened around a cart piled high with winter apples. Hands grasped at him, ripping his sleeve. He headed down an alleyway and ran blindly, the winter air searing his throat. As he raced along, he concealed his purse inside his trousers. He would need the money if he escaped with his life.

The shouts and footsteps drew closer. A sharp burn started in Armando's side. His breath huffed like a smithy's bellows. At the end of the street loomed a stack of barrels. He scrambled over the pile and then toppled it, filling the alley with rolling barrels and the reek of spilled olive oil.

The alley led to a wharf area where brigantines and galleys rode at their cables in the deep harbor. White spume from the incoming waves erupted against the granite coastline. Seizing his lead, Armando ducked between bales and crates stacked for loading. His luck lasted only seconds; the ruffians had raised a cry up and down the docks. A pair of longshoremen spied him.

Rolling their sleeves back to reveal beefy arms, they started toward him. Armando stumbled over a coil of thick rope, picked himself up, and began running again. A man appeared at the other end of the row of crates. Cornered and panting, Armando leaned against a tightly bound bundle of sugarcane from the Canary Isles. Shit! Now what? He was trapped.

"Psst! This way, *busno*!" Miguel poked his head between two crates and beckoned.

Too desperate to question Miguel's sudden interest in protecting him, Armando followed. Ducking low, Miguel led him through a maze formed by the goods lined along the wharf. They came to a sail-rigged galleasse, already laden and riding low in the water. The hull bristled with outriggers supporting long oars. The ramps to the hold had been drawn up. Sailors stuck like spiders in the ratlines, unfurling canvas at the yardarms.

Armando's pursuers came at them from both sides.

"This way!" Miguel said, beckoning toward the galleasse. They pounded up a narrow gangplank and leaped over the rail.

A bearded man stood at the binnacle, one elbow propped atop the compass housing. His hard, narrowed eyes coldly assessed Armando. "You didn't tell me he was a gypsy, too."

Miguel took a step back toward the gangplank. "You didn't ask. His back is strong. I thought that was all you wanted."

Armando's blood turned to ice water. The anger he felt was at himself, for trusting Miguel. He lunged for the rail.

Three sailors leaped on him, pinned him down, pressed his ear to the slanting deck. He could hear the ominous rattle of chains, an occasional plea to Allah, and knew he was listening to the galley slaves below.

"Gypsies." The bearded sailor spat onto the deck. "Nothing but trouble."

Cables ground loudly, and the ship's timbers shuddered as wind plucked at the sails. Armando struggled to raise his head. "You bastard," he hissed at Miguel.

The sailor flipped Miguel a silver *real*. "I hope I won't regret this transaction."

Miguel snatched the coin from the air. "I'll be long gone before you do." With athletic grace, he braced one hand on the rail, jumped down to the dock, and disappeared.

A sense of unreality slithered over Armando as he was shoved below. In a dark hold that stank of sweat, blood, and bilge, he was chained with five convict rowers to a giant oar and forced to row in rhythm with a thudding drum.

By the third day out, his back was raw with weals from a spiked lash applied to motivate the rowers. By the fifth day, he became aware that the man beside him had died, his body borne like a puppet with the ceaseless motion of the oar. Armando's cry of horror earned him an extra beating, and he quickly learned to keep his mouth shut.

By the eighth day, he forgot all that he knew in the world. His only awareness was of the bell that rang every four hours, signaling the new watch and the chance to swill spoiled food and wine, to steal a nap in the filthy hold. His universe narrowed to the banks of twenty-five oars on each side, a dark tunnel where a man's death was no more than a minor annoyance.

On the tenth day, he spoke for the first time to the man on his right, a Moorish slave who insisted his name was El Hakim, the Learned One. "What ship is this?" Armando gasped out.

"She's called *Princesa de Aragon*." Despite the muscle-tearing work of rowing, El Hakim spoke with ease. "Didn't you check when you signed her manifest, Infidel? How do you like the stateroom they assigned you to?"

It took a moment for Armando to catch the Moor's humor. He could not find it in him to smile. "What's she carrying?"

El Hakim grinned. "Treasure. Silks and brocades, jewels and horses. Gifts from King Ferdinand."

Armando's gaze followed the broad reach of the oar. The wood was slick with fluid from his blisters. "Gifts for whom?"

A black lash snapped across his back, then El Hakim's. "You slaves, pipe down there!" bellowed the sergeant at arms.

Armando's interest flagged beneath the fiery pain of the whip. His thoughts clung to his master's words: *You slaves.* Christ Jesus, he was a slave. Just like Paloma, snatched from her island paradise. Back then, he had believed slavery was an injustice. Now he knew better. It was a living hell.

The next day, the man on his left side lost his mind. Sentenced by the Holy Office for the crime of lighting a candle in his window on a Friday night, he began to babble about his wife, his young children, his aging parents. He swore he knew nothing of Jewish practices, swore it by the name of every saint he could think of. Then he begged for death.

Armando roused himself from his pain-filled stupor and turned to El Hakim. "Er, where are we bound?"

"Deliverance! Salvation!" screamed the man on his left.

El Hakim's grin glinted in the shadows; then he burst into laughter. "Why, it's about time you asked, Infidel. We're going to the richest island in the world!"

CHAPTER 6

Durham House, London
January 1509

"This is surely the poorest island in the world!" Doña Elvira Manuel's staccato voice snapped into the plainly furnished room.

Hoping the tirade would be brief, Gabriella Flores continued to strum soft chords on her lute.

Doña Elvira paced the floor and paused at a finger's-width crack in the flags, shivering when a draft sneaked up her black skirts. "Scandalous, that a princess of the blood royal should be treated like a guest who's overstayed her welcome. Jesus wept, that Henry Tudor sent us no one to help with the packing. I can't believe that after eight years we're going home." Doña Elvira poked her sharp nose at Gabriella, who sat under the archway linking the outer room to the main bedchamber. "The least you could do is summon those sluts from the kitchen to help. You're the only one whose English they understand."

Suppressing a sigh, Gabriella stilled her fingers on the strings of her lute.

"Let her continue, Elvira," said a soft voice from a chair by the hearth. "Her music comforts me."

"You flatter me, Your Grace." Relieved at being rescued from a row with the English servants, Gabriella picked out an arpeggio of haunting minor notes.

Elvira's lips thinned. She put her hand to her hair, which was oiled and scraped back into an old-fashioned rolled coif. "Better you should console yourself in prayer, Your Majesty."

The princess Catherine of Aragon stood, her black silk skirts rustling as she paced the bare floor. "Elvira, I have prayed until there are no words left in me. His Holiness the pope has consented to my marriage to the dead Prince Arthur's younger brother, but apparently a papal bull is not enough for King Henry to offer up his surviving son. My ambassadors have parleyed with him for—my God, seven years it's been! My father has sent a fortune in treasures as a token of our good faith."

"Indeed he has," Doña Elvira agreed. "I'd like to know what became of the shipment last year, the one from the galleasse *Princesa de Aragon*. I've certainly seen none of the riches here at Durham House." Seeing the princess stiffen, Doña Elvira added, "Be patient, Your Grace. The Lord will provide." The words rang hollow in the chill, nearly empty chamber.

"And what has patience gotten me?" Catherine whirled, making an angry gesture with her hand. "A few cold rooms in this unfurnished old house? Having to sell my plate to buy food?"

Gabriella thought the princess most attractive when she was angry. Her grayish eyes flashed, and color suffused her usually pale cheeks. It made one remember she was but twenty-three, surely the youngest royal widow in Europe, and a pawn in a shabby political game. "I came to take the throne of England," she said. "And now, thanks to that tight-fisted fence sitter Henry Tudor, I shall leave penniless and humiliated, widowed by his weak-willed son Arthur.''

Gabriella's fingers stroked the strings, filling the cavernous dayroom with quivers of sound. Moved by Catherine's anguish, she stood and glided to the window embrasure while playing a melody she had heard at the Frost Fair on the Thames below Durham House.

She played best when she moved. Perhaps some traveling player inhabited her blood, a minstrel who performed on her feet. The thought made her smile. Mama would have been shocked by the suggestion.

Her mother, Doña Mercedes de Montana, was a grandee's daughter, and Gabriella's father was a noble martyr to the Christian cause. Roman de Flores had been killed in the Moorish wars only months before Gabriella's birth. She knew little of her father. All her life, she had been warned of the treachery of males. Her mother, who had retired to a convent in Spain two years earlier, would neither look at nor speak to any man.

Perhaps, Gabriella thought, her mother was not far wrong. Witness the princess Catherine, a royal prize in the power struggle between her father Ferdinand, King of Spain, and King Henry, her father-in-law.

Thank God, Gabriella mused, that she herself would never have to submit to a man. She was content to serve the princess as maid of honor, and had no ambition to marry.

Catherine came to look over Gabriella's shoulder through the diamond-shaped panes of the window. "Open it, Gabriella," she said. "It's already beastly cold in here. At least we can enjoy a draft of fresh air."

Gabriella set aside her lute and unlatched the dormer window, throwing it open to the chill winter afternoon. The long privy garden, its trees denuded, opened out to a grand view of the river Thames. Coaches and tottering sedan chairs crossed the frozen water between Lambeth

Marshes and Westminster. Very close to the water steps of Durham House, two traveling players had drawn a small crowd. A fistfight—obviously staged—had broken out between the players. Catcalls, amplified by the clear air, carried across the ice, which had been strewn with straw to prevent slipping.

Both men appeared foreign; one wore brown and had a swarthy face with a beard and mustache, and a turban on his head. The other, in a green tunic, was clean-shaven, tall and slim, with long dark hair. He wore the high red boots of a gypsy.

"Rabble, the lot of them." Elvira shivered. "This is a country of ill-mannered rabble. I for one shall be glad to get to the civilized folk of Castile." She touched Gabriella's shoulder. "Your mother was lucky Her Majesty allowed her to return to the convent of Santa Inez."

Catherine of Aragon took Gabriella's hand. "She was so unhappy here, I felt I had no choice but to let her go. Do you miss Doña Mercedes very much, child?"

"No, ma'am. I wanted to stay here with you. Truly, England has been my home for more than half of my life. I should feel like a stranger in Castile, and lost without your friendship."

Below, one of the combatant's faces had blossomed with blood. The crowd went wild. Other passersby gathered to watch. Bookmakers moved through the mob, taking bets.

Doña Elvira hugged herself and shook her head in revulsion. "Rabble," she said again, turning away. "It's a sin to watch."

To Gabriella's delight, the princess sent a look of mischief at her duenna. Catherine planted her elbows on the stone sill and leaned forward. "Which one, Gabriella?" she asked. "I'll lay you ten thousand ducats it's the one in brown, the Moor."

"Really, madam," scolded Doña Elvira. "A princess of the blood royal should never gam—"

"You're on," said Gabriella, raising up on her knees. She would not let the dour Doña Elvira spoil a rare moment of fun. "I'll bet on the other—the one in green."

"He hasn't a chance," Catherine assured her. "All that blood! Look, it's stained his shirt to the waist."

Gabriella shrugged. "A nosebleed is nothing. Look, He's better on his feet. See the way he presses the attack."

"But the Moor is quicker with his fists. Another five thousand ducats says he'll lay your man out flat before the Bow bells toll again."

"Done!" said Gabriella.

With their knees on the padded embrasure seat and their elbows on the sill, the two women, both honored guests and forgotten liabilities, leaned out to watch the fight. Doña Elvira grasped her rosary beads like a lifeline.

"Get him," Catherine shrilled in her heavily accented English. "Don't be taken in by his fancy moves, you fool. Get some meat behind those punches."

"Duck!" shouted Gabriella in English as clear and precise as an Oxford scholar's. "Don't be a bloody fool, he's using your height against you!"

The bearded man absorbed a blow to his gut. The man in green moved in. He pummeled his opponent about the head, the stomach, the kidneys. The turban fell to the straw-strewn ice.

The Moor roared with pain, lowered his head, and rushed his opponent.

"This is better than a bullfight," the princess declared.

"It's certainly more sporting," said Gabriella. "But there are similarities." Even from a distance, she could hear the dull thud of impact and the rush of breath from the man in green.

Catherine's man had been hit too hard. He put a hand to his head and reeled. Gabriella's man doubled forward. At the same moment both keeled over and hit the ice like sacks of grain tossed from a barge. Breath rushed from them in streams of white smoke.

"A draw!" Catherine cried, lifting the hem of her petticoat to dab the tears of mirth from her eyes.

"A bloody draw," said Gabriella, clutching her sides. "Every last bettor is bilked."

"Including us," the princess said, chuckling. "And a good thing it is, too. We've neither of us fifteen thousand ducats."

Gabriella gazed dreamily out the window. "They're good, those two men."

"It's one thing men are good for—fighting."

"Really, madam." Doña Elvira bustled forward and shooed Catherine from the window. "Your behavior is most unseemly."

"Unseemly?" Catherine's laughter took on the shrill edge of hysteria. "Jesus wept, Elvira! I have been wed and widowed. I have been for seven years a virtual prisoner because my father has sworn to put the crown of England on my head. I have lost my youth while waiting for young Prince Henry to grow up enough to wed me. Merciful heavens, the lad's seventeen. How long does it take for an Englishman's ballocks to drop?"

Doña Elvira put her hands to her flushed cheeks. "Madam!"

"I'm good enough to serve as diplomat, but not to marry a second English Prince," Catherine continued, her voice rising in pitch. "Seven years I've guarded Spain's interests in England. Seven years I've waited to wed. Seven years of worn clothes and poor food, and you dare to call me unseemly?"

The princess's laughter turned to wild grief, and she ran from the room. Gabriella heard the creak of a divan as Catherine flung herself, weeping, onto its threadbare cushions.

With tears of compassion in her eyes, Gabriella started

toward the bedchamber. Doña Elvira's clawlike hand
pulled her back. "Leave her to me. 'Twas your foolishness
that set her off." Elvira stalked into the bedchamber and
slammed the door.

Her own mirth chased off by Catherine's misery, Gabriella picked up her lute and turned her gaze back out the
window. The combatants were being helped to their feet
and given mugs of ale.

Princess Catherine had spent her youth in the cold in-
hospitality of Henry Tudor's court. Eight years earlier, she
had arrived amid fanfare worthy of her rank. The celebration of her wedding to Prince Arthur had spanned weeks.
But a few months later, the man Gabriella recalled as a
weak, pale youth had died, leaving Catherine a virgin
bride.

Though interested in a betrothal to his second son, King
Henry took care not to show Catherine too much favor.
Rumors said he was considering a Hapsburg alliance for
the seventeen-year-old Prince of Wales. Nearly as wily as
Ferdinand himself, Henry would keep his options open
and his coffers shut.

Idly Gabriella's fingers strummed a mournful soft cloud
of sound from the lute. Neither monarch spared a thought
for the princess in the next room, in a mended gown on a
faded divan, weeping for her lost youth.

Discomfited, Gabriella turned her attention back to the
Frost Fair. The bearded performer had made a speedy
recovery; he reappeared with his turban in place. To the
discordant screech of a reed flute, he performed a graceful
saber dance.

A few moments later, a man led a slender horse across
the ice. The front of his green tunic was smudged in red,
identifying him as the gypsy brawler.

At first Gabriella watched with only passing interest;
then her attention was caught. One moment he was leading his gray mare by the reins; the next, he stood on its

back, his tall, slim frame outlined by the colorless after-noon sky.

The performance appealed to her musician's sense of beauty and balance. She felt the willful freedom in his every move, recognized his powerful confidence and joy in his own skill.

He finished the breathtaking routine with a smooth can-ter around the cheering crowd while he stood on the horse's back, one hand at the reins, the other arm outflung. The audience cast dried posies and ribbons and coins in the center of the ring.

After a time the crowd dispersed, and the horseman dismounted. Gabriella expected him to snatch up the take immediately. Instead, he led his horse to a bucket and curried her while she ate and drank.

As the noise of the crowd abated, Gabriella heard again the sounds of Catherine's weeping. Melancholy swept over her, then firmed into resolution. King Henry had made the princess miserable; Gabriella refused to let her own youth dry up while he vacillated. She snatched up a shawl and drew it over her head. The distant echoes of her mother's voice warned her away from men, but she ignored caution. This was England, where people did not look askance at a young lady walking out alone.

She hastened down the stairs, letting herself out through a servants' door. She ran across the privy garden, enjoying the rush of wind on her face as she sped toward the river.

She stopped cold. The dark-haired horseman held a woman in his arms. While his bearded companion waited some distance away, the horseman kissed the woman as if he would devour her whole.

Dark longing, as dangerous as it was inevitable, rose through Gabriella, stealing her breath. Never had she felt a man's embrace, a man's mouth hard upon hers. Never had she yearned for it—until now.

At last she understood the depth of Catherine's frustration, her shame at having to return to Spain. With numbed awareness, Gabriella watched the man break away from the smiling woman, mount his horse, and ride after his swarthy companion.

Well-favored in face and form, the girl scuffed her feet along the ice, then snatched a coin from the trampled straw. Gabriella felt a prickle of resentment. If *she* had been kissed like that, she'd not forget it so quickly.

"Where did they go?" she asked the young woman.

The girl gave a vague jerk of her thumb. "West, somewheres. To Richmond in Surrey where the court is, I think 'e said."

Gabriella bit her lip, forcing herself to speak boldly. "What was his name?"

The girl laughed. " 'Ow would I know, eh? One man's the same as another."

Turning back toward Durham House, Gabriella felt a chill gust of disappointment. Then she scolded herself. What had she expected? To boldly flirt with the man? What business had she, a Spanish gentlewoman, with an itinerant carnival trickster?

The pounding of hooves invaded her thoughts. She looked up to see a troop of soldiers in livery of Tudor green galloping along the Strand toward Durham House.

Royal messengers, she realized, lifting her skirts to hurry back across the garden. What news did they bring this time?

"Pity about the girl," El Hakim said as he and Armando rode away from London, toward the flat, frosty fields of Saint Martin's. "She was right pretty."

Armando grinned at his friend's affected English speech. "It's just as well we get away from London for a while. She was too tempting by half."

"Aye, a bit more time with her and you'd've had to marry." El Hakim shook his head, blew out his breath in a puff of frozen air. "They're always on you like a leech on a camel, yet you never do more than kiss and fondle them. Tell me, Infidel, how in Allah's name do you keep your women happy?"

Armando grinned. "That's my secret."

"Allah preserve me from ever having such a secret."

Keeping an easy smile in place, Armando turned the subject. "The take was poor in London."

"Must be that sickness they call the sweat. People are afraid of contagion. Keeps the cautious ones away from the crowds."

"And it's the cautious ones who have the coin to spare for a pair of performers like us."

"England," El Hakim said as they rode over the rocky roads along the Thames and past sere, terraced hills dotted with miserable-looking sheep. "What a place. Hard-drinking infidels and practical-minded women." He sighed. "At least their character is shaped by ambition and greed, not by fear of the Inquisition as it is in Spain."

They rode on in companionable silence. If, a year earlier, someone had told Armando he would become best friends with a Moorish outlaw, he would have laughed at the absurdity of it. But their bondage at an oar of the galleasse *Princesa de Aragon* and their harrowing escape during the off-loading at the Thames, had bound them with the unseverable ties of danger, shared adventure, hardship, and the desperate need to live free.

On the outskirts of the town of Sheen, they stopped at an abandoned croft on the banks of the river. At sunset, El Hakim spread out his prayer rug and bowed toward Mecca. To the singsong strains of the Arab prayers, Armando fed Esmeralda and Bayard, the horses he had won in a sword fight in Greenwich. Then, in the fast fading winter light, he took out needle and thread to mend his shirt. *Dios*, it was only three hours past midday and already darkness crept upon this cold north country.

El Hakim finished his prayers and came to join him. They sat in the lee of the half-tumbled stone building, warmed by their fire and by the breath of the horses tethered nearby.

"Ah, for a whiff of Andalusian jasmine," El Hakim sighed.

"You'd more likely be treated to a whiff of the *quemadero*," Armando reminded him. "We'd both surely be burned alive for escaping a royal galleasse."

"You are twice a fool," El Hakim chided. "The son of not one, but two rich *hidalgos*. You should never have left."

As his chilled fingers plied the needle, Armando battled a familiar surge of anger. "If I'd stayed in Spain, I'd be straining my eyes over scholarly texts at Salamanca, preparing for the life of a gentleman scholar. Spare me the boredom."

"Perish the thought, O wise one," said El Hakim.

"Not for a moment do I regret leaving Spain."

"So you're happy with this empty, wandering life we lead?" El Hakim asked.

"It's better than being chained to an oar."

"You could go back," El Hakim suggested.

"No. Rafael and Santiago destroyed who I thought I was. At least here I'm free. Cold and ill mended, but free." No matter that lonesome yearnings pulled at him, plagued his sleep and tormented his waking hours. "I answer to no man."

"And love no woman," El Hakim lamented. In the icy twilight, he polished their weapons: a curved scimitar, a sword, an array of razor-sharp daggers. "Our stock in trade," he said, drawing a length of silk along the curve of the scimitar. "But I'm a farmer at heart. By Allah, I'd trade this for a herd of sheep if I could."

"Fortunately for me, you can't," said Armando. Unlike El Hakim, he loved sword fights. Even when none but crows and stray cats witnessed his feats, he tossed daggers, battled tree stumps and sheaves of grain to keep himself in practice.

"You've perfected every trick, every move," said El Hakim. "I wonder why you drive yourself like a crusader on a quest and leave the women panting for your virgin soul."

Even to his only friend, Armando would not confess the truth. He honed his fighting tactics for one reason, and one reason only. To surpass the skills of Santiago.

Because the day would come, Armando knew, when he would face a reckoning with the father who had abandoned him.

The next day dawned damp and chill. Stamping their feet to warm themselves, Armando and El Hakim ate a meal of stale bread and river water. Then they saddled their horses and rode to the city gate. Fishmongers and tinkers lined up to pay their entry tax and make their way to the main square in front of the church of Saint Mary Magdalene.

Armando parted with a copper to enter the city, shadowed by the glittering new Richmond Palace and surrounded by a royal deer park and terraced gardens running down to the Thames.

"Good poaching to be had here," El Hakim commented.

Armando tucked the information into the back of his mind, but already his thoughts moved ahead to the possibilities offered by the town. Their trek eastward had exhausted their funds. El Hakim's thin face and dark eyes haunted Armando. His friend was wearying of their wandering life. As they tethered their horses on the side of the church, he wished there were some way he could reward the months of loyal friendship.

The marketplace rocked with activity. Costermongers

and fish sellers hawked their wares, while jewelers and clothiers presented their offerings from stalls and shop fronts. Women purveying everything from silver buckles to a roll in the hay called out in rusty voices. Alemen stood by their tall kegs and offered a swig for halfpence. Armando bought a leek tart and ate it without relish. ''The English,'' he said around a mouthful of doughy pastry, ''have the unique ability to take perfectly good food and render it tasteless.''

El Hakim nodded. ''One of the many things I miss about Spain is the food. By Allah, onions so strong they make a warrior shed tears, heavy cream and sugared dates and fruits sweet enough to move a maiden to sighs.''

Eating mechanically, Armando scanned the crowd for possibilities. He nudged El Hakim. ''That grassy sward there. We could cry up a show, maybe stage a fight.''

El Hakim shrugged without enthusiasm. He had begun to shiver with cold. ''I suppose. Let's do it honestly this time. I've no wish to be chased out of town like we were back in Kew.''

Armando cocked his head. ''Do you hear music?''

El Hakim pointed at a wagon with a sign bearing a musical instrument. Beneath the sign stood a young man with bright red hair and a harp carved of yellow wood.

The lively melody, plucked effortlessly from the quivering strings, drew a small gathering. Armando eyed the musician speculatively. His song worked magic on the rapt listeners.

''He'd make a fine partner in our enterprise, El Hakim. His music calls like a siren! He could draw the crowds. Then we could dazzle them into showering us with gold.''

''You dazzle them, Infidel. I won't be able to perform at all if I don't stop shivering. Oh, for the warmth of Andalusia.''

''Andalusia?'' came a deep, good-humored voice. Armando turned to see a man coming toward them from the ale barrels. He had chestnut hair and a two-pronged beard, and moved with the grandeur of a ship in calm waters. "Now, how is it that two goodly fellows like yourselves come to speak of so fair a place?"

El Hakim's eyes narrowed in suspicion. "Who wants to know?"

The man pointed his toe and bowed elaborately. "Sebastian Cabot of Bristol, at your service. I'm a man of the sea, but I keep my ear to the ground."

Armando felt a spurt of interest. "Sebastian Cabot, the explorer? I've heard of you."

Cabot swung his arm out, showing cloth of gold in the slashes of his sleeves. "Hasn't every mother's son heard of me?"

"I haven't," said El Hakim.

"He sailed across the Ocean Sea," Armando explained.

"Ah, like your father's friend, Colón," said El Hakim.

"Colón." Cabot sniffed. "Lunatic Janney couldn't sail his way out of the London Pool."

"Janney?" asked El Hakim.

"Aye, a scheming Genoese."

Armando bristled. "The admiral found the Indies, sir, while you encountered only isles of ice and some fishing grounds."

"Ha! A lot you know, whelp. I'm heading for the Indies myself before long." He aimed a glare at Richmond Palace, the brickwork grim in the winter light. "I just came from an audience with King Henry. He's too stingy by half with his coin, especially now that he's too sick to see another year. Perhaps there's hope for your countrywoman, Catherine of Aragon."

"Truly?" El Hakim scratched his head beneath his turban. "The last gossip we heard, she was being shipped back to Spain."

"The king's too ill to banish her now. Only two days ago, he sent riders to halt her from departure. Not that he'll let his son Harry marry her, but he's enjoyed the gifts from King Ferdinand. I mean to ask him for a charter."

"Ferdinand?"

"Aye. Too many incompetents bumbling around in the Indies these days. *I'll* find the way to Cathay, mark my words."

El Hakim folded his arms across his chest. "Why are you telling us this, sir?"

Cabot gave a wolfish grin. "I just thought two likely gents of Andalusia might enjoy accompanying me to a land of warm sunshine. I'd pay you a wage and take care of the passage in exchange for your complete loyalty."

Both Armando and El Hakim reacted instantaneously, Armando with a swift, "No," and El Hakim with a rapt, "It is my fondest wish." Armando jabbed his elbow in the Moor's ribs. "You'd risk your neck by going back to Spain?"

"Better that than die of cold in this nation of barbarians."

Cabot clapped him on the shoulder. " 'Tis done, then. Come along, my friend, and we'll be about arranging the crossing."

Armando blinked at his friend. "Just like that? You'd leave?"

El Hakim drew a long, shivery breath. "I can no longer be a man of the road, Infidel. Please. Come with us."

Armando was tempted, but only for a moment. Over the past years, he had perfected the art of holding people at a distance; even El Hakim had never breached the wall of his self-imposed isolation. Still, the impending sense of loss hurt more than he would admit. He forced out, "No. You're free to go, El Hakim. I ask only that you watch your back."

"I'm not without influence," Cabot huffed. "I'll keep your friend safe. And if ever you change your mind about leaving England, seek me out. If I'm not in the court of the Great Khan, I'll be sailing the Indies with El Hakim at my side.''

Armando studied El Hakim's bleak expression. With a groan, he reached out and hugged his friend hard. "I won't hold you back. Good luck, my friend.''

"Allah's blessings on you." As he followed Cabot toward an inn that faced the square, El Hakim looked back, a strange glitter in his eyes. "We'll meet again, Infidel."

"Southampton!" Cabot called over his shoulder.

"What?" Armando yelled back.

"It's the best place to take ship these days. Use my name, and you'll find a likely vessel to bring you home." He gave a dazzling grin. "When you decide to follow in our wake."

"I'm not going back," Armando warned. With Cabot's laughter echoing in his ears, he watched until they disappeared into the inn. Trying to ignore the yawning emptiness inside him, he shrugged, then moved off to an herbalist's stall to examine the sacks of dried roots and flowers.

Four young noblemen, in clothes resplendent with jewels and family crests, came strolling across the square to listen to the musician. The tallest one, with hair the color of wheat ripening in the sun, stepped close to the wagon. His handsome young face wore a look of pure rapture, and high color painted his cheeks.

"By God," he cried when the harpist finished, "you could move a standing stone with your music, my friend."

The harpist tugged his red forelock. "William Shapiro, instrument maker, at your service."

"Are you looking for a patron, Will Shapiro?"

The musician gaped. The color fell from his face, leaving only a spray of freckles across the bridge of his nose. He bowed deeply. "Is that an offer?"

"Harry, don't be a fool." A sharp-eyed young man,

nearly as elegantly dressed as Harry, put a hand on his companion's arm. "He's a Jew, for God's sake."

Harry scowled. Then he dug in his bulging purse, extracted a coin, and flipped it to Will. "Jew or not, Neville, his art exalts all mankind."

Armando recognized the coin, both from its appearance and from the goggle-eyed look of Shapiro. The piece depicted Henry VII on his throne.

A sovereign. A bloody gold sovereign. Christ Jesus.

He moved before he was aware of making his decision. His dagger dropped from his sleeve into the palm of his hand. He threaded his way through the crowd, his gaze fixed on the heavy purse. Pickpocketing had never been his forte. He remembered the stories of Santiago's bungled attempts at thieving. More than once the reckless gypsy had nearly swung for purse cutting.

As Shapiro started a new melody, Armando seized the chance to prove himself better than the man who had fathered him.

He drew close to Harry. The young man stood with his arms crossed over his chest and his eyes shut tightly as if to close off all awareness save that of the music.

Foolish gull, thought Armando, passing behind his quarry. In a movement as smooth as warm oil, he angled his blade toward the purse strings.

The playing stopped. "Beg pardon, my lord," Will said. "But that dark foreigner is about to clip your purse."

Faces frozen in shock, hands grabbing for him, a moment in which Armando felt a pure sharp flash of rage before he ran for his life. He bolted across the marketplace. His horse trailed her reins at a stone post by the church. Shouts rang across the square. Hands clawed at him, tearing at his hair and clothes.

But his moves had been taught to him by a master, perfected by years of training. He placed his palms on the horse's rump and vaulted into the saddle. With one fluid movement, he whipped the reins into his grip. Esmeralda reared, raking the air with her forelegs. Armando dug in his heels. She clattered across the marketplace toward the town gate.

A flurry of movement erupted in the gate tower. To Armando's horror, he saw the iron spikes of a portcullis slowly descending over the opening.

Holy Christ, he might be trapped. He leaned down over the horse's pumping neck and gritted his teeth.

The gridiron crept lower. He gauged the distance and hissed a prayer between his teeth. The clamor of pursuit became a dull, urgent pounding in his head. With pikes extended, guards moved into the gateway, but faltered when his pace did not slacken.

He was almost there; he could feel the cold rush of triumph whipping over him. Almost . . . A small child wandered out into the roadway. Directly in his path, to be trampled like a grape.

Cursing, Armando sawed on the reins. The mare slid to a panicked stop. A woman snatched the child out of the way. Men ran at Armando from all sides. They grasped at the bridle and hauled him roughly to the ground.

With a deafening clang, the portcullis slammed home.

The bone-grinding weight of guards and townsmen pressed on Armando. His lungs screamed for air. God pity him; for the price of a purse he would die beneath a pile of sweating Englishmen. A fitting end to the son of two deceitful *hidalgos*.

"Let him up." The blond youth's voice penetrated the sounds of the scuffle.

The weight left Armando, although the smell of damp woolen clothes and beer breath lingered. He scrambled to his feet and cast a glance over his shoulder to assure himself that Esmeralda was not injured. The mare stood, tense at the withers, held fast by two men.

Thick-fingered hands clamped onto Armando's upper

arms. He jerked his chin up to glare at the man called Harry.

Harry's blue eyes were round and shining with interest, not anger. "Where the devil did you learn to ride like that, man?"

Surprised, Armando did not think to lie. "In Spain, from the gypsies."

"By God, you were a sight. And that horse! Where did you get her?"

"I won her in a sword fight."

Harry rubbed his chin. "A sword fight, was it?"

"Aye."

"What's your name?"

"Armando Vis—just Armando."

Harry slapped his hands, bright with rings on each finger, on his hips. "Well. I suppose you know the penalty for theft."

His insides chilled. "I do, sir."

"Hang him high!" shouted someone from the back of the crowd. "Let him rot in the gibbet!" More voices joined the chorus.

With a regretful look on his face, Harry spread his hands. "It seems public sentiment is against you. Guards, take him—"

"Wait!" Will Shapiro's voice cut through the noise. "Begging your pardon, but this man's not guilty of stealing."

"Shut up, you," said Neville. "Nobody asked your opinion."

Ignoring him, Shapiro indicated the purse that swung from Harry's belt. "He merely created a small disturbance."

Harry touched his smooth-shaven chin. "Good point, my man. Very well, we'll spare our foreign friend."

Even as Armando sagged with relief, he had to keep

from laughing at Harry's air of authority. The nobility were taught arrogance young in Surrey, it seemed.

"Now, Harry," said one of his companions, speaking loudly over the mutterings of the crowd, "surely you won't let the young devil get away with making a fool of you."

"He's committed no crime, Compton. That may not count with my father, but with me it happens to—"

"No crime?" Compton aimed a glance at the long sheath at Armando's thigh. "Since when is it legal for a commoner to carry a sword?"

Armando blurted, "I am no commoner, but the son of a *hildalgo* of Seville."

Compton and Neville swept skeptical glances over his frayed tunic, his worn boots and poorly mended hose. "Lying gypsy."

But Harry merely grinned in delight. "Then we shall settle the matter as gentlemen. Trial by combat."

Whispers of admiration rose from some of the girls.

Neville's face darkened. "Harry—"

"A sword fight, I think," the blond youth said blithely. "First to draw blood wins. If you best me, you go free."

Armando darted a glance around. Surely someone would object. But everyone seemed in awe of Lord Harry. Christ Jesus, why had El Hakim picked this day to abandon him?

"And if I lose?" he forced himself to ask.

"Then we let justice take its course."

Armando was suddenly keenly aware of the winter chill sweeping down from the slope where Richmond Palace brooded. Harry swept the black velvet toque from his head, pointed his toe, and bowed with inborn grace.

"Done," said Armando.

Within minutes he was swept back through the marketplace to the sward. Children drove a small flock of grazing sheep off to one corner.

Armando spat into his palm, wiped it on his shirt, and gripped the hilt of his sword. He felt cold no longer, as if

he had never known cold at all. Hot blood raced through
his veins. He would best the foppish, handsome nobleman.

Santiago had schooled him well in swordsmanship. But
that had not been enough for Armando. Every day he had
practiced, determined to make himself better than the man
who had sired him. Over the past years, Armando had
beaten highwaymen, gamesters, and arrogant nobles. From
one of the latter he had won his sword. Ironically, it was
a Spanish weapon from Toledo, its square pommel ornate
with exotic Mudejar designs and its blade as sleek and
smooth as damask silk.

Harry relinquished his fur-trimmed murrey cloak to
Compton. Armando noted the hard-muscled breadth of
Harry's shoulders, the quick spring in his step as he drew
his sword. It was a magnificent *épée de Passot*, the hilt
aglitter with colored jewels and gold filigree, a Latin motto
etched in the blade. It would be a pity to damage the
sword. Armando decided not to toy with Harry, but to
blood him quickly and leave Richmond in his dust.

A movement beneath a tree caught his eye. It was the
Jew, Will Shapiro. With a jolt of anger, Armando decided
that perhaps he wouldn't leave town as quickly as that.

"So it begins," Harry said, snapping into an offensive
stance.

Armando bit the inside of his cheek to keep from grinning. These noblemen were always so precious, so affected in their adherence to form and convention.

Extending his arm, Armando sketched a challenge in
the air.

Harry laughed with delight. Still laughing, he made a
lightning thrust, his blade streaking past Armando's defense. The attack was so swift, so unexpected, that Armando nearly felt the icy cut of the blade. Just in time, he
leaped back, feeling the rush of air disturbed by the blade.

He forgot to cover his astonishment. Harry—and most all of the onlookers—laughed uproariously.

"Took me for a gull, did you?" Harry chuckled, pressing on. With that same nonchalance, that same unexpected speed, he attacked again. Armando brought his sword up, crossing it with Harry's, then disengaging and mounting an attack of his own.

If Harry fought with humor and guile, Armando countered with fire and determination. His life hung in the balance. The knowledge burned inside him, honing his every move with precision, lending speed and faultless agility to his defense.

Only vaguely did he hear the gasps of the audience. For him, the world had narrowed to this frozen patch of grass, its parameters defined by the reach of his opponent's sword.

Beads of sweat sprang out on Harry's brow. Still he smiled, but he panted, too. "Very good, Armando," he said, eluding an expert backward lunge. "Very picaresque indeed."

Armando cared nothing for the man's flattery. He cared only for the expensive blade singing past his shoulder. Too damned close. One nick, and he'd not see another sunrise. Aflame with near panic, he parried, desperate to storm his opponent's defense. But Harry's restless blade sketched a fortress around him. He was as impregnable as the stone walls of the Alhambra.

Armando tried every trick he knew—false attacks, stoccados, even risky acrobatics. Harry beat him into a retreat against the cheering, shouting crowd. They pressed back to give him room.

"He tends to drop his hand," a voice, speaking Spanish, whispered in his ear. "Elevates his point too much."

Who had spoken? It must have been the voice of God, he decided, for Harry did have a weak spot, invisible to all save the most practiced eye.

Like a marksman, Armando aimed for the subtle hole in Harry's defense. He passed his blade over his opponent's. The contact with living flesh filled Armando with a dark, hot, pagan joy. *"Tocada,"* he whispered. "At last, a hit."

Harry gave a small exclamation and put his hand to his chin. "First blood!" he shouted, holding his reddened hand high.

Uncertain murmurs rose from the crowd. Harry threw back his golden head and shouted with laughter. "Go on," he urged. "Cheer the man who bested me!"

"Huzzah!" The voice was soon joined by others. "Huzzah for the Spanish champion."

Harry wiped his chin on his sleeve. "Damn, this will surely leave a scar. I shall have to grow a beard to cover it. Aye, a beard would be good . . ."

Flushed with victory and weak with relief, Armando sheathed his sword. The crowd began to disperse. Harry stuck out his hand. "Your skill does me honor, sir."

"And your skill nearly did me in," Armando admitted.

Harry kept hold of his hand and studied the frayed cuff of Armando's woolen tunic. Impulsively, he twisted a ruby ring from his finger and handed it to Armando. "You've given me a good sport on what had promised to be a bleak winter's day."

"Thank you, sir." Armando pocketed the ring. Good God, he thought, the token given so casually was worth a princely sum.

"I say, do you ride in the lists?"

Armando hesitated. He didn't think Harry believed his tale of being a *hildago*'s son. As far as the English were concerned, he was a commoner, prohibited from competing in tournaments. Which was not to say he had stayed away. But the gleam in Harry's eye, not to mention the glint of more jewels on his hands and around his waist and neck, proved hard to resist.

"Yes," Armando admitted. "When I can."

"Then I should see you there anon. You're too good a swordsman to be a thief."

"I'll try to earn my living honestly from now on," Armando lied. His arms and shoulders ached from exertion. He could not remember the last time an opponent had taxed him to true fatigue.

"I say, would you be willing to teach some of those tricks to a few laggardly Englishmen? I should like to see a patent offered to masters of defense, so all the nobles could learn the same methods."

Armando lifted an eyebrow. What a self-important young man Harry was. "An interesting notion, sir."

"Harry, we'd best be going." Compton cast a worried eye at the blood still dripping from his friend's chin. "Your father—"

"Can wait," Harry cut in, grimacing. "For God's sake, Compton. Haven't I been at his beck and call all my life, and he only found me worthy after Arthur died?"

Armando winced at the hurt in Harry's voice. He knew too well the ripping pain of familial conflict. "Go on," he said. "When you defy your sire, don't let it be on my account."

Harry stared at Armando, then grinned and clapped him on the shoulder. "I'll remember that. I'll wait for something of large consequence. Then I'll defy him. Keep you well, gypsy."

Armando winked. "Stay precious, good sir."

Harry guffawed. "Think about my offer. Come see me if you ever decide to display your skills properly."

"Where will I find you?" Armando called back.

"Why, I'll most likely be at Richmond Palace."

"And to whom shall I address myself?"

Harry brayed again with laughter. His companions elbowed each other in the ribs. "Ask for Harry," the blond man cried. "Harry Tudor!"

CHAPTER 7

Armando sagged against Esmeralda's broad flank. "Harry Tudor," he breathed in disbelief. "I just won a fight with the Prince of Wales."

"You really didn't know?" Will Shapiro grinned at him.

Armando curled his hands into fists. "Why, you little bastard Jew. If not for you, I would have been halfway to London with a small fortune in my purse."

Will shrugged. "If I'd not spoken out before you stole the prince's purse, you'd've been caught and hanged before you could say *Ave María*. You didn't do so poorly." He gestured at the ring. "That ruby's as big as my thumb. You're a wealthy man. I did you a favor."

The Jew's complacent manner dug at Armando's temper. "Forgive me," he said, drawing back his fist to strike, "for not showing more gratitude."

Something went wrong. His fist, scarred tough by dozens of brawls, should have landed with shattering accuracy on Will's nose. Instead, Armando felt a blinding pain in his jaw. He stumbled and struck the frozen ground with a thud.

Half-dazed, he stared up at Will. The Jew stood frowning at his hand, flexing his fingers as if to assure himself he had not broken any of them.

"Demonios!" Armando exploded, bracing his hands behind him to lurch to his feet.

It happened again, too quickly for him to see or to defend himself. Will's foot clipped him under the chin. Armando lay supine with a large, booted foot pressing on his neck.

Will regarded him mildly. "Let's not do this anymore. I dislike brawling." He cocked a rusty eyebrow. "Truce?"

Armando made a strangled sound in his throat. He threw off Will's foot and jumped up. But he didn't try to attack again. "Where the devil did you learn to fight like that?"

Will grinned and spread his arms. "In Spain."

"Spain?"

"Toledo, to be exact." Will spoke perfect Castilian. Armando realized with a start that it had been he who had pointed out Harry's weak spot during the sword fight. "My family name is Chávez. My uncle David and I are the only ones left. Let's go. You're probably hungry." He turned to stroll away.

Armando hesitated. His stomach griped for food, for the tart he had eaten was but an unpleasant memory. Appetite overcame pride. Muttering a curse under his breath, he grabbed Esmeralda's reins and fell in step with Will.

"It's well you're not in Spain," he said, touching his jaw. "We arrest your kind and burn them at the stake."

Will nodded. "Don't forget the strappado, the rack, and the wheel. An admirable civilization. Remind me never to go back."

He spoke blithely, but Armando sensed an undercurrent of rage. Suddenly the fog in his brain cleared. "*Dios!* You fled Spain because of the Inquisition, didn't you?"

Will's silence hinted at terror and loss, at hiding in the dark and fleeing in secret, never to return.

Armando felt an unpleasant stab of shame. He had never believed the Holy Office to be just. Rafael had taught him differently, had taught him that the Church of Spain had become an institution ruled by fear, ignorance, and suspicion.

"And after we eat," said Will, "we'll leave for London."

"I just came from London. And who says I want to travel with you?"

"You can't stay here. You won your freedom today, but word is out that you're a cutpurse. The Prince of Wales won't always be around to protect you from the town watch. They'll be looking for you. Besides, I need your help. Prince Harry just gave me enough money to open my own shop."

"I don't know anything about commerce," Armando said.

Will laughed. "You really are a *hidalgo*'s son, aren't you? Nevertheless, you can help me establish a shop. Although they don't ordinarily burn 'my kind' in England, there are some who hesitate to do business with an outlawed race. We'll use your name to procure special leases and licenses."

"Why should I help?" Armando demanded.

"Because you've nothing better to do."

Almost against his will, Armando found himself with a full belly, Will riding pillion behind him on Esmeralda, heading back to Londontown.

Bow bells rang incessantly, their rusty throats calling through the smoke-laden mist of late afternoon. In the marble solar of Durham House, Gabriella swept back her skirts, curtsied deeply, then offered her hand to an imaginary partner. Only the empty air, throbbing with the discordant peals, and a gray cat, sunning itself on the windowsill, witnessed her dazzling smile.

"Another dance, Don Gitano?" she inquired with a gamin wink at the dark-haired suitor who smiled at her from her mind's eye. "Oh, but I couldn't possibly accept your favors again."

"Honestly, Gabriella!" Doña Elvira's staccato voice clipped the fantasy short. "A royal wedding tomorrow, and you do no more than flit about, talking like a magpie to thin air."

Flushing, Gabriella froze in midcurtsy. "Doña Elvira, I didn't hear you come in. But is it not wonderful? After all these years, our lady is going to marry. And she'll be crowned queen, not Princess of Wales." Gabriella swept up the sleeping cat and cuddled it to her cheek. "Think of it! No more drafty chambers, no more horrible meals, no more threadbare clothes. Why, now we can burn candles just for fun if we wish."

"Deo gratias." Doña Elvira made the sign of the cross. "And to think we almost departed for home only a few months ago."

Gabriella would always remember that day, for it had been the same day a dark horseman had captivated her fancy and sent her running across the privy garden to see him. The fact that she had no idea who he was only made her dreams more delicious, more tantalizing. She had lived on the memory of his graceful movements, his stern command of himself and his smoke-colored horse, his passion when he had swept a pretty girl into his arms.

A third event crystallized that day in her memory. A messenger had arrived from Richmond. King Henry would not live to see the spring.

He had lingered on into April with the same stubborn will that had won him a crown on Bosworth Field.

Now his handsome son, seventeen years old and bursting with possibilities, had succeeded to the throne as

Henry the Eighth. Filled with notions of chivalry, he had brushed aside his father's Hapsburg negotiations and declared that he would honor the betrothal to the Princess Catherine of Aragon. Tomorrow they would marry at Greenwich; in a fortnight they would be crowned at Westminster.

Like all royal alliances, it was a betrothal of strangers. As a lad of nine, Henry had stood proxy by Catherine for his brother Arthur. Since then, they had encountered each other only a few times. Still, both Henry and Catherine were young, handsome, and energetic. The new reign held out the promise of a golden age. The coronation feasts and tournaments and festivals promised to go on for months. It would make all the long years of waiting worthwhile.

"Gabriella?" snapped Doña Elvira. "You've not heard a single word I've said." She moved about the room, fussing at an arrangement of daisies on a glossy-topped table, trying the latch of a jeweled coffer beside the flowers.

"Indeed I haven't," Gabriella admitted. "Do pardon me."

Doña Elvira clucked her tongue. "I was commenting on the wedding plans. Jesus wept, but the ceremony at Greenwich is to be so small, it seems an almost clandestine affair. Why cannot our lady have a grand state ceremony?"

"She already had one—to King Henry's brother." As soon as the words were out, Gabriella clapped her hand over her mouth.

Doña Elvira's eyes kindled. "Where did you learn to say such hateful things? You're no better than a scullery maid."

Gabriella sensed real distress in Elvira's strident tone. She waved a conciliatory hand. "I spoke out of turn, Doña Elvira. Please forgive me. It's just the wonder of it all— the wedding, then the coronation. . . ."

"You'll live at court now, and must learn to guard your tongue." Scowling, Doña Elvira opened the coffer.

"What is that?" Gabriella asked, crossing to the table.

"The king's wedding gift to Her Highness."

When she spied the contents of the silk-lined box, Gabriella gasped. "Jesu, have you ever seen anything so beautiful?"

"Beautiful?" Dona Elvira snorted. "Pearls are the symbol of tears, of sorrow. Hardly appropriate for the occasion, and the king has insisted that she wear them."

"Surely it's just a superstition." Gabriella ran her finger over the string of matched pearls, each the size of a Jerez grape. "Truly, the king must love her."

Doña Elvira made a grumpy sound in her throat. "I want you to sit with the princess for a while. I have countless details to go over with her new English ladies-in-waiting and with the Spanish ambassadors. I just got word that the Duke of Albuquerque has sent an emissary and some sort of lavish wedding gift. Lord above, I don't know what I'll do with everyone. . . ."

"You'll manage." Gabriella took up her lute and glided into the inner chamber. Velvet hangings insulated the room from the clamor of the bells. The muted sound only served to underscore the silence of the figure on the bed.

A pair of candles set in niches at the head of the bed bathed the princess in a golden glow. Catherine had one arm flung over her face. Clutching the slim neck of her lute, Gabriella made an obeisance.

"Your Highness? Doña Elvira said you might like me to sit with you."

At the sound of Gabriella's voice, Catherine moved her arm, revealing eyes that were puffy and pink from crying.

"Mother of God, look at you," the princess murmured.

Flushing, Gabriella put up a hand to straighten her coif. As usual, her riot of black curls had escaped the stiffened linen. "I'm sorry. I should have stopped to comb my—"

"Never mind," said Catherine. "Sit down where I can see you better. You've changed, child. When was the last time you looked in a mirror?"

Gabriella lowered herself to a stool beside the bed. She noticed the coral rosary twisted in Catherine's pale hands. "Until recently, we could afford no mirrors. But I confess, Your Grace, that when the plate looking-glass arrived from the Duke of Mantua, I couldn't resist a peek."

"Of course you couldn't." Catherine pushed herself up and sat back against the pillows. "You are utterly beautiful."

Gabriella heard no warmth in the princess's voice. Catherine's eyes narrowed. "Your skin is as white as a lily but colored at the lips and cheeks as if you'd used carmine."

"Your Grace, you know I'd never submit to vanity."

"Your hair is like black silk, and your eyes as big as pansies. And look at your figure, Gabriella!"

Gabriella glanced down at the square-cut bodice of her gown, cinched in above the full skirts. "I've outgrown most of my clothes, Your Highness. Thanks be to God, we all have new costumes for the wedding and coronation feasts."

"Your pretty breasts would tempt a saint. There are men who would lay down their lives for a glimpse of your slim ankle."

Hearing the bitterness in Catherine's voice, Gabriella shifted uncomfortably. The princess had changed over the past tense months. As the day of her wedding approached, she grew more and more withdrawn. Gabriella missed the moments of gaiety and intimate friendship they had once shared.

Gabriella pondered Catherine's words. Lavish compliments indeed—if they were meant as compliments. But her musician's ear was tuned to nuance; something in the princess's speech gave Gabriella the urge to apologize.

She laid her hand on Catherine's arm. "Shall I fetch you a posset?"

"No! I'll not have you wait on me as if I were an invalid, creaking with age." She glared at Gabriella's hand until, blushing, Gabriella drew back. "It's not fair," Catherine burst out, slapping the counterpane. The rosary beads whipped like a snake over the brocade covering. "Seven years I've waited, and in those seven years you've blossomed like a rose. The footmen trip over their tongues each time you pass by. But what of me?"

"They would never presume to stare at a princess of the blood royal."

"Wouldn't they? *Wouldn't they?*" Catherine snatched a loose thread from the coverlet. "I was as pretty as you when I first came here to marry Arthur. It's true!"

"Surely you were much more beautiful, more refined."

Catherine waved her hand. "Don't give me platitudes. *Jesu*, since the old king's death I've heard nothing but insincere flattery." She wound the thread around her finger, pulling until the tip was bloodless. "The years of waiting in this miserable climate stole my youth. Stole it, Gabriella. I'm twenty-five years old! My face is sallow, my hair dull, and my waist thick."

"That's not so, Your Highness. Besides, England will love you for your fine mind, your commitment to the True Faith."

Catherine sagged back against the pillows. Gabriella wanted to offer a damp handkerchief to ease the puffiness from her eyes and the mottled color from her cheeks. She dared not. Catherine was like a vessel filled to the brim. Her emotions would slosh over if Gabriella upset the balance.

"You should join our diplomatic corps." Catherine's spine stiffened. "Aye, a queen's looks count for naught when all is said and done. I'll give them a queen such as England has not seen since Eleanor of Aquitaine."

Gabriella smiled. "You are your mother's daughter, ma'am." The one time she had met Queen Isabel, Gabriella had been only seven, but the impression of steadfast strength, implacable will, and uncompromising intelligence lingered in her memory.

"Thank you." Catherine gave a watery smile. "Best I get all my passion out now. Henry—and England—expect a queen who can govern herself."

What an odd thing for a bride-to-be to say, thought Gabriella. Surely the young ruler craved just a small measure of passion from his bride.

"Will you play and sing for me now, Gabriella? In sooth it does calm my nerves."

Gabriella spent a few minutes tuning the lute. She thought of the feast being planned for the coronation. Thanks to William Cornish, master of revels, armies of musicians would play. Thanks to Catherine's influence, Gabriella, too, would perform. She felt no nervousness at the prospect. Her talent was a gift from God. He would not take it away the moment she stood before the royal court of England.

She strummed a chord and took a deep breath. While she sang, the princess lay still. Gabriella believed Catherine had gone to sleep, lulled by the slow song. Finishing with a final shivery plaint, Gabriella looked up at the princess.

Her heart lurched in sympathy. Catherine was not asleep, but weeping silently, the only movement that of great tears sliding down her cheeks.

Tucking her lute under her arm, Gabriella went down on her knees. "Your Majesty! Please, what's amiss?"

Catherine began to speak—slowly, in measured tones, as if unburdening herself to a confessor. "If I enter into this marriage with Henry, I will be guilty of a hideous sin. 'To uncover thy brother's nakedness . . .' "

"No, Your Grace!"

"I was married to his brother Arthur."

"That was no true marriage at all," Gabriella objected. "Doña Elvira has certified that you are *virgo intacta*. You have a papal dispensation to wed Henry. The marriage to Arthur was never consummated."

Catherine inhaled as if she had been struck. "I lied."

Gabriella thought she had heard wrong. "Your Grace?"

"I lied, God forgive me, and one day a reckoning will come. For pity's sake, Arthur was sickly, but he was young and eager for all that, as was I. Of *course* the marriage was consummated!"

In shock and fear, Gabriella stood in horrified silence.

Catherine leaped from the bed, her eyes blazing. "Get out!" she shouted. "How dare you invade my most private thoughts!"

Gabriella backed away. "Your Grace, I'm so sorry, I—"

"Nothing! You heard nothing!" She picked up the lute by its strings. Two of them snapped with a discordant twang.

In sudden, sick understanding, Gabriella took the instrument and edged toward the door. "I heard nothing," she repeated, then scurried out. The ceaseless clamor of the bells thudded against her temples. The princess's confession pressed on Gabriella's chest like a load of stones. Consummated! Catherine's first marriage had been consummated! No wonder the approaching wedding had so unnerved her. She was going to the new king's bed with a lie in her heart.

Nothing good had ever come of a lie.

But it was Catherine's lie, Catherine's sin, Gabriella told herself as she hurried to her own chamber. She must banish the memory from her mind as if she had never heard the confession.

She closed her door, set down the lute, and rubbed her temples. She refused to let herself think of the dire information that could destroy a kingdom.

To occupy herself, she searched her Moorish coffer for lute strings to replace the ones that had broken. Think of other things, she told herself, inhaling the cedary smell of the coffer. The ornately inlaid box had been taken as booty by her father, a hero of the reconquest. She wished she had known him.

What had he been like? Gabriella had asked her mother many times, but Doña Mercedes would only give the vaguest of answers.

She had dared not press her mother for more information. Just the word "father" sent Mercedes to her knees, saying the rosary like a chant against evil.

Frustrated, Gabriella dumped the contents of the box on her bed. Not a string to be had.

She donned a light cloak and tucked the instrument under her arm. Properly, she should send a household page on the errand. But the need to escape pressed at her. Besides, the English lads, sent by King Henry, tended to dawdle. Best to buy the strings herself. She could be down to Maestro Martelli's on the bridge and back before Elvira noticed her absence.

The years of living in poverty at Henry the Seventh's sufferance had made Catherine's women into independent souls. Stepping out into the street, Gabriella drew up her hood and walked eastward. Shop girls and apprentices hurried through the streets, their faces merry and exhilarated from the holiday air created by the tolling bells. The Thames was a forest of masts, for visitors had come from far and wide for the coronation. Laden with carpets and spices, vessels from Venice and the Levant bobbed amid ornate barges and wherries. A flock of the king's great white swans glided through the fleets.

In five minutes she stood at Maestro Martelli's shop and knocked with a growing sense of futility. He was gone, probably for the next month, for all of London would go on holiday in honor of the coronation.

Gabriella leaned her forehead against the shop door as if the wood pressing into her skin would help her think. She reviewed the names of other craftsmen she knew of, but all would have closed their doors in honor of the royal nuptials.

Then she recalled William Cornish, master of revels. He had told her of a talented new instrument maker just north of the bridge. Passing beneath the drawbridge gate, she hurried toward Eastcheap. The buildings, shoulder to shoulder, their gabled brows arching out over the lane, nearly obliterated the waning light. Over the shop hung a wooden sign in the shape of a viol.

"Are ye lost, miss?"

"No." She saw a wizened man moving a twig broom over the stoop of the herbalist's shop next door. "I need some lute strings and it's rather an emergency," she explained. "Do you know if this shop might still be open?"

"Give Will Shapiro a knock, miss. He's new to London and hungry for business. He and his partner went out earlier, but they might be back by now."

"Shapiro . . ." Gabriella tested the name; then awareness slammed into her. "A Jew, is he?"

"I doubt he bites, miss." He turned to go back into his shop. She noticed the small embroidered cloth circle he wore on his sleeve. A Jew's yellow badge.

She opened her mouth to apologize, but the words stuck in her throat. She came from a country that had been ripped apart by warring Christians, Jews, and Moors. Her mother had raised her to believe that Jews threatened Christian souls.

She rapped at the door. The idea of spending good coin on a Jew rankled, but she was determined to perform before royalty. She would not let even prejudice stop her.

Securing her hood more tightly over her head, she waited. When no one came to the door, she pushed it open, stepping into a small shop lit by a fanlight over the door. A workbench littered with vises and tools and pots of glue stood at the rear. One wall was lined with shelves covered in wool felt. On a side counter lay musical scores hand-inked and illuminated on vellum.

Gabriella took a deep breath, and her senses filled with the scents of rosin and lacquer and fine wood, clean horse hair and ink and parchment. The smells of the instrument maker's trade.

Her gaze fell on a small lady's lute that lay on a velvet cloth on the worktable. The lute was made of pale wood polished to a golden sheen. Gabriella set down her parcel, untied her cloak and slung it onto a stool. She touched the strings and found the instrument perfectly tuned. With a faintly guilty air, she picked out a melody of her own creation. No one but she knew that the song captured the vigor of the gypsy horseman and her own unfocused yearning.

The sound of the instrument astonished her. The sweet resonance vibrated like the echo of an angel's voice. Holy Mother of God! Never had she heard such a glorious sound.

She picked out another melody, this one from the stack of printed music with the words penned beneath the notes. It was a simple lay, unremarkable, yet there was an appealing innocence in the poem. The composer was no Abelard, but the words rang with a direct and naive idealism that caught at her heart.

No longer a girl hurrying in search of lute strings, she felt transported by the gifted artisan's creation and by the simple love song. Doña Elvira would be shocked. She believed Gabriella should use her art solely for the glory of God, performing only sacred music.

But why had God given her the gift if not to allow her to explore every facet, sing every song in search of perfection?

All her girlish dreams, all her anguish and joy sprang from her throat, then died on the last, magical chord.

A footstep sounded behind her. She turned and saw that she was not the only one caught up in her performance.

A young man in an apron and shirtsleeves stood gaping at her. Gabriella's first impression was of warmth and openness. Aye, he exuded the quality from the top of his unruly red hair to the toes of his soft leather knee boots. He was slim, of medium height, and looked strong in his upper body. His face, guileless and dotted with freckles, was not handsome. His eyes were the warm gray color of her favorite cat. He greeted her with a smile. "Hello, miss."

"Is . . . the master in?" she heard herself ask.

"Aye, miss."

She laid down the lute. "Did he make this instrument?"

"Aye, he did."

She brushed her fingers over the neck of the instrument. "His artistry is without peer. Will you tell him that for me?"

The smile widened. "You just told him yourself, miss."

Her jaw dropped. "You? You're Master Shapiro?"

Enchanted by the flustered young woman, Will made a half-bow. She was surely the most appealing customer who had crossed his threshold yet. "William Shapiro, at your service."

She took a step backward and clutched at the cross hanging round her neck. "But you're not—you don't look like—"

"—a Jew?" He felt a flicker of pain, for her obvious distaste disappointed him. Recovering himself, he reached around behind him. "I've got my pointed tail here somewhere . . ."

"Don't," she snapped. Even in anger, her voice had a honeyed resonance. "Don't you dare make sport of me."

"I'm sorry. I have a sense of humor. Bad habit of mine, or so my uncle David tells me."

"Your uncle David is the herbalist next door?"

Will could see that she had been none too pleased with that encounter, either. "What can I do for you, miss?"

She seemed grateful for the change of subject. Her face was like a flower, the skin soft and tinted pink at the cheeks. She picked up her parcel. "I need some lute strings."

Will removed the shroud from her instrument. As he stepped close, he caught a soft, exotic fragrance that reminded him of large, thick-petaled blossoms too lush to grow in England. From a drawer, he took a fine length of spun gut. He wrapped the end around a peg. The lute was of rosewood, the neck well worn. A mediocre instrument, but her talent would overcome its flaws.

"You play and sing beautifully, miss . . ."

"I am Gabriella Flores, of the household of the princess Catherine of Aragon."

Will gave a low whistle. "You're a Spanish girl?"

"A maid of honor," she corrected him. He found her prim manner endearing.

"Of course." He threaded the end of the string through the tailpiece. "Who taught you music?"

"I taught myself."

He glanced up from his work. "Indeed?"

A smile played about her lips. "You don't believe me."

"I do. I recognized an untrained quality in your voice."

"You couldn't have," she retorted. "I take great pains to sound as refined as Jane Shippen or Dorian Amity. I do not—"

"I found it enchanting," he interrupted, enjoying her bursts of temper almost as much as her smiles. "Very refreshing, like the springtime after a long winter."

A smile softened her scowl. Her black hair fell in waves

around the shoulders of her dark green gown. "Thank you. That lute is truly a masterpiece."

"The Duke of Buckingham commissioned it for his daughter."

Her dark eyebrows shot up. "Buckingham's your patron?"

"One of them." Will turned the peg to tighten the new string. "King Henry sends them."

"Jesu, the king?"

Will nodded. "Unlike his father, King Henry takes a great interest in art and music." He indicated the manuscript on the counter. "He wrote that song you just played."

Almost reverently, she touched the gilt edge of the parchment. "Really? I'm astounded."

"King Henry's a very accomplished man."

"But the song is so tender. So emotional."

Will shrugged. "So's the king, some people say." He plucked the new string, cocking his head to hear the pitch as he turned the tuning peg. The lute had a thick, flat sound that grated on his sensitive ears. He replaced the other string, then handed it to Gabriella.

She smiled openly and broadly. "What do I owe you?"

"A ha'penny," he stammered out, dazzled by her smile.

"Don't be foolish." She put tuppence on the counter. "Martelli on London Bridge would have charged half a crown, and I'd've been glad to pay it. I'm to perform at the feast at Westminster Hall after the coronation."

Will indicated her lute. "You're going to play for the royal court on that?"

"Of course."

"No."

"No?"

"You can't." Without thinking, he took her hand. Her bones felt small and fragile. "Gabriella, you can't."

"I beg your pardon?"

"The lute's inferior. Oh, your face and your voice will surely charm them out of their chairs, but it's not enough."

She stared at the hand capturing hers. "Sir, you touch my person. You use my given name. And you call my lute inferior."

Will jumped back and struck himself on the chest. He almost blurted mea culpa but stopped himself just in time. "I'm sorry. But I want you to shine, my lady."

"Why?"

"Because you can. With the right instrument, the right music." He snatched up Buckingham's lute and pushed it into her hands. "Play this." Then he shoved the manuscript toward her. "And perform this."

"Will. Master Shapiro. I couldn't."

"What greater honor could you do the king?"

"I don't know . . ."

"I do." Heedless of her earlier warning, he curled her hand around the neck of the lute. "Now. Play it once more . . ."

A flower. She was a veritable flower, blossoming beneath his gentle instruction. He coaxed her through the piece, stopping her, giving encouragement. He leaned close, growing drunk on the fragrance of her hair. Her face loomed close enough for him to see the fine down of hair at her temples and the spears of light that glinted in her eyes. Close enough to kiss.

Will reared back, astounded at himself. He, a commoner and a Jew, daring to contemplate kissing a gentile noblewoman. To cover his chagrin, he glanced out the window. "It's late."

She followed his gaze. "Jesu, it's fully dark out."

"I'll walk you home."

"We'll have to run. If I'm missed, Doña Elvira will have me doing penance for a month."

"I have a better idea." Will hurried to the rear of the shop and yanked open a door. A stairway rose into darkness. "Armando! Armando, get down here and fetch your horse. There's a lady in the shop who needs a ride home."

"Armando?" asked Gabriella.

Will nodded, turning back to face her. A moment of apprehension seized him, but he dismissed it. Though brash and irreverent, Armando lived by a strict code of honor. That code would govern his behavior with a lady like Gabriella.

"My partner," Will explained. "He'll have you home in no—"

The clumping of footsteps interrupted him. A slim shadow moved down the stairs. "Damn it to hell, Will," Armando grumbled. "I can't be expected to squire every idle dame who . . ." Emerging into the light, he spied Gabriella. His eyes widened, and he clutched at his heart. "Mother of God, I've died and gone to heaven!" He rushed to her and sank down on one knee. "I am your servant. Your slave. Your will alone rules me."

She giggled. He raised his face to gaze up at her.

It happened as Will had expected. Her laughter stopped. Her face softened, and she stared. Will had seen the look a hundred times since he and Armando had left Richmond together. Ladies could not resist Armando's devilish good looks, his smooth tongue, his air of insouciance, his flair for drama.

Will ignored a hot stab of jealousy. Just for a moment, when Gabriella had been singing, their souls had touched. Just for a moment, she had belonged to him. But Armando's arrival had eclipsed the encounter like the sun's brightness burning away the light of the stars.

"Just like that?" Gabriella asked, craning her neck to peer around Armando's broad shoulder. "You simply struck your chains and escaped the galleasse?"

Guiding Esmeralda past the guildhalls of the joiners and vintners on Thames Street, Armando grinned into the darkness. She rode pillion behind him, her small hands clinging to his worn jerkin. He loved the breathless quality of her voice, the gentle pressure of her arms around him. He loved everything about her.

"It seemed prudent at the time," he said offhandedly. "Being chained to an oar for six weeks doesn't exactly make one eager to obey."

"Oh, Armando." Her sigh against his neck was the breath of an angel. "You left so much behind—your fortune, your family, your noble status."

"But in return, I gained my self-respect."

"Your decision has forced you to live in poverty."

"There are worse things than poverty, Gabriella."

"I know. You must think me shallow."

"No, you're thinking like a true Spaniard."

"Which doesn't say much for us, does it?"

He reached down to clasp her hand in his. Her skin was soft, but callused at the fingertips, the badge of her art. "We've broken away, you and I. Don't you see? We don't bow to the constraints of society. We're kindred spirits."

A second story window opened, and a woman dumped a pan of washing water into the street. Armando grimaced. "Londoners. No wonder El Hakim hated it here. The Moors could teach the English a few lessons in cleanliness."

"Where is El Hakim now?"

Armando felt a pang as he thought of his friend. "He took ship with Sebastian Cabot—first to Spain, then to the Indies."

"What a wonderful adventure!" She leaned her cheek against his back. "My mother would swoon if she knew I was having this conversation—*any* conversation—with a man."

"Would she?"

He felt her nod. "She's very strict in her rules of proper behavior." Her voice dropped in pitch as she added, "She despises all men. She hardly ever spoke of my father, and then only when I badgered her to tell me about him. His name was Roman de Flores. He was a *hidalgo*, and a hero in the Moorish wars. A Saracen cut him down before I was born.'' Her tone turned wistful. ''That's all I know. Now it's your turn. Tell me more about your family, your father.''

Bitterness rose in his throat. ''Both of them?''

She gasped. ''I'm sorry. I wasn't thinking.''

''It's all right.'' He angled the reins, guiding the mare around a muddy section of the street. ''The man who fathered me dishonored my mother before leaving with Colón on the first voyage. The man who raised me married her when they returned. I could have forgiven them had they been truthful. But they lied by omission, let me find out the truth from Colón himself.''

''Surely they had your interests at heart.''

''They had their own interests at heart!'' He could not keep the tension from his voice.

''Tell me what they're like, Armando. I want to know.''

He sighed and glanced down an alley to the right. Barges and lighter boats with lanterns burning in the windows slid slowly along the river Thames. The story poured out of him—his mother, who had defied convention by studying medicine with a Moorish physician; Rafael, who had made the voyage of discovery, then was content to head the trade office; Santiago, who had fled responsibilities like heretics from the Holy Office.

''What you say doesn't surprise me, Armando. From the first moment I saw you, I sensed a nobility in you.''

''A self-exiled noble,'' he cautioned.

''Someday,'' she said, ''you might realize they did what they did out of love for you. I had no father at all, Armando. You had two. One to teach you fighting skills and horsemanship, and another to teach you scholarship and family love.''

Part of him yearned to believe her; then he waved away the suggestion. "Enough about me. I want to know everything about you. I want to know what color your shift is. I want to know what you think about in church. I want to know what makes you laugh and what makes you cry."

Her sounds of mirth chimed into the night. "So many questions. And most of them highly impertinent, I might add. Well. My shift is saffron yellow. In church I think about music, mostly. And at the moment, what makes me laugh is you, Armando." She moved her cheek against his back. "I think you could probably make me cry, too," she added softly.

"Oh, my God," he muttered under his breath. This was serious. He could feel himself teetering on the precipice, then tumbling, the wind rushing past him as if he were plunging over a cliff, his heart left behind. He knew it was love. It had to be. Because for the first time since he had vowed to abstain from coupling with a woman, he was glad of the decision. He wanted to be clean and pure and new for her.

"You'd best put me off here," she said, pointing to a line of torches that reflected in the river.

"I should see you to your door. I should tuck you into your bed and kiss the stardust from your eyes."

She laughed again. "Doña Elvira—she's Princess Catherine's chief lady—would lock me up if she knew I came home with a man."

"Very well." Armando drew up the horse and dismounted, then reached to grasp her around the waist. His hands lingered there, cradling her slimness, his eyes filling themselves with the dusky vision of his destiny. "My God, Gabriella, I—"

"Hush. Hand me my parcels, Armando."

He detached the two bundles from the saddle. She was right to stop him. The attraction was too strong, the temp-

tation too great. They needed time. Time to savor falling
in love.

"I'll see you at the coronation feast, sweet Gabriella."

"Oh. Does Will need the lute back so soon?"

"No. I think he'd give it to you if he could afford to.
The man's half in love with you."

"He can't be. He's a—" She pressed her mouth shut.

"I used to think like that, too. But we were wrong.
Will's a man of honor. Jews are no different from us when
it comes to love and hate and passion and art."

"I know. It's foolish of me."

"What I meant about the feast is that I'm taking part in
the festivities, too."

Her lips parted in delight. "You're surely not!"

He nodded vigorously. "Some acrobats will be performing before the grand tourney. I'll be doing some riding tricks."

"Riding tricks?" She looked at the horse and then back
at him. "Armando! I should have seen it before!"

"Seen what?"

"You're the one!"

He bent over her hand, pressing a kiss to her wrist. "Oh
yes, *querida*. I *am* the one."

CHAPTER 8

"That's a very handsome nose, *amigo*," Armando whispered to the palace guard who stood at a side door of the hall of Westminster Palace. "I assume you wish to keep it that way."

"Sir, I have strict orders not to let—"

"To hell with your orders." Armando brandished a large fist. "Let my friend and me pass, or I'll break your nose."

Will fished in Armando's purse for one of the coins earned after he and Esmeralda had performed for the court in the yard. "There's no need for violence," Will said. He pressed a coin into the guard's sweaty palm. "Think of it, my friend. A half crown and your handsome nose besides."

The guard snapped to attention, thumped his halberd on the floor, and stared straight ahead.

Exchanging grins, Armando and Will stepped into the great hall. An explosion of color and light greeted them. Three tiers of candles hung from the ceiling. Tapestries ablaze with scenes of glory wafted against the walls and served as a backdrop for the long tables draped in red velvet. One hanging depicted the king's father on a snorting charger, seizing the crown of England on bloody Bosworth Field.

Armando's gaze traveled to the dais. Twin thrones caparisoned in cloth of gold and embroidered with the lions of England and the castles of Spain framed the royal couple.

"Feast your eyes, Will," he said, grabbing two goblets of wine from the tray of a passing servitor. "The start of a new age for England."

And an auspicious age it would be, too, if the young king and queen could be judged by their splendor. Jewels in rainbow colors winked from Catherine's bodice and coif. Golden cloth peeked from slashes in her fitted sleeves. Her face was like the center of a flower, overshadowed by the grandeur of its petals.

The only thing more dazzling than the queen was the king. He radiated power like the sun at high noon. He sparkled from the crown on his head to the spurs at his heels. His doublet hugged him like a jeweled crust, and displayed in its center a diamond the size of a walnut. The padding magnified the breadth of his shoulders and accentuated the narrowness of his hips. A beard, darker than his golden hair, framed his smiling mouth.

Armando smiled too, recalling the scar concealed by the king's beard. "Come on," he said, watching the master of revels scurrying to and fro, directing the jugglers, minstrels, fire eaters, and acrobats who would provide the evening's entertainments. "I hope to God we haven't missed her performance."

"We're probably breaking six laws by barging in here," Will muttered, but followed Armando to the end of one of the tables.

"Shut up," Armando said through his teeth, and bowed

to a red-robed papal nuncio. "And wipe that furtive look off your face. Act as if you own the place." He broke into a gracious smile. "Ah, Lady Trevelyan," he exclaimed, jumping into a narrow space on the bench beside the startled noblewoman. "How good of you to keep a seat warm for your two most ardent admirers."

"Do I know you?" Lady Trevelyan's nostrils thinned in disapproval. Her two-horned headdress poked at Armando's face.

Leaning out of reach, he clutched at his heart. "Madam, you cut me to the quick. How can you not remember that I wore your"—he glanced at her sleeve—"Kentish kendall favor at the Rushton tourney?"

Her features pinched in skepticism. "Sir, I was not even present at Rushton."

"No wonder you don't remember me wearing your colors. My lady"—he grabbed her hand and pulled it to his chest; beside him, he could feel Will shaking with mirth— "my admiration for you spans a hundred leagues and more." Letting go of her hand, he seized her wine goblet. "I am not worthy to kiss you, but let my lips touch the place where yours have been."

Her expression melted into helpless enchantment. A strangled sound issued from Will. Armando brought his foot down hard on his friend's instep.

Troubadours blared a bright salute. A troop of minstrels in particolored costumes tumbled onto the center floor. "The Doge of Venice sent the acrobats in honor of the royal occasion," said Lady Trevelyan, turning her attention to the center floor. The assemblage laughed and clapped at their antics.

"I don't know how you do it," Will said under his breath. "You stroll in here as if you were to the manner born."

Armando polished off the last of Lady Trevelyan's wine

and thumped the goblet to call for more. "My dear Will," he said. "Has it ever occurred to you that perhaps I am?"

"Perhaps you're what?"

Armando grinned. He felt warm and expansive, full of his own charm and easy enough with Will to reveal a long-guarded secret. "To the manner born."

"I'll be damned. I should've guessed."

Armando hesitated. He and Will had lived as brothers. They had traveled miles together, founded Will's shop, shared a home. But never in all that time had Armando spoken of his past.

Gabriella had changed all that. Now revealing his secret was no longer a danger to his closely guarded heart; it was a way to free himself from past hurts. A way to prove himself worthy of a blue-blooded lady.

"Will, my tragical boyhood could fill the verses of a hundred mournful lays. I am a *hidalgo*'s son, run away from a betrayal too deep to be borne."

He could tell by Will's thoughtful expression that the comical tone of his confession did not fool his friend. While a group of mummers from Westphalia performed, he related his revelation at the deathbed of Colón, his travels with the gypsies, his enslavement on King Ferdinand's treasure ship.

"I'll be damned," Will said again, raising his voice over a fresh blast from the troubadours.

Armando's head felt light after his fourth glass of wine. "Don't swear in the company of your bet—"

"*It's her.*" Will clutched Armando's arm.

Armando followed his gaze to a draped side portal. Tasseled blue and gold curtains framed a vision that brought a hush over the entire assembly. Armando's jaw went slack. The fawn-colored gown and stiff white coif were as plain as a nun's habit. But the beauty of the girl transcended the lack of ornament. Any fool with eyes could see that her figure was as lush and ripe as a peach about to fall from the limb. The coif spread out like a pair of angel's wings, framing a face of heart-stopping beauty.

A smile curved her ruby lips as she glided across the floor and, holding her lute, sank into a deep obeisance before the royal couple. The king's eyes widened; then he leaned over and whispered something to Catherine, who responded with a restrained inclination of her head. Gabriella stepped back, cradling the lute to her bosom like a precious babe to its mother's breast.

Her small hands skimmed over the strings. A sigh gusted from Will as if he had been holding his breath. The instrument he had crafted sang with uncommon clarity.

Armando had expected her to be nervous, but she stood and faced the most powerful grandees of England with the confidence of a seasoned courtier. Indeed she was, he reminded himself. She had been a member of Catherine's household since the age of eight. When she began to sing a haunting song from the sunny *vegas* of Andalucía, he understood another reason for her poise.

Magic touched her. She had a pure voice to please even the most jaded of listeners. The melody glowed with Spanish fire, yet seemed tempered by English precision and balance.

Though few besides Catherine and her entourage of Castilian nobles and diplomats could understand the words, the song wrapped around the audience, holding dukes and prelates spellbound until the final notes shimmered up to the candlelit rafters.

Gabriella dipped her head to acknowledge the huzzahs and the pleas for more. Then, smiling a smile that sent Armando's heart to his throat, she performed a sacred song that made even the papal nuncio clasp his hands and lift them to Heaven.

If the first two songs had captured the hearts of the court, the final one shattered them, for Gabriella lent her art to the king's own song:

As the holly groweth green and never changeth,
So I am, ever hath been, unto my lady true.

"My, how charming," whispered Lady Trevelyan. "She does homage to the king."

The song was as heartfelt as a prayer, as gentle as a lullaby, and yet at the same time as compelling as a lover's endearments whispered in the dark. Beneath the open, clear notes throbbed a distant sensual passion. Listening to the words springing from Gabriella's milk-white throat, Armando felt a sting of heat in his loins.

You're the one. Her statement echoed like a melody in his soul, more dulcet even than the song she performed. Plans and practicalities meant nothing. He would have her. Forever.

He glanced up at the dais. The avid heat in King Henry's eyes made him catch his breath.

"*Demonios,*" he muttered. "King Henry's smitten with her."

Will made no response. Armando turned to his friend. The look on Will's face stopped him dead.

Will Shapiro rested his chin in his hands. He gazed at Gabriella, not with infatuation, but with pure, unabashed adoration, as deep and abiding as the currents in the sea.

Will's response to Gabriella frightened Armando more than King Henry's. Will was his best friend, his only friend now that El Hakim had followed Sebastian Cabot to the court of Spain. Could their friendship survive a rivalry over a beautiful woman?

Anger and confusion lent weight to Armando's elbow as he jabbed again at the man beside him.

Will's breath left him in a whoosh. "Hey!"

A dozen glares shushed him.

"Did you hear what I said?" Armando whispered. "The king's smitten with Gabriella."

Will glanced at Henry. "I'm afraid you're right."

"Can you credit such a thing?" Armando snorted.

"Not at all," Will said without conviction.

"Surely Queen Catherine will have the sense to keep the two of them apart."

"Surely," Will echoed.

The melancholy in his voice awakened Armando's sympathy. He touched Will on the shoulder. "Nothing will come of it. Except, perhaps, enough orders for your lutes that you'll have to take on a dozen apprentices."

"Wonderful," Will said dully.

Guilt stabbed Armando. The love that transported him into the realm of dreams was making Will miserable.

Still, he felt compelled to stake his prior claim. "I'm going to marry her," he declared. The words were out before he had a chance to consider, to plan. But the conviction rang in his soul, as sweet as a song from Gabriella's lips. He stroked his thumb across the ruby ring he had won from Harry Tudor.

Will pressed his hands on the table. "Yes, I suppose you shall." His gaze riveted to her as she sank into a curtsy amid a storm of applause, then withdrew through the curtained doorway.

The merriment continued with more performers from as far away as Rome and Constantinople. A Flemish giantess, a coal-eater from Northumbria, and a saber dancer from the East regaled the royal court. Then came the presentation of gifts from princes and emperors. A tiny monkey from the Azores, a piece of the True Cross, strange and wondrous treasures, all presented with pompous grace. Flushed with gratitude and magnificence, King Henry bade one and all to attend the upcoming tournament.

Fabulous platters of dressed peacock, roasted boar, and spun-sugar subtleties came in an unending stream from the busy kitchens. Armando had no appetite for the delicacies, no ear for the breathless conversation of Lady Trevelyan.

"I've got to see her," he said to Will.

Will toyed with a wine-soaked plum on his dish. "She might appreciate being informed about your plans for the rest of her life."

Warmed by wine and new love, Armando laughed. "Don't be so dour, Will. One would take you for a bare-assed Scot. She likes me. She said I was the one. Where do you think she's gone?"

Will gestured at the nervous master of revelries. "Ask Master Cornish. He's in charge of the performers."

Far across the hall, King Ferdinand's agents started to move en masse toward the dais. With a shudder of revulsion and bitter hatred, Will regarded their black and silver costumes, their pointed beards and thin mustaches. "You go on alone," he said. "I'll meet you later."

Armando rose to seek out Gabriella. He bent gallantly over Lady Trevelyan's hand, then moved off. As he squeezed between seated revelers and the serving boards, he watched pages in livery of the House of Aragon bring forth a heavy coffer. With faultless Spanish grace, they set the wooden box on a tasseled pillow before the dais. "From Ferdinand," a scribe read from a scroll. "King of Aragon, Regent of Castile, León, and Asturias, Lord of Naples and Sicily, and Supreme Ruler of the Indies."

Sighs of greed and pleasure soughed through the room. The box overflowed with jewels and gold. Catherine of Aragon looked on with heartfelt pride.

Then the sighs turned to fascinated murmurs. Two Spanish officials stepped forward with a tall, slim woman between them.

"From His Grace the Grand Duke of Albuquerque, I bring you greetings," one of the officials announced.

Momentarily forgetting his quest, Armando edged toward the dais. He pushed past two Blackfriars to get a better look.

He sensed something familiar about one of the black-

clad emissaries. When he positioned himself for a better
view, he knew that intuition had not failed him.

That great mane of auburn hair, the broad shoulders and
the cruelly handsome mouth hurled Armando back across
the years, back to the offices of the *Casa de Contratación*.
Back into the presence of his old rival, Baltasar de León.

Yes, it was the bastard, wearing the crimson sash of the
time-honored Order of Calatrava and gripping the arms of
the slim woman. Armando craned his neck to view his
nemesis more clearly.

A hot stab of satisfaction bored into him. Baltasar's nose
sat decidedly off-center, and a bump marred its profile.

While a notary read a lengthy salute from the grand
duke, Armando wedged himself through an opening beside a pair of diplomats from Saxony and moved closer to
the front of the hall. Who was the woman with Baltasar?
Surely a creature so exquisite of form must be an important lady indeed.

She stood taller than the two men who flanked her. Her
gown was cut to hug her willowy form, flaring at the
sleeves and belling out into a wide skirt below the hips.
An exotic design, vaguely Moorish in flavor, rimmed the
hem and the parted edges of the overskirt. Her blue-black
hair shone like a veil of satin and hung dead straight down
her back to brush the tops of her hips. She stared at the
floor. Baltasar gave her arm a jerk, and she flung up her
head.

A shock of recognition froze Armando, then drew a
tortured gasp from him. *He knew that face.* Four years
earlier, he had looked upon this girl with pity. Now he
looked upon her with awe.

Her dusky skin, flawless as lustrous wood, glowed in
the candlelight. She had brown eyes tilted at the corners,
high cheekbones, and a full, sensual mouth. About her
hung an air of melancholy as potent as perfume.

He recalled her disappearance, the frantic, fruitless

search conducted by Rafael and Santiago, the bitter conclusion that the girl was lost forever. And yet here she stood, a woman garbed in costly raiments and staring at the King and Queen of England with a faint haughtiness that Armando recognized as fear.

Had she become a great lady, then?

He forced himself to focus on Baltasar's words. "She is called Paloma," he recited in smooth-toned English. "She is an island princess from the Indies. She has served his grace of Albuquerque in the kingdom of Naples; now he sends her as prized chattel to serve your needs for diversion."

The words thudded like a death sentence in Armando's mind, driving out the latent effects of the wine. Paloma had become an exalted, exotic slave, a pampered and polished plaything.

King Henry gawked, his mouth an astonished red O in the middle of his gold-streaked beard. Queen Catherine curled her pale hands around the arms of her throne. She drew a breath, then spoke. "My good lords, we do not keep slaves from the Indies. My mother forbade the practice. On her deathbed, she—"

"Peace, my lady." Without taking his eyes off Paloma, Henry waved his beringed hand. "It would not be seemly to insult a great Spanish lord by refusing his gift."

Catherine fell silent. Unlike her mother, who made a practice of defying her husband, the new queen seemed at a loss.

The murmurs from the crowd rose to a feverish buzzing sound. "God! A true island wench!" said a portly lord from Hampshire. "Can you credit that?"

"She's so comely, she frights a man," someone else said in a reverent whisper.

"She looks dangerous to me."

"Nay, I've heard these savage women are like turtles,"

came a sneering voice. "Just flip 'em on their backs, and they're helpless."

A low chorus of ugly chuckles greeted the remark.

Baltasar led her toward the retiring chamber. Even from a distance, Armando could see Baltasar's grip biting into her arm.

Fury propelled Armando through the throng, back to Will.

"Well?" his companion asked, tugging at a lock of rust-colored hair. "Did you get to see her?"

"See her?" Armando blinked; even his eyelids felt hot with blinding rage. "By God, I—" He broke off as realization dawned. "Oh, you mean Gabriella." He grabbed Will's arm and pulled him toward the doorway. "I don't have time for her now."

Will rolled his eyes as Armando propelled him from the hall. "Damn. I understood you better before you fell in love."

"Your scheme will never work." In the dimly lit shop, Will scowled at the message Armando had penned so laboriously. "No one challenges the king."

Armando sifted sand over the message. "I do."

"What makes you think he'll accept?"

Armando lifted the paper, sprinkling the floor with fine blotting sand. He angled the page toward the light. "Not bad penmanship for an indifferent scholar, eh?"

"You didn't answer my question."

Armando read aloud: "Meliadus, Lord of the Southern Star, challenges His Highness Henry Rex to a joust on the field of honor at Westminster, to provide exercise to them that honor desireth, the prize being the slave girl, Paloma of the Islands."

"Meliadus?"

"*Miles a Deo*, soldier of God. Do you like it?"

"The soldiers of the Inquisition call themselves thus, too. How could I like it?"

Armando grinned. "It's not you I want to impress. You think Harry Tudor could resist a challenge to his honor from a phantom noble? Curiosity alone will get the best of him."

"You'll hang for this."

"If the king doesn't skewer me first. I've heard he's a terror with the lance, and I've never had much practice with it." He thought fleetingly of Santiago, and was surprised to feel a small measure of gratitude. "But I once had a good teacher."

"I don't get it, Armando. You've pledged your life to Gabriella, and now you're gallivanting off on a quest for an island princess. What is this woman to you?"

"She's a promise I once broke." Armando's face sobered, and he told Will of finding the runaway girl, giving his pledge to see her returned to her people, and then discovering that she had vanished without a trace. "Baltasar," he spat in conclusion. "The bastard left the *Casa* at the same time Paloma disappeared. He must have been involved in transporting her to Naples."

Will's freckles stood out starkly across the bridge of his nose. "And now you've found her again, after all this time."

"It's like a net of interconnecting threads, isn't it? Tug on one, and the rest tighten." Armando folded his challenge and sealed it with softened wax. "How much money do you have?"

Will shrugged. "Enough for tomorrow's breakfast and next month's rent. I would have had the price of Buckingham's lute, but I wanted Gabriella to use it. You *do* remember Gabriella?"

Armando ignored the sarcasm. "I need a suit of armor—very light, for Esmeralda is no war-horse—and a caparison for her." Armando counted off the items on his fingers. He paused when he came to his ring. No. That was for Gabriella.

"My own sword will do, and the lances are provided at the lists, but I'll need a shield."

"You need an exorcist, for I fear you're possessed by madness," said Will. "We can't afford a pair of gauntlets, let alone armor and the rest. And even if we could, you could never get everything in time for the tournament."

Armando tucked the challenge and a letter to Gabriella into his belt and started to go. "I'll have to steal it, then. It'll be easy. London and Westminster are so overcrowded with visiting nobles that they've set up a city of tents outside the palace."

Will grabbed his arm and hauled him back. "You're an incompetent thief."

Armando bridled. "I can't fail, Will. Paloma is depending on me."

"How do you know she even wants to go back to the Indies?"

"Did you get a good look at her? Did you see her face?"

Will stared at the floor. "Yes. Yes, I did, as they were leading her out."

"And was it the face of a woman who is pleased to be given as a gift like a prize monkey?"

Will leaned over and blew out the candle. "All right. I'm coming with you."

The lists had been built in front of the north facade of Westminster Palace. Legions of spectators packed themselves into double-tiered viewing stands around the long tiltyard. Seven-foot fences, painted Tudor-green and white, surrounded the area. Heralds scurried between the fences, carrying messages from challengers to tournament officials who perched on their lofty posts above the lists. The tilt barrier, situated east and west, had angled ends to help the heavily encumbered combatants turn their armored horses.

Gabriella moved with a wave of illustrious courtiers toward the viewing stands. Dignitaries, nobles, ambassadors, and tournament judges streamed into the yard by way of the King's Bridge, a pier that extended out into the Thames.

Doña Elvira screamed for order among the queen's ladies and the Spanish contingent, but her voice drowned in a sea of song and chatter. Gabriella found the excitement wildly intoxicating. After years of confinement at Durham House, the prospect of viewing the king's first public tourney held the allure of a siren song. She responded to the jostling with merry laughter, earning herself a glare from Doña Elvira.

Nothing could dim Gabriella's mood. She had performed brilliantly at her first court appearance. Master Cornish had assured her of an important place with the king's revelers. But the giddiest tidings of all were tucked into the bodice of her new green court gown. It was a love letter from Armando. Unbeknownst to her, he had sneaked into the hall to watch her perform. Her songs, he explained, smote his heart.

A smile stole across her face, and she reached up to touch her bodice, to press the parchment closer to her heart.

"All this confusion does steal a lady's breath, does it not?" said a voice in her ear.

Gabriella's smile took on the stiffness of forced politeness. "Indeed it does, Don Baltasar."

Since her performance in the hall, de León had singled her out for his attentions. She found him well-mannered enough. He would have been almost too handsome, but for his crooked nose. He caught her staring, and turned his head away. She wanted to tell him not to worry. The flaw lent character to an otherwise inhumanly perfect face.

"I thought England the dreariest of nations," he said, taking her by the elbow and steering her toward the Court of the Exchequer, where the royal family would make its entrance. "But today gives lie to the notion."

"We have many such days, I assure you," she said.

"The air brings roses to your cheeks, Doña Gabriella," Baltasar said, hurrying after her.

She threw another smile over her shoulder. She should probably blush like a coy maiden, but she felt wise and confident. She had ever since the night she had met Armando. "Doña Elvira would say you are too familiar," she chided.

"Life is too short for outmoded conventions. Alas, I might have wasted my best years moldering in the House of Trade in Seville, but for a stroke of fortune."

She eyed his velvet doublet and silken hose, the heavy gold brooch in his Spanish toque, and his cordovan leather boots. "Fortune does indeed seem to favor you, my lord." His mention of Seville piqued her interest, for it was the home of Armando's family. "How did you escape the House of Trade?"

The front of his doublet expanded as he drew in his breath with pride. "I helped to capture a runaway slave."

She caught her breath. "Was the runaway a dangerous man?"

He laughed. "He was no man, but the princess Paloma."

Gabriella stepped out of the way of a passing bishop. She thought of the mysteriously beautiful young woman, remembered her haunted eyes and the sense of barely repressed tension that hovered around her. Gabriella's regard for the handsome Spaniard slipped. "So," she said, "capturing her was an act of heroism?"

"Indeed so. We can't have heathens running free! As it happened, his grace of Albuquerque was going on an extended diplomatic mission to Naples, and King Ferdinand offered him the girl. I myself went along as the duke's chief deputy.''

''So the princess helped him in his diplomatic mission?''

Baltasar laughed indulgently. ''My lady, your innocence touches my heart. No, she served him in a capacity which is not licit for me to describe to you.''

Gabriella suppressed a shiver. Seeking a way to abandon the topic, she paused to regard the fountain of the Great Conduit, dressed like a royal bride for the occasion. The cupola wore a Crown Imperial; the embattling bore gilded Tudor roses and pomegranates; sheaves of arrows and Tudor-green lozenges decked the octagonal base. The initials of the royal couple graced the turrets that flanked the conduit. Gargoyles and griffins spewed streams of wine into the cups of waiting dignitaries.

With as much grace as she could muster, she accepted a cup from Baltasar. ''Tell me, do you know this Meliadus?''

Baltasar slashed a brow upward. ''No. I'm surprised King Henry would agree to such an unconventional challenge.''

They moved to the palace yard, where the scaffolds around the field were rapidly filling with spectators. On one side, the stand for the mayor and aldermen rose above the challengers' pavilion. Opposite was the elaborate viewing stand of the queen. Its roof and columns bore royal badges and hangings of green and white. A gold canopy extended out over the tiltyard. Catherine had not yet made her appearance, but a number of courtiers, including Doña Elvira, had gathered already.

''King Henry loves jousting, whimsy, and spectacle,'' Gabriella explained.

Baltasar downed his wine and seized another cup from a passing servitor. ''Dr. Álvarez tells me he's never jousted in public before.''

''Which accounts for the size of the crowd.'' She swept her arm outward. The stands for the common folk bowed in the middle and swayed ominously with the movements of the onlookers. Rickety awnings supported by posts billowed in the breeze.

''His father never allowed him to ride in the lists,'' Gabriella added. ''He feared injury to the prince.''

A red-hooded horse litter moved into view beside the royal scaffold. ''Perhaps,'' said Gabriella, eyeing the elaborate conveyance, ''everyone's eager because of the stake.''

The twist of Baltasar's mouth marred his attractiveness. ''For a slave, the wench travels in grand style. She's terrified of horses and dogs, you know. All the savages are.''

Gabriella peered at the red drapery and caught a glimpse of the woman's silky black hair. ''How frightened she must be. She's a beautiful lady.''

Baltasar's gloved hand tightened around her elbow. ''You can't really think so.''

The urgency in his voice confused her. ''Of course I think so. She's different—so tall and slender, and the lines of her face are so sharp. Yes, I think she's very beautiful indeed.''

Baltasar scowled. ''The wench isn't worthy even to be mentioned by your sweet voice.''

''Oh, don't be—''

''She's a whore, Doña Gabriella. You must pardon my bluntness, but it's true, and I should have explained that earlier. Just because she's been used by grandees doesn't make her any better than the lowest slut in the Southwark Banksides.''

Shock drained the color from Gabriella's cheeks. ''Oh, that poor woman.''

''She's a heathen wench and deserves no better than she's gotten.''

''Heathen? Surely she's been baptized.''

"Of course. They all are. But the True Faith means nothing to a savage."

Feeling a strange tightness in her throat, Gabriella watched as guards conducted the island princess to a special draped pavilion near the royal viewing stand. Four of King Henry's personal Gentlemen Pensioners flanked the pavilion.

Wishing for any companion but Baltasar de León, Gabriella took her place in the queen's gallery by the front rail.

Baltasar slid onto the tapestry cushion beside her. "My lady," he said, his gloved hand closing around hers, "I know we have only just met, but my heart tells me we are kindred souls. Will you do me the honor of encouraging my suit?"

She looked at him in surprise, then cast a furtive glance at Doña Elvira. To her amazement, the elder lady gave a slow nod of approval. "Don Baltasar, surely you speak prematurely."

"Only because I fear so many men are smitten with your charms. Say you'll accept my suit, Gabriella." His leather-clad fingers pressed at her knuckles. "My family is wealthy. I am kin to the Marquis of Cádiz. My other cousin, Juan Ponce de León, has captured Boriquen, the richest island of the Indies. I can give you everything your heart could crave."

She should be flattered. A grandee, offering for her. But a memory whispered through her soul, of a dark London night and a dark Spanish horseman.

You're the one.

Oh yes, querida. *I am the one.*

She withdrew her hand. "You flatter me, Don Baltasar. But no, I cannot. My heart belongs to another."

"Who?" he demanded, capturing her hand again. "Name the villain, and I shall duel him to the death over you."

She laughed and tugged her hand away. "Really, Don Baltasar. A battle to the death will certainly not win me."

"We'll see about that." A latent cruelty flowed beneath his voice. Gabriella tried to edge away from him on the bench.

A blare of trumpets announced the arrival of the queen. Catherine and her sister-in-law, Mary, emerged from the chamber of the Court of the Exchequer and paced with stiff ceremony to the royal viewing stand. Heads bowed in deference to the queen.

A parade of champions came to honor her. Under a rainbow of banners and pennons rode gentlemen from as far away as Constantinople and as close by as Sussex. The presentation of a floral wreath and of the knights' shields, followed by the reading of the rules, drew out the tension.

Leaning forward beneath the gold canopy, Gabriella peered anxiously at Catherine. Though the queen accepted every tribute with a smile of inborn grace, lines of strain bracketed her lips. She and Gabriella had not spoken since Catherine's confession about her marriage with Arthur. As quickly as the thought came, Gabriella thrust it away, an unwelcome burden.

"No sign of the mysterious challenger," Baltasar remarked.

Gabriella shrugged. The first match was a clash between a Swiss lord and an English earl. The men were well matched, their rebated lances breaking almost with each pass. Squires hastened to replace them. On the sixth pass, the Swiss champion's buckler splintered. At the same moment, he unhorsed his opponent, and the match was declared a draw.

Next came two Spanish grandees performing the *juego de canes*. The English watched the play of stout poles avidly, always on the lookout for new sport.

The afternoon wore on. Whispers declared that the

Spanish challenge was a hoax. Just as ladies began to fan their faces in ennui, a fresh clarion called from the gate.

Gabriella's sensitive ears detected a melodic artistry in the salute. The trumpet blared again, clear and liquid, perfectly pitched. At the challengers' gate she spied a herald in particolored doublet and hose and feathered hat, his long brass trumpet aimed at the cloudless sky.

"Will," she whispered, focusing on the curl of red hair peeking from beneath the hat.

"What?" asked Baltasar.

She leaned forward, burning with curiosity. "Nothing. I thought I recognized that herald." Her woman's instinct and her dislike of Baltasar kept her from revealing Will, for Baltasar could make trouble if he knew a Jew attended the tourney.

His nostrils thinned. "Surely you don't consort with common heralds."

"I am a musician," she reminded him.

"In you, it's a gentle accomplishment." He spoke as if her achievement were no more important than her ability to ply a needle and thread. She tucked away her annoyance and turned her attention back to Will. He had set aside the trumpet and picked up a buckler and lance. The picture made her smile. In the role of herald he acquitted himself with grace; as a warrior's squire he lacked hauteur. Now why would Will Shapiro be acting the squire? she wondered. Was he truly so in need of money?

"It's the phantom challenger!" cried a voice in the back of the pavilion.

Gabriella half stood to crane her neck. At the west end of the list she could see a man in a black frog-mouthed helm. His armor consisted of a breastplate alone, and an iron manifer on his left arm and hand to hold the lance in place. The horse wore a quilted caparison of black with a fringe of gold.

The challenger's visor was clamped shut and his shield,

handed up to him by Will, bore a blank field of black. He rode directly to the pavilion where Paloma of the Islands sat under guard. Gabriella could see the woman stiffen at the sight of an approaching horse. The knight flung out his arm, then clapped it over his armored chest in a time-honored gesture. The romantic gesture caught at Gabriella's heart.

"He's dedicating himself to the savage wench," Baltasar said in disbelief. "That's an insult to the king."

The challenger's defiant salute to the island princess inflamed the noble spectators. "How dare he challenge the king!" "Who can he be?" "Lord of the Southern Star, he calls himself. I say he's a Spaniard." "He sits the horse boldly enough." "Not for long. Here's the king!"

Wild cheers burst from the spectators. A long double line of trumpeters, their instruments flying royal pennons, announced King Henry's arrival. Clad in full armor and mounted on a destrier in silver bard, he rode through a flower-decked pavilion. At the center of the yard, he saluted his queen. High color graced her cheeks as she tossed a green scarf to Henry.

The English king and the Spanish challenger took their places at opposite ends of the tilt barrier. Each raised his lance to a vertical position. At the blare of a trumpet, each spurred his horse.

The lances dropped down into position.

The horses shot forward.

Gabriella sent a glance at the queen and caught Catherine's eye. In that moment, a memory passed between them, a memory of a dreary day at Durham House, when the two of them had leaned out a window and cheered a pair of brawlers. How far they had come in just a few short months. How much had changed.

The challenger's horse was smaller and swifter, straining beneath the weight of its burden. Why, thought Gabriella, it wasn't a war-horse. Its gray legs were too dainty, too graceful.

"Jesu," she breathed, her whisper nearly lost to the thunder of hooves over the ragstone paving on the yard. "I know him."

Baltasar leaned down to hear. "What did you say?"

"That's . . . never mind." There was a reason Armando had appeared in disguise; it would not do to expose him to Baltasar. She was filled with pride that the man she loved would challenge the king. Then a thought iced over her pride. He had demanded the slave woman as the prize. Dear God, why?

Surely, she told herself, Armando had a purely honorable intent. Still, she could not stifle a bitter surge of jealousy.

"What were you saying?" Baltasar demanded. "Do you know something about this challenger?"

"No," she murmured, only half attending. "Of course not."

The combatants clashed at midpoint. The shields bore the brunt of the simultaneous blows. Gabriella knotted the strings of her fan. King Henry kept his seat as if the horse were part of him. Hollow, infectious laughter wafted from his helm.

Armando's lighter horse faltered, but he checked her and thundered on to turn for the next attack.

"Dear God, Armando, be careful," Gabriella whispered, her gaze fixed on him, her mind heedless of the man beside her.

So intent was she on the high sport of the lists, she never noticed Baltasar's burning look, the recognition flashing in his eyes. She never noticed him leave the pavilion almost furtively, slipping down the tiers in search of the king's marshal.

* * *

Armando watched the rebated tip of King Henry's lance, driving at him like an arrow shot from hell. Christ Jesus, he thought in the split second before contact. Help me.

Angling his shield, Armando caught and deflected the thrust. The pain of impact streaked up his arm and wrenched his shoulder. He bit his tongue to stifle a cry.

His own thrust hit wide of the mark, throwing him off balance. The movement slammed his tender parts against the high-cantled saddle, eliciting a low groan from him.

Fool, he thought, with Henry's laughter echoing in his ears. He'd been mad to think he could best a man who had been trained for jousting from the cradle. Worse, this was not the jovial young prince he remembered from Richmond; this man was king, determined to show his power to all of London.

Armando was risking his life in a hopeless enterprise. Esmeralda was no war-horse. After only two passes she blew high, her sides fanning with exertion. He would be unhorsed, humiliated, found out, punished. Paloma would remain a slave. Gabriella would lose all faith in him.

It was too late for regrets now.

Gritting his teeth, he turned the mare at the angled end of the barrier and prepared to spur her for another encounter. He felt the lithe, acrobatic dance step of her motion. What a fine animal she was. This cavalry riding degraded her.

With that thought came an idea as ripe and shining as an apple in autumn. Armando could have kicked himself. Of course! He was trying to play by conventional rules, trying to make a destrier of a palfrey.

He should have trusted his horse's own strengths. In speed and agility—and probably intelligence—she outranked King Henry's bulky charger. He should have capitalized on that instead of hurling Esmeralda and himself into a battle in which they were outweighed and outskilled.

Filled with new hope, he prepared for the next charge.

"All right, my girl," he murmured under his breath. "I shouldn't have forced you into that charge. I'll trust you next time."

He slackened his grip on the braided reins. He bounced his spurred heels against her caparisoned hide. Sensing new freedom, the mare shot forward along the divider. Armando felt the fiery ache in his torn shoulder, saw Henry's lance speeding at him.

But this time, instead of forcing the mare to drive headlong into the thrust, he let her instinct take over.

Just before the instant of contact, she shied from the hedge divider. Her movement took Henry by surprise. His lance passed harmlessly by. His curse floated on the breeze.

That's it, Armando urged silently. Get mad. Mad enough to do something rash. He turned his horse. At the other end of the tilt, King Henry did likewise. In a pause before the charge, Armando let his gaze sweep the viewing stands.

Gabriella shone like a beacon, brighter than the gold cloth that draped the scaffold. She stood with her headdress snapping in the summer wind like the wings of an angel. His angel.

Then he sought Paloma. Viewed through the iron bars of his visor, she appeared more a prisoner than ever. In her bower of red she sat, flanked by Gentlemen Pensioners and looking cold and lovely and frightened and lost. The prize. How very strange this spectacle must seem to her. Did she understand that he was fighting for her?

Two beautiful women directed the course of his destiny. One he had pledged to marry. The other he had vowed to set free.

He would fail neither. Filled with the vigor of confidence, he spurred his horse. The reviewing stands sped past.

Henry would be expecting a trick this time. But he could

not anticipate Armando's next move. The armor encumbered him, but with a creaking of joints, he dipped low over the pommel. At the same time he brought up his lance.

The rebated tip slammed home, hitting Henry's round shield. The king rushed past, his splendid buckler splintering. Behind him, Armando heard a metallic clatter and a bone-jarring thud. The spectators drew a collective gasp.

He pulled the mare up short and turned. Squires and nobles had streamed on to the field. Even the Gentlemen Pensioners left their post to aid their fallen sovereign.

Henry wrenched the helm from his head and hurled it away. It struck the ground and rolled, the bright plume gathering dust. For a moment, Armando had the image of a severed head tumbling from the block. Suppressing a shudder, he forced himself to look at Henry's face. To his credit, the monarch grinned. "I yield the battle," he announced. But his eyes conveyed a grimmer message. *You have bested me in my first public joust.*

Armando's mind raced. If things went awry, Will would create a diversion. He prayed his friend would realize that the victory was not so simple as besting Prince Harry on a greensward. Armando had humiliated a king before the noble heads of England and Europe.

He urged the mare through a break in the barrier. "Sire," he said loudly, thickening his Spanish accent, "you are undoubtedly my superior on the field of combat."

Murmurs of assent breezed through the crowd.

"But this day," Armando added, "I was your superior in blind beginner's luck." He raised his hand. "I salute you, my liege."

Damn! Where the devil was Will?

"Long live the king!" "Long may he reign!" The cheer roared from the stands. Gabriella made the sign of the cross. Paloma recoiled when a mounted marshal rode past, his horse's tail flicking close to her face.

"Your Majesty, I humbly beg your indulgence," Armando called. Ah, there was Will. His gay costume concealed by a cleric's hooded cloak, he moved inconspicuously to the side of the queen's reviewing stand and propped his shoulder against an awning pole. "About the prize . . ."

Henry's coloring deepened. Atop the broad shoulders of his armor, his head appeared small and neckless. "I accepted the terms," he said with forced expansiveness. "Of course, it's customary to buy back the booty won in combat." A jerk of his head ordered two lackeys to bring Paloma to her feet.

Like hell, thought Armando grimly. His nerves quivered with the anticipation of trouble. He surveyed the area. No one stood at the west gate, which opened out to King Street. Everyone had surged toward the center to witness the conciliation.

Two Gentlemen Pensioners stepped forward, Paloma between them. His foot flashing out from the hem of his cleric's robes, Will inconspicuously kicked at the pole of the awning.

"Dismount, sir," called Neville. "Let us see the man whom God gave victory over the king."

Armando's natural flair for showmanship tempted him. But the handsome Spaniard standing beside the king's marshal made caution rule.

Damn! Baltasar! How did he get into the thick of things?

Armando touched his visor but did not lift it. It was the signal to Will. "I'll see the prize delivered first."

Baltasar spoke quietly to the marshal, who bellowed, *"Wait!"*

Suspicion tore through Armando. Spurring the mare, he slammed his buckler onto a pensioner's head. At the same instant, a shove from Will pushed a corner support out from under the awning.

With a sound like a ship breaking apart in a storm, the

rickety wooden structure gave way. The cloth awning flapped free, cloaking the queen and her ladies and the men—including, God be thanked, Baltasar—from view. Aldermen and councillors toppled over clerics and notaries in the wild scramble. Screams filled the air. Dust flew, and panicked horses ran wild.

Escaping her guards, Paloma burst from her draped seat and ran blindly through the dust-laden yard.

Galloping toward her through the scene of pandemonium, Armando cursed his armor. He had scooped gypsy girls into the saddle many times, performing the Abduction of Psyche. But he'd had freedom of movement then. And the girl had been willing.

With terror stark in her eyes, Paloma cast a glance over her shoulder and kept running. Armando reached out and down. He caught her across the chest, hooked her under the arm, and scooped her off the ground. The move lacked the grace of a performance, but he didn't care. He slammed her belly down over the saddlebow and rode for their lives.

Cries of "Stop!" and "Traitor!" streamed from the offended Englishmen. Armando gave the mare her head and prayed her instincts would save them. The horse seemed eager to flee the lists. With single-minded purpose she drove toward the opening and burst through, clattering down King Street.

Armando knew he could count on only a few moments' lead. The confusion would clear, and he would have an army after him.

Damn, he thought, barely noticing the breathless sounds of panic issuing from the girl slung across the saddlebow. It wasn't supposed to happen like this. The phantom knight was supposed to claim his prize. Armando would take her to a smuggler's ship and back to Spain, where he would secure her passage to the islands. He would return to England and

pose of my visit. Tell me where he is, so I can throw this in his face!'' She yanked out Armando's letter and slammed it on the table.

''How did you manage to get away alone?''

She would not let herself think of Catherine's coldness, the warm friendship turned to icy reserve because of a confidence given freely. ''What with all of the queen's new English ladies, I might as well be a piece of furniture.''

His gaze coasted over her high-backed lace collar and her stiff bodice of green velvet. ''You don't look like a piece of furniture to me.''

She couldn't help smiling. ''Well, no one notices me since the queen has so many English ladies. I simply walked out of Westminster the first moment I could. Now. Where is he?''

Will set down the pumice stone and held out a stool for her. Sanded wood dusted his hand. ''You mean Armando, of course.''

She took a seat. ''I deserve to know. Surely he left word.''

''It's hard to know where to begin.'' Will shook his head, and a lock of hair spilled over his brow. ''He once knew the slave woman. She has connections to his family back in Spain.''

Gabriella's mouth rounded into an O. ''You mean that poor woman belonged to them?''

''No, it seems Armando and a man he calls Santiago—''

''Santiago? He told you about Santiago?'' Dismayed that Armando had shared a confidence with another, she traced her finger along the neck of the rebec Will had been working on. ''I remembered something after I met Armando. Years ago, my mother spoke to me of a gypsy warrior called Santiago. She accused him of the most unspeakable behavior with her. But then again, she speaks favorably of no man.'' Gabriella waved away the recollection. ''It's not important now. They could not be the same person. You were saying?"

"The two of them somehow found out that Paloma's the daughter of a friend of theirs in the Indies."

Gabriella's eyebrows shot up. "Jesu! She's Spanish, and a slave?"

"On her father's side. Her mother is a"—Will thought a moment—"a Taino Indian. Apparently Paloma was seized in a slave raid four years ago. Armando vowed to help her get back to the islands. But the authorities took her away, and that was the last Armando heard of her, until she was brought to England."

Tears stung Gabriella's eyes. "How like Armando. And I doubted him," she said past the thickness in her throat. "He kept a vow made when he was still a youth. How wonderfully, foolishly gallant of him."

Will looked deflated. "I don't know how the plan went wrong. We thought Armando's disguise was impenetrable, but someone recognized him and gave him away."

Gabriella's mind swept back to the joust. She remembered suppressing an unseemly cheer when Armando had unseated the king. She remembered whispering a caution to Armando, then turning to say something to Don Baltasar.

But Don Baltasar had been gone.

"Jesus wept," she whispered, grabbing for Will's hand as if she were drowning. His fingers tightened around hers, but she barely noticed. "Will, I betrayed Armando." She struck her free hand on her thigh, making her underskirts rustle. "Stupid, stupid me. I told Don Baltasar."

"Who?" Will's grip tightened. "You told whom?"

"Don Baltasar. An emissary from the Duke of Albuquerque."

"Baltasar." A troubled frown scored his brow. "He's Armando's worst enemy. They knew each other in Seville."

Misery slipped over her. "After eight years of living with Catherine of Aragon, I should know to guard my tongue."

"So you think Don Baltasar revealed the truth."

She nodded glumly. "It's all my fault."

He lifted her hand to his chest, and her fingers brushed his leather jerkin. Just looking into his sane gray eyes gentled her emotions. "Gabriella, no." The pounding of his heart met her palm. "You couldn't have known. Don't blame yourself."

"Thank you. But I always will. I'm a fool."

"No. You're tenderhearted and trusting."

"Armando will hate me."

'No.' Caught in an emotional snare, Will pondered his choices. Damn Armando for entrusting him with Gabriella's heart. Damn Armando for foisting this temptation on him.

He sat in silence, his mind running over the possibilities. With a few words, he could denounce Armando, declare him faithless, and destroy Gabriella's love for him. If her heart was free then maybe, just maybe, she would turn to Will.

The fantasy danced through his mind, then vanished like a wraith. He was the fool, not Gabriella.

Hating himself, he relinquished her hand and forced a smile. "Armando is going to Spain to send Paloma back to the Indies. He'll face his family, make amends if he can."

"He will?" A warm feeling rose through Gabriella, banishing her curiosity about the sudden melancholy that darkened Will's face. "But he swore he'd never go back to them."

"For you, Gabriella. For you, he means to stop running. Only a nobleman is worthy of you."

The romance of the notion seized her heart and brought a sigh to her lips. She glanced up to see Will gawking at her. He looked as if a mule had kicked him in the stomach.

"Will? Are you all right?"

He blinked. "Aye. Armando means to marry you."

Pride and adoration filled her. "Marry me," she whispered in wonderment. "Marry me!" In that instant the plans of a lifetime dissolved to nothingness. And out of that nothingness a new dream was born.

Will shifted uncomfortably on his stool. "Er, that is, if you'd have him." A look of almost unbearable hope lit his eyes.

She kissed his cheek. "What a good friend you are. You want the marriage almost as much as Armando and me."

He shrugged. "If it makes you happy."

"I'd have him," she stated slowly, her voice strong with conviction. "I'd have my Armando if he were the most beggarly thief in Bartholomew Fair."

Will's shoulders slumped. He fished in his pocket and brought out a ruby ring. "He left this for you."

She turned the jewel over in her hand. "Jesu, it's beautiful. How could he afford such a gem?"

Will's gaze shifted. "Royal indulgence, I suppose you could call it." He took the ring from her. Gazing into her eyes, he slid it onto her finger and closed her fist.

"A ring of promise. Will, I must see him. Where is he?"

"If he follows our plan, he'll take Paloma to a smugglers' port in Southampton. From there, they'll find passage to Spain."

"I want to go to Spain with him."

"He'd never allow you within a furlong of a smugglers' ship. Wait for him. Keep yourself safe. He'll find his way back."

"I must see him one last time," she said. "If you won't

help me, Will, I'll manage on my own. Even if it means my life, I must go to him.''

"She'll never come." Armando scowled into the coals of a low-burning fire. "I shouldn't even think of it."

Bemused, Paloma looked up from stirring a dark brew in Armando's helm over the fire. The low orange light of evening played over his features, sharpening and sculpting them into a visage so uncompromisingly Spanish that she shivered. His eyes—dark, burning, conquistador eyes—reflected the embers.

"What does it matter," she asked in crisp Castilian, "whether she comes to . . ." She paused, trying to recall the word. "To Southampton?"

He studied her, now looking nothing like a conquistador. He seemed vulnerable, unsure of himself. For two days they had traveled together, riding by night and speaking little. She tried to liken this stranger to the merry boy she had met at her disastrous first landing in Seville. His handsomeness had a hard edge now, but the eyes were the same—full of compassion and intensity. "It matters because I love her," he said.

"Then trust that she will wait for you."

His scowl deepened. "You don't understand love, do you?"

The question stirred a rush of bitter memories. "In my years at court in Naples, I saw the Spanish concept of love. Women sigh behind their fans; men kiss the hems of their gowns." She removed the helm from the fire and set it aside to cool. "If that is what you mean by love, then no, I do not understand."

He eyed the brew in the helm. "That's not what I mean. Gabriella and I . . . even when we're apart, our hearts beat as one."

She shrugged. "I see no advantage to that."

"Then I pity you." He snapped a twig in two and tossed

it onto the coals. "I pity a woman who doesn't know how
to love."

Years-old rage boiled inside her. "I never said I didn't
know how. I do know, Armando Viscaino. I love the way
a bird catches the wind beneath its wings. I love the sound
of the rain spattering the ground, and the hiss of the waves
on the sand." She hugged her arms across her chest. "I
love the memory of my mother stroking my hair, and my
father telling me stories of ancient prophets." She caught
her lip in her teeth. Never had she revealed to any Spaniard what ached inside her.

Armando stared back, his face soft, his eyes warm. "I'm
sorry. I wasn't thinking. There's so much about you that
I don't know, and you hardly talk to me."

"I'm talking now," she said, surprised at how easy it
was. She remembered the boy listening beneath the window at Doña Antonia's house. "I know you love gossip."

His face reddened. "What happened to you and Doña
Antonia? When I returned from Córdoba, it was as if you'd
both been plucked from the face of the earth."

"A group of men came in the night. Baltasar was with
them."

Anger kindled in Armando's eyes. "The bastard."

"He killed the blind servant, Mateo. I never learned
what became of Doña Antonia."

"Where did they take you?"

She frowned, grappling with memories like beasts in
the dark. "First to a castle belonging to the Duke of Albuquerque. Soon after that, his household—including Baltasar and me—took ship for Italy."

He slammed his fist into his palm. "Damn! No wonder
we couldn't find you. Was it hard for you there?"

She sat back on her heels. "Slavery is hard," she said
simply. But the whole truth she would keep from him.
That was her own nightmare, to be taken out and agonized over in private. She did not want to think about her

years in bondage, the stolen years of her childhood, the pain and terror and confusion and loneliness. Like a monster, the worst of the horrors that had befallen her leaped out of memory. She thrust it aside. She must never, ever think of that or she would go mad.

"Were you forced to work?"

She stiffened. "I was not made to labor in fields and mines as my people in the islands are."

"You were a maid, then. A lady's maid." He seemed anxious to reassure himself.

"My duties were . . . varied."

"Paloma." He sat forward, his fists planted on his knees. "Did they force you—"

To stave off more questions, she asked, "What of you? How did you come to be at the court of the English *cacique*?"

"I broke away from my family. They lied to me, betrayed me. I spoke words in anger. . . ."

With dawning amazement, she listened to a tale of illicit love, of dark secrets, of a young man's pride and his pain. And she saw now the resemblance to Santiago in Armando's distinctive, dark-featured face. She heard the hatred in his voice when he spoke of the man who had dishonored his mother.

"But if you take me to Spain," she said, "you'll have to face them again."

Armando nodded. "I must. No matter what Santiago and Rafael did to me, they'll help you."

Wild hope rushed over her. She pushed the feeling away. It was foolish to hope when she was so far from home. Bemused, she tested the concoction in the helm and found it tepid, slightly oily. She picked it up, moving away from the fire.

"Is it ready to eat?" he asked, walking to her side.

She cocked her head. He gestured at the helm. "That—er—soup, or whatever it is. Can we eat it now?"

She felt an unfamiliar tugging at the corners of her mouth. It was not quite a smile; she had not smiled in years. "I don't think you'd want to eat it."

"Then what is it?"

She set down the helm. "It's dye." Bending, she dipped a torn swatch of her petticoat in the warm, red-brown liquid. Then she lifted the dripping cloth and approached Armando's horse. Her every instinct told her to flee. No islander would willingly touch a horse. They were iron-shod demons; since the conquerors had arrived, the beasts had been used to hunt down and kill people. Some clans persisted in the notion that a Spaniard on horseback was a single beast, a monster from the Dark Place.

But this animal, calmly chewing a mouthful of summer grass, was different, she told herself. Esmeralda had carried her to safety. She touched the cloth to the mare's pale neck.

"Christ Jesus!" Armando burst out, rushing to her side. "What the devil are you doing to my horse?" He gaped at the bloodred smear on the pristine gray hide. With an oath, he grabbed Paloma's wrist.

Chilled to her heart, she flinched.

He seemed taken aback by her reaction.

"It was you who said we must travel to the coast in disguise," she explained.

"And so we are," he said. "As a merchant and his wife."

"On a horse as gray as the sky," she added, a note of sarcasm in her voice. "The king's men will be looking for this beast."

As quickly as it had come, the anger left his eyes. He let go of her. "God, what a prize dolt you must think me."

"What is a dolt?"

With a self-deprecating grin, he spread his arms. "Look your fill. A dolt is a man who never thinks matters through, who lets pride and sentiment rather than reason rule his thoughts.''

"Oh." Once again, she was tempted to smile. "I've met many such men before. They were all Spaniards.''

"I'm only part Spanish—the other part is mongrel gypsy. So perhaps there's hope for me.'' Taking out his handkerchief, he helped her dye the horse from muzzle to rump. "Paloma, where did you learn to make dye?''

"From my mother, and the other women of the clan.''

The throb of emotion in her voice silenced him. They finished and stepped back to admire their handiwork. Armando gave a gasp of horror. "*Dios*! She's as red as a harlot's lips!''

A strange tautness gripped Paloma's throat. Armando was right. The horse was the color of a ripe berry. Oblivious to the abomination, Esmeralda cropped at a clump of grass.

The pressure in Paloma's throat built, then burst forth as a rusty bark of laughter. The sensation was one she had not felt since she had been a child, running free across the beaches of Cayo Moa.

Armando shot her a furious look. She pressed her knuckles to her mouth to stop her mirth. "Perhaps," she said carefully, "the color will not be so bright once it dries.''

He muttered an unfamiliar word and flung himself down by the fire. "God," he said, "my horse. My beautiful horse. This journey has been nothing but a series of disasters.''

"I didn't ask you to snatch me from the king's games.''

He waved his hand. "I'm sorry." Pressing his hands to his middle, he added, "What I wouldn't give for a bite of meat.''

Paloma brightened. Perhaps he would forgive her for dying his horse red if she fed him something other than roots and berries. She slipped deeper into the woods and began to hunt.

Less than an hour later, she returned with her quarry in the iron helm. Armando lay with his arms crossed behind his head. His eyes were closed, his breathing regular and deep.

She stopped for a moment, studying him. The beginnings of a beard shaded his jaw and chin. His nose was slim and straight like those of the grandees in the portraits that lined the halls of the great houses in Naples. Dark curly hair spilled over his brow. Her gaze kept straying to his mouth, to the full, sensual lips that made her remember something she had been forcing herself to forget: that she was a woman.

She blinked away the thought, but could not take her eyes from his face. Clear and unlined, it was the face of a man who had known pain and hardship, but never true despair. Life had not challenged him yet.

If he continued on this unlikely course of rescuing her, he would certainly be challenged, possibly scarred forever. She did not want to be responsible for ruining his life.

With a sigh, she sat down beside him. "Are you asleep?"

He started, jerking upright and closing his hand around his dagger. "Christ Jesus, Paloma, don't sneak up on me like that."

"I did not sneak up on you."

"I didn't hear a sound. You make no noise when you walk."

She stared at her bare feet, free now from the hated slippers. "It's habit, I suppose. Are you still hungry?"

"I was hoping I'd fall asleep and dream of fresh meat."

"I found something." She placed the helm in her lap. "It's not exactly roast goose, but—"

"Did you snare some game?" He scrambled closer.

She lifted the cloth covering the contents of the helm.

His dark eyes glazed in horror. "My God! Those are . . . grubs!"

"They're quite edible and give great strength to the body."

He edged back, the dry leaves crackling beneath him. "You've eaten these before?"

"Yes."

"I don't believe you."

Bedeviled by impulse, she picked one up and ate it.

His face paled. "But it's raw and—and alive."

"Not anymore."

He sagged back onto the grass. "Holy Mother, but you are a strange female. You look so—so civilized, and you speak like a lady. Yet there is another part—a wild, savage part that can move soundlessly through the woods and eat raw grubs for supper."

"As shocking as that part of me is to you, it is a part of myself that I cherish. It is the life I will return to." She pressed her hands on the pad of grass. It felt moist and cool, a welcome sensation after the years of living in palaces with hard stone walls and manicured gardens. "I have come to a decision."

He regarded her hopefully. "You're going to give up eating bugs?"

Her fingers itched to smooth a curl of inky hair from his brow. "This is serious. I've decided to go on without you. To find my own way back to the islands."

Something flashed in his eyes. Hurt? Anger? "Don't be ridiculous. You speak no English. You know nothing about the countryside. You'd get lost. But even if you did find your way back to Spain, you'd give yourself away and be caught."

She suppressed a shiver and lifted her chin. "I will manage. I must."

"Not without me, you won't."

''You have great plans for your life. You'll claim Doña Gabriella as your mate. I'll not keep you from your dream.''

He sat forward, gripping her shoulders. He seemed not to notice the coldness that took hold of her at his touch. ''Four years ago, I swore I would help you get back to your home, and I mean to honor that promise. A Spaniard's honor is everything.''

She wrenched from his grasp and scrambled to her feet. ''Do not speak to me of Spanish honor.'' Bitterness poured from her broken soul. ''I have seen it, seen how thin and shallow it is, a façade for black deeds against people you consider beneath you.''

He took a step toward her. ''You speak as if I were one of them. One of those who hunt your people like game and make slaves of you. Damn. Why did I bother rescuing you?''

Lifting her cumbersome skirts, she struck out into the woods, the branches streaking past in a blur of green. Her feet moved swiftly over the moss and dead leaves.

Armando grabbed her around the waist. The assault awakened memories of other hands grasping at her. Wild with panic, she kicked and scratched and bit. He wrestled her to the ground. The jarring fall emptied her lungs of breath.

He threw himself atop her, trapping her flailing wrists and holding them above her head. She arched her back, but he held her fast, stretching his body along the length of hers.

Through a haze of terror, she saw his face flush and his eyes widen. He seemed startled by the press of her breasts to his chest, her pubic bone to his groin. With a jolt of horror, she felt him swell to hardness.

Oh please no. Not again, please.

She did not realize she had spoken aloud until he eased

off her, still holding her wrists in one hand while the other, with aching tenderness, smoothed the hair from her face.

"Christ Jesus," he whispered. "What did they do to you?"

"Let go," she said, gulping for air. "I beg of you."

"Don't you dare beg," he said softly. The pressure on her wrists eased. She saw him tense, ready to pounce if she tried to bolt again. "Answer me." His voice was gentle, urging. "You were ill used by a man."

She chewed her lip. If it were a matter of just one man, perhaps she could have a chance to heal. But it had been more than one, and more than just her innocence had been taken from her. She thrust aside the dark memory. "I just don't like . . . being touched," she said, then looked away.

"I think I understand." He stood, reached out, then dropped his hand to his side.

You'll never understand, she thought.

"Promise you won't try to run away. I mean to take you to Spain, put you on a ship bound for the Indies. Nothing you can do will stop me. Do you understand that, Paloma?"

She nodded and came to her feet. "I still think you're a fool to get involved with me."

"And you're a fool to resist my efforts." He gave a half-smile. "By the way. You were running in the wrong direction. Southampton's that way." He gestured behind him.

She looked in the direction he pointed. Her eyes widened. "Armando, the horse!"

He turned and gave an exclamation of delight. "You were right. She's turned a beautiful shade of chestnut." Impulsively he pulled her into his arms. When she stiffened, he let go and shook his head in chagrin. "I'm sorry, Paloma. I forgot myself already. But there's something you must understand about me. I like touching. I do it all the time. I touch a child's head when he smiles at me as I pass by. I pat stray dogs that wander the streets. I am a person who likes to touch.''

"I am a person who likes to be left alone."

"Look, I'll tolerate your strange dietary habits if you'll allow me an occasional touch."

She hesitated, her gaze measuring his sincerity. "Very well, Armando." She stuck out her hand and he clasped it.

With a wide grin, he said, "See, some touches aren't so bad. Let's get ourselves to Southampton."

"We're almost there," said Will.

Gabriella peered at the yellow dirt road framed by the ears of her plodding jennet. The rough stone wall, surmounted by a score or more of towers, sheltered a town of thatched dwellings and an abbey church. Salt marshes and ripening grain fields ran down to the mouth of the river Test.

"You can see the masts of the ships," Will said, pointing. "And I've been told the Isle of Wight is visible on a clear day."

She tightened her hands on the reins. The hard saddle pressed into her buttocks much as it had for the past three days. "Oh, Will! You didn't tell anyone where we were going."

"Of course not. But I struck up a conversation with a tinker in Petersfield. He gave me directions." He eyed her fretfully. "It's you we should be worrying about. The story you gave Doña Elvira is as thin as watered broth."

She tossed her head, her homespun wimple chafing the back of her neck. "Nonsense, Will. Doña Elvira was impressed by my newfound devotion when I informed her I'd be joining the Little Sisters of Saint Agnes on a pilgrimage to Chichester. What better way to honor the coronation of the new king and queen?"

"What better way to find yourself punished by that

dragon? She's bound to find out you never joined the Little Sisters.''

"I'll manage Doña Elvira when the time comes." She lifted her nose and sniffed the salty air. "If it ever does." She cast her gaze about the road. During the long ride on the jennets Will had procured, they had passed wayfarers and wandering lay priests, merchants, and peasants. But in the past half-day, they had encountered no one but a drover with a flock of sheep. "Do you think we'll get there in time?''

Will sighed. "I can't say. They might have been caught—''

"I won't believe that, Will Shapiro.''

"—or they might have lost their way.''

"Not Armando," she said stoutly. "His father was a great cosmographer and navigator.''

He regarded her with that odd, quiet look she had come to associate with him. "Do you realize, Gabriella, that most of what you know about Armando has come from me? You've spoken with him directly only once.''

She clasped the ring suspended on a leather thong around her neck. The circlet of gold had been too large for her finger, and she thought it prudent to conceal such a rich prize. Closing her eyes, she pictured a handsome face, a velvet voice calling to her out of the darkness. *Oh yes*, querida. *I am the one*.

"That's the magic of it, Will." She opened her eyes and looked directly at his plain, freckled face. "In that one moment, something happened. I looked at him, and it was as if my soul had found its missing half. Do you believe that, Will? Do you believe two people can meet by chance, and yet feel as if they've known each other forever, as if they were destined to love against time and distance?''

He hesitated for so long that she thought he might not have heard her. Then at last he spoke, quietly, his voice like the breath of the wind. "Yes," he said, looking at her with an unreadable expression. "Yes, I believe that, Gabriella."

She smiled brilliantly. "You're a true friend, Will Shapiro. When Armando and I are married, and living at our estate in—where did you say that was?"

"Jerez."

"Yes, Jerez. When we're living in Jerez, you must come and stay with us. Will, think of it. You shan't have to toil away, but you'll be free to build your instruments, sing songs—"

"Aren't you forgetting something?"

"What? Oh. If you want a wife, of course she'll be wel—"

"Damn it, Gabriella, listen to yourself, spinning fantasies as if life were a bard's ballad. I'm Jewish, remember? Guillermo Chávez of Toledo. Jews have been banished from Spain for almost twenty years." With a jerk of the reins, he guided his jennet past a deep rut in the road.

Gabriella swallowed hard, immediately contrite. She felt as giddy and foolish as the vapid English ladies who had joined Queen Catherine's household. "Oh, Will. Can you forgive me?"

His mouth curved in a smile that was both wistful and mocking. "There's nothing to forgive."

"You're so understanding. One day you'll find a girl—"

"All right, pipe down. We're here."

She closed her lips, although she was curious about his poignant fatalism. Stiffening her spine, she assumed the role she had played since they had left London. Will was a wandering minstrel, and she his sister who sang in taverns for the price of a meal and a bed.

They entered through Bargate. A single track of dirt a peculiar shade of yellow ran from the north of town to the wharf area. The houses and market halls huddled together as if the fog surrounding the port held them in a dreamlike state. Gabriella felt the cool mist settle on her wimple, making its wings droop and causing her hair to pull into tight, unruly curls.

"I must look a sight," she grumbled. "No self-respecting innkeeper will have me to entertain his patrons."

Will drew up his pale brown mount. "You look like an angel, Gabriella. You'll have them tossing gold at your feet."

She laughed. "I don't agree. But thank you for saying so. Now, where do you suppose Armando is?"

Armando sat on the only dry spot in the middle of a bog outside of Southampton. A mosquito buzzed near his ear. He slapped at it; his hand came away smeared with blood. Paloma was off somewhere, convinced she could find something he was willing to eat. Squinting through the mist, he saw fieldworkers in the distance, scything an early crop of hay. A green stick marked every tenth sheaf for the church. He did not worry about Paloma. She had common sense and woods-craft; she would not stray too close to the workers.

To pass the time, he took out the small purse of coins from the folds of his baldric. He made two short stacks. The coins represented the total of his worldly goods, he realized bleakly. Most of Paloma's rich clothes—the head-dress and mantle and stiff overskirt—had been sold to a gentleman merchant in Petersfield. Armando had sold his breastplate to a blacksmith, accepting a pittance in exchange for the man's silence. Esmeralda had gone to a trader for a fraction of her worth. His chest tightened at the thought of his horse. For years she had been his constant companion, the source of his income, a comfort when memories of the past washed him in melancholy, and a swift escape when trouble threatened.

One by one, he was casting off the pieces of his former life. First he had lost El Hakim to Sebastian Cabot's dream;

then he had left Will. And now Esmeralda. Armando
squared his shoulders. He would never lose Gabriella.

The first stack of coins was for the purser of the swift,
low-waisted bark called—he hoped for good reason—
Fortune. As Sebastian Cabot had predicted, Southampton
was a smugglers' haven, and his name hissed in the right
ear had brought results. Armando had already given the
purser an equal sum, the balance to be paid when he and
Paloma stole aboard at dawn. The rest of the coins would
pay their keep on the journey to Seville.

Armando glared at the ground. Here he sat with two stacks
of coins worth a fraction of the price on his head, awaiting a
baffling woman who could not abide his touch.

He put away the coins, shifting restlessly as he thought
of her—the pagan allure of her face, the hunted look in
her eyes, and the dark red lips that offered rare, fleeting
smiles like shy gifts. His traitorous body remembered the
moment he had wrestled her to the ground. His ears went
hot. His heart belonged to Gabriella, and yet when he had
held Paloma, his body had jolted to life, as ungovernable
as a ram's in rut.

She was a young woman, he told himself. A strange
and lovely woman with a body as ripe as an autumn peach.
Any man would desire her.

Love and desire were distinctly different matters. What
he felt for Gabriella was as lofty and pure as the blue skies
of Andalucía. He closed his eyes, counting the days until
he could return to England and claim her as his own.

"She must be very dear to you," came a soft, husky
voice.

Armando started and reached for his knife. "Damn,
Paloma. You keep doing that. You keep sneaking up on
me."

Her feet and the hem of her skirt were muddy from her
trek through the bog. "You looked so dreamy and content

just now. Surely you must have been thinking of your Gabriella.''

He forgave the intrusion with a smile. "I was. Ah, if you could only see her—"

"I have."

"—with her dark curls and pink lips—"

"I have."

"—and hands so dainty they couldn't span a— *What*?" Snapping to attention, he gaped at Paloma. "You've seen her?"

"I think so. I saw a young woman traveling with a man with bright red hair—just like your friend Will's."

Armando scrambled to his feet. "When? How? Are you sure?"

Paloma's mouth softened in one of her mystical almost-smiles. "Just a short while ago. I crept up to the main road to watch the travelers going in and out of town."

"Christ, Paloma! Someone might have seen you!"

"You know how unobtrusive I can be."

He acknowledged this with a nod, and she went on. "I saw them entering the town. They were riding small brown horses, and Will had a guitar slung over his back."

"It's them." Armando paced the ground in excitement. "Bless them, they've found a way to come and see us off. We've got to risk going to town, Paloma. We have to find them."

She nodded, and with a surge of gratitude, he took a step toward her. Seeing the alarm in her eyes, he stood still. His gaze coursed over her, taking in the disarray of her hair.

"You look a sight. You'll attract less attention in town if you plait your hair."

Again, the almost-smile toyed with her lips. "I don't know how to plait hair in the English fashion."

"You're joking. Every woman knows that. It's the same as braiding harness."

"I can't braid harness, either."

Armando rolled his eyes. Paloma was a jumble of con-
tradictions. She was innocence and ignorance and intelligence and exasperation all at once. "Turn around," he
said.

"What?"

"Turn around. I'm going to braid your hair."

She set her jaw and sent him a mulish look.

"Please," he said. "The less you look like a woman
from the Antilles, the better."

She presented her back to him. The sun struck the long
fall of her hair, igniting subtle flames of blue. He recognized her smell—he had first caught it the day she had run
away in Seville. It was a feral scent of wind and water and
sweat, intriguingly spiced with feminine musk.

His hands fumbled with the thick black locks as he separated them into three strands at the nape of her neck. The
silky slide of her hair between his fingers nearly made him
wince. In a movement that seemed contrary to the wary
woman he had come to know, she arched back her neck
and sighed, as if his touch pleased her. Despite the refine-
ment of her speech, she was a savage, he reminded himself, with a savage's lack of regard for mortality. No doubt
this unconscious sensuality came naturally to a promis-
cuous island woman.

But an inner voice insisted that she had been hurt—
probably worse than she would ever confess to him. He
had offered his protection, and that included protecting her
from his own lust.

Blinded by the indigo gloss of her hair, he did not realize how hard he was tugging until she flinched. "Sorry,"
he muttered. Braiding harness was one thing; Paloma's
slick hair challenged his dexterity. The result was a shining, uneven braid from her nape to her waist, secured with
a bit of string.

"There. You look the ordinary country wife. Just remember not to say anything and pretend you understand all that's said."

She tied a kerchief over her head. When she turned slightly, he caught a glimpse of her profile. Ordinary country wife indeed, he thought darkly. Everything about her screamed that she was a captive princess.

"We probably shouldn't go into town," he said.

Paloma swung around to face him squarely. Nearly as tall as he, she could stand almost nose to nose with him. "Your woman has traveled far to see you. Will you repay her efforts by hiding in a marsh while she wonders if you are dead or alive?"

First anger, then humor, jolted through him, and he grinned. "I'm beginning to like this reckless streak in you, *chica*. Let's go find my woman."

CHAPTER 10

Each time he played music, Will Shapiro put a piece of his heart into the song. For him, the wharf-side tavern full of unwashed sailors and painted doxies was no different from the royal court. All the tenderness and secret adoration he felt for Gabriella radiated from his eight-string guitar as he strummed out the opening strains of the song she would sing.

Not that the rough-and-tumble patrons of the tavern would appreciate his art. He could barely be heard above the banging of tankards, the cursing of gamblers hunched over parchment playing cards, and the loud, foul conversations of sailors.

Damn you, Armando, where are you? Will wondered. He had made discreet inquiries about a young traveling couple, and had been met with open-palmed shrugs and closed-mouth suspicion. Which meant nothing, he realized. Men of the sea were a different breed, men who could steal and kill without blinking, but who followed their own system of honor among themselves.

Shadowed by the dark timbers of the taproom, the ale-man regarded Will dubiously. Will had promised the proprietor half the coin they took. So far, not one copper penny had been tossed in their direction. But the sailors, with their purses fat with shore wages, had not yet heard Gabriella sing.

He glanced at her while his nimble fingers coaxed a chord from the guitar. She stood before an empty table at one side of the plank bar. Her eyes were closed, dark lashes shading her cheeks. She swayed, letting the soul of the music enter her. She absorbed sound like a flower drinks in sunlight. Will was glad for her plain garb, for in clothes of a more revealing cut she would tempt the rollicking gamesters and sailors.

His introduction rose to a shivering crescendo. His own playing, he knew without vanity, was as superb as the instruments he crafted. But perhaps he should have let Gabriella play. While Will's art teased the intellect, hers seized the heart.

She opened her eyes. Her lips parted in a half-smile, and she drew breath. She started singing softly, an exhalation as sweet as a spring breeze. Her skill pulsated with passion, the emotions naked and accessible to the most untrained of listeners.

Patrons stopped talking to stare at her. The noise ceased in stages, like birds falling silent at evening. Within moments the room held only the sound of Gabriella's voice, subtly underscored by Will's playing. Her voice rang like a clarion bell, reaching out to snare her listeners.

My bonny blithe William did carry me far
On wings of the morning by light of a star . . .

The old lay was one of many Will had taught her during the long hours of their ride from London. The song recounted, as most ballads did, a heart-rending tragedy.

More precious than rubies my William shall be,
My bonnie blithe William from over the sea.

He had taught her the melody because the aching, minor strains both challenged and flaunted a gifted voice. Because secretly he wanted to hear his own name on her lips, knowing her voice would caress the word like a lover's gentle hand.

Performing together was as close to making love as they would ever get. What a moonstruck fool he was, to yearn and lust after a Catholic Spanish gentlewoman whose heart belonged to his best friend. Will was worse than the troubadours of old, laying their souls bare for idealized and unattainable ladies. If ever there was a woman ill-suited for Will Shapiro, common Jewish instrument maker and fugitive from the Spanish Inquisition, she was Gabriella Flores.

The last velvet word trembled from her throat. The final minor plaint vibrated from his guitar. In the hush that followed, men paused with tankards half raised to their lips. The alewife and her daughters dabbed at their eyes. Even the most crusty of sailors gawked. From Gabriella's knowing look, Will could tell she felt the power of her hold over the listeners, the magic that could come from her alone.

Then hands slapped the tables and feet pounded the floor. Coppers showered the table in front of Gabriella. The alewife's daughters scrambled to retrieve them.

Gabriella gave a smile, sweetly distant as if she were still caught in the ancient charm of the song. Will could see she had wrung too much emotion from the hard-drinking patrons. Deciding to lighten the moment, he strummed out a lively melody.

Gabriella launched into the piece with full-throated gusto. Clapping and stomping accompanied her. The aleman grabbed his wife around the waist and pulled her into a jubilant reel.

As the evening passed, Will and Gabriella alternated between mournful ballads, soothing lullabies, and playful dances. In the midst of a song about a white witch whose kiss healed a fallen knight, Will noticed a newcomer, a tall, slim man standing with his shoulder propped on the low door frame. The curve of his arm sheltered a dark woman whose face lay in shadow.

Even as Will rejoiced to see Armando and Paloma alive and hale, his heart took a sudden leap into ice water. How simple it would have been to refuse to accompany Gabriella on this reckless quest. With a word in the right ear, he could have ensured that she stayed in London under the watchful eye of Doña Elvira. But no, he had done the noble thing and brought the two yearning lovers together. Keeping her in London would have been useless anyway. Time and distance could not quiet their passion.

Will knew the precise instant Gabriella spied Armando. Her tones became even clearer, her delivery more impassioned. She sang for Armando and Armando alone, her voice reaching across the dim room to caress him.

The song ended. While the patrons threw coins and shouted for more, Armando gave a jerk of his head to summon Will and Gabriella outside.

"She needs some air to cool her throat," Will explained to the tavern keeper. He scooped up a handful of coins. "Here, quench their disappointment with your good barley ale."

The aleman, jubilant over the coppers that littered the table and floor, nodded gratefully. Will and Gabriella slipped out through the kitchen door and emerged into an empty yard.

He expected her to lift her skirts and race to find Armando. Instead, she stopped and turned to face Will. The moon sparkled in her eyes. She reached up, laying her hand on his cheek, her thumb brushing the tender flesh beneath his eye.

"My bonny, blithe William," she whispered. "Thank you." She lifted herself on tiptoe and kissed him, her lips fluttering against his mouth. Then she moved away, running around the side of the wattle and timber building.

And Will Shapiro stood alone beneath a full moon in a strange city, and felt his heart break.

Gabriella tumbled, laughing and weeping at once, into Armando's outstretched arms. Wordlessly he pulled her between the high, concealing stacks of hay in front of the town tithe barn. He drew her close, and she reveled in the taste of the salt air at his neck, and then his lips as he kissed her. It was their first kiss, ripe with passion and the startling newness of discovery. Immutable dreams passed across the bond of their clinging mouths. Despite her lack of experience, Gabriella was filled with the sublime conviction that no woman had ever been kissed like this before.

After a long moment they broke apart. "God," said Armando, and Gabriella was touched to hear the trembling in his voice. "My God, that was worth the wait."

Laughing with joy, she leaned against a sheaf of hay and reached up to cup her hands at the sides of his neck. "I had almost given up hope of seeing you before you sailed for Spain."

"Where's Will?" Armando asked.

She glanced around the mound of hay to see him walking toward them with his loose-limbed, shambling gait, his guitar slung over his back.

"*Compadre!*" Hurrying to meet Will, Armando clasped him in a hug and gave him two loud smacking kisses, one on each cheek.

Will pulled back. Gabriella giggled. Staid Will Shapiro had never gotten used to his friend's demonstrative affection.

Sensing a presence nearby, she turned to see Paloma, the young woman from the islands across the sea. How strange and lovely she looked, thought Gabriella. She felt a flicker of jealousy, but conquered it and held out both hands. "My name is Gabriella. I've been so worried about you both."

"I don't speak English," Paloma said in Castilian.

"Oh! I'm sorry. English has become so much the language of my thoughts." She repeated the introduction in Spanish.

Paloma stared at her hands for a moment, then squeezed them briefly. "I'm grateful for what Armando is trying to do. I've told him he should let me go on alone, but he won't hear of it."

Gabriella's heart swelled with admiration. "He will do the honorable thing and see you safely home." She sent him a glance of pure affection. "I can wait for him. A lifetime, if I must."

"Hush, *querida*, you mustn't talk like that," Armando warned. "It will be only a few months. I'll be back by Christmas."

"Let's go someplace more private," Will said, speaking Spanish in the cultured tones of Toledo. "The patrons will drag her back inside for more singing if they find her out here."

Armando took Gabriella's hand as they hurried out of town by way of the Westgate. Will and Paloma followed at a discreet distance. "What were you doing singing like a common minstrel in a tavern?" Armando asked.

His vehemence surprised her. But the adoring expression on his face banished resentment. "We're traveling incognito. When Will requested beds for the night, the innkeeper hired us to entertain his guests."

"I see. It's clever. Will is always clever. But I don't like it. Everyone knows a sailor's lust can turn dangerous."

She giggled. "You would have made a good priest."

"This is serious, *querida*. I worry about your virtue."

"My virtue! Armando Viscaino, how dare you—"

"Hush." He touched a finger to her lips. "I just can't stand the idea of any other man even looking at you."

She smiled, her heart awash with pleasure. Moonlight painted the salt marshes in silver and flashed through the gases rising from the bog. Sharp salt smells mingled with the piquant tang of wildflowers opening their blossoms to the night. A nightingale called, and she could hear the creak and rattle of a marsh bird in the reeds.

She tucked her hand around Armando's arm, glorying in the muscled strength of him. His handsome face bore no traces of hardship. He wore a workingman's tunic and jerkin; his only concession to vanity was his tall red Moorish boots, the cuffs turned down above the knees. "Let's not quarrel, Armando. You've found a way to get back to Spain?"

He nodded. "We leave with the dawn tide. There's a ship called the *Fortune*, manned by smugglers, bound for the Middle Sea through the Pillars of Hercules."

"Smugglers! I hate to think of you with that rough lot."

"They don't ask questions, don't demand credentials and passports, only unclipped coin."

"Can you afford to pay?"

Another nod. "I sold nearly everything—the armor and the sword and trappings. Most of Paloma's clothes. And my horse," he added with regret.

"Oh Armando." She rested her cheek against his sleeve. "I know you'll miss that mare."

He stopped beneath the twisted branches of an old water oak and caught her in his arms. "Not half so much as I'll miss you."

Reaching into her bodice, she drew out the ruby ring

and traced her finger around the letters that circled the stone. The motto read *Dieu et mon droit*. "Will gave me this from you. I think you should take it back."

He caught his breath sharply, the quiet sound of a man in pain. "You don't want it, *querida*?"

Unlike Don Baltasar and his sort, Armando was unafraid to show his vulnerability, and she loved him for that. "I'd rather have you," she explained. "What I meant was that I wanted you to take the ring to exchange for whatever you need on your journey."

"No." He tugged at her linen cascade and tucked the ring back inside. "This is for you. Wear it always here, close to your heart. It's my promise to wed you, if you'll have me."

"Armando, there was never any question of that."

Their kiss was long and searching and hungry. She pressed against him, arching back until her wimple drifted to the ground and her hair came loose in a tumble down her back.

Breathing hard, Armando took her face in his hands. "Can this be only the second time I've held you in my arms?"

She laid her palm against his heart. It beat in racing counterpoint to her own. "We've known each other forever."

They sank to the ground, cradled by the soft grass and wildflowers beneath the towering oak. Gabriella grew drunk on his kisses, the way his hands skimmed her throat and shoulders. His palms found her breasts, and she flamed with lust and longing. The sounds in her throat were alien, the discordant utterances of a wanton woman she did not know. A woman she longed to become in Armando's embrace.

She strained closer to him, her fingers exploring the texture of his hair, the smoothness of his shoulders. She reached down, shaping his waist and then his hips. The stab of his tongue in her mouth was shockingly delicious, and she sucked at it as if to draw the essence of him into her.

"Armando," she whispered between kisses. "I want to be closer to you, to feel your flesh on my flesh, to be lovers." Pulling at his lace points, she parted the neck of his shirt and threaded her fingers into the hair on his chest.

A groan ripped from his throat. His body tensed, and he pulled back, propping himself on one elbow while she gazed up at him through a haze of passion and confusion.

"Gabriella, I want that too," he said. "Christ Jesus, you don't know how much I want it. But we can't. Not yet."

"Yes," she insisted, tracking the shape of his pectoral muscles with her fingers. "There's no one else about, and we have until dawn."

"No." The word seemed wrenched from him as he pressed kisses to her brow. She wanted to feel his lips elsewhere, at her throat and breasts and belly. But he drew away, brushing the hair from her cheek. His movements were studiously chaste.

"Listen to me, Gabriella. There is so much we don't know about each other, so much that needs to be said."

"Ah, talking!" She rose up to lick the moisture from his lips. "This may be the only night we ever have."

He threw back his head, gritting his teeth like a man in the last stages of torture. "Please, Gabriella. Hear me out." He leaned against the trunk of the tree, pressed her cheek to his chest, and rested his chin on top of her head. "It's not enough to tumble you in the grass like a tavern wench."

"It's all we have now, Armando."

His finger went beneath her chin and guided her gaze to his. "I wish to honor you, not simply claim you. I couldn't live with myself if I did. I've never taken love-making lightly."

Jealousy bedeviled her spirits, and she ducked her head down to hide the expression on her face. "I hate to think of you with another woman. How can you refuse me?"

She felt the curve of his smile against her temple. "Ah, Gabriella, how little trust you have. You think a man will lie with any likely woman who comes along."

She recalled the stern lectures of her mother and Doña Elvira. "It's true of all the men I've heard of."

"And you place me in their ranks?"

"Armando, you're passionate, and you're a man of the world."

"Only in dreams, *querida*. Only in dreams."

Her ears rang with his statement. "You mean you've never been with a woman?"

His soft laughter tickled her ear. "Not in the way you mean, *mi vida*."

Stunned and weak with tenderness, she lifted her head and kissed him. "You could give me no greater gift than that, Armando. Beloved, I could not feel more married to you if we had been wed by the Archbishop of Canterbury himself."

"Ah, Gabriella, you tempt me sorely. But we must wait. It's too risky to bed together before we're married. Believe me, I know. Learning the truth about my parentage was a blow to my pride, and not a legacy I'd pass on to my own child."

The dark pain in his voice brought tears to her eyes. "I'm sorry," she whispered. "I'll respect your wishes. We have only this one night, so let's not spend it quarreling."

After Paloma had told him the story of her life in a place called Cayo Moa, Will Shapiro gaped in astonishment. "I can't imagine it," he said, leaning back in the cool grass to stare at the stars. "Being ripped from your family at such a young age—"

"Eleven rains is not so very young."

"Rains?"

She nodded, her glossy braid falling over her shoulder. "We measure our age by counting the spring rains. A girl of eleven is almost a woman. I would have been mated within one or two more seasons, as soon as my bleeding started."

Will's ears caught fire. He had scant experience with women, and none at all with one as forthright as Paloma. He cleared his throat and tried not to think about Armando and Gabriella clasped in an embrace by the riverbank. "It's a crime that you were captured. The years must have been hard on you."

"Yes. Have you ever been so angry, Will Shapiro, that you wanted to tear out your hair, to fling yourself off a cliff?"

He closed his eyes. In his mind he saw images of his family in their Toledo house, his mother thrown upon a table and raped while he and his father were forced to watch and a fat Dominican chanted prayers. "Yes," he said. "Do you know what a Jew is?"

"A Christ killer. A defiler of the True Faith."

The color drained from his face. "Where did you learn that?"

"In the household of the *cacique* of Albuquerque. There was a Dominican monk who taught me the catechism."

"Did he also teach you that Christ himself was a Jew?"

She stared, the moonlight gliding over her uncommon features and her strange, uptilted eyes. "Brother Buil never told me."

From Armando, Will had learned that her father was a *converso* who had adopted island ways. Apparently he had never told her that part of his past. First Will felt resentment; then he realized that the man called Joseph had discerned the methods of the Holy Office. Wisely, he had kept his daughter ignorant of Jewish ways so that if she were ever questioned, her innocence would be genuine. My God, he thought. She was half Jewish herself and didn't even know.

"I've seen the Jews they call *Marranos*. They are made to wear special robes and hats, and are marched through the streets to an auto-da-fé. Sometimes they are lashed with a whip. Sometimes they are burned alive." Her stark horror made him want to gather her to his chest and weep with her.

But she was not a woman to weep in a man's arms. Vulnerable, yes, even frightened and confused, but strength was evident in her straight-backed posture, the proud tilt of her chin, the quiet dignity with which she comported herself.

"When I was made to watch the auto-da-fé," she continued, "I saw that these people were men and women and children, not demons from another world. It was the anger I felt for my own clan. By what right did the Spaniards claim our land and the seas around them? By what right do they make slaves of us?"

"I can't answer that. But I want you to know, I am a Jew."

Her expression betrayed no condemnation. "Ah, so that's why you left Spain. You're not persecuted here in England?"

"The Jews were banished from England two hundred years ago. But for the most part, the Christians here tolerate us."

"Why are Jews so hated? Is it because you do not worship the Christ god?"

Will nodded, enchanted by her unusual way of speaking. "That's part of it. We're stubborn about our religious rites, our rich heritage. People fear those who are different."

"I know."

He glanced at the moon. It had begun its slow ride into

the deepest part of the night, the dark before the dawn. Soon the tide would turn and Armando and Paloma would make their escape. The finality of it struck Will. He would never see this remarkable young woman again.

"Paloma, do you still remember your life in that other world?"

"It's the same world, Will Shapiro."

"But have you forgotten the language you spoke, the way things look and smell?"

"No. I remember every member of my clan—the toothless elders, the women at their chores, the babes strapped to their boards. I remember the flowers that bloom on Cayo Moa, the patterns of the waves on the beach." She plucked a reed from the roadside bank and separated it into strands. "You know a lot of songs, Will Shapiro. You remember every word and every note."

"True, because I practice them. I play and sing, over and over, until I know them without thinking."

"So it is with my memories of Cayo Moa. I can close my eyes and be there, racing along the beach with the wind in my hair."

Impulsively he took her hands in his. "Don't ever lose those memories, Paloma. They're precious."

"I know, Will Shapiro." She carefully removed her hands.

"What will you do when you reach your island again?"

She drew her knees to her chest, heedless that her skirts fell away to reveal her bare thighs. "I'll try to find my parents again. It might be a long search, for the islands are many and the waters are wide."

"You're not afraid?"

Her mouth curved. He thought she almost smiled. "Afraid? After four years as a slave, what could possibly frighten me?"

"What happened in those years?"

She looked away. "I will not speak of it."

And in that instant, Will knew. She was young and wildly beautiful, lacking the practiced coyness of Spanish ladies and the brittle artfulness of Moorish concubines. The nobles of Castile must have used her, often and hard.

"I'm sorry," he said. "I still consider myself a Spaniard, and you've made me ashamed of that."

"Sorrow never helped a thing, Will Shapiro. Strength and wisdom—these are the things I cling to."

"I'm glad you'll have Armando with you until you're safely away from Spain."

"I'm glad, too. He's rash and innocent in many ways, but he has what my people call *ceiba*."

"What's that?"

"It is hard to explain. A burning, here." She pressed her hand to her chest. "A flame that never wavers."

Will smiled. The description suited Armando once he had chosen a course of action. "He'll do his best to protect you."

"I wish he would not risk himself. I wish he would just stay and make Gabriella his mate."

Will's Adam's apple bobbed as he swallowed. "Armando's not one to take a promise lightly. Besides, it's probably a good idea for him to leave the country for a while."

"Because he defeated the English *cacique* and stole me away?"

"Precisely."

"Will it be safe for him to return one day?"

Will wished he could reassure her. But King Henry was a man of high spirits and even higher temper. "Safe or not, Armando will come back."

Somewhere in the marshes, a lark filled the air with morning song. Will stood, stretching. The night had passed in the blink of an eye. "Will you remember me, Paloma?" he heard himself asking. "When you close your eyes will you see a picture of me?"

Her lips parted. "Yes, Will Shapiro." And then she

smiled, a genuine smile. "You will not be hard to remember with all that red hair. Most unusual in—"

The thud of hooves on the road cut off her words. Grabbing Paloma, Will tumbled into the ditch and lay still. When the horsemen passed, he scrambled up the ditch bank.

"Oh, shit," he said under his breath, staring at the rich saddlery, the gleaming harness, the flowing tabards of Tudor-green and white.

"I do not understand your English words."

"Those are king's men. Come on. We'd best get you and Armando on that ship."

Ducking low, they rushed along the road to find Armando and Gabriella in the shadow of a water oak. Oblivious to the passing search party, they were locked in an embrace so hot that just looking at them singed Will's eyelashes. He stopped, feeling a tightness in his chest.

Bridling his emotions, he called, "Time to go, *amigos*. The king's riders just went into town. They'll be looking for you."

Armando and Gabriella broke apart. He swore softly and took her hand, drawing her down the steep, muddy bank. They found a half-dozen wherries moored in the tall reeds.

Armando watched Will help Paloma into the boat; then he took Gabriella in his arms. "One last time, *mi vida*," he whispered. He pressed his mouth to hers, passion mounting like a banked fire stirred to life. What a fool he was to go racing off on an adventure, leaving this precious treasure behind.

And yet, even as he flayed himself with regrets, he felt something inside him spring to life. It was the surge of excitement he felt moments before a race or a fight. Trying to deny his love for challenges, he anchored himself to Gabriella.

Will cleared his throat. Armando pulled back, pausing to touch the ring nestled between her breasts.

"Wait for me, Gabriella."

"I will," she pledged.

Armando put his arm around Will's shoulder. His best friend was everything the *hidalgos* of Castile had been taught to despise. But Armando would trust Will with his life. "You'll look after her," he stated.

"Of course. Hurry, Armando. I'll try to distract the king's men while you get yourselves aboard the *Fortune*."

Armando slid into the wherry and picked up the oars. Pushing off the bank, he began to row. He had learned the skill in the belly of a Spanish galley, and for the first time he saw that something good had come from the betrayal of his adopted gypsy family. The galley had brought him to Gabriella, had reunited him with Paloma. A man's life took some strange turns.

He was oblivious to the feel of worn wood in his hands, the quiet plash of the oars drawing through the water, the salt smell of the creeping tide, and the light in the beacon of Netley Abbey to the east. His gaze stayed fixed on Gabriella, a dark shape leaning on Will for support.

He watched until the darkness swallowed them.

He and Paloma said nothing as they cleared the mouth of the river Test and turned westward toward the quays. They passed over the great, deep rudder of the *Fortune* and came alongside the weather side of the ship, the side facing out to sea.

Sailors hung in the ratlines, unfurling sail. The hull of the ship rose steeply, bowing out so Armando could not see the rail when he looked up. A rope ladder hung down the side.

"We'll have to climb. Can you make it, *chica*?"

With a round-eyed stare Paloma regarded the ship. Her skin seemed stretched taut over her cheekbones, and her lip trembled before she caught it firmly with her teeth.

"This won't be like other voyages," Armando assured her. "This time, you're sailing to freedom."

She stood, bracing her feet against the swells that caused the wherry to bob. "I'm ready."

Above decks, the ship's master called orders that were echoed from stem to stern by the mates. Warm with exertion from the climb, Armando found the purser. The thin, cat-eyed man stood amidships with one elbow propped on the binnacle while he spoke with the captain.

They glanced up at Armando's approach. The purser said, "I thought we'd be sailing without you—" He broke off and gaped at Paloma. "You never said your companion was a woman!"

"Does it matter?"

His deep chest swelling with indignation, the captain planted his hands on his hips. "Of course it matters, you fool. Everyone knows a woman aboard brings bad luck. "I won't have her on my ship."

"Then, I'll tell the king's men about that undeclared wine and gunpowder you've hidden in your hold."

The captain's face flushed to a livid shade of red. "Get her below," he ordered curtly. "And not one mother's son is to see her face until we make port and put you off."

The king's men and their dark, foreign leader had awakened the town with the church bell. By the time Will and Gabriella reached the Westgate, people in hastily donned robes had come to see what the commotion was about.

The lieutenant of the guard had cornered the tavern keeper. "Haven't seen anyone answering that description, sir," the stout man was saying. "On my honor, I haven't."

Similar denials murmured from the others.

"Search every plank of every ship in the harbor," the lieutenant ordered.

From the corner of his eye, Will saw Gabriella make the sign of the cross. The soldiers formed up to fan out over the wharves. "Wait here," Will whispered, pulling her into the shadow of the church porch. "Don't draw attention to yourself." Slipping into the tavern kitchen, he snatched a pair of bowl lamps and hurried back out, taking care not to slosh the oil.

Keeping to the shadows, he went to the tithe barn, where sheaves of hay lay stacked for the church. The sweet, dry scent of it mingled with the smell of burning oil. He hesitated, swallowing hard. The huge stack represented one tenth of the bounty of the land. One tenth of the toil of the people.

The Church was rich enough, he told himself. Not allowing any more hesitation, he threw the lamps in the dry hay and dove for concealment at the side of the stone barn.

"Fire!" The call sounded over the milling crowd.

Startled, Gabriella hurried out into the main street to see the bundles of hay ablaze. Soldiers and townspeople raced back from the wharves. Lines formed from the river to the church front. The lieutenant issued orders while the village lay priest wrung his large rosary of olive-wood beads.

Will must have set the blaze, bless him. Standing calmly in the midst of confusion, Gabriella watched the *Fortune* slip out to sea. She hugged herself, threw back her head, and laughed out loud. Armando was free! He had made it!

She raced across the market square in search of Will. She found him being hauled off by a raw-boned, lantern-jawed soldier.

"Look what I've found, sir!" the soldier brayed.

Gabriella skidded to a halt. The lieutenant subjected Will to a long, assessing look. "You're the man who abetted the Spanish challenger, Armando Viscaino."

Will put on a doltish expression. "Surely I don't know what you mean, er, my lord. Your Grace. Your Excellency."

A gloved hand smacked him across the face. Gabriella winced, then shot a glance at the harbor. The *Fortune* was just clearing the banks of the Test and heading for the misty rise of the Isle of Wight.

"As I see it, the situation is simple," the soldier said. "Tell us where the thief is, or we hang you for a traitor."

"You'll hang me for nothing," Will said defiantly. "For I can tell you nothing."

The lieutenant turned to the coarse soldier. "Get a rope."

"No!" Gabriella rushed forward to clutch the lieutenant's arm. Will shot her a warning look but she ignored it. "You prevail upon an innocent man! He knows nothing! I know where the fugitive Spaniard went.'Tis what I came to tell you."

Stunned, the soldier loosened his grip on Will.

Run, Gabriella urged him with her eyes. She prayed he would realize he could help her more by escaping with his life. He hesitated a moment too long. The coarse soldier hauled him off to a horse-drawn tumbril.

"Very well, miss," said the lieutenant. "Where's the fugitive?"

She pointed randomly at a cog. "Aboard . . . that one, I think." She gave him her most charming smile. "Or perhaps that other one there, the one with the shields hanging down its sides. It's so difficult to tell one ship from another, and—"

A high-pitched whistle pierced her recitation. Someone from the port began shouting. A group of men stood pointing at the fast-receding shape on the horizon to the south.

"Such a pity."

The sound of the velvety smooth voice froze Gabriella. With her heart pounding in dread, she slowly turned to see, shouldering a path through the crowd, the formidable shape of Don Baltasar de León.

"Such a pity," he repeated, taking her hand in a tight grip. "You showed great promise as a queen's lady. But I see you've strayed from the path of virtue, Doña Gabriella."

The crowd gaped at the melodrama unfolding so deliciously before their eyes. With a flick of his wrist and a curt command, Baltasar ordered a pinnace to be commandeered to give chase to the *Fortune*. "I'll give a silk doublet to the first man who boards her," he offered. "And ten gold sovereigns to the first man who lays hands on Armando Viscaino."

"Let go of me," Gabriella demanded. She wondered how she could ever have found him handsome. In the firelight he appeared loathesomely cruel.

"Oh, no, my lady. I mean to escort you to London. I'm certain Her Majesty will be most gratified to find you safe." He leaned down and dropped his voice to an intimate whisper. "Gratified enough, I expect, to offer you to me as my bride."

CHAPTER 11

"Here." In the cramped storage berth of the *Fortune*, Armando handed Paloma a ship's biscuit. "I found some that the worms haven't gotten to." He grinned. "Although you never seem to mind the worms."

Ignoring his attempt at humor, she ate in silence. "I wish you'd eat more," Armando said. "You've got to keep up your strength."

"I've strength to spare." She spoke without vanity. Despite the weeks at sea, despite the confinement, she had remained stoic, powered by sheer determination. Her limbs were sleek and muscled, her eyes clear and calm. Even during the harrowing hours during which a pinnace from Southampton had chased the bark, she had remained unruffled. A lesser woman would have succumbed to despair. Paloma accepted the danger and discomfort with an indifference he found vaguely chilling.

"We'll spy the Pillars of Hercules within the next day or two," he said.

"What is that?" She finished the biscuit, and he handed her another.

Compassion welled in Armando. For days, she had endured the darkness. He became her window to the churning blue world outside. "The pillars are a pair of great rocks that rise from the sea between the tip of Africa and the coast of Andalucía. The farthest one, which the Moors call Jebl Musa, is almost always visible. A very important spot, *chica*. In ancient times, men believed it the end of the earth."

"How is it important to us?"

"We'll leave this ship when we reach it, for it's only a short way from the coast. I'll bribe the master to send us ashore in a ship's boat."

"And if he refuses?"

"I'll set fire to his ship if I have to. Just think, within a day we could be coming ashore in Spain."

The glow from the candle lantern accentuated the pallor of her skin. Armando felt a strange tightness in his chest. In some ways he still did not know her at all. "Forgive me, *chica*. I forgot. Spain holds no particular allure for you."

"No."

"Paloma, I wish you would speak of your ordeal. No good can come of letting a wound to the soul fester."

"How can giving my troubles to you ease my mind?"

"The gypsies have a saying: A burden shared is lighter." His own words sparked pain and an unsettling sense of anticipation. He had left Spain a confused, tormented youth. He was returning as a man of purpose.

She regarded him placidly. Her strange, light eyes missed nothing. "You have burdens of your own, Armando."

He nodded, then leaned back on his elbows against a mildewed coil of rope. "I never thought to see my family again. I didn't want to. I still don't."

"Hatred within a clan is poison."

"It wasn't I who caused the trouble."

"No? Then tell me who did." A smile flirted with the corners of her mouth. He was familiar with the expression by now, familiar with its sad charm.

He took a sip from his wine flask. Awful stuff, and hardly worth the trouble of smuggling. "I grew up believing Santiago was my godfather. *Dios*, but I loved the man!" Armando pounded his fist into the damp rope. "He was everything I thought a *hidalgo* should be. Brave and strong and honorable. But it was all a lie. And Rafael was part of that lie."

"You Spaniards use so many words. I don't understand."

"I can't forgive them," he explained. "Their lies took my identity, my honor. Can you blame me for leaving them all?"

"A family is precious and fragile, Armando."

"My parents should have considered that." He tunneled his fingers into his hair, then raised his tormented gaze to her.

She plucked at the coil of rope. "In my clan, men and women mate for life. They do not mate with any others."

"That's as it should be."

"Still, if it weren't for Santiago, you would never have been born."

He couldn't help smiling. "Well said, *chica*. Perhaps when you get back to the Indies, you'll be a jurist."

"I don't want that. I just want to be . . . as I was."

"And what was that?"

"A child of the morning. My mother called me that— Kairi."

"Kairi." The word tasted sweet and exotic on his tongue. He found himself reaching for her, pulling her against his chest. As always, she stiffened and resisted. As always, he made a soothing sound in his throat and held fast to her. She smelled of apples and mildew and the faint muskiness he always associated with her. He wanted to break down the wall she had built around her heart. He wanted to probe the mysteries she kept hidden behind her eyes. He did not pause to wonder why this was so important to him. "Paloma, I—"

A faint shout sounded from above. Armando leaped up, banging his head on a rafter. "You might get your wish sooner than you thought. I think we've spied the Pillars of Hercules."

He rushed up three decks until he reached topside. The captain, the pilot, and the navigator were clustered in earnest conversation. Sailors ran to and fro in confusion.

"What is it?" Armando asked a passing seaman. "Have you sighted Gibraltar?"

"Hours ago," the sailor said.

"Then what's all the shouting about?"

"Oh, a minor matter," the sailor said contemptuously. "You and your fancy lady are going to get us all killed. Look." He pointed. "That's a fighting galley chasing us."

Flaming with apprehension, Armando raced to the rail. Closing in fast was a galleasse, bristling with long sweeps and scudding beneath yards of wind-filled canvas.

The mainsail bore the ensign of Castile and a familiar device of a lion rampant. Armando's heart dropped to his knees. It was the banner of the House of De León.

"Damn!"

"They're after you and the wench, aren't they?" said the captain. He took Armando's silence for assent. "I thought so."

"Can you outrun them?"

"They're shipping no cargo save ballast. They're carrying sail as well as oars, while we're at the mercy of the wind. What do you think, my friend?"

Armando remembered the hours of back-breaking rowing, and knew the Englishman spoke true. It was one thing to outrun a small pinnace, yet another to elude a sleek galleasse.

"What will you do?" Armando asked.

"I'll raise a flag to signal that I wish to parley. Then I'll surrender you and the wench."

"No!"

"I've already given the signal."

Armando clutched the weathered wood of the rail. Looking eastward, he could see the great rock, its sheer face plunging into the surging sea. Looking right, he spied the hazy mainland of Spain. Christ Jesus, to get so close . . .

"Go and fetch the wench," the captain ordered.

Armando hurried back down to the storeroom. Oblivious to the drama above decks, Paloma had fallen asleep on a damp floor mat. More and more these days, she sought refuge in slumber. She looked lovely when she slept, her face smooth and untroubled.

He knew what awaited them. For him, torture followed by death. For her, torture followed by . . . more torture.

She would never see her island home again.

He would never hold Gabriella in his arms again.

Chilled by the certainty of their fate, he shook her awake. His expression must have betrayed his sick fear, for she said, "Something's amiss."

"Yes." He explained about De León's galley. Her face paled, but she showed no other response. During the years of her captivity, she had learned to bury her emotions.

"Damn," he said, brushing a lock of hair out of her eyes. "And we're so close! I can see the coast of Andalucía."

The color rushed back to her face. "All's not lost, then."

"What do you mean?"

"We'll swim."

He clutched her shoulders. "You've been cooped up too

long in this room. You've lost your mind. It can't be done."

"Why not?"

"It's too far. Besides, I can't swim."

She regarded him with pity. "Most of you Spaniards can't. I always thought it foolish for seagoing men."

"I agree, but it can hardly be changed now."

"So we should simply submit to Baltasar de León?"

She was as close to true anger as he had ever seen her. Fire glittered in her eyes, and a tiny vein throbbed at her temple. He spread his arms. "It's either that or drown."

"And which do you prefer?" She drew her knees up to her chest. "I won't go through it again. I'll die first."

A group of sailors crowded into the passageway outside the room. Armando and Paloma were dragged above decks. She blinked at the dazzling light of the sun touching the Middle Sea.

Through a red mist of fury, Armando watched a sailor brush his chapped hand over the front of her blouse. He tried to tear himself from the grip of his captors, but they held him fast.

Something strange came into Paloma's eyes. A blankness that was frightening, achieved with chilling ease.

This had happened to her before. Men had pawed at her, abused her. She had learned to gird herself with indifference, to appear aloof, to remain immobile. If she let go of her emotions, she would lose herself in horror and misery.

Armando marveled at the inner strength it must take to erect that wall of indifference. At the same time, he wanted to exhort her to fight back.

He strained against the sailors' grip while his gaze swept the main deck. Apparently the English did not trust de León to be content with taking just two prisoners. The crew prepared for battle, manning the bombards at the sterncastle, swiveling a pair of falconets at the fast-approaching galley, and stirring embers in braziers for igniting slow matches and crossbow bolts.

"God help you if we have to fight this out," muttered an English sailor. "We're no match for a galley rigged for battle."

The galleasse bounded closer, so close Armando could make out the slim, well-dressed *hidalgo* on the quarterdeck. How far we've come, Baltasar, he thought. What had begun as a boyhood rivalry had grown to unmitigated hatred.

The galley loomed less than a cable length away. Paloma's gaze was no longer empty and dull. With bright, avid eyes she watched a muscled blue swell rolling toward the two ships. Armando remembered that her people lived close to the sea; they read its moods and nuances like seasoned mariners.

She glanced at the brazier, then looked at Armando. A silent message of hope and defiance passed between them.

The captain lifted a hollow horn to his mouth. "We're lowering a boat for the Spaniard and his wench," he shouted. "We have no quarrel with you."

The incoming swell struck. The deck listed sharply.

Armando spared no time to think. While his captors stumbled, he twisted out of their grasp and kicked out at the brazier. The coals spilled across the deck. A sack of corned gunpowder made a fount of sparks. Flames licked along the tarred wooden decking. The boatswain's whistle shrilled an alarm.

Armando looked around for Paloma. To his astonishment, she picked up a flaming crossbow bolt and tossed it like a spear at the rigging. A few shrouds broke free and canvas snapped in the wind, fanning the small fires that had broken out on the decks.

Enshrouded in smoke and panic, Armando fought by reflex, barely thinking about the knee he drove into a sailor's gut, the elbow he smashed into someone's rib cage.

He reached the rail in time to see Paloma dive headfirst into the water.

The churning, depthless water.

Fear coiled inside him. A burly sailor charged, a barrel hefted on his shoulder, ready to launch at Armando's head.

He ducked. The barrel sailed overboard.

Giving himself no time for contemplation, Armando followed it. He was surprised to discover that leaping to his death was exhilarating. He knew a momentary weightlessness, the wind screaming through his hair, the steel-blue and foamy water rushing up to meet him.

He smacked the surface. Another surprise. He hit hard, as if the water were solid as packed earth.

But then he sank, a blur of bubbles racing across his field of vision, burning his eyes. And the coldness, the bone-deep coldness embracing him in a death grip.

Visions streamed through his consciousness. The kind green eyes of Rafael, pleading . . . the sin-dark eyes of Santiago, laughing . . . And then Gabriella's round sweet face, so vivid for an instant, until another face replaced it: pale brown, haunted eyes, stark features, a mouth that broke his heart with its attempts to smile. . . .

The images dissolved into endless blue. The matchless, eye-smarting azure of the Andalusian sky. His last sight on earth was stingingly beautiful . . . and empty.

"Take hold of this."

Armando gasped; he had not realized that he'd surfaced. Bitter seawater rushed into his mouth. He choked, floundered, until something grabbed his arm.

"The first rule of swimming," called a familiar voice, "is that you don't inhale the water like air."

"Paloma?" Her face came into focus, then shimmered away again as a wave crested over his head. He came up sputtering and saw her there, riding the lift of a wave, holding the bobbing barrel with one arm. Holding him with the other.

"Gracias al cielo!" he heard himself shout. "We're alive!"

The popping of a falconet punctuated his statement. The sound jolted Armando's faculties to full alert. The bark was on fire, the crew out of control. The ship heeled. Her jutting prow slammed the galley broadside. The sound of splintering wood and screaming men mingled with the roar of fire and sea.

Paloma thrust the barrel at him. The stench of spoiled contraband wine had never been more welcome, for the barrel floated like a cork-filled buoy.

"Kick your legs," she commanded, coiling the barrel rope around her wrist. "Kick hard and fast."

Armando followed her lead. In a small corner of his mind rose a feeling of sheer wonderment. Paloma was a marvel, her strong arms pulling them through the water. Within moments he was able to match the rhythm of her stokes.

He glanced behind. Along with flaming pieces of canvas and fallen timber, men leaped over the sides of both the bark and the galley, swarming around a flotilla of hastily lowered boats.

Armando kicked faster, the rudder to her tiller.

"It's a long way," Paloma called over her shoulder, not breaking her stroke. "Can you make it?"

Her endurance and skill challenged him. Armando threw off the last of his fear. "I can make it."

Aching and exhausted, nearly blind from the glare of the sun, they flung themselves onto a gravelly beach strewn with fly-ridden seaweed.

Through cracked lips, Armando tried to utter a prayer of thanksgiving. His parched throat protested, and he abandoned the effort, settling for a rakish grin of gratitude.

Alert as a doe, Paloma darted her gaze at the ocean.

There was no sign of shipwreck survivors. "I'm thirsty," she said.

Armando raised himself on his elbows, then lumbered to his feet. Every muscle, from the large, aching bands in his thighs to the tiniest ones about his eyes, constricted in fiery protest. He nearly pitched forward onto his face. No, he thought, steeling himself. Paloma was thirsty. The woman who had saved his life was thirsty.

He pulled her to her feet. She leaned into him briefly, her weight curiously welcome despite his burning muscles, his heaving chest, the gasps of air rushing down his throat.

"Come," he said, his voice rasping yet gentle. Together they staggered across the unfamiliar beach, cresting a hill studded with spiny plants. Far in the distance rose an ancient stronghold surrounded by steep, cobbled streets and densely packed houses. Tarifa, he thought. The southernmost point in Spain. Christ Jesus. *Spain.*

They came to a vineyard; he led Paloma down the espaliered rows. She paused, grabbing a cluster of hard green grapes.

"Don't," he cautioned. "They're bitter, and will make you more thirsty than ever." Reluctantly, she dropped the unripe grapes. He guided her deeper into the vineyard. At the center was a cistern surrounded by unmortared stone. Half-running, half-stumbling, they reached the rock-walled cistern. Shaking in his haste, Armando drew a bucket, and they devoured the cool water.

He drank until he nearly retched. Then he threw back his head and laughed with the sheer joy of being alive. "Look at us, *chica!*" he shouted. "We've made it! We're home!"

She did not smile, but her eyes glowed with warmth. "You are home, Armando Viscaino. Not I."

He took her hands, fingers that were wrinkled and raw. Ignoring her aversion to being touched, he pressed his mouth to her palm. "Let God witness my vow. I'll get you home."

Not "I'll put you on a ship." His vow had, without volition or conscious choice, changed from a matter of honor to something deeply personal. He shivered with the enormity of his decision. And shivered again when he thought about facing his family.

With ice-cold fingers, Gabriella tied a wispy linen cap beneath her chin. The cavernous antechamber throbbed with shadows. She told herself she mustn't be nervous about the queen's summons. Catherine had been more a parent than Gabriella's own mother. Surely the years of friendship were ample reason to hope for a pardon.

The door of the queen's bedchamber swung open. Black-garbed and looking like a buzzard circling for a kill, Doña Elvira descended on Gabriella. Swooping close, she peered at Gabriella's dove-gray gown, the austere white cap on her head.

"Her Majesty will see you now."

Gabriella lifted her chin and glided past Elvira. Although the woman was now one of the most powerful in the realm, Gabriella refused to be intimidated by her.

She stepped into the queen's bedchamber. Servitors and English ladies-in-waiting fluttered about the room. Furniture draped in dark green velvet made the room a dim forest. Unspoken censure hung like a suffocating veil over the oppressive air.

"*Come.*" Catherine of Aragon's voice summoned from the straight-backed chair facing the hearth.

The English ladies edged looks of resentment at their queen. To their annoyance, Catherine always spoke Spanish. No doubt they feared missing out on bits of gossip and court intrigue.

The distance from the door to the chair seemed like a furlong. A pair of nervous whippets cowered on cushions at the queen's feet. A lay sister knelt on a prie-dieu in a corner, her eyes lifted to a shrine of Mary.

Gabriella crossed the room and sank to her knees. The dogs snapped at her, but she ignored them. "I am your most humble servant, Your Majesty."

Catherine wore a dressing gown woven of paned gold velvet with black silk peeking through the openings. Her face was a pale oval framed by a peaked headdress. Surrounded by luxury, she should have been drowning in comfort.

Yet the rigid way she held herself made it seem as if the chair was made of nails. "Rise and be seated," she commanded. Her hand came up and ran around the neckline of her gown.

Gabriella's eyes widened. A rash circled the queen's neck. A dark garment peeked from within the neckline of the robe.

Jesus wept, Gabriella thought. The queen was wearing a rough nun's robe. A garment of self-induced torture to remind a sinner of her past misdeeds.

Gabriella alone guarded the dangerous secret. As keeper of the queen's conscience, she embodied the nun's robe. The constant, chafing reminder of Catherine's sin.

Resentment simmered in the queen's eyes, and Gabriella knew that Catherine regretted the moment of weakness in which she had blurted the truth to her reluctant listener.

"What be your pleasure, Your Majesty?" Gabriella forced herself to inquire.

Catherine pressed her mouth into a flat line. "In causing me this embarrassment, you have humiliated all of Spain. For eight years I have stood as the symbol of Spanish decency and piety in this land. I have spoken out for Spain's interests. I've learned the diplomatic cipher in order to better serve our mother country. Eight years of toil, Gabriella. And now you have called my reputation into question."

Gabriella twisted her hands into the folds of her gown. "No, Your Majesty, I can explain—"

"I'll hear no explanations from you. The facts speak for themselves. You professed to go on a pilgrimage. Instead, you traveled alone with a Jewish artisan to Southampton. You sang secular songs in a tavern. You abetted a common thief."

"Armando is no thief!" Gabriella blurted. "He has stolen nothing. His honor demanded that he free the slave woman. I applaud his bravery, Your Grace. He follows a higher law than the law of the king's pride." On a surge of defiance, she added, "Were she alive, your lady mother would applaud him, too."

Outrage burned in the queen's eyes. "People have been put to death for lesser impertinences." Gabriella steeled herself for condemnation; then Catherine tempered her voice. "However, up until recently you have served me well. I am prepared to be lenient. I've the situation in hand."

A cold fist of dread took hold of Gabriella's stomach. "What's to become of me, madam?"

"You're to be married. Even as we speak, a royal notary is drawing up the betrothal papers."

The fist squeezed tighter. "Don Baltasar?" Gabriella asked.

"Aye. He's willing to ride out the scandal and attempt to piece together your reputation. Quite a good match, considering your mother will not offer a dowry."

Gabriella's vision swam, and she reached up to press at her breastbone, where Armando's token lay in the warm valley between her breasts. Blessed Virgin, she was to marry Baltasar de León, the man who had betrayed Armando, the man who had stared at her with ugly promises in his eyes.

"No, please, Your Majesty, I beg of you—"

"My decision has been made."

Courage stiffened Gabriella's spine. "Do my years of

devoted service mean so little to you, then, that you would force me to marry a man I do not want?''

''You should have thought of that when you acted like a common trollop.''

Gabriella crushed her fists into the folds of her gown. She found herself thinking of Will. She always did when she needed steadiness. But Will could not remedy this situation. He was rotting in prison, maybe dying. Armando was running for his life. She faced the possibility of losing both men.

She lifted her agonized gaze to the queen. And an idea tiptoed into her mind. She had the power to throw off the yoke of obligation to Catherine, for she possessed a secret that could rock the monarchies of two mighty nations.

One word whispered in the right ear, and King Henry would dissolve his illegal marriage to Catherine of Aragon. For she had lain with his brother.

The vengeful words stuck like a sour note in Gabriella's throat. She could not bring herself to ruin the queen's life, nor bring further shame upon Spain.

Catherine of Aragon stared implacably back. ''You are dismissed, Doña Gabriella,'' she announced.

Gabriella managed a graceful obeisance, then withdrew. The stares of the other ladies of the bedchamber seared her. Only when she reached the cool emptiness of the antechamber did she give in to her weak knees and her tears.

She sank to the flagstones, burying her face in her hands. Her tears flowed freely, bitter and burning. She faced a life with a man she hated, a man who believed in enslaving women and betraying his countrymen.

A light touch on her shoulder pulled her from her misery. The King of England helped her to her feet.

''Oh, sire!'' She clutched her skirts to make a curtsy. The disdainful stares of Neville and Compton reflected the picture she made, her nose red and her cheeks streaked with tears.

"Here, what's this?" Without taking his eyes from her, Henry put out his hand. Lord Neville produced an embroidered silken handkerchief. "Dry your eyes, my lady," commanded the king. His voice was gentle and kind.

Gratefully, Gabriella obeyed. Not knowing what to do with the sodden handkerchief, she tucked it into her stomacher. "Thank you, sire. Please forgive me."

He took hold of her hand, squeezing it when her fingers trembled. "Only if you'll confess what is wrong, my dear. Your grief pains my heart."

He was a virtual stranger, and the king besides. She had abetted the man who had humiliated King Henry in public. Yet she found herself admitting, "I have offended your lady wife."

He frowned at the closed bedchamber door. "How so?"

Her gaze strayed to the king's companions, Neville and Compton. Like the king, they were mere youths, yet chains of office draped their chests and ponderous parchment scrolls burdened their arms.

"Gentlemen, if you please," Henry said.

His advisors stepped out the main door. Henry led Gabriella to a window seat. "Will you confide in me, my lady?" he coaxed.

She bit her lip. "I . . . my troubles are small to a man who rules a kingdom."

"A kingdom is made of subjects. If I lack the time for one lady's grief, how will I make treaties with whole nations?"

"I should unburden myself to a confessor," she demurred.

"Aye, a confessor could absolve you from sin. But I am the king. I can order a subject put to death . . . or grant her enough wealth to let her live free for the rest of her life."

Warmth kindled in her heart. He leaned forward, centering his full attention on her. As if he truly cared.

"I lied to the queen about making a pilgrimage. Instead, I went to Southampton to help Armando Viscaino escape with the slave girl Paloma.''

A muscle leaped in his gold-bearded jaw. ''I've been informed of your escapade. You used poor judgment, Gabriella.''

''I went because I love him. And also because I believe it's wrong to hold a woman in bondage.''

''You've a noble spirit.''

''No, sire. I'm selfish and vain. The queen was right to censure me. I'll get used to the betrothal—''

''What betrothal?'' he asked sharply.

She gripped the window ledge. Was it possible the king didn't know? Of course! The years of waiting had taught Catherine independence; she had not consulted her husband.

''The queen has arranged a betrothal between me and Don Baltasar de León. We're to be married when he returns from his voyage.''

King Henry's eyebrows knit. ''I mislike it,'' he muttered. ''You're too young to be married, far too young.''

Although it was not true, Gabriella nodded in agreement. ''I don't wish to marry Don Baltasar, sire.''

''Fine.'' He gave a decisive nod. His glittering doublet moved stiffly with the motion.

Gabriella hardly dared to breathe. So simple. Was the king really susceptible to a woman's tears? Impulsively she took his hand and planted a fervent kiss on it. ''Thank you, sire! I am speechless with gratitude.''

When she raised her face to his, she saw something in his pale blue eyes, something that touched her spine with fingers of ice. Then the king smiled, and the look vanished. Gabriella called herself a fool for questioning her good fortune.

''My lady,'' he said, ''you have but to ask me for anything, and it is yours.''

She felt like a princess in an old ballad, granted a wish

by an indulgent fairy. And like the princess, she felt re-luctant to test her good fortune by demanding too much.

"There is," she began hesitantly, "one other matter." She wanted to beg him to absolve Armando and let Pa-loma go free. But there was another issue, more immedi-ate. "It's about Will Shapiro, sire."

"Ah, a gifted man indeed. A credit to his race."

"He's been put in Billingsgate Prison. Your Grace, the escape was all my doing. Will shouldn't be punished."

"I admire your sense of justice. Yes, Master Shapiro will be released. You have my solemn promise on that." He took her hand and kissed it. His beard and mustache abraded her skin. Then he left her, moving with stately grace to join his companions outside. His ambergris per-fume lingered in the air.

Gabriella sagged back against the window embrasure. Far below, boatmen called to each other on the Thames, and gulls screeched in the summer sky. Unthinkingly she spread the handkerchief over her knee and closed her eyes. She vowed to dedicate a month's worth of devotions to King Henry.

A sound disturbed her reverie. She opened her eyes to find Doña Elvira glaring down at her, or more accurately, at the handkerchief draped over her knee.

Before Gabriella could speak a word, Doña Elvira turned away and marched out of the chamber.

Stung, Gabriella glanced down at the wisp of silk. When she inspected it, she understood Doña Elvira's speechless fury. Embroidered in gold on the white silk were the words HENRY REX.

CHAPTER 12

Dragging in a slow, steadying breath, Armando stepped into the *zaguán* of his parents' house. The smells of his childhood hit him: lemon and herbs and faint medicinal scents from his mother's surgery. The sitting room glowed with light from a pair of cresset lamps set in the plaster wall. Her head bent and her hand tucked under her chin, his mother sat on a leather slung couch. She had not heard him come in. In the weeks of traveling with Paloma, of living hand to mouth and moving by stealth, she had taught him to move soundlessly.

He stood behind his mother in a room that belonged to his earliest memories. Here he had toddled his first steps, spoken his first words. Here he had stood before Rafael to face chastisement for boyish transgressions, or more often to be drawn into an embrace by loving arms. Home. He was home.

"Better, Clara?" Catalina asked.

A child sat up on the couch. Armando gaped. Clara!

His sister, the mewling babe he had left behind, was a little girl.

He nearly ducked back out of the room. This was not his home. He was a stranger here. Then he thought of the hungry, weary young woman waiting outside, and he cleared his throat.

Catalina turned. He heard the hiss of her indrawn breath; then she said, "San—"

"No!" Armando slaughtered the mistaken word forming on his mother's lips. Seeing the pain on her face—a face that bore the seams of hard years—he said, "It's me. Armando."

His mother leaped to her feet, rushed forward, and took him in her arms. "Oh, thank God," she said in a voice thick with tears. "Oh, thank God." Her strong, gentle hands relearned his person, smoothing over the breadth of his shoulders, the width of his chest, the length of his hair, the shape of his beard. Finally she stepped back, brushing at the tears on her cheeks. "You're a grown man. I was afraid I'd never see you again."

At a loss for words, he shrugged. The light picked out threads of wiry silver in his mother's golden hair.

Over her shoulder, she said, "Clara, fetch your papa."

The little stranger gaped a moment, then scampered off.

"Er, I have to . . ." Armando gestured at the door. "There's someone . . ."

"Paloma?"

He blinked. "You know?"

She nodded. "Baltasar de León has half the *Santa Hermandad* hunting you. They've already been here once. They'll come again. Bring her inside. Quickly."

He ducked out the door. A shadow detached itself from the gloom of a twisted old olive tree. "It's all right," Armando called softly. "Come in."

In the few seconds it had taken him to fetch Paloma,

Catalina had dried her face and removed her worn apron. And Rafael had walked into the room.

Armando had an urge to put his arm around Paloma. But she stood rigid and alert; he knew she would not welcome his touch. And so he stood, staring across a strange yet familiar room at a tall, thin man with kind green eyes. Hurting eyes.

I hurt, too, thought Armando. He nodded curtly. "My mother says you know what's happened." He stood with his chin up, his feet planted wide. See what I've made of myself, he wanted to shout. I've become a man without your help.

"We know the official version," said Rafael. "Probably thick and stinking with the lies of Baltasar de León. Even as a lad, that one was nothing but trouble. It's bad."

"How bad?"

"A death sentence. But I had it commuted to banishment."

Armando refused to acknowledge Rafael's faith in him.

"You are welcome," said Catalina, holding out her hands to Paloma. The young woman merely stared at the floor. "Come into the kitchen," Catalina suggested, dropping her hands and rubbing them on the front of her skirts. "We can talk while you eat."

A few minutes later, they sat at a table laden with bowls of fruit and cheese, bread and wine and smoked meat. Paloma ate and drank with the delicate manners that had been forced on her during her captivity. Armando had no appetite except for the wine. Before long, Paloma's shoulders drooped and she swayed against the table.

"You're tired," Catalina said. "Please, let me take you to a guest room."

Paloma looked hesitantly at Armando. He forced a smile. "It's all right. My mother will make you comfortable."

"I have one question," said Paloma, rising from the table.

"You may ask us anything," Catalina assured her.

"Is there any news of Doña Antonia?"

Catalina's eyes misted. "No, I'm sorry." As they left the room, she put her arm around Paloma's shoulders, and the young woman did not pull away.

Armando refilled his wine cup. When he glanced up, he saw that Rafael's eyes shone with cautious joy. He and Catalina were loving, all-forgiving in their welcome, as if Armando were the prodigal son. He would have preferred censure; at least that would have stopped his uncomfortable sense of guilt.

Instead, they accepted his story of taking ship to England, of living as a gypsy and attracting first the admiration, then the fury, of the man who was now King of England.

"You would have lived out your life in England, then," Rafael said, "but for your vow to Paloma."

Armando shook his head. He felt hot under Rafael's hungry stare. "I had already decided to come back and claim my birthright." He unsheathed the blade of his resentment and drove it deep. "From you, and from the man who sired me."

Rafael clutched at his wine goblet. "I wish you had stayed to listen to us."

"Santiago took my mother's honor. You saved it by marrying her. I suppose you expect thanks for that."

"We're not asking for thanks."

"Fine, because you won't get it."

"We—all three of us—had always meant to tell you one day, but as time passed, it became easier and easier to put it off. And you must believe this, Armando. There was never, ever a time when I did not consider you my son in every way."

Armando refused to acknowledge the sentiment behind

Rafael's words. "I suppose it's presumptuous of me to assume the birthright is still mine to claim."

"Not at all, my s— Not at all. You're heir to my properties and to Santiago's as well, both in Andalucía and the Indies. However, the fact that you've caused an international dispute and have been declared an outlaw complicates things."

Armando searched Rafael's face for a hint of anger, but saw only a willingness to help. He wanted to leap across the table, grab Rafael and scream at him: Chastise me! Punish me! Give me a reason for this rage that boils inside me!

"You mean I'm to have nothing?" he demanded.

"I didn't say that. Both Santiago and I have influence with Diego Colón. He's governor of the Indies now. We won't be able to manage complete clemency, but we've made a plan."

"Without consulting me?"

"I still consider myself your father."

"I'm not interested in your plans for my life."

"Armando, I don't think you have a choice. The de León family is influential as well. Juan Ponce de León has made himself master of an island called San Juan in the Indies. Baltasar nearly died in the shipwreck you caused. They'll not see you go free. I think it best if you and Paloma sail with the next fleet to the Indies. You'll make your home there."

Excitement leaped in Armando's chest, but before he could hold the high feeling, he thought of Gabriella. "No," he said. "I can't stay in the Indies."

"Why not?"

"I have other plans." He thrust up his chin. "I mean to marry a noble lady." He tried not to smile at Rafael's amazement. "She's one of Queen Catherine's maids of honor."

"Don't you think you're still too young to—"

"No!" Armando cut in. "I've made my own way. I started with nothing except a legacy of lies from you and my mother and Santiago. I think I can take on the responsibility of a wife."

"You'd be in danger and so would the girl."

"I've been in danger many times," Armando retorted. "Where were you then?"

For the first time, anger sparked in Rafael's eyes. "You claim you're ready to be a husband. What about a father? Armando, there's still too much rage in you. Children should be nurtured on love and security and trust—"

"As I was nurtured on trust?" he cut in.

Rafael waved his hand, and his anger dissolved into sadness. "You've made it clear you welcome only my money and title, not my advice. Who is the woman?"

"She is Doña Gabriella Flores."

"Flores." Rafael rubbed his chin. "I don't know the family."

"Her father died in the Moorish wars before she was born." The discussion depressed Armando. A man telling his father about the woman he wants to marry should be joyous. The occasion should not be strained and underlaid by accusations.

"Armando, I don't want to stand in the way of your happiness. But if you stay here, you'll be arrested. Go to Española. Establish yourself there. Then you can send for Gabriella." The name seemed to prod a memory awake in Rafael, for he paused and mouthed the word again.

"What is it?" asked Armando.

"Nothing. I once knew someone who had a daughter named Gabriella. But she didn't belong to the Flores family."

Armando barely heard. He was thinking of Rafael's plan to banish him to Española. He had practically grown up in the House of Trade. He had seen firsthand that the islands to the west were not the gold-littered paradise Colón claimed to have found. Armando himself had copied reports of native uprisings, infighting among the colonists, arguments among the clergy.

"So," he said, "you'd have me squatting in some jungle river, straining the mud for gold, dying of tropic fever."

"Don't be foolish," Rafael snapped. "There isn't enough gold in the Indies to sustain all the men who go there seeking it. It's far more profitable to raise sugarcane."

"Me, a farmer?"

"Have you a better plan? It's an honorable profession, provided you pursue it with honor."

Armando finished his second glass of wine. He sat for a long time, thinking. Ever since he had met Gabriella, he had dreamed of living in grand style in the lush hills above Jerez. But now the dream had changed. He saw wild jungles, fields hacked out of the hillsides on a far-off island rimmed by a turquoise sea. What would Gabriella think of such a life?

He could not answer. Destiny had thrown them together, but circumstances had allowed them little time to talk and plan and dream. He suddenly realized how little he knew her, and how great his faith was in their love.

"It seems I have no choice," he said. "I shall have to write to Gabriella and pray she'll agree to join me in exile."

Catalina stepped into the room. A wisp of silver-gilt hair drifted across her brow, and her face was soft with a maternal look that chipped away at Armando's defenses. Yet on the heels of sentiment came the ugly truth that, long ago, she had given herself in sin to Santiago.

"Paloma's sleeping," she reported. "Armando, does she speak at all about what's happened to her since she was captured?"

"No, but surely you can guess."

Catalina shivered. "I can do more than guess, my son. I can feel what she's feeling."

The statement stopped Armando cold. With a shaking hand, he set down his wineglass and put up a hand as though to ward off the thoughts that came at him like an advancing army. But he failed in his effort. With blade-sharp clarity, he recalled a tale Catalina had told him years before. She, too, had once been taken captive back when the Moors still ruled Granada. She had said little of her suffering at the hands of the emir Boabdil, but now that Armando was grown, he understood.

He rose from the table, ignoring the bench that crashed backward at his sudden, swift movement. He pulled his mother into his arms, amazed to find that he had grown tall enough to tuck her head under his chin. "Mama," he whispered, the dam of his reserve breaking, "you do know, don't you? Christ Jesus, Mama, I'm sorry. I'm so sorry." He spoke from the heart, apologizing for what had befallen her, and for abandoning her.

She drew back, taking his face between her hands. "You're old enough to understand now. I was like Paloma, a shell that was aching inside. It was Santiago who broke through to me, who taught me to feel again, to love again. And that, my son, is why I shall never apologize for what we did. Not even to you. Do you expect me to regret having a son like you?"

Agony washed over Armando. "I'd never ask you to, Mama. But can you forgive me?"

"Only if your apology is for your father, too."

Armando turned and looked at Rafael, who stood waiting, his ink-stained hands pressed to his sides. Armando went to him. The words stuck in his throat, but he forced them out. "Yours was an act of generosity and love," he admitted. "I was too angry to acknowledge that."

Rafael gave a gentle, weary smile. "I tend to forget. I was once an angry youth, too. Come here, son." They embraced, and Armando felt peace and warmth settle over him. His past was a morass of mistakes, his future was uncertain, but the present moment glowed with the feeling that all was right.

Rafael leaned back against the table and crossed his feet at the ankles. "I've told him the plan, Cat."

She looked expectantly at Armando. "And?"

"I'm going."

"The captain general will see you in his quarters."

Armando and Paloma followed the young page to the cabin in the afterdeck of the flagship *Ciervo Volante*. Armando stood to one side of the door to let Paloma in first.

"Close the door," said the captain general of the fleet.

The man who had sired Armando was as handsome and insouciant as ever. Santiago sat with his feet propped on a writing desk, his arms folded behind his head and a cigar between his teeth.

When he saw Paloma, he came to his feet. "God, look at you! Both of you!" He spread his arms wide.

There had been a time when the sight of Santiago with arms outspread would have sent Armando running to him. Now he merely took off his hat and nodded curtly. Armando had forgiven Rafael and Catalina, but Santiago still had much to answer for.

Santiago dropped his hands to his sides. "Well then," he said. "We've plans to make. Sit down." They sat on a bench beneath the diamond-shaped stern windows, and he addressed Paloma first. "I owe you an apology. I gave my word that I'd take you back to the Indies. I did not mean for it to take so long."

"I understand," Paloma said softly. "There was little you could have done."

"I searched for you; but if anyone knew what had become of you, they kept it a secret. What happened, Paloma?"

"I was . . . given to the Duke of Albuquerque. He traveled to Naples for an extended stay."

"Albuquerque." Santiago spat the name. "No doubt he considered it a grand gesture to ship you off as a wedding gift to Henry of England." Finally he turned to Armando. "It was a good thing you did, risking yourself for her."

Armando fought off a flush of pride. "I, too, made a vow."

Santiago puffed on his cigar, filling the stateroom with a cloud of pungent smoke. "Here's the plan—"

A knock at the door interrupted him.

"Come," he called.

His page poked his head inside the door. "The new comptroller of the fleet has arrived, sir."

"Fine. Take him to his private quarters. I'll see him later." The page ducked out, and Santiago explained, "The comptroller broke his leg in a bad fall off his horse last night. I had to send to the House of Trade for a new man. Now. For our purposes, Paloma belongs to me."

Her back snapped like a bow, and her eyes narrowed in suspicion. Santiago clasped his hands in a placating gesture. "It's the only way I could explain your presence, Paloma. That, and the fact that you're to share my quarters."

Armando surged to his feet, smacking his head on a rafter. "I won't allow it."

"*Cálmate, hombre.*" Santiago appeared to be fighting a grin. "She's safest that way. She gets her privacy, and our shipmates believe our little fiction."

"You'll compromise her. I won't allow it."

"Fine," Santiago snapped, his mood changing like the wind. "Shall I send her out on the decks to sleep among the sailors?"

Armando exhaled slowly. Santiago was right. But the thought of Paloma sharing quarters with him rankled.

Santiago indicated a length of canvas hung from the

rafter. "She'll have her own hammock behind this hanging. Is this agreeable to you, Paloma?"

She nodded without hesitation.

"Better she share my quarters," said Armando. "My strength has protected her all the way from England."

"You'll have no quarters on this voyage." Santiago's voice was flat and uncompromising.

"What?"

"You'll sleep anywhere you can find a clear patch of deck."

"Like a common seaman?"

Santiago sent him a cheerful smile. "Like the lowliest gromet. You see, *hombre*, that is to be your position on this expedition. I'm captain general of a fleet of three ships. We're shipping a hundred colonists, livestock I haven't bothered to count yet, and enough cargo to fill the warehouses of Santo Domingo. It's taken me two years to snare this post. I can't be worrying about people accusing me of nepotism."

Armando went very still. He heard the distant creaking of the ship tugging at her cables. He heard the mewing of a gull, men's excited voices, the rustle of Paloma's skirts as she shifted on her seat. But none of the sounds made any sense. Nothing in the world made sense.

"For Christ's sake, why?" he demanded.

"Because it'll teach you things."

"Yes!" he burst out. "It'll teach me the feel of the ship's master kicking me awake after four hours of sleep. The taste of poor rations, the—"

"By God, you're a spoiled bastard," Santiago said matter-of-factly.

"Yes, I'm a bastard. Because of you."

"Rafael and Catalina begged me to give you a higher rank on this voyage, but I stand by my decision."

Armando stalked toward the door.

Santiago's arm lashed out like a whip. He caught Ar-

mando by the collar. Armando tried to twist away; he was
appalled to discover that even now he was no match for
Santiago's iron strength. His gypsy father seemed to read
his thoughts. "You call yourself strong?" he drawled.
"You don't even know what it is. It's crawling out on a
yardarm in a storm. It's enduring pain beyond bearing.
That's what strength is. You'll need it where you're going.
Make yourself a sheep and you'll find plenty of wolves."

"I believe I've found one," Armando said through
clenched teeth. "I'm leaving."

Santiago let go of him, put his face very close, and
whispered, "What of your vow, *hombre*?"

Armando drew a deep breath that hurt his lungs. "To
help Paloma, I'll sail with you. I will take whatever abuse
you heap upon me." The concession tasted bitter in his
mouth. "But be warned, *Capitán*. I will never, ever forgive you."

Santiago tossed his head. "I'll take the wind as God
has sent it."

Armando stormed out, ducking beneath the lintel and
nearly colliding with a well-dressed man on the break ladder.

"Well, well," said Baltasar de León. "Is that any way
to welcome the new comptroller of the fleet?"

"Would you prefer my fist?" Armando shot back,
planting his feet on the gently shifting deck.

"You're listed on the manifest as a gromet," Baltasar
said. "Your dear papa saved you from the *Hermandad*,
but I could order you whipped for insubordination."

"You could." Armando felt sick. "Remember, all voyages come to an end. When we step off this ship, we're
equals again."

Baltasar swept his cloak to one side to keep the fabric
from touching Armando. "Out of my way, dog. I've business with the captain general."

Armando thought of Paloma behind the sailcloth hanging in Santiago's cabin. It was too late, he told himself. Too late for Baltasar to report the escape. It had to be.

Six days later he knelt on the forecastle deck, his sweaty forehead pressed to the rail, his clammy hands gripping a pair of belaying pins. Dying. He was dying. He wished death would claim him quickly, sparing him the awful sickness that had seized him the first moment the ship had broken out into open water.

"Mother of God," he muttered, heaving nothing but salty spittle from his empty stomach. "Mother of God, help me."

A wave broke against the hull. An icy plume of spray slapped him in the face. Armando was too weak to recoil from the stinging droplets, almost too weak to blink them away.

"Master Niño, what ails this man?" Santiago's voice knifed into Armando's misery, opening it like a gutted fish.

"On your feet, gromet," the ship's master barked.

Some inner reserve of pride gave him the will to stand, to salute, and to keep his gorge from rising. "Aye, sir."

"The captain general wishes to know what ails you."

The high wind chilled his face. He could feel his wet hair plastered to his forehead and neck. "Nothing ails me," he shouted into the wind. "I'm perfectly fine . . . sir!"

Niño and Santiago exchanged a dubious glance. "Watch your mouth, sailor," Niño said. "It'll get you in trouble."

"Fine," said Santiago. Pitiless, he planted his hands on his hips. "You've an hour left on your watch. And those grates and coamings aren't clean yet."

Armando aimed a look of hatred at Santiago, but the older man was already striding down the deck, his red shirt snapping in the wind. "Yes, sir," said Armando, curling his fingers around a long rope attached to his wooden bucket.

He drew water from the surging sea and knelt beside the broad grate. Even more than the drudgery of the work, the humiliation of it nagged at him. All the officers and crew knew he was Santiago's godson. They looked enough alike for some to bait Armando about their true kinship. The ship's master assigned him only safe and tedious tasks, never challenging him.

He observed the higher-ranked sailors working sail from lofty perches. Only the foremast man sat idle, warming himself by a sand-lined firebox. While securing the buntlines the day before, he had broken his jaw when the ship pitched.

Armando eyed the jutting bowsprit, aimed dead west at the horizon and bucking like an unbroken horse. Of all the tasks under sail, working the foremast was the most treacherous. Even as he watched, one of the bowlines sprang loose with a discordant twang. The spritsail luffed. The sailors who observed the catastrophe wove a verbal fabric of curses so vivid Armando could almost see it flying on the wind. The chaplain of the expedition sank to his knees and prayed with some of the colonists.

The ship's master yelled an order to the foremast man. He rose wearily to his feet, reeled, and pitched to his knees.

"Get up," yelled Niño. "You're to make that bowline fast."

Armando stopped working and eyed the other sailors. Surely one of them would step forward and help the injured man. But the men of the *Ciervo Volante* offered only averted glances and shuffling feet. Cowards, thought Armando. He abandoned his bucket and brush and approached master Niño. "I'll do it," Armando said.

The seasoned sailors gaped at him. "That's a bad jest, pup," muttered the second mate.

But nothing—not one solitary blessed thing—on this sea voyage was a joke. Armando had come to that conclusion in the middle of the night, when his meager supper had been stirred to a deadly squall in his stomach.

"Do what, gromet?" asked Niño.

"Secure the bowlines," he said.

"You'll do no such thing," Santiago cut in, taking the ladder to the foredeck two rungs at a time.

"I beg to differ with you, sir," he muttered, brushing past the two men. The horizon tilted in his swimming vision.

"What's that, gromet?" Santiago spun him back around. "I didn't hear you. Speak up when you address your superiors."

For a moment Armando forgot the churning, dizzying sickness. He thrust his face inches from Santiago's. "I'm going out on the bowsprit, sir!" Pivoting, he stalked forward.

"By God," said Santiago, "I'll—"

Armando missed the rest. The bowsprit thrust out like a giant monolith, pointing at the burning horizon to the west. It rose and fell with the terrible rhythm of the waves, lifting to the blue marble sky, then dipping toward the surface where white foam veined the iron-colored water. In defiance of the elements, a boatswain bird perched on the very tip.

The gray and white bird seemed to mock him. It roosted as if the treacherous, sucking waters far below were nothing.

Armando wiped his sleeve across his clammy forehead. He could feel the heat of his father's stare pierce his back.

Leaning forward, he laid his palms on the hot, weathered wood. If it was his fate to plunge to his death in the seething Gulf of the Mares, he would meet it with courage, embrace it with honor. He pressed his knees to the huge beam. Thick as a tree trunk, it tapered to a point.

The end still held the little boatswain bird, unconcerned about the doomed man crawling out above the swells.

Armando thought fleetingly of Gabriella. His illness had claimed every moment, leaving no room for dreams. Now he remembered her, an angel's face cowled in silky dark curls, a siren's voice calling across the miles to him. He wished he had taken her body when she had offered it. But now, trembling, half-dead and facing peril, he could not imagine ever desiring a woman again.

She would be fine, he thought with the certainty of a man at the end of his life. Will would take care of her.

And Paloma? Inching along the bowsprit, he thought of her sequestered in Santiago's quarters. Armando had brought her this far. He could do no more. Of Rafael and Catalina, he had only fond memories and a newfound sense of peace. Of Santiago he would not think at all.

Splinters jabbed into his hands and bare feet. Thick rope in coils impeded his progress, dragging at his thighs.

He lifted his head. The bowlines flew free, still out of reach. The boatswain bird watched from its perch.

Armando pulled himself along the ever-narrowing length of wood. He glanced at the water, roiling foam cut by the sharp wedge of the bow. He imagined his body falling, cleaved in two by the huge ship.

A swell rolled toward the hull. Somehow, in the days of misery, he had learned to reckon the size and impact of incoming swells. This one was big.

He twisted his legs together at the ankles, hugged the bowsprit with his arms, and laid his cheek on the weather-beaten wood. He closed his eyes, gritted his teeth, and waited.

The ship climbed the wave. Higher and higher still, until Armando was almost upright. The timbers shuddered for an awful moment, then plunged into the trough.

He heard the sound of his own voice screaming. The wind snatched the red seaman's cap from his head. The sudden downward motion gave him a sick feeling of weightlessness. Then the impact crushed him against the great beam. The wood bruised his jawbone. He opened his eyes to see the white beard of the wave crash beneath the bow. Cold water pelted him like driving rain. He blinked away the stinging salt water.

The bird still rode the tip of the bowsprit. The lines still snapped in the stiff wind. Armando was vaguely aware of shouting behind him, hoarse voices calling above the wind.

Inch by treacherous inch, he conquered the bowsprit. He had set himself to the task. It was his duty to see it through.

At last the ropes flew within reach. His feet found the foot ropes, which pulled taut with his weight. Keeping one hand on the mast, he pushed himself to a sitting position, straddling the beam. He felt slight, a mere speck of humanity vulnerable to the caprices of the wind and the boiling sea.

He had the sensation of breaking a wild horse. Likening this treacherous situation to that familiar one gave him a small measure of confidence.

He reached for one of the flailing ropes. The twisted hemp burned his palm. With a bellowed curse, he held fast, then threaded the end of the rope through a deadeye. His wet, cold fingers fumbled as he made a knot. A few days ago he had been ignorant of the uses of the seaman's knot. Now he was glad for the dogged practice that Vargas, the sailmaker, had forced on him. He secured the line with a decisive tug and reset the spritsail. The luffing of the canvas quieted. Half sick with relief, he dropped his chest to the timber beneath him.

The boatswain bird cocked its head, then spread its wings and wheeled away. Behind him, Armando heard a cheer go up.

Aye, cheer for me, he thought darkly as he shinnied back toward the deck. Cheer for the captain's bastard son.

His bare feet touched the wet planks. He stumbled a little, his thigh muscles quivering, and wiped the plastered-down hair from his brow. Most of the forward watch had gathered. All were cheering, waving their caps. Except Santiago. He stood to one side, his fist closed around a shroud. Staring. Just staring.

Shivering with cold, Armando walked to Master Niño. "Bowlines are made fast, sir."

"Well done, gromet."

Armando started to walk away to his post. Master Niño called out, "Viscaino!"

"Sir?"

"A bit of watered lime juice, Viscaino."

"Lime juice, sir?"

"Drink it before you get to your feet, first thing when you wake up. It's the best remedy for seasickness."

"I'll give it a try, sir." But as he made his way back to his post, he realized that his hands were no longer clammy. His throat no longer felt thick and full.

He simply felt empty.

Dear Gabriella,
We have been six weeks at sea, and the navigators of the fleet reckon that we will reach the island of Española in a fortnight.

Armando paused to dip his pen. The written word had never come easily to him, as it did to Rafael. Emotions pulsed hard in Armando's heart, but he could find no graceful way to commit his feelings to paper. He closed his eyes, pressed the back of his head to the rail of the foredeck, and summoned her image. A serene Madonna face, dark eyes, round and open as pansies. Small, soft hands and moist ruby lips. Lips that had smiled, he hoped, when she had received his letter from Seville. He opened his eyes and started writing again.

My heart, you cannot know the strangeness of life under sail. We are a little universe unto ourselves, living beneath the masts and canvas that define our tiny, moving space. Prayers and songs and the call of the sandglass boy count the hours for us. I fear you would not recognize me. I did not either, this morning, when I caught a glimpse of myself reflected in the glass of the binnacle lamp. My hair and beard have grown long and wild. I have become very quick and agile, for men who move slowly or hesitate cause accidents.

Christ Jesus, you would not believe the wonders I see each day. Dolphins leaping beside our bow, little winged fish that skim the surface and then disappear, clouds piled like mountains of wool on the horizon. At night the sky is a great bowl filled with more stars than the imagination could conjure. The motion of the ship makes the sky seem to spin, so that it is the same, yet not the same. The wind may shift and the sea may change, but the stars are our constant.

As you are my constant, my guiding star. No matter how far I travel, you are with me in my thoughts.

The woman Paloma keeps much to herself in the privacy of the captain general's quarters. I do not know what she thinks of on this voyage. It troubles me that Baltasar de León is aboard as comptroller of this fleet. He has a big mouth and no doubt will try to stir up trouble when we make port at Santo Domingo. He is quite proud of his lofty position.

I know we dreamed of a life in Jerez, but if you received my letter from Seville, you will know that circumstances have changed. I am an outlaw in Spain and in England. I will not fault your judgment if you choose not to join me. But if you love me still, Gabriella, please come to me. My parents have given me their word that they will help you.

The words are so simple, yet I know what I ask. I ask you to abandon the country you love and your position with the queen. I ask you to cross the Ocean Sea and be my wife.

I smile as I write this, because my heart tells me you will do so. And so think of me, my Gabriella. I will be in Española, building a life for us and for our children.

A thousand kisses from your

Armando

He stuck his plume into his belt and corked his inkhorn. Gabriella would not receive the letter for months. It would take even longer for her to make her decision, address herself to his parents in Seville, and come to him.

His restless heart pounded, a captive beast rattling its chains. He held up the letter, watching the page luff in the wind while the ink dried.

The boatswain's whistle shrilled across the decks, heralding the changing of the watch. Armando sang the Salve Regina with the rest of the crew and prepared to undertake his duties.

Santiago, he had been surprised to learn, was scrupulous about clean and well-ordered decks. Though he often joked that he had been nurtured by grubby, itinerant gypsies, he insisted on decks free of dirt and clear of coiled rope and barrels.

Armando lowered a bucket into the sea and drew up water. The school of dolphins that had accompanied them for the past several days was still in attendance. Silver-gray bodies flashed just beneath the surface and, from time to time, one graceful animal would arc upward, emitting a cheerful chittering sound before it dove again. As he watched, Armando sensed a dark presence like a chill wind at his back. Being at sea sensitized a man, awakened the nerve endings of alertness.

Armando swung around, seawater sloshing from his bucket. Baltasar de León stood there, a wolfish grin on his face and a loaded crossbow in his hands. A frisson of fear tiptoed up Armando's spine. "What are you doing?"

Baltasar swung the weapon. For a moment the razor-sharp tip pointed directly at Armando's chest. At this range, the bolt could skewer him through as if he were a slab of butter.

Baltasar laughed. "A good day for a hunt, no?"

At first Armando was confused; then he saw Baltasar aiming at the school of dolphins. He took a step forward. "Don't."

Baltasar jerked back on the trigger. The bolt leaped forward with a buzz like an angry bee, and embedded itself with a wet thump into the sleek, blue-gray side of a dolphin.

A shrill sound, half whistle, half scream, came from the animal. Blood clouded the water and spread as the creature floundered. Armando expected the others to scatter in fear. Instead, they clustered around the wounded one, their chittering noises sounding like the concerned clucks of nursemaids.

"An excellent shot, no?" Baltasar leaned over the rail to watch the animal die. He fitted another bolt into the bow and wound the crank tight. "It lacks the high sport of deer hunting on the *vegas*, but a man must always stay in practice." He took aim again.

"Don't shoot." Armando planted himself in front of Baltasar. The dolphins were friendly and harmless, possessing more humanity than the man who hunted them.

"Step aside," Baltasar ordered. "You'll spoil my aim."

"Put the weapon down," Armando said through clenched teeth. Hearing the rage in his voice, a few sailors gathered to watch.

Baltasar shouldered Armando aside. He leaned out over the rail. His thumb tightened on the trigger.

Without pausing to think, Armando lifted the bucket and dumped the cold seawater on Baltasar's head. The crossbow bolt flew awry, speeding aft. It thudded, quivering, into the mizzenmast, only inches from the head of the sandglass boy.

With a shriek of terror, the lad dropped his *ampolleta*. Shattered glass and sand spread across the deck.

"Damn you!" Baltasar spluttered, rubbing his eyes with his fists. "By God, Viscaino, you'll pay for this."

Armando lowered the bucket. Slowly he became aware of the crew members gathered around them. The sailors' expressions conveyed the enormity of what he had done.

"Master Niño!" Baltasar's outraged cry rolled across the decks. "This man is guilty of assaulting a superior and endangering a crewman. I demand that he be punished."

As Baltasar complained loudly of the assault upon his person and his dignity, Armando could think of no words to say in his own defense. The killing of dolphins was senseless, but it was no crime. Dousing the comptroller with a bucket of cold water was, on the other hand, an offense punishable by—

"—seventy-five lashes," Baltasar declared. "We cannot allow lawlessness and disrespect among this crew."

"That's severe," the ship's master said. "With all due respect, sir, it was only a bucket of water."

"Only?" One dark eyebrow slashed upward. His fine mane of hair was drenched, and a drop of water hung from his crooked nose. "Mutiny has been started with less."

Santiago arrived, his long hair flying free about his grave face. Several witnesses, including the offended sandglass boy, related the offense. At first the captain general said nothing. He picked up the spent crossbow and flung it into the sea.

"*Dios!*" Baltasar swore. "That was a perfectly good—"

"Any hunting from this ship will require my permission," Santiago said coldly. "We do not hunt for sport, but for food. Is that understood?"

"I do as I—"

"Is that understood?"

Baltasar gave the slightest of nods.

"Don Baltasar," Santiago went on, "if you are in need of something to relieve your boredom, I'm certain Master Niño will find a diversion for you."

"So you intend to let your precious godson go unpunished?"

"On this expedition, he is a crew member first, and my godson second."

Armando stood staring at the stony face of the man who had sired him. He saw nothing in his father's sleek black eyes, no emotion at all.

"For the crimes of insubordination and endangering a crewman," Santiago said, "fifty lashes."

Like all great cruelties in Spain, the sentence would be carried out with great ceremony. As Armando awaited the punishment, it did not seem real to him. He stood in the midst of a dream world of fluffy clouds and the sea hissing past the hull, the drum beating like a giant heart and Fray Tomás exhorting heaven to forgive the sinners of his flock. There was a stately dignity to the proceedings, with the notary reading out the sentence, the master counting the knots to be certain there were no more than nine tarred ends of the lash.

Santiago had dressed for the occasion, Armando noted wryly. He had pulled a black velvet doublet over his familiar red shirt.

Even when two sailors came forward and pulled Armando to a timber beam, lashing his hands high above his head, he had no sensation that this was actually happening to him.

Even when the sergeant at arms grasped the back collar

of his shirt and ripped it asunder, and the wind rushed fast and cool across his back, he did not accept his fate.

In the waiting silence, while the notary who would record the proceedings and count the strokes settled himself with his wooden lap desk, Armando's awareness heightened. He heard the snap of canvas overhead, the song of the wind in the rigging. He heard his heart beating and the pulse of the drum. He tasted a light dusting of spindrift on his lips, felt the warmth of weathered wood pressing into his bound wrists. There was a certain beauty in the tense silence of the men, in the full sails tugging at the shrouds.

Then the boatswain's whistle shrilled. The whip cut through the air, whining, black knots spreading over the bare flesh of Armando's back. Out of the corner of his eye he could see the notary with his white ledger spread on his lap. Spots of red spattered the fresh white paper.

Blood. His own blood. Armando finally became aware of what was happening to him. The pain cut so deep that at first he did not recognize it as pain, but a powerful separate enemy with a life of its own. Someone cried out, a horrible gagging sound, and he realized it was himself.

The whip clawed at his back, raking through flesh and muscle and bone to his very soul. The force was like the blow of a cudgel with gnarled teeth. The pain was heat and ice, full of inexhaustible energy, pounding at the door to his being to get at the naked, cringing creature inside. Stinging agony radiated to the tips of his fingernails.

His body became a bleeding, sobbing stranger. He felt himself urinate, felt himself bite his lip, tasted the hot, wet rust of his own blood. He felt himself dying by inches, the life ripped out of him with each killing stroke of the lash.

His thoughts stopped; his mind ceased to function. Only one part of him lived: a small entity, hard and cold as a stone, which fed on the dark elixir of hatred.

Hatred for the man who had caused him to be here, hatred for the man who had given him life and who had ordered his death.

His consciousness wavered from agonized awareness to dull, throbbing listlessness, the half-sleep of a man close to death.

After an eternity of torture, the tentacled beast fell into stillness, an animal bloated with the blood of its prey. There was a moment of awed silence in which the observers stood staring at the bloodied carcass that had been Armando.

His lips moved. He was blinded by blood, blood from the sticky wound he had sustained by bashing his head against the beam. He saw only darkness pierced by white pain. He heard his pulse in his ears and the ceaseless sound of the sea.

And then footsteps hurrying, the sound of a man dropping to his knees. "Doctor Sanchez, come quickly." Santiago's voice. Armando could not fathom why he sounded so concerned.

Hands grasping his wrists, a tug on the ropes. With a groan, Armando melted to the deck. Santiago spoke again, coldly this time. "I hope you're satisfied, de León."

"For now," Baltasar answered.

Rage exploded in Armando's head. He tried to speak past his swollen lips, but only managed a terrible, strangled sound. Someone called for water. A bucket of stinging ice sloshed over him. Rivers of salt water coursed deep into the raw wounds.

Armando's eyes rolled up in his head, and he fainted.

CHAPTER 13

He awakened to darkness and the familiar creaking sound of shrouds tugging at timber. As awareness crept over him, he realized that he lay prone on his stomach. A hundred fiery remembrances of the beating scored his back.

He heard a quiet ticking sound; then a dull yellow glow lit the area. He recognized the piles of rope and canvas in a 'tween decks storage room. Laboriously turning his head, he spied Paloma. Her face was pale and drawn, her eyes frightened.

The sight of her struck a spark in his spirits. "Hello, *chica*," he croaked, the word trickling from his cracked lips.

She hung a small lantern from a nail and settled herself on her heels beside him. "Are you thirsty?"

He tried to nod. The smallest movement awakened thunderous echoes of agony. "Yes," he managed.

She put a goatskin flask to his lips. Brackish water mingled with the taste of his own blood. Gagging, he moved his head away. "How long have I been like this?"

"A few hours."

"I didn't think I'd last that long."

"You'll live, Armando. You know you will."

"I must." Talking grew easier. "At least long enough to avenge myself on Santiago and Baltasar."

"If your need for revenge helps you survive these wounds, I won't quarrel with you."   .

Concern softened her voice. Concern and . . . something else. In another woman, he might have called it affection. He hoped to God it wasn't pity. "What are you doing down here with me?"   .

"I asked the captain general's permission to sit with you and tend to your needs. Doctor Sanchez put some herbal unguent on your back. He says I must keep the wounds clean and uncovered. He assures me you'll heal faster that way."

The ship listed, and Armando rolled onto his side. "God . . . oh Christ Jesus, it hurts."

She reached out to touch his hair, but seemed to think better of it and dropped her hand. "I know, Armando. Close your eyes. Try to sleep."

"I can't. I have to talk about what they did to me."

"Spaniards talk so much. I have often wondered why."

"I need to remember every second of this day. I need to remember every stroke of the lash, because one day I mean to give this pain back to Baltasar and to Santiago."

"You believe they are both equally responsible for the beating."

"You think they're not?"

"Baltasar means you harm. But Santiago . . . I have come to know him. We speak of my father, and of the situation in the islands. Did you know Santiago opposes the conquistadors?"

Armando was not prepared for the searing jealousy he

felt at hearing the gentle tone of her voice, at seeing the softness that came over her face. What had Santiago said to her, all those nights, closed in the comfort of his cabin? Did he prey on her sympathy? Was he able to touch her when she welcomed the touch of no man?

"I know him, too, *chica*. I know him well enough to suspect him of making you his lover."

Her gasp sounded like a flame touching water.

"God, Paloma, I'm sorry," Armando said quickly. "I spoke out of turn." If he could have, he would have touched her cheek, traced the cool curves with his finger. But it hurt even to blink, to swallow. "My hair hurts," he muttered.

"What?"

"Never mind. I have no right to involve you in my problems with Santiago."

"Don't hate him, Armando. It is not healthy. Hating Baltasar . . . that is a strengthening thing. The people of my clan purify themselves with hatred for their enemies. But to hate your own father . . . it is like one of these wounds getting infected and poisoning your blood."

"The man ordered me flogged. Me! His son!"

She gave him another drink and spoke as he struggled to swallow. "He is commander of three ships. A gromet attacked the comptroller of the fleet and caused an accident. He had no choice but to treat you as he would have any other man. Armando, your father tormented himself over this punishment."

Damp canvas pressed into his cheek. He closed his eyes, plagued by the realization that Santiago had spoken of the matter to Paloma. "In Spain," he said angrily, "many atrocities are committed in the name of righteousness."

"I made that discovery long ago. That is the world you live in. What if Santiago had refused to punish you? What then?"

He opened his eyes. "Then I'd be up on deck singing the Salve Regina with the rest of them."

She shook her head, her hair glossy and luminous in the candlelight. "No. You would have been taunted by the other members of the crew."

"Believe me, I could suffer taunts better than a flogging."

"Your wounds will heal. But the resentment of the crew members would stay with you always. Santiago maintains his leadership in the Spanish way, the only way these men understand. By upholding discipline."

"When did you become so wise in the way of a Spanish fleet? Did Santiago take you on his knee and whisper the secrets—"

"No! You are hurt, Armando. Don't strike out at me."

He blew out a long breath. His lungs and throat ached. From screaming, he remembered. "Don't tell me to forgive him."

"I would never tell you that. But I was there, Armando. I saw his face. He looked almost as ravaged as you. Every lash on your back was a lash to his heart."

Her testimony tore at his convictions. He did not want to consider the fact that she could be right. "I'm tired, Paloma."

"Sleep, then. I'll stay with you."

He closed his eyes and listened to the quiet sea outside the hull, and the faint, comforting sound of her breathing. Just as he was sliding toward the oblivion of wounded slumber, he felt a lock of hair drop onto his abraded forehead. And then, like the brush of silk, her hand smoothed back the hair.

Armando was too exhausted to ponder the warmth that flowed through him at her touch.

Every moment she was not sleeping, Paloma stayed by his side. On the first day they had met, she recalled, he had promised to help her. She could not have known then what cost the vow would inflict, what price her freedom would demand. For her sake, he had offended two powerful *caciques*, left behind the woman he loved, and confronted the family he had sworn to forsake. He had gambled his future for her sake.

In return, she wanted to heal his body as well as his soul.

Gazing at his face, shadowed by a thickening beard and framed by a dark spill of curls, she tried to will him to mend. For three days he had lain virtually motionless, senseless, eating and drinking little.

He came awake with a deep shudder. She knelt beside him, ready with the water flask. "Thirsty?"

"Mmm." He sipped from the flask and opened one eye. "How does my back look?"

Hideous raised weals and open wounds furrowed his flesh. In accordance with Dr. Sanchez's instructions, she had cleansed the wounds each day and coated them with unguent salve.

"Still bad," she told him. "But the healing is starting."

"Look," he said suddenly. "I can lift my head today."

She smiled. "Truly, you are a wonder, Don Armando." She felt an ease with him that she had never expected to feel with a Spaniard. Of course, she told herself wryly, it was safe to be with a man who couldn't move.

He looked from side to side in slow, tentative movements. He winced, then braced his elbows on the cushion, lifting his torso. "Maybe I'm not dying after all."

"You were never even close to dying, Armando."

"So you say." He raised himself higher. The cloth covering his hips slipped downward with his movement. "Christ Jesus!"

Paloma jumped. "What? What is it?"

"I'm naked!"

She sat back on her heels. "You have been since the flogging."

"I've been lying here naked! Why didn't you tell me?"

"This is the first time you've been fully conscious, I think."

"Paloma, you've got to leave. Now. Hurry. You can't sit with me while I'm naked."

A rare warmth glowed in her heart. She smiled because he was so afraid of lying in his natural state and being tended by a female. She smiled because his earnest protests meant he was getting well.

"I mean it, Paloma. This is wrong. It's no joke."

"You worry about the strangest things, Armando."

Dear Gabriella,

A fortnight has passed since the flogging. A few of the deeper wounds on my back turned putrid. Dr. Sanchez treated me with leeches. This helped the swelling to subside, but I think my mother would be appalled. She eschews leeches and bleeding. Like the Moorish physicians, she believes Nature put a certain amount of blood in the body, and no one should remove it.

The unguents and poultices have helped. I go about my usual duties, but I am still unable to wear a shirt. This does not trouble me, for the weather is balmy.

Baltasar de León keeps clear of me. The captain general and I have not spoken at all.

The men are more animated these days, for we shall sight land soon. The ones who will settle in the Indies have grandiose plans. Some, like me, will take control of land grants. The Crown exempts us from taxes for twenty years. We pay only tithes to the Church. Prizes will be awarded to the men who produce the best crops. I am told that my encomienda

*was started by a man who turned from farming after
the discovery of gold high in the mountains of Española. Gold does not lure me as it does most colonists. For me, the lure is the chance to build a home
and a life for us—*

"Tierra!" The topman's call jolted Armando to his feet.
His pen fluttered away on a wisp of wind. He tucked his
letter to Gabriella in his belt.

A lombard roared the signal to the rest of the fleet.
Armando raced through a fog of gunpowder smoke toward
the prow. Gripping the rail, he squinted at the horizon.

"I see nothing," he said, disappointed.

"Get yourself up into the rigging," the sailmaker ad-
vised.

Armando climbed with practiced ease, feeling the
breeze on his injured back. He strained his eyes until at
last he picked out a hazy bump, greenish in color.

"It's the isle of San Juan," called the boatswain. "Always the first place we spot."

Armando squinted at the island that had been conquered
by Juan Ponce de León, Baltasar's kinsman and the man
who had enslaved Paloma. Master Niño called Armando
back to his duties, but his mind stayed fixed on the islands
rising out of the sea to greet him. They shone like jewels,
emerald and turquoise and deep amber, a glittering necklace draped around the cool blue chest of the sea. The
new lands were alien and exotic, lush with a vague, forbidden wonder.

Paloma, he thought. We're here. He longed to seek her
out, but the ship's master kept every hand busy furling sail
and making ready for the landing. The docking of the fleet
raised a flurry of activity at the port. A flotilla of canoes
propelled by naked, cinnamon-skinned men glided toward
the fleet.

A coldness moved through Armando. The paddles dug

like entrenching tools into the turquoise swells. The natives were shouting, screaming . . . Armando glanced aft, where Santiago stood on the high deck. The fleet was under attack. Why didn't Santiago do something?

Within minutes, Armando saw how wrong he was. The shouts were cries of greeting. Some of the natives scaled the great hull and cast themselves at Santiago's feet in welcome.

Shaking his head in wonderment, Armando turned his attention to the island. His new home. White sand fringed the beaches. The town of Santo Domingo was a cluster of thatched wooden buildings and rubble-built edifices crouched around a tall stone structure. A stout cross marked the single church. Beyond the town rose green-cloaked mountains in layered profile. A huge tree reached heavy branches toward the incoming fleet.

The docking passed in a blur. Many of the crew fell to their knees and kissed the ground, then raised their hands to heaven and prayed with the priests who came to greet them.

Uninterested in pious gratitude, Armando moved along the sandy shore where soaring palm trees waved in a steady breeze. He faced the mountains and spread his arms wide as if to embrace the whole vast, mysterious island.

His soul felt as if it were opening with a demand for adventure. Gone was the hand-to-mouth existence he had endured in England, the stifling correctness of life in Spain, the cramped confines of the ship. Here the sun glinted like new gold on the sea; here all things were possible.

He went in search of Paloma. She stood beside Santiago and glanced around uncertainly, as if she weren't ready to believe she had reached the islands at last.

Brushing past his father, Armando rushed to her. Without forethought, he grasped her about the waist and swung

her around, then set her down and planted a resounding
kiss on her mouth.

"Isn't it wonderful, *chica*? Here we are in the New
World!"

She eyes him dubiously, shaken by his exuberance.
"This world is as old as time. The *cacique* Colón claimed
he discovered it. But my people knew all along where they
were. It was Colón who was lost."

He took her by the shoulders, wishing he could see more
joy in her eyes. "Paloma, I came here to build a farm.
But also to help you find your people." He glanced at the
natives helping with the off-loading. "Do you see them?
Could they be here?"

"No." Her face went soft with yearning. "They would
never come here. I will have to search for them."

For the first time, Armando faced the thought of saying
good-bye to her. He was not prepared for the pain, the
strange emptiness in his chest. Yet he had always known
that his success in bringing her here would end with a
parting.

London
January 1510

"Gabriella, what is that you're reading?" Doña Elvira's
voice snapped into the silence of the antechamber.

With a guilty start, Gabriella crushed together the pages
of Armando's letter. "Nothing, my lady. The words to a
new song."

Doña Elvira sniffed. "More of that heathen drivel, no
doubt. You should use your talent to glorify God, not to
entertain drunkards and sentimental dames."

"Yes, ma'am." Gabriella put away Armando's letters.
How amazing that they had come all the way from the

New World, through Seville, and finally, by special messenger, to England. Discovering that Armando had been outlawed in Spain had been shocking enough; learning that he planned to be a sugar planter in a far-off place called Española stunned her beyond speech.

In the privacy of her chamber she would caress every word, clasping each thought to her heart. And then she would plan. He made it sound so simple: contact Rafael Viscaino of Seville, let him book her passage across the Ocean Sea.

She had not paused for a moment to consider. Of course she would go. She had pinned her future on Armando. *Wither thou goest, I will go.* A bard named Nettoye had set the words to music. Gabriella longed to sing them aloud.

"Truly, Gabriella, your behavior has been most distracted," Doña Elvira said. "You have distressed Her Majesty. Perhaps that is the reason her labor started three months prematurely."

Gabriella surged to her feet. "How dare you blame me? It is no one's fault that the queen has gone early to her confinement. It is God's will."

"You distressed her," Elvira shot back. "First with your deception in the matter of the pilgrimage, and then with your pulling pleas to the king."

"I did not plead with him."

"Then why did he destroy the queen's plans for a match between you and Don Baltasar?"

"Because King Henry is a just man," Gabriella retorted, remembering his tenderness that day. "Because he would not force a woman into a marriage she doesn't desire."

"Because he's yet a lad of eighteen"—Doña Elvira's voice lowered to a hiss, the sibilance of a snake sliding beneath a rock—"and susceptible to the charms of a pretty face."

Gabriella regretted for the thousandth time that Elvira had seen her holding King Henry's handkerchief. The woman had a brittle mind full of suspicion and doubt. It was possible that Elvira had confessed her thoughts to the queen, for each day Catherine grew more chilly and distant.

The queen! The thought dropped Gabriella to her knees. She squeezed her eyes shut and prayed hard for the woman in the next room, the woman attended by her physician and confessor.

They waited to witness something—but what? The tragic birth of a half-formed child? The death of the mother herself? And where in heaven's name was the king?

"She calls for you, Gabriella." Father Diego Fernández stood in the wedge of light cast by the half-open door.

Gabriella hurried into the room. It was the queen's own privy bedchamber, for her lying-in chamber was not ready. The heavy curtains, the musky smell of body fluids, holy oil, and melting candle wax transformed the room into a forbidding and sinister place. With her heart battering her breastbone, Gabriella moved toward the bed.

The drawn-back curtains revealed the pale, straining figure of the queen. Catherine's face was still save for her bloodless lips moving in ceaseless silent prayer. The small mound of her belly rose beneath the coverlets as she arched her spine.

"Your Majesty." Gabriella knelt beside the bed.

"There you are." Catherine's voice was a wisp of sound. "Gabriella, I want you to do something for me."

"Of course, madam. Anything."

"If it be God's will that I live through this, I must give thanks." A tear leaked from the queen's eye and anointed her pillow. "A punishment . . ." Her voice trailed off and Gabriella remembered the confession. "But my own life might be spared."

"Your Grace, that is the earnest wish of all England."

Catherine twisted her lips in an expression of irony. "Well said, my dear. On the floor there is an inlaid box. Open it."

Gabriella picked up the box and set it on the edge of the bed. She flipped the iron latch and lifted the lid. Soft gasps of admiration sounded from the queen's attendants. Inside the box, in a nest of bloodred satin, sat a fabulous headdress.

"This is one of the gifts from your father," said Gabriella.

"It's wrought of Indies gold," said Catherine. "The balas rubies are from the Doge of Venice. Gabriella, I want you to take this as a gift to the shrine of Saint Peter."

Behind Gabriella, Doña Elvira cleared her throat, a sound eloquent with disapproval. Defiantly Gabriella closed and latched the coffer. The jeweled headdress was the queen's to give. Catherine, risking death while birthing an English heir, should shame Elvira with her generosity.

"It is done, Your Grace," said Gabriella.

"Hurry, please—" Catherine's face contorted. Her back arched, and she emitted a high, thin scream, ancient in origin, a woman's cry of the singular agony and grief of losing a child.

Clutching the box, Gabriella curtsied, made the sign of the cross, and backed toward the door. Elvira followed her out and gave her hasty directions to the shrine. "Be certain you take the Dover road," she cautioned. "It's the quickest way and—God have mercy—there might not be much time."

Gabriella prayed when she wanted to curse the law that had sentenced woman to bring forth children in pain and blood, to damn a nation for magnifying Catherine's agony with their scrutiny, and to rail against Henry Tudor for bringing the ordeal upon a troubled woman who belonged rightly in a Spanish convent, not on the throne of England.

The halls of the palace passed in a blur of tears. Henry

had turned his father's cold, utilitarian kingdom to dazzling gold. Outside the chapel of Henry V, she paused. Strange, harsh moans issued from the darkened interior. Poking her head inside, she saw a single candle burning on the altar, a single man kneeling with his bare head bowed in prayer. Instantly she recognized the golden mane of the king.

The faint light gilded the helm and buckler of Henry V, hero of Agincourt a century before. The reflected light spread over the praying man. The chill stone walls echoed a single word, uttered over and over again: "Please, please, please . . ."

Tenderness touched her heart. At that moment, she saw him not as an ambitious king, but simply as Harry Tudor, a frightened young husband whose wife lay dying. Gabriella left the chapel, his hopeless incantation and ragged sobs echoing in her ears.

Blue dawn lay over the frosted fields of Horsleydown. Gabriella's fingers and toes, and the arms she kept wrapped tightly around the box, had long gone numb. The pain would come later, like the sting of grief once the shock had worn off.

Her gaze picked over the ice-clad fields, seeking a glimpse of the shrine where she would make the offering on Queen Catherine's behalf. She saw only clumps of bare trees and a thatched shepherd's hut crouched in the distance.

She shook her head, glad at least that the cold kept her from falling asleep. She could have taken a horse litter from the palace. She could have sat swathed in miniver while attendants bore her in comfort to the shrine.

But, although she had made her life in England, Spanish blood pulsed in her veins. Spanish discipline shaped her beliefs. Spanish training guided her in matters of faith.

A pilgrimage was not to be made in luxury, but alone

and in agony. It should hurt to give of oneself to the Lord. And since the queen could not do it, the task fell to Gabriella.

She bent into the driving wind that skirled off the river. The temptation to rest plucked at her will. She longed to huddle in the lee of a hedgerow, to hide from the wind that tore at her, from the pale dawn stars that seemed to wink with secrets.

She began to sing to revive her spirits. Sacred songs to the glory of God, love songs that branded her mind with images of Armando, and laments for the unfulfilled promise of Catherine's firstborn child. Her voice broke through the silence of the dawn; her breath made smoky trails in the biting air. The strength and clarity of her own voice reassured her, drew her along the road, step by step. So loud and so fervently did she sing that she failed to hear hoofbeats behind her.

The appearance of four armed horsemen took her by surprise, a sudden storm in the cold peacefulness. The horses blew out clouds of warmth. She stumbled back, her mouth agape, her gloved hands clutching the box.

"There you are, you thieving wench!"

"Guard your tongue, sir." Indignation brushed past her confusion. "How dare you address me as—"

"Take the box."

A soldier leaped down and wrenched the box from her. One of the men opened it. Gold and jewels glinted in the blue light.

"This is it. The piece what was stolen."

"Stolen? Nay!" She recognized the men's livery now. It was the Kendall green and silver of the royal guards.

"Oh?" The man's eyebrows lifted. "This belongs to you?"

"It belongs to Queen Catherine. I am Gabriella Flores, her maid of honor, and I'll thank you to give it back."

"God, it's a heartless bitch you are," the soldier muttered, grabbing her arm and yanking her toward his horse. "Stealing from your mistress as she lies bleeding . . ."

The tragic news held panic at bay a moment longer. *"Ave María,"* whispered Gabriella. "My poor dear lady."

"You'll not fool us with your false tears. You're a thief, and no big-eyed, pretty pleading will save you now."

"I tell you, I'm no thief," Gabriella stated, balking as he pushed her closer to his horse. "Who sent you?"

"That's no business of yours, wench."

She tried to twist from his grasp. "Queen Catherine gave me the box with instructions to make an offering to the shrine of Saint Peter. It's to save her life and her immortal soul!"

"Then what are you doing on the Dover road, my lady?"

She glared into his accusing eyes. "Going to the shrine."

"A pretty pretense. Aye, you're miles from your goal. God help you, wench, when the queen discovers your betrayal."

"But Doña Elvira told me to come this way. I must get to the shrine before it's too late."

"Oh, no. We're going back to London. You see, my lady, you're under arrest."

The damp walls of the small tower chamber were curved like a cold embrace. The few faded hangings did little to keep the moist seepage at bay. The stale rushes on the floor did nothing to sweeten the smell of mildew and rodents.

Gabriella's keeper, a small, secretive man called Orrin Specter, bustled in with a tray as the bells tolled a dirge.

With a gasp, Gabriella ran to the window. It was not properly a window but an old-fashioned arrow loop, giving her a strange, narrow view of the smoke and spires of London, the half-frozen bend of the Thames.

"Is it the queen?" she demanded. "You must tell me! Do the bells ring because the queen is dead?"

Specter edged his finger around his crisp white collar. "Nay, for the child. The stillbirth is supposed to be a secret, but Londoners won't be fooled." He lowered his hands to his heart, his fingers crossed against evil.

"Tell me," said Gabriella.

"A changeling it was, or so they whisper at the palace. Blue and malformed, a female by the reckoning of some." Specter made a dismissive gesture with his hand. "The thing had no soul. It was buried in unconsecrated ground."

"When?" Gabriella's voice rose with urgency. "Tell me when it was born. Please, I must know."

He stared across the circular room at her. His crossed fingers tightened. "They say it happened at dawn."

Gabriella sank against the stone wall. "Oh, my poor lady." She crushed her fists into her eyes. "Oh, Lord, it's my fault. I took the wrong road and never reached the shrine. If I had, perhaps there would have been a chance."

"Aye, you shouldn't have stolen that crown."

"I didn't steal it, damn your eyes. And furthermore, I demand to see the steward of this house. I was on a legitimate errand at the behest of the queen. If it's not resolved, it will go hard on those of you who are involved in this travesty."

Orrin Specter scratched his head beneath his slouched hat. He sniffed and rubbed his nose on his sleeve. "Well, you talk like a fine lady." Moving to the hearth, he fanned the bellows at the banked fires. "The proper authorities have been notified. If there's a mistake, it'll soon come out."

She stared without appetite at the food on the tray. "I suppose you're right. I must be patient."

Specter left her alone.

Patiently she stared out the window. The stillbirth scudded like a storm cloud over the sun-gilt reign of the new king. People went about their business sluggishly, their cloaks rucked up around their necks. For days the sky remained a joyless shade of gray. There was no merry-making in London.

Patiently she sang songs to keep herself company during the endless days of her illegal confinement. Patiently she exorted Orrin Specter to speed the process of justice. Patiently she read and reread her letters from Armando, and prudently sewed his ring into the hem of her gown to conceal the jewel. It was bad enough that she was accused of one theft.

And patiently, she speculated about her whereabouts. From the view out the window, she had deduced that she was imprisoned in a private house on the north bank of the river Thames. To her right, she could see the corner of Baynard Castle; far to her left rose London Bridge, crowned by its clusters of handsome merchants' houses.

Who, she wondered feverishly, was responsible for this travesty? Could the queen herself, resentful and suspicious, have arranged the arrest? The thought cut like a surgeon's knife into a boil. Catherine had been her friend, a mother to Gabriella after Doña Mercedes had returned to Spain.

But what of Elvira? Had her dislike of Gabriella taken a sinister turn? Perhaps the conspirator had been a jealous English lady, or one of Cornish's players?

With a sigh, Gabriella conceded that she might never know the truth.

After a few weeks, confusing things began to happen in the secluded tower room in the strange house. An army of laborers appeared. They had obviously been instructed not to speak to Gabriella, for each time she tried to question them, she was rebuffed, her efforts slapped down by a quelling glare.

Descending on the chamber with zealous energy, they ripped down the faded hangings and brushed the walls with earthy-smelling lime wash. They swept out the rushes and strewed the floor with braided mats. They hung beautiful tapestries, the central one of a fierce unicorn, penned and gentled by the magical presence of a virgin. The straw pallet was carried off, and a massive tester bed set up in its place.

The workers left and four women arrived, silent and purposeful. They erected a dainty screen of carved ash, then heated water over the fire, slowly filling a small wooden tub.

Gabriella went willingly to the bath. She accepted a change of clothes, recognizing with a thrill of hope that it was her own gown, the one she had worn at the coronation feast. She expected her case would be heard soon. Surely that must be the reason for the frenzied preparations.

And yet that evening, she found herself alone. Bathed and freshly gowned, her hair a glossy mantle of curls, she sat in an upholstered chair and stared in confusion at the fire.

Tomorrow, perhaps. Yes. Tomorrow she would be free.

At nightfall she heard footsteps outside.

Probably Specter, bringing her supper. Food was the sole pleasure of her confinement. It was good and plentiful and the only thing she had to look forward to.

But it was not Orrin Specter who came into the room and stepped into the pool of light cast by the hearth fire.

It was the king.

CHAPTER 14

The winter wind nipped at Will's ears as he made his way toward Windsor Palace. His breath frosting the air, he rehearsed the words he would say to Doña Elvira. Over the past several days, he had sought an audience with the tight-lipped duenna in order to find out what had become of Gabriella.

But so far, he had learned only one fact. He and Doña Elvira despised and distrusted each other. Like all proper Spanish ladies, she loved the Lord and hated Jews with a virulence that was almost laughable.

The new king had brought an abundance of ceremony and protocol to his reign. Will was stopped three times by officials of the palace warden. All wore expressions of self-importance and black armbands of mourning. Finally, in exasperation, Will bribed a page and was conducted to the chamber of the queen's ladies. Standing with his hat in his hand, he studied the receiving room and tried to picture Gabriella here.

The cold stone and stiff portraits made an inhospitable place for a gentle, gifted artist to spend her days. Will moved to a window and peered through diamond-shaped panes of glass. Ah, he thought. There was her escape. The room overlooked a rose garden. Even in winter, when frost glazed the walkways and dusted the rose bushes and box hedges, a pristine beauty permeated the scene. He imagined Gabriella seated in the shade of a yew arbor. Her hands would strum music from her lute as if she were plucking petals from a rose. *My bonny, blithe William from over the sea* . . . Her voice would join breezes and bird song, creating music to charm men's souls and break their hearts.

I love her, he thought.

Will shook his head. What a fool he was. He found a curious comfort in the agony of his unfulfilled dreams. At least he was safe from other women. He would be spared the trouble of falling in love with another, being trapped in a marriage that time would dessicate like a corpse in a crypt. His love for Gabriella would always be as ripe and painful as a fresh wound. An artist could ask for no better inspiration. Thanks to her, he had enough pain to lend feeling to every instrument he fashioned, every song he sang, every note he played.

Coming here would only twist the knife. But Will could not help himself.

"Yes? What is it?" The voice, dark and rich with the accents of Castile, broke into his thoughts.

Will bowed to Doña Elvira, savoring her gasp of outrage when she spied the yellow Jew's badge pinned to his doublet. He knew it was wrong to take pleasure in inspiring hatred and prejudice, but he couldn't help himself. "I am William Shapiro of—"

"I remember you." Each syllable was a dagger tapping a tabletop. "The king thinks highly of your skills." Doña Elvira turned toward the window and spoke half to herself. "He has brought so many strangers to court. Erasmus, More, Whytford . . . Men who put human values above God. It makes no sense to me."

"It makes no sense for a king to surround himself with the greatest minds of the age?" Will inquired politely.

"He should surround himself with men of God," Doña Elvira declared. "A king needs no more than men of the True Faith to advise him. He should follow the example of King Ferdinand."

"Ah, yes." Will sent her an ingenuous grin. "Just think, without his grand cardinal, without the Dominicans, Ferdinand would have no public tortures and burnings."

"He punishes heretics in the name of Christ Jesus, the son of God. And God has blessed Spain with a whole new world."

"True," Will admitted. "But is that good fortune due to the influence of the Church, or did it come about in spite of it? I've heard that Colón's first voyage, the one that started it all, was financed almost entirely by Jews."

"The thieves controlled the purse strings of the realm."

"The Inquisition put a swift end to that," Will said.

She completely missed his irony. "Yes, thanks be to God. Now. What business have you here?"

"I've come to see Doña Gabriella."

Elvira's face darkened with a look he could not fathom. She said: "Doña Gabriella is no longer in England."

Shock stole his breath. His mind pawed through the possibilities. Had Armando returned and spirited her away already? How could they have left without saying goodbye?

Damn them both. He had been a better friend to those two than they deserved. "She's gone back to Spain, then?" he asked.

Doña Elvira would not meet his gaze. "Yes," she said,

her voice quiet and strained. "Good day, Master Shapiro. I have packing of my own to do."

He glanced at her sharply, but she left the room before he could question her further.

As Will wandered the cold, quiet streets of London, he burned with rage. He had been Armando's friend. He had been his partner in business. He had introduced Armando to the woman he loved. He had risked his neck to help him carry out a dangerous plan.

Armando and Gabriella had thanked him with complete disregard. Will pictured them now, probably man and wife already, basking in the sunshine of Andalucía, surveying their bountiful vineyards while the blue Middle Sea lapped at the white coast of their kingdom. A kingdom that had expelled Will Shapiro.

Damn them. Damn them both.

"Damn." Armando slapped at a mosquito that fed on his neck. "They suck more blood from me than Saint Xavier's leeches." He glowered across the crumbling wall of unmortared stone. "They don't bother you at all."

Paloma lifted her chin. "That's because I bathe."

He studied her for a moment. As always, he was grateful that she had stayed with him while Santiago went in search of her parents. She wore Spanish garb haphazardly, a bleached cotton skirt hiked up and tucked into the waistband, a blouse opened wide to the cooling breezes off the sea.

"Bathing's for Moors and other heathen." Armando saw her gaze drift away, and he instantly regretted his words. Bracing one hand on the wall, he leaped over and landed in front of her. "Paloma, I'm sorry."

"It's nothing." She spoke with the flatness of a woman inured to abuse. Someone else had hardened her. He caught himself wondering who. He caught himself wanting to choke the culprit.

"It's something," he countered, keeping hold of the stone wall to stop himself from touching her. "It's me, being careless of your feelings because of my own troubles." He swept his arm across the ruins of the *encomienda* that had been granted to him.

"It is beautiful here, is it not?" she asked, completely missing his meaning.

Yet her words forced him to look at his new home. Beyond the reaches of the plantation, the island hills bombarded the senses. Blossoming trees exploded like fire from lush forests. The green-cloaked hills were sliced open by cascades. Azure lagoons pooled in the mysterious shadows, and waves smashed on secret, underwater reefs.

"Aye, it's a wonder," he admitted. "But look at this place." He kicked at a loose rock. "The house is a mere hut that the wind tore down. The fields are neglected. The jungle is overtaking the cane. How am I supposed to make a proper farm of this?"

"Not with your own hands." A deep voice, rich with laughter, called from the drapery of cassia vines below the hill.

Armando stepped in front of Paloma. "Who's there?"

A man rode out of the trees that shaded the rocky path from the coast up into the hills. The newcomer had dark brown hair threaded with gray, and a pointed beard. He was broadly built and favored with the cold handsomeness Armando recalled of King Ferdinand's high-bred grandees. But this was no court dandy. He wore his vermilion doublet flapping open and his shirt unlaced to the waist.

Behind Armando, Paloma gasped.

The man reached the boundary of what had once been the beginnings of a yard, where plumes of acacias waved in the wind. The visitor dismounted and came forward, his hand extended.

"Juan Ponce de León of San Servas, governor of San Juan. I'd heard you'd laid claim to Montoya's *encomienda*.

Welcome to Española." Juan glanced around at the wild terrain. "Little Spain, we call it. God preserve Spain if she ever gets to look like this."

Armando barely heard. He was thinking fast and hard. De León. Ponce de León. Baltasar's kinsman and . . . the bastard who had captured Paloma. Tamping back his fury, he said, "I am acquainted with your çousin, sir. Baltasar made the crossing on the *Ciervo Volante*."

"I've not seen him yet." Juan fingered his beard. "He's taken over my first plantation, Alta Gracia in Higuey. No doubt he's as eager as you to get to the business of farming, and has gone off to find laborers to work his land." Juan clapped his hands sharply. From the underbrush trotted a small native boy in ragged sailor's trousers. He had a bag slung over his shoulder and carried a smoldering torch. Without a backward glance at the child, Juan put out his hand. "So. You are Armando Viscaino."

Armando nodded. "And this is Paloma."

"Ah, your wife is as beautiful as the sea at sunset." Juan bowed low. Paloma looked as if a scorpion had stung her in an unseen place.

"She's not my wife."

Juan straightened. A smile of boyish charm shone through his dark beard and mustache. "I see. Forgive me for staring, señorita, but there are so few Spanish ladies in the islands. I hunger for the sight of a female who—if you'll forgive me—doesn't wander around naked and offer her favors to any man who happens by. The Indian women are born whores, I tell you."

Armando nearly choked with rage. "Don Juan, I must ask you to govern your tongue in the presence of a lady."

Paloma simply stared at Juan, her gaze unwavering.

Chagrined, he looked away. "Forgive me. But now, Don Armando, let's talk of you and your plans."

"I mean to rebuild the house and harvest the present

cane crop. It's overgrown, but mature. I hope to establish a mill here as well.''

''An admirable enterprise, to be sure.'' Juan spoke with a certain irony. ''My life would be easier if I had the soul of a farmer. But alas, I'm cursed with an insatiable appetite for adventure. I conquered Boriquen, named it San Juan.''

''Congratulations,'' Armando said wryly.

Missing the sentiment, Juan went on. ''There are plans to take the island of Cuba, you know.''

''I heard the talk in Santo Domingo.''

''Are you a fighting man, Armando?''

Ask your cousin, he thought; then he said aloud: ''I don't know yet.''

''Then you've come to the right place. The Indies have a way of stripping a man bare and showing what he truly is.''

Armando felt both drawn to and repelled by Juan. He managed to seem both ruthless and charming at the same time.

''What do you know about this farm?'' Armando asked.

Still without looking at the slave boy, Juan snapped his fingers. The child took out a tube of tobacco and held the glowing end of his stick to the tip. He handed the cigar to Juan, who took a deep puff. ''Montoya brought a good deal of cane from the Canaries, but he failed. Didn't know how to get his Indians to work for him. He didn't understand that they're like children. You have to have a firm hand, avoid spoiling them. Montoya let his slaves eat too much and sleep too—''

''Slaves?'' Armando cut in.

''Of course. Montoya's all took off into the hills, but there're plenty more. Forty head per section is necessary for cultivating cane.'' He paused, studying Armando's expression. ''Do you not have the money to buy slaves?''

"I'll hire islanders as laborers, if they're willing," said Armando. "But I will not have them as my chattel."

"Wealth takes many forms, *amigo*. A biddable savage is worth his weight in gold." Juan leaned forward and eyed Paloma, who had moved off toward the run-down house. "She's a beauty, to be sure." His eyes kindled in a way Armando found disturbing. "Not your wife, eh? Your betrothed, then?"

"No." Armando thought longingly of Gabriella.

Juan flashed another of his charming grins. "Then you won't mind if I—"

"Yes," Armando said, surprising himself with his ferocity. "Yes, I'd mind very much. She's off-limits, Juan."

Juan turned, one eyebrow slashing upward, a question mark above the gleaming black orb of his eye. "Oh? She carries the French pox, then?"

The devastating sexual pox had, in recent years, swept the ports of the Middle Sea and penetrated to most of the major cities of Europe. Many believed its origin to be here, among the natives of the Indies. But Spaniards were quick to blame the disease, as they did so many ills, on the French.

Armando hesitated. It would be a simple thing to allow Juan to believe Paloma was tainted. But he heard himself saying, "As far as I know, she's healthy. But she's not available to you, Juan. Not to you, nor to any man."

"Well said, *amigo*. You sound more like a knight than a farmer." Chuckling, Juan mounted his horse. *"Hasta luego,"* he said and rode off, the slave boy hurrying after him.

Armando returned to Paloma's side. She seemed pale and shaken. "You remember him, then," said Armando.

She nodded. "I could never forget Juan Ponce de León."

"But he didn't recognize you."

She lowered her eyes. "He captured a frightened island girl. That girl lives no more."

The bleakness of her words touched Armando's heart. "People change. Some more than others. You're a beautiful woman now. You have the graces of a Spanish lady—"

A shadow passed over her face. "My family won't recognize me."

"Ah, I'm sorry. I know you don't value what you learned during your time in Spain and Naples. But hold on to that knowledge, Paloma. It could serve you well one day."

"Perhaps." She aimed a wistful gaze at the distant horizon, a filament of gold strung along the turquoise sea.

Impulsively he took her hand. "Soon, Paloma. Santiago sent messages with natives all over the islands. Soon your parents will know you're back."

"I wish he had let me go with him."

"No. I rarely agree with Santiago, but this time I do. Your clan most likely left Cayo Moa. It would be a tragedy to bring you this far only to lose you. It's safest to stay here and wait for your parents to come."

She nodded slowly. She looked lovely when she was solemn and thoughtful. But then, she looked lovely when she was laughing or melancholy or angry.

"In the meantime," he said, "you'll stay here with me. We've got a farm to build."

Her head snapped up. "You'd put me to work like a slave?"

He laughed. "No, Paloma, that's just the point. We're going to attempt something no one's ever done in the islands. We're going to run a farm without slave labor."

Her eyes softened. And then, like the sun breaking from the clouds, a smile came over her face.

In the third week of her imprisonment, King Henry brought Gabriella a gift. She was lying on the comfortable tester bed when he entered the chamber and locked the door behind him.

His face alight with a boyish smile, he held a large dome-shaped object draped in dark linen. "This is for you," he said, setting the object on the low table below the single narrow window. "Come and see your gift."

Silent and apprehensive, Gabriella went to his side. She no longer bothered with the formalities of greeting the king with an obeisance. He neither noticed nor objected to the slight.

With a flourish, he swept the covering from the dome. Gabriella stared at a cage fashioned of steel filigree. Its inhabitant was a small yellow bird huddled on a roost.

"It's a canary," Henry said proudly. "From the islands of that name. Its song is said to be extraordinary, but I've never heard this one sing."

"Why should he sing?" Gabriella inquired. "Being trapped alone in a cage gives a songbird no reason to sing."

Henry's piercing blue eyes seemed to pick her apart. "You're speaking of yourself, aren't you, Gabriella?"

She saw no point in denying it. In the past weeks she had lost her innocence, her naïveté, and her faith in the benevolence of kings. "Sire, I beg of you. Let me go free."

He reached out and fingered a strand of her hair. She never braided it anymore, though she bathed often and scrupulously, only because it was a way to pass a few of the lonely hours.

"Gabriella." He spoke softly, his voice as rich as mead. "You stand accused of theft."

"Then let me face my accusers. I'll go to the queen. She'll explain that she gave me the jeweled headdress to take to the shrine as an offering."

"She has already admitted as much. But when you were found, Gabriella, you were nowhere near the shrine. Suspicion is, you were making your way to the coast in order to run away to meet your lover, the outlaw Armando Viscaino.''

"I took the wrong road. Doña Elvira told me to do so."

"Doña Elvira denies doing so. One of her last acts before she left for Spain was to sign a statement avowing that."

Startled, Gabriella backed against a slender bedpost. "Doña Elvira has gone to Spain?"

King Henry tucked his thumbs into the top of his wide baldric. "Aye, I banished her. The woman's treacherous."

"She is," Gabriella said eagerly. "She misled me on purpose. I think she was jealous of my friendship with the queen." *She sold me like a whore to you.*

He regarded her with faint regret. "She had no reason to lie in this matter. And why were you traveling alone?"

"Sire, one does not make a pilgrimage in the company of bodyguards."

"No court in the land will believe your excuses."

She fixed him with a brave stare. "Do you believe me?"

He blinked. For a moment he looked very young. "I could give you a royal pardon and that would be that."

"Then why—"

He held up his hand. "I have promised to show impartial justice, to allow the courts their independence. I won't go back on my word, Gabriella. Not even for you."

Hard words, tenderly spoken. She could make a point, too. She dropped to her knees beside the cage. "This bird is mine?" she inquired. "Truly, entirely mine?"

An indulgent smile curved his lips. "Entirely, my dear."

With a swift movement of her hand, she unhooked the tiny door. The canary hopped out of reach, but she took it gently in her hand. The bird's tiny heart fluttered against her palm. Its cold little feet trembled in her fingers.

"Gabriella?" said Henry. "What are you—"

She brushed past him and set the canary on the sloping window ledge. The wind off the river ruffled its feathers.

Then the bird loosed a note of pure, shattering sweetness, spread its wings, and soared.

Henry stepped up behind her. "Gabriella, I went to a great deal of trouble to bring you a rare gift."

"You said it was mine. Mine to keep, or mine to set free."

The canary flew in joyous loops, and its flight was a wonder to Gabriella. She clasped her hands to her breast. For the first time in weeks, she smiled. She started to turn away.

"Watch," King Henry commanded.

She turned back to the scene outside the window. The canary swooped in and out of her narrow field of vision. A shadow rose from the river. It was one of the sea eagles that nested in the walls of the great houses along the river. The large bird made a dark streak across the sky. Its strike was swift and clean, instantly deadly. The canary plummeted toward the river.

Horrified, Gabriella covered her face with her hands.

King Henry touched her shoulder. "You see, Gabriella. Freedom can sometimes be a dangerous thing."

She spun around to face him. "You've made your point, sire. How satisfied you must be. But you're an intelligent, educated man. Surely you don't liken my fate to that of a canary."

"Gabriella." His hands moved from her shoulders to her upper arms. "I want you to realize that the safest place for you is with me." His breath was sweet and clean with fennel, his young face earnest as a postulant's. And yet here he stood, a wall between her and the golden future she planned with Armando.

"What you want," he said with the voice of a king but the words of a spoiled child, "is not as important as what I desire."

"You've never said exactly what it is that you want. You come here day after day to hear me play and sing, yet you never say what is in your mind and heart."

He dropped his hands. "I have lost my firstborn child," he said, his voice thin with real grief. "And nearly my wife as well. I'm a king, Gabriella, but I'm also a man. I need comforting, same as any man."

"Then take your comfort from your courtiers."

"I get nothing but insincere platitudes from my courtiers."

"Sire, I don't believe your sole purpose in detaining me is to have me as your personal songbird." Aye, she would force him to admit his purpose. Spoken aloud, it would sound as sordid as it truly was. Perhaps it would shame him into freeing her.

"How did you become so wise at such a young age?" he asked.

"The same way you did, sire. By bitter experience. And you still haven't answered my question."

He turned away, his shoulders hunched. "I thought if I gave you a beautiful room to live in, if I brought you gifts and became your sole companion, you would come to love me."

"No more than that bird would have come to love me," she stated. "You are King of England. Thanks to your father, you've the richest treasury in Christendom. Your wish has the power to bring armies and palaces and fleets of ships into being. But all your wealth and your royal will can't win a woman's heart."

He looked amazed as he scratched his head. "Am I ugly?"

She laughed. "Your Grace, honest men have described you as the fairest prince England has seen since Arthur. The warrior, not your brother, God rest his soul."

"Your compliments don't warm me, Gabriella."

"They're not meant to, Your Grace."

He crossed the room and lowered himself to the bed, cradling his head in his hands. "I find myself a king before I had a chance to be a man. Everyone wants something from me. My nobles, my captains, my clerics . . . They're taking me apart!"

"What does that have to do with keeping me imprisoned here?"

He shook his head. "I don't know. I only know that I desire you. I want to make love to you."

"No," she said in a low, shocked voice. In her heart she had known the truth from the very first time he had stepped into her secret chamber. But hearing the words from his own lips shook her to her soul. "You cannot mean that, Your Grace."

He looked at her with his heart in his eyes. "I do."

"You would betray your wife, the most saintly woman God ever put breath into."

He stood and paced in agitation. "That is exactly the point. Catherine is saintly. She submits to me like a postulant to a penance. She's more sister and friend than wife and lover."

"You ask treason of me. She is my queen."

"And I am your king." Henry crossed to her side and pulled her against him. She felt the strength in his arms, the silk of his shirt. "I mislike games of seduction. Perhaps in a few years I shall, but not now."

She tried to twist from his embrace, from the scent of his spicy perfume and the grasping of his hands. "Then go cut your teeth on some other woman. There are plenty who are willing."

"No." He held her tighter; she felt his vigor and implacable will. "Gabriella, a woman of your charms is not safe at court. If I set you free, you'll die like that bird. Tell me, am I truly worse than dying?"

"Having experienced neither you nor death, Your Grace, I don't know."

He chuckled. "Your humor is black, my Gabriella. As black as your beautiful hair." He leaned down to kiss her. She turned her head away. His hungry mouth fell upon her cheek, then dipped lower to her neck, his beard abrading her flesh. "How soft you are," he murmured. "Dark and soft like a ripe plum."

For a moment, his kisses held her spellbound. She saw herself as the king's mistress, pampered by his gifts and attention. Shocked by her errant thoughts, she pushed against his chest. "Your Grace, please. Do my feelings mean nothing to you? Do you care nothing for my life, my ambitions, my desires?"

"Your dreams are everything to me. That's why I'll give you everything. Your own estate in the country. A room filled with all the instruments in the world. A troupe of musicians to accompany you whenever you wish. I'll hire a composer to serve you, to write songs such as none has ever heard before."

"These promises mean nothing," she said, pulling out of his embrace. Anger and resentment consumed her, made her utter words that, a few weeks earlier, would have shocked her. "They are gifts a man gives a whore in exchange for the use of her body."

He sent her a wounded look. "You're more to me than that."

"No," she said with quiet certainty. "I'm less to you than that. At least a whore is free to come and go as she pleases."

He shook her hard. "You mock my passion!"

"No." His vehemence frightened her but she forged on. "I do have dreams, Your Grace. I wish to marry one day and have children. I wish for the peace and contentment of a family."

He let her go. "What is mere contentment compared to the love, the riches I can give you?"

She pressed her lips together and looked away. She must

never speak aloud of Armando. Evening darkened the sky outside her window, and faintly she heard the call of bell-men crying out the hour of sext.

Henry sighed, moving to her side again. "Gabriella, I will make love to you." He spoke so gently that she almost failed to hear the threat. His strong, pale hand came up to lift her hair from the nape of her neck, to caress the sensitive flesh there. "In tenderness or in violence, the choice is yours."

The days blurred into weeks. From the tower window Gabriella watched harsh winter yield to warm spring, even as she yielded her body to the king. She watched the ice break from the edges of the river, and likened the melting and shattering to the turmoil in her heart.

King Henry was radiant. He emerged stronger from the tragedy of his lost child; his will and his pride were more lofty than ever. His golden vibrance chipped away at Gabriella's defenses. He awakened her body even as her soul slept the troubled sleep of guilt. She responded to his bold caresses like a sleek, well-fed cat—conscienceless, with no thought of the future Henry had stolen from her. She took to sleeping too much, to relishing every rich meal. Her body was a finely tuned instrument and Henry a gifted musician. Her senses sang for him, a melody of surpassing yet soulless sweetness.

But a small, cold part of her stood aloof from the seduction. That part was angry. That part had a plan.

Henry had promised her a country estate. She would demand the prize from him.

And then she would leave him.

"No," he said one April day, when budding trees masked the stink of the river, and the king's swans drifted in a snowy flotilla along with the currents. "Not yet, Gabriella. I cannot give you a house of your own."

"But you promised." They lay together, naked and entwined upon the counterpane, their bodies cooled by the breezes from the window. She reached up to run her hand over his chest. He was massive there, furred with gold. It was a young man's well-conditioned body she held, yet with his fondness for food and drink it might someday run to fat.

Her own body seemed to belong to a stranger. Her muscles were flaccid from inactivity. Her appetite had run rampant, nearly matching the king's.

"Henry? Did you hear me? You promised me a house—"

"Yes, yes, my nightingale." He seemed agitated, bursting with some secret. "You shall have a place of your own. But not yet. I have to stay in London to plan the invasion of France."

He spoke as if a full-scale war were no more complicated than a stag hunt. Once again, his youthfulness struck her. He was only a boy, playing at being a king, toppling foreign armies like ninepins.

"I'll take a house in London," she said, blinking prettily in a way she knew he admired. "I simply need more room."

Tender as a priest, he kissed her temple. "I don't relish the thought of sharing you. You're the one part of my life that belongs to me alone. Do you know that I require the services of six men—three of them dukes or better—just to put me to bed at night? Think of it—six grown men. With you I can drop my doublet on the floor and put it on again with my own hands."

"You talk of everything except what really matters," she said in annoyance.

He laughed, reached for the goblet of claret he always kept on the floor beside the bed, and drained the cup. Then he cradled her face in his hands, letting her silky black curls tumble through his fingers. "God's mercy, Gabriella, you are lovely. I've brought a new painter from

Saxony. Very gifted. One day I'll have him paint your portrait.''

"I don't want my portrait painted." Of late she had been moody, her temper ungovernable. "I want—''

He stopped her words with a long, slow kiss as deep and intimate as their couplings were. She could taste the wine he had drunk and feel the gentle abrasion of his golden beard. As if with a life of its own, her passion awakened.

When he lifted his mouth from hers, he was smiling. His hands glided downward, mapping the generous contours of her body. "Ah, Gabriella, I like you like this, all plump and soft and angry with me." His hands cupped her breasts, and her heightened sensitivity drew a moan from her lips.

"Harry." She sighed out his name in helpless desire and exasperation. "About your prom—''

He kissed her again and suckled her breasts, then turned her so that his face was between her legs and he was licking her while she writhed in shock and delight, and finally cried out in a shattering climax. Henry slid upward and entered her, his beard and lips moist and musky with the taste of her.

"Aye, I like you like this," he repeated, starting to move within her. "Alone in your room, growing fat and sleek, my own nightingale in a cage . . .''

Even as her hips rose to his thrusts, even as her body sang like a rebec beneath a curved bow, Gabriella despaired. His immovable will and seductive ways held her captive; she had no notion how she would ever escape him. And even if she did, she knew she would always be a prisoner of her own shame.

Much later, when the red light of a cool evening fell in a cruciform bar through the window, Henry rose from the bed and started dressing. Gabriella reached for the purple robe he had once given her as a gift, but he snatched it from her.

"No. I want to leave you unclothed, my darling. I like to imagine you like this, always, just waiting for me."

The bells of London started to toll, signaling the closing of the city gates. Henry quickened his movements. "I must hurry. I'd nearly forgotten that I'm dining with the queen tonight." His boyish grin shone with whimsy and charm. He was, Gabriella realized, utterly unaware of his own cruelty.

"We're celebrating, you see." He took Gabriella's hand and placed a fervent kiss in the middle of her palm. "It's wonderful news. The queen is once again with child."

He left her lying naked and stunned, the cold click of the lock echoing in her ears.

And then Gabriella turned her face into the bedclothes and wept. Not because Henry lay with his wife. She would have been a fool to think he had forsaken Catherine. And not because of his careless announcement, not even because he had refused to give her a house.

Gabriella wept long into the cool April evening because she, too, was expecting the king's child.

CHAPTER 15

"It's magnificent!" Santiago stood on the hill overlooking Armando's plantation and spread his arms wide. Behind him the river rushed down from the mountains. To his right and left the cane rippled in the breeze. "You've worked a miracle here!"

Tamping back a surge of pride, Armando gave a curt nod. He gazed at the green fields, the stone fence encircling the *trapiche* powered by sturdy horses plodding around the mill wheel. Close by stood the sprawling hacienda with its towering thatched roof and a curl of smoke coming from a new plaster chimney. A small army of natives, free to come and go as they pleased, worked in the fields, the stockyard, the kitchen garden.

Armando had lived for this day, when he could throw his achievement in his father's face, but instead he felt only a sour satisfaction. The scars on his back stung with the memory of the flogging he had endured at Santiago's command. "It's hard work, not a miracle," he said.

Santiago's head snapped up, and his hands tightened into fists. Then he laughed, his sun-browned throat moving. "And what does a gypsy know of hard work, eh? I bought you some cows from the fleet that just arrived. Someone will bring them up later. Cattle thrive on the green tops of sugarcane."

Armando's words of thanks stuck in his throat. He did not want to be beholden to Santiago. Since his arrival in Santo Domingo, he had labored to assert his independence. The plantation represented months of toil and sweat. In exchange for the *encomienda*, Governor Diego Colón had sought Armando's word that he would not make trouble with either Santiago or Baltasar de León. The promise turned Armando's stomach.

Unruffled by Armando's lack of response, Santiago strode to the level area of the mill, where a native boy patiently led the tethered horses in a circle. Armando followed reluctantly.

The sweet, damp fragrance of fresh-cut cane perfumed the air. The open door of a lean-to revealed a copper boiler with a fire lapping at its sides. Two natives and a Spanish boy, the son of Rosa the cook, fed the fire with Coconut husks. Icacos, the father of the two island boys, skimmed the boiling cane. By sunset, the bubbling syrup would turn yellowish. The women would strain it through cloth to yield wet sugar.

"Most impressive," said Santiago. "The other planters are still making their slaves crush the cane with rocks and clubs." He lifted an eyebrow and turned to Armando. "Your doing?"

Armando shook his head. "The *trapiche* is the work of El Hakim." The Moor was, Armando reflected, yet another obligation owed to Santiago. In his travels in search of Paloma's parents, Santiago had encountered Sebastian Cabot, sailing in King Ferdinand's service in the Lesser Antilles. Disillusioned with the blustering English adventurer, who refused to admit he could find no way to Cathay, El Hakim had been delighted to hear from Santiago that Armando was in the islands. Some months earlier, the Moor had taken ship to Española.

Santiago leaned over the pot and fanned the sweet fumes to his nose. "Ah. So your Moorish friend likes the farming life."

Better than I do, thought Armando. "Yes," he said. "I've made him my partner here at *Gema del Mar*."

"Jewel of the Sea?"

"It's what we call the plantation." Disliking the pretense of civility, Armando crossed his arms over his chest and glared at his father. "Look, you're no more interested in my progress than I am in telling you about it. It's time we spoke of Paloma's parents."

Armando glanced back at the house. She would be in the kitchen now, helping Rosa, a soldier's widow he'd hired from town. If any miracle had taken place, it had been brought about by Paloma. She had negotiated with the native laborers; she had calmed their fears and persuaded them to work for Armando.

Santiago scratched his chest through his thin red shirt. As always, he eschewed the doublet, hat, and pantaloons most Castilian men found fashionable. He wore tight trousers, and knee boots of black cordovan leather. He was forty-one years old, and to Armando's great annoyance, still resembled a young adventurer in the prime of life.

"Well?" Armando prompted. "Did you find out anything at all?"

"Only unreliable hearsay." Santiago rolled an unlit cigar between his palms. "As I'm sure you've noticed, the islanders are a strange lot."

"We're the strangers here, not them."

Santiago smiled with an approval Armando did not crave. "You can't trust what they say to a Spaniard, even one they like. Some are so eager to help that they'll make up information just to please you. Others are so wary that they'll lie to throw you off course."

"But you traveled with a small army of native guides," said Armando. "Do they lie to each other?"

Santiago shrugged. "Maybe, maybe not. We went first to Cayo Moa, the place where Paloma grew up." He blew out his breath. "Deserted. We visited all the cays to the north. A Taino merchant mentioned some huge tribes on Cuba, and some on a vast land to the north. Seems they've gotten wind of what the Spaniards are about. Years ago, the natives welcomed us as gods. Now I fear they're not so agreeable."

"It's our own fault," Armando said.

Santiago went into the shed to light his cigar from the boiler fire, then returned. The steady trade winds snatched at the blue-gray smoke. "I don't dispute that."

"Did you go to Cuba?"

Santiago nodded. "The natives took up arms against us, wouldn't let us land. I sent a message to the *cacique*. I have to believe that if Joseph had been there, he would have responded."

Armando's lips thinned. "So you've found out nothing."

"Could you have done better, *hombre*?" Santiago swept his arm toward the distant, sparkling sea. "It's a new world out there, *hombre*. It doesn't work like our—" He broke off, and his mouth fell open.

Armando turned to see Paloma on the rise in front of the villa, her form vivid against the plaster and thatch building. She wore a plain skirt and blouse that enhanced her height and slimness; her feet were bare, her hair braided. Her cheeks paled as she hurried down the hill.

Armando looked back at Santiago and felt a rush of anger. The elder man's eyes were sin-dark and shadowy with desire.

"She's under my protection," Armando warned in an undertone. "So don't even think about it."

Santiago flung his cigar away. "Easy, *hombre*. I know what you think. I was just surprised at . . . how grown-up she's become." As she approached, he held out his hands to her. She sent Armando a look of uncertainty, then clasped Santiago's hands.

"I couldn't find them, Paloma," Santiago explained in a voice hoarse with regret. "We searched the islands, but we encountered no one who would speak of Joseph and Anacaona."

She dropped his hands and held herself stiff and proud, her face expressionless. But Armando could read her moods. Her eyes were dry, but her heart wept.

"You found no sign of them at all?" she asked. "Not the *cacique* Guyati, or my half-brother Malak?"

"Nothing, *cara*. We'll reprovision the canoes and set out again within the week. I want to try Cuba again, and we heard rumors of a great land to the north."

Her chin came up a notch. "I'm going with you." She turned and stalked off, skirting the cane fields as she headed toward the estuary that flowed to the west of the *encomienda*.

"Stay here," Armando said to Santiago. "I'll talk to her." He reached her just as she flung herself onto a patch of grass beside the rushing stream. They sat for a while, listening to the gurgle of water over the rocks. A parrot squawked in the mangrove trees, and the breeze, scented by wild *poui* flowers, stirred the feathery coconut palms on the far bank of the stream.

El Hakim rode into the mill yard from the fields and joined Santiago in conversation. The Moor wore a burnoose to shield his neck and back from the strong island sun. The Indies sun had deepened the color of his skin to the rich shade of polished chestnuts. Armando quelled a surge of resentment. El Hakim was *his* friend, *his* partner.

Yet from his easy stance upon the horse, he looked taken with Santiago's smooth charm.

"I don't want you to go," said Armando.

She laced her arms around her knees and shot him a dark look. "I must. Don't try to stop me. You are not my master."

"No, just the man who left the woman I love—"

"You've sent for her."

"—incurred the wrath of two kings—"

"You escaped."

"—and crossed the Ocean Sea to bring you home."

"I am not home yet." Her face softened. "I will always thank you for what you have done. I've tried to repay you by lending my help with your enterprise."

As quickly as it had risen, his anger retreated. He could never hold on to anger where she was concerned. "You have, Paloma. Your people have taught me new ways to cultivate the land, to fish from rivers and lagoons. But what you don't understand is that I never expected payment from you. I did what I did as a matter of honor."

The breeze plucked a strand of silky hair from her braid. Armando had an urge to tuck it behind her ear, but he resisted. Summoning restraint was getting harder and harder these days, for the better he came to know her, the more he longed to touch her, to break through the shell of her private pain. He could never erase her past, but he wanted to help her build a future.

She braced her hands on the grass behind her and tilted her face to the sky. He tried not to notice the way her breasts thrust against the fabric of her blouse. As usual, he failed.

"You're a fair man," she said. "Other Spaniards talk much of honor. Your actions are more honorable than their prattle."

"Then you won't go chasing around the islands with my—with him? You'll stay?"

"Armando, I must go."

He ripped out a clump of grass by the roots and flung it aside. "Damn it, Paloma, it's dangerous. Do you want to be captured again? Let Santiago find your parents."

"He's tried. And he's failed."

Armando took a dark satisfaction in that. He wanted Paloma's clan to be found, but he did not want to give her into Santiago's care. Nor, he admitted, did he want to lose her.

He leaned back on one elbow and studied her. He liked the way the light danced in her hair. He liked the shadows her eyelashes made on her cheeks. But most of all, he liked her remarkable human spirit.

Guiltily he checked his thoughts. It was Gabriella he pined for, Gabriella he missed. He prayed she had received his letters. He had sent several with returning fleets. Surely by now she knew where he was and how desperately he needed her.

"Your world is changing, Paloma. Before Colón came, it was safe to travel the islands. But now, slavers might seize you. Your own people might harm you, for they can't trust anyone."

She stretched her legs so that her toes touched the water. Her shins were smooth and brown. As always, her lack of modesty startled and discomfited him. No lady, Spanish or English, gave a man a glimpse of her bare feet and ankles, much less her legs.

His thoughts grew hot and dark; his loins tightened and his hands itched to caress her. He had vowed to keep himself pure for the woman he loved, to avoid the heartbreak that Santiago's promiscuity had brought to his own life. But he was young and lusty, and base urges pounded away at noble reason.

Inexplicably, startlingly, he needed to hold her. In an act of instinct as irresistible as breathing, he found himself moving swiftly toward her, pulling her into his arms and pressing her back onto the grass. A gasp of surprise escaped her; then he closed his mouth over hers.

Her lips felt as soft as they looked. Her mouth tasted of the *yaruma* fruit from the little grove behind the villa. A powerful desire devoured him and he pressed his body to her supine form. She moved beneath him, brushing him with fire. At first he fancied she shared his mad hunger. But the choked moan she made in her throat had the guttural ring of terror.

Her fear cooled his ardor. Armando rolled away. Her face was white, her eyes large and sleek with a hunted look. Without shifting a muscle, she withdrew from him, her spirit disappearing behind a wall of past hurts and distrust.

Armando spoke her name.

She jumped up and fled, swift as a rabbit, darting beneath the dense canopy of *bihao* leaves into the forest. Hurrying after her, Armando tripped over a root, cursed, and increased his speed. Just as she plunged up a hill toward the source of the spring, his hand closed around her arm.

She struggled in his grip, but he held fast, even when her fingernails raked his arm. "Enough!" he said sharply, his grasp tightening. "I'm sorry. I didn't mean to frighten you."

She tried to tug away. Her eyes held the glazed terror of a stranger. She said something in her language, and to him it sounded like a plea for help.

"Paloma, I'm your friend. I swear I won't force myself on you. If I let you go, you won't run?"

She shook her head. When he released her, she shrank back against the rough trunk of a ceiba tree.

He ran an unsteady hand through his hair. "That was stupid of me. I should know better. I had no right. . . . But you seemed so lonely. God, I'm lonely, too."

Her shoulders trembled. He fought the impulse to take

her into his arms again, not in desire, but to soothe her fears.

"Why must my touch always frighten you, Paloma?"

"I don't like your way of mating."

He laughed. "Mating? It was just a kiss, a—" He broke off, trying to fathom the nightmares she would never talk about. "I know you've been hurt, Paloma. But you can't let it poison the rest of your life. Someday you'll have to talk about it."

"Never." She pressed her hands to her stomach in a gesture of self-protection that tore at his heart. "That part of my life is over."

"Is it? Then why do you flinch when I touch you?"

She threw back her shoulders, and her show of pride stung him with guilt. "Because your countrymen taught me a lesson in cruelty and mistrust. They saw me as a savage, chattel, a person who couldn't feel hurt or fear."

Armando imagined her years as a captive and saw truths he had been too stubborn to face before. She was young, exotic, and astonishingly beautiful. He imagined other men's hands pinching her body, other men's mouths stealing her sweetness.

"God damn it," he snapped. "You keep too much to yourself."

"How will talking to you, accepting your kisses, heal me?" She lifted her hands to her chest. "I will never be free of what they did to me."

He ached for her. She looked so vulnerable, with only her pride as a fragile shield against the ugliness that haunted her.

"Let me into your life, Paloma," he said quietly.

Ignoring his words, she started toward the house. "I'm going with Santiago."

"Then so am I," he answered with grim reluctance.

She stared at him. "You cannot. What about your plantation?"

"El Hakim can manage." He matched her long strides. "He's far more inventive than I, and your people like him. Rosa will see to the house. The sun and the rains will do the rest."

"You sound like a *guahiro*."

"Like one of you?"

She nodded. "My people place their faith in the sun and rain."

"So must I, Paloma. Together we'll find your parents."

She stopped walking and turned to him. "No."

"Yes."

"You are stubborn and foolish. A"—she paused, retrieving the word from memory—"a dolt." Despite her words, her mouth softened in an almost-smile. A rainbow of colors, reflected from the water, jeweled her shining eyes. "But I suppose it is better to have a stubborn fool for a friend than no friend at all."

Gabriella stroked the strings of the new lute Henry had given her. The sweet-sad plaint drifted into the quiet of her tower room, echoing the melancholy in her heart.

Her music, once a refuge from the days of poverty before Catherine became queen, failed to cheer her anymore. She no longer took much enjoyment in food, yet she felt fat and slow and listless. The illness of new pregnancy roiled through her, and each morning she vomited a colorless liquid into her chamber pot. There was no sign yet of the baby, but she knew she had only weeks before Henry would notice.

When she thought of the baby, she encountered only a vast white blankness. The idea that she would soon give birth to a child was not real to her yet.

Henry visited less and less frequently. He was bursting with hope for Queen Catherine's pregnancy and busy with plans to defend Pope Julius from attacks by Louis XII of

France. He had little time to spare for Gabriella, and little sympathy for her repeated pleas for freedom.

But he was young and golden and handsome, and his touch stirred her. She told herself it was because her isolation made her hungry for any company. But the truth was, she missed him.

No, it was Armando she missed. But she was losing him. His memory faded like a half-remembered dream. The days melted together, and nothing outside her chamber seemed real anymore.

Sighing in despair, she picked out a mournful melody on the lute. The tones saddened her, and so she stopped. She ran her finger over the craftsman's mark on the bottom of the lute.

A row of stars. Will's mark. She should have guessed he was the craftsman of such a fine instrument.

Oh, Will. Suddenly she missed him fiercely. Her deadened emotions awakened, and she hugged the instrument. Missed his easy smile, his wry humor, his extraordinary talent as a musician. When they played together, her heart exulted in music that was bright and full of hope. When she played alone, she could coax only her cheerless laments from the instrument.

As she sat touching his mark on the lyre, a thought tiptoed into her mind. *Will.* He was always so clever. . . .

As the thought firmed into decision, she set aside the lute and picked up a book of hours Henry had brought her. The calfskin volume fell open to a beautiful handpainted page. The illustration depicted a rustic scene, peasants working in the fields with a vast manor house sprawling across the background. The illuminator had embellished the page in gold leaf. The value of the book could feed a large London family for a year.

Savagely she ripped out the page, went to the grate, and scrabbled through the ashes for a piece of blackened wood.

It was a crude writing tool, but she had only a few words to write.

She finished her note, folded it, and dropped it inside the hollow body of the lute. Then, with tight-lipped purpose, she took hold of the bridge of the instrument. The wood broke with a loud snap into the heavy silence of her prison.

Will stood at the back of his shop, surveying the empty counters and bare shelves. In his hand he held a purse containing all the money he had earned from selling every last trenail and lute string. He prayed it was enough.

Enough to pay his passage to Spain. To Gabriella.

"You're making a big mistake," said his uncle David, who stood behind him. "She could still be in London."

"No. Doña Elvira said she went to Spain months ago."

"Then leave her be. She is with her own kind there."

"I have to do this," Will said without turning.

"You're a fool."

Will shrugged. "Probably."

"Your parents would hate this, had they lived to see it."

"Hate that I'm facing my fear of Spain?"

"You're leaving a prosperous business behind, and for what? For a woman who is Catholic. A woman who loves a rich *hidalgo*'s son. For her you abandon your livelihood? It makes no sense to me, Guillermo."

Stung by the memories stirred by his Spanish name, Will stared out the window. Evening lowered like a smoky shroud over London. "I never said it made sense, David."

David snorted. "You'd walk into the arms of the Inquisition—"

"Jews are outlawed in England, too."

"The English borrow money from us; they don't burn us alive."

"It's a chance I'm willing to take."

"For God's sake, why?"

"Because I love her."

"This is crazy. What good will chasing the woman to Spain do? She went there to join her blue-blooded lover. They're probably married by now."

"I have to find out for certain. . . ." His throat aching, Will let his voice trail off.

"And then what? Assuming you're not caught and hanged from the *strappado* by the Holy Office—"

A knock at the door interrupted him. Both turned to see a messenger with a lute tucked under his arm. David took a step toward the door.

"Don't answer it," said Will.

"The man's wearing royal livery."

"I'm no longer in trade."

David gave a snort of disgust and strode to the door. Before Will could protest, he pulled it open. "Welcome, sir," he said heartily, stepping aside while the messenger entered.

"Richard Wolf of the Royal Windsor Guard." The visitor blinked into the dimness. "You're Master Shapiro?"

"No, I own the herbal shop next door."

Wolf glanced dubiously around the empty shop. "I did address myself to the right place?"

"No," said Will.

"Certainly," said David. He made a grand gesture at his nephew. "Here's Master Shapiro now, at your service."

"Good. Master Specter told me to come here and only here."

Will released a sigh of exasperation. He had paid dearly for a forged passport and traveling papers. A delay could jeopardize his whole enterprise, for the papers would expire soon. "I'll do the repair," he said, quelling his impatience.

Wolf settled himself on a bench against the wall. His gaze moved dubiously over the empty shelves. "I'll wait."

Will carried the lute to the worktable while David lit a lamp. Will assessed the damage. This was one of his own instruments; he had crafted it not a fortnight ago. Rescuing discarded clamps and glue from the rubbish bin, he set to work.

David brought Wolf a mug of herb-steeped wine from next door, and the two of them sat amiably discussing the unseasonable cold weather, the impressive glitter of the young king's reign, the promise of the queen's new pregnancy.

Will paid little heed. His mind leaped to the long and dangerous journey ahead. David was right. He was a fool. He was going to get his heart broken; he could possibly lose his life. But the alternative—growing old on stale dreams here in London—was unthinkable.

He glued and clamped the lute, turning the instrument to check for other damage. A faint rattling sound came from inside. Angling the lute toward the light, he saw what looked like a wad of parchment inside.

He shook it out. Someone had scribbled on the paper. A pity to have damaged a nicely illuminated page. The owner of the lute must be very careless indeed.

Preoccupied with his plans, Will started to toss the scrap into the grate.

But curiosity claimed him. He glanced at David and Wolf, who shared another round of wine and London gossip. Will smoothed the paper out on the table. The charcoal had smudged. He bent close to read it, starting with the initials at the bottom. G. Flores y de Rascon.

Gabriella.

His eyes devoured the page, each desperate word an arrow in his heart. Doña Elvira had lied. Gabriella had not gone home to Spain. She was a prisoner in a house on the banks of the Thames.

As Will committed her words to memory, the slow burn of anger kindled to the unholy heat of rage. He rose, picking up the lute and advancing toward Wolf.

"Leave the clamps in place overnight," he instructed in a bland voice, laying the lute on the counter. He tried not to appear nervous as he eyed the royal soldier. Will was by nature a peaceable man. He had been in few brawls; he rarely struck another living thing save the rump of a recalcitrant jennet.

Gabriella was in London. Gabriella needed him.

His hand clenched into a fist.

Richard Wolf stood.

Will drove one fist into the man's gut while the other clipped his jaw. The impact nearly broke Will's fingers, and he had the fleeting thought that he would never work again.

Wolf stepped back, scowling and shaking his head. "Here now, what're you about?" David regarded his nephew with a stunned expression.

Will panicked. It wasn't supposed to happen like this. Wolf was supposed to fall senseless to the floor. He tried again, fists flying. Wolf's face darkened, but he held his ground like a water oak rooted to the floor.

Will saw the large fist coming toward his face. He also saw a pewter wine cup crash downward from behind Wolf.

Wolf's blow numbed the entire lower half of Will's face. David hit the soldier twice on the head with the wine cup. Wolf staggered, cursed, and pitched forward to the floor.

David set aside the cup, shaking his head. "With fighting skills as pitiful as yours, you want to go to Spain?"

Will worked his jaw to ascertain that it wasn't broken. "Thanks for your help. But you didn't even know what I was about."

David shrugged. He knelt and touched the large artery in Wolf's neck. The royal messenger groaned softly. "True. What did the note say?"

* * *

Gabriella heard footsteps outside her door. She tensed, her fists pressing her stomach in a gesture that had become instinctive in the past weeks. It could be Specter with her supper. Or King Henry, bleary with drink and hungry for her.

Or perhaps her desperate message had reached Will.

She stood beneath the window, with the golden sunset spreading into the room and trepidation pounding in her chest.

A murmur of male voices drifted through the thick door. She heard the jingle of keys, the metallic click of the lock, and then a thud she could not identify.

The door opened. A man in royal livery stepped over the fallen body of Specter and into the room.

"Your lute, my lady," he said, leaning the instrument against the open door, then striding toward her.

She shrank back. But her gaze clung to him, to the tufts of red hair peeking from beneath his hat, the spray of freckles across his nose.

"Will!" She rushed forward, letting his strong arms enfold her as she pressed her cheek to his chest. Giddy joy blazed through her. At last, she thought. At last she could hope for freedom. Will lifted her off the floor and swung her around, whispering meaningless words into her tangled hair.

"Oh, Will," she said when he set her down. "It's a miracle. You've come to me."

"How could I not?" Nervousness edged his voice. "Come, we haven't much time. Have you a pair of shoes and something discreet to wear?"

She nodded, hurrying to the chest at the end of the bed. "You have a terrible bruise on your jaw," she said.

"Rescuing damsels in distress is a dirty business."

While she shoved her feet into a pair of felt slippers and tucked her hair into a coif, he gazed around the room.

'' 'Tis a strange, gilded cage Henry has furnished for you.''

''Is Specter dead?'' She was surprised at the lack of emotion in her voice.

''God, I hope not. I don't need a death on my conscience, too. It's bad enough I left Uncle David to concoct some story for the messenger who brought me the lute.'' He grasped Specter under the arms and dragged him into the room. ''Is there anything you need to take with you?''

She glanced around the elegant prison, the brocaded counterpane on the bed, the jasper goblet—all gifts from Henry. Her fingers sneaked to the inner seam of her skirt and touched the small bulge of Armando's ring.

''No, Will,'' she whispered, reaching for his hand. ''I have everything I need.''

He locked the door behind him and they hurried down the stairs. The gathering evening dimmed the long corridors of the house she had never seen save for the locked tower room. A vaulted ceiling and columns of stone, dark rooms and high windows facing the river. For the first time, she realized just how isolated she had been. If Will had not come . . .

''Through here,'' he whispered, pulling her into a small passageway that opened out upon a garden. Roses and asters perfumed the air. A low gate, its latch rusted with age, stood between the wall and the river. Will pushed it open, and they fled into the night.

CHAPTER 16

"I can't see a thing," grumbled Armando, crouched low on the sand of a strange beach. In the moonless night, the forest behind them was impenetrable, a black curtain. He jabbed Santiago in the ribs. "We're lost, aren't we?"

His father groaned. "A gypsy is never lost so long as he can feel the earth beneath his feet."

Armando cursed under his breath. He could not see Paloma, but sensed her presence nearby. "I'm sorry, *chica*," he said into the darkness. "We've been separated from the others since the storm. Our boat leaks and our supplies are gone. And we seem no closer to your parents than we were a fortnight ago."

He heard the soft sound of her breathing, and then her voice. "At sunrise, we'll take on fresh supplies and water."

Santiago snorted. "What makes you think there's fresh water nearby?"

"I can smell it."

"Oh? Then how about smelling your way to the source? We haven't had water in days, save the rain we swallowed in the storm."

"Leave her alone," Armando snapped. A mosquito roared in his ear. "She's just as thirsty as you are."

"No," said Paloma. "Santiago gave me his bottle of water."

The gentle gratitude in her voice rankled Armando. Almost as much as it rankled him that he had not thought to share his own rations with her. He rolled over on his back. The stars sparkled in a milky band across the sky, so thick and brilliant that it seemed they must light up the world. Yet he could see only the white ribbons of the breaking waves on the shore.

"Very well," he said, tasting blood from his cracked lips. "This island—whatever it is—seems huge. Let's start looking."

They rose to their feet. Dizziness engulfed him; the lack of water was getting dangerous. He heard the swish of Paloma's tattered skirt. He could not pick out her form; she was an indistinct shape slightly more dense than the forest ahead.

Something brushed against his cheek. Shivering, he wondered what sort of venomous creatures haunted the night. In the weeks of searching, he had encountered snakes and scorpions, asps and adders, lizards and terrible spiders that could fell a grown man with one secret, unfelt sting.

Apprehension fueled his anger. "It's your fault we're lost, Santiago. If you hadn't insisted on pressing on when the storm came up, we never would have lost the guides and ended up here—wherever here is."

Behind him, Santiago said with exaggerated courtesy, "Oh, pardon me, Your Highness. I didn't realize you were leading this expedition."

"I didn't say I was—" A horrible sticky film brushed

his face, and he gasped, clawing at the clinging threads of
a large spider web. "Jesus!"

"Hush!" Paloma's voice cut in. "Listen."

They stopped walking. Armando cocked his head. He
had heard the sounds many times in the past: the hiss of
sand tumbled by the waves, the rustle of broad, thick
leaves, the strange clicking and buzzing of nocturnal insects, the scurrying of rodents hiding from owls. "Well?"
he asked.

She put her hand on his arm. "Listen harder."

He strained to sift through the sounds, and at last he
heard it: a steady, quiet gurgling.

"Water!" he cried, lifting her hand to his mouth and
pressing a kiss to her palm. "By God, you've found it!"

They moved faster, stumbling over rocks and roots. Before long, Armando could smell the water, too—a fresh
blue smell borne on the steady breeze. As they hurried
along, the moon rose. Pale fingers of light slipped through
the canopy of trees. Soon they saw a stream bursting out
of the heart of the hill.

The travelers fell to their knees and scooped the fresh
water into their mouths. Never had plain water tasted so
sweet to Armando. He swallowed hard, until his throat
ached. Flanking him, Paloma and Santiago drank just as
greedily.

After a few moments, she raised her head. He sensed
her tension. "What?" he asked between gulps. "What's
wrong?"

"Smoke," she whispered. "I smell sm—"

"Ahh!" A howl of pain burst from Santiago. Armando
jumped up to see a black shape tumbling down the hill.

Instinctively his hand went to the hilt of his sword. He
had the blade halfway out of its sheath when another shape
flew at him, hurled him backward into the stream. His
hands felt the dried *bija* dye on the islander's skin.

He heard Paloma cry out in her native tongue. His head

slammed against a rock. For a moment, the same stars
that lit the sky winked behind his eyes. Then his vision
cleared. He could see the arc of the spear's path as it drove
toward his gut. He could see Paloma lunge for his attacker.

The spear pierced his flesh. He felt the livid burn of the
poisoned tip, and then he could see nothing, nothing at
all.

A ring of grave-faced islanders watched Paloma.

She sat in the middle of the village while the sun rose
over a cluster of thatched *bohíos*. The settlement was nestled in a clearing surrounded by a cypress swamp on three
sides and a stand of mangroves on the fourth. She was
reminded of the moated fortresses in Naples. So secluded
was the village that a traveler a bow shot away might pass
by without noticing it. Beyond the swamp rose hills
cloaked in green, layer upon layer of lush mountains, the
peaks fading into mist. Armando had been right about the
immensity of the island.

"Where is the *cacique*?" she asked in her native tongue.

"No questions, woman," said a man, toying with the
cotton strap woven around his bare ankle.

"Please, just tell me where we are."

"No questions," he repeated.

Shifting restively on the cool earth, she craned her neck
to see Armando and Santiago. Her friends lay wounded,
maybe dying, some yards away. Their hands were bound
and tied to stakes pounded into the ground. Neither man
moved. Blood soaked into the ground from the wound in
Armando's side.

"I wish you'd let me help my friends," she said.

The man looked up at her, and she studied the shape of
his mouth, the set of his shoulders. Like the landscape,
he seemed familiar to her in some vague, unfathomable
way. And yet he had shown no recognition when she had

told him her Arawak name, Kairi, and the names of her parents, Anacaona and the Spaniard called Guahiro.

"No," he said at length. He seemed to be of an age with Santiago, about forty rains, with leathery skin and coarse, straight hair. "If it's the will of the gods that they live, then they will live."

"Then cut them loose and give them water."

"No."

Paloma sighed and sank back on her heels. The man's statement bothered her, for it pointed out how vastly she had changed during her years of exile. No longer could she accept unquestioningly the custom of the island clans. The infirm were put out in a hammock, given food and water, and left alone. If they died, it was because it was time, and they would go to the island of the Otherworld.

But living with the clans across the sea had opened her eyes to a world of differences, had shaken the totems that had guided her, had disrupted the central core of her girl-hood beliefs. If Doña Antonia had left Paloma alone with the smallpox, she would not have survived.

"How long have you lived like the Outsiders?" asked the man.

She blinked; she had not realized her thoughts were so transparent. "It has been many rains since the slavers took me."

"You should have killed yourself," he suggested matter-of-factly. "Crossing over to the Next World is better than living in bondage with the Spaniards."

She nodded, neither shocked nor insulted by his sug-gestion. "I was young and frightened. I had no weapon."

He eyed her bedraggled skirt, her blouse worn thin by days in sun and sea. "You admire the Outsiders."

"No!" Her response came swiftly, almost violently. "I . . . some of them are my friends." She gestured at the unmoving forms tied to the stakes. "Those two—they helped me escape. If not for the younger one, I would this moment be on an island called England, serving the *cacique* Henry Rex. If not for the older one, I would not have been permitted on the caravel that brought me back to the Cays of the Clear Sea.''

The man—captor or companion, she was not certain which—nodded mildly and dug his fingers in the sand, extracting a tiny spiral shell. ''So they're helping you find your parents.''

''Yes. We had guides, but we lost them in the storm.''

''More Spaniards?'' He looked hopeful. ''I would not mourn the loss of the iron-heads.''

She shook her head. ''All *guahiro*. I hope they survived.''

He rubbed the pad of his thumb over the shell, exposing its shiny inner pinkness. ''I, too.''

''You talk too much to the strange woman,'' grumbled one of the older men, this one dark, his back and chest ornate with ritual scarring.

''I'm no stranger!'' Paloma said fiercely. ''I am clan born!''

''Ha!'' The scarred man snorted. ''Look at you, with your pale skin and long garments, your worry for your Spanish captors. You don't belong with us.''

Paloma pressed her lips together to seal off a retort. It was no good to argue. She studied the village more closely. A palisade of hollow reed palm stalks, camouflaged by living vines, surrounded the cluster of *bohías*. Tiny flies hovered in a gray cloud above the kitchen midden at the edge of the settlement. Near an opening in the palisade were stacked bundles of spears and arrows. Her gaze drifted idly over them; then she blinked, suddenly grasping the significance of them.

''You're a war clan,'' she said.

''Be silent, woman,'' the scarred man ordered.

Paloma stuck her chin in the air. ''I have a right to know.''

The man made a guttural sound in his throat. He drew back his hand to strike her. Paloma did not shrink or flinch. She had endured far worse from her masters in Spain.

The younger man's hand stopped the other's fist. "Don't be a fool," he whispered. "Her fate is for the *cacique* to decide."

"What if the *cacique* doesn't come?"

Paloma pounded her fist in the sandy earth. "Doesn't come? You mean he's not even here, not even in the village?"

The scarred man narrowed his eyes. "The *cacique* will come when the time is right. Until then, you must speak no more."

Perhaps the war clan was too big for one camp, she thought. Frustrated beyond words, she closed her eyes and listened to the breeze in the tamarind trees, the mangroves and cypresses, and the distant roar and swish of the sea. She must have dozed off, for the sun had begun its ascent when she opened her eyes.

She immediately sought her companions. Armando and Santiago still lay where she had last seen them. Santiago was cursing softly—gypsy words drawn from his parched throat. Armando had not moved. The pool of blood was the size of a platter.

Paloma made a strangled sound of despair. The man who had spoken to her earlier dropped to his knees beside her. His tone was mild as he said, "The young one suffers from poisoning. The bleeding drains the venom out."

His words failed to comfort her. Her gaze clung to Armando. How pale he looked, how thin and vulnerable. Always, he had been strong and sure of himself, even tender with her when she allowed it. She had not liked his touch. She did not like remembering all the ways she had been brutalized. It made her ache in her heart for the treasure she had lost.

But she had found contentment working with him on his

farm. The inevitable tide of Spaniards was an evil thing, but men like Armando could live peaceably with the clans of the islands. He treated the natives with respect. Guiltily, she bridled her thoughts. The Spaniards—Armando included—were destroying life as she once knew it.

The low boom of a drumbeat caught her attention.

"The *cacique* comes," said her companion.

Villagers lined up on each side of the opening in the palisades. A man and woman entered the settlement. The scarred man hurried to them, spoke and gestured at Paloma.

The man and woman turned toward her and broke into a run. A trembling started inside Paloma, a moment of awe and disbelief. She shot to her feet. Her knees buckled, but the younger man snatched her arm to steady her.

Mother. Her lips formed the word but no sound came out. Then she was running, the sand burning her bare feet.

They met in the central plaza of the settlement. Paloma froze. Tears streamed down their faces; lines of sorrow and heartbreak bracketed their eyes.

Then the moment of painful confusion passed. Joseph and Anacaona took her in their arms. She felt their strong, desperate embrace. She drew in a deep breath; the smell of her mother's hair and skin was so poignantly familiar that fresh tears stung her eyes.

"Look at you," said her father, speaking the language of the islanders. "My little Kairi, my child of the morning."

A wave of grief rushed over Paloma. The Spaniards had stolen all innocence from her. But she would not darken the moment with old horrors. Her gaze went to her father. "You are *cacique*?"

Joseph stooped and touched the ground by his wife's feet in an ancient gesture of deference. "Not I, my daughter."

Paloma turned to her mother. "You?"

Anacaona nodded, her shell and feather headdress brushing her bare shoulders. "After the slavers raided Cayo Moa, we came here to live with the tribe of my brother, Caonobo. When he died, I became *cacique*."

"Here? I don't even know where we are."

Joseph and Anacaona exchanged a covert look. "You're on Española. Many leagues to the east of Santo Domingo. The Spaniards don't know we've made a settlement here."

Stunned, Paloma caught her breath. All the weeks of searching, and her parents had been here, on Española. She grew light-headed with a feeling of futility. "We have been searching for months. We sent messages all through the islands. How could you not have known I was looking for you?"

Joseph took her hands. "We've been away. Far away."

"Searching for a place to live in peace," Anacaona added, "and to fight for our freedom, if we must."

Seeing Paloma's worried gaze stray to the piles of weaponry, Joseph hugged her again. His beard, streaked with white, chafed her cheek. "Tell us everything."

"I will," she said. "But first we must see to my friends. One of them was your friend, too, long ago." She pointed at the two men lying on the ground.

"Dios!" Joseph shouted.

The three of them hurried toward Santiago and Armando. The latter lay unmoving, but Santiago dragged himself up on one elbow and shook the hair from his eyes to stare up at Joseph.

"So, *compadre*," he said, jerking at his bound hands. "I bring your daughter back and this is the thanks I get?" His tone was teasing, and in spite of the large bluish lump on his head, he managed a broad, engaging grin.

Joseph dropped to his knees to saw at Santiago's bonds with an onyx knife. "Still the same worthless gypsy, I see." He, too, spoke lightly, but once the bonds were cut, he gathered Santiago in an embrace and exhaled in a shuddering sigh. "By God, it's been nineteen years! I never thought to see you again."

Santiago kissed him loudly on each cheek. "Don't worry, *compadre*, you'll be sick of me soon."

"And you brought Paloma home. How can I repay you?"

Santiago reached for Armando's hand. "Help me. My son caught a poisoned spear."

"Your son?" Joseph gaped at the unconscious man.

"This is Armando," Paloma explained, cradling his head upon her knees. Unthinkingly she stroked his hot, dry brow and directed a pleading look at her mother. "Can you save him?"

Anacaona's smile was cautious. "If the gods will it."

Panic gave way to anger. "*Not* if the gods will it," she snapped. Seeing her mother's face pale, Paloma tempered her tone. "Please, I meant no offense. But I have learned that healing is not always a matter of letting an illness run its course. There are things we can do. . . ."

Anacaona turned away.

I've found her only to realize I'm still lost, thought Paloma.

To her surprise, Anacaona called over her shoulder. "Malak! Bring help!"

While Anacaona untied Armando's bonds, Paloma stared at the man who had sat with her through the night. "Malak?" she said as he and two others ran forward to bear Armando away. "You're my brother?"

He nodded. Now she saw clearly the resemblance she had only suspected earlier. Her older brother had their mother's smooth brow, her delicately formed lips, and strong-limbed grace. She had known him only through her mother's stories, for he had gone adventuring with Colón himself, years before.

"I wanted to tell you," he said. "But the times have

made us cautious.'' He and his companions started to lift
Armando.

"Be careful,'' Paloma begged, the concern in her voice
drawing a sharp look from her mother. "He's been badly
wounded.''

They took Armando to the *cacique*'s *bohía* and laid him
in a hammock. Malak left while Anacaona, Joseph, and
Santiago gathered around. Morning sunlight made shifting
patterns on the floor mats. There was a stillness, a long,
breath-held moment.

Then Joseph spoke. "Tell us.''

Anacaona busied herself with cleansing the wound while
Paloma poured her story out, a flood unleashed. Out of
habit and out of deference to Santiago, she spoke in Castilian. She told of her capture, of falling ill from smallpox,
of a lady who had healed and sheltered her.

She sent a questioning look to Santiago. He gave a tiny
shake of his head. Antonia had begged them never to reveal her existence to Joseph; they felt bound to honor that
request.

She told her parents she had been sold in servitude to
the Duke of Albuquerque. She saw her father's shoulders
stiffen, saw his eyes flash with comprehension and then
rage. She rushed on, hoping to divert his anger, and explained about her voyage to England, her brief stay at the
court of Henry VIII. Of her most painful torment, she said
nothing at all.

She stared at the ravaged face of the man in the hammock. "He battled for my freedom, and won,'' she said.
"He had to leave everything behind to get me home. I
owe him much.''

"Then we cannot let him die,'' Anacaona vowed.

The pain in his side burned like a glowing brand. His
eyelids felt thick, his lashes gummy as he tried to open
them. And the thirst, *Dios*, the thirst! His throat was

parched, his lips cracked, and his tongue hard and dry as a block of wood.

Perhaps he was in Hell. But no, he heard voices speaking the Arawak tongue; the smell of roasting fish hung in the air. For a moment, he savored the pleasant, suspended sensation of lying very still in a hammock.

Armando put out his tongue to wet his lips. It felt like dragging sandpaper over rough timber. Something hard pressed at his mouth. The edge of a drinking gourd, the trickle of cool water. Armando drank until he choked. A hand lifted him, patted him sharply on the back.

Revived from the half-sleep of fever, he rubbed his eyes until they opened. He saw dark hair surrounded by a nimbus of light. "Gabriella?" His muddled thoughts spoke his yearning.

"It's me, Paloma."

Her rough velvet voice brought memories rushing back: The search for water, the surprise attack, the bright agony of a spear thrust, the blackness of poisoned oblivion.

He lifted his head. "More water. Please."

She moved close, steadying him by cradling the back of his neck in her hand. Sunlight flowed through the reed walls; the sky was a patch of blue through the low doorway. He drank convulsively, then grasped the ropes of the hammock.

"Please don't move." Paloma leaned forward, placed her hand over his. "You're wounded."

He scowled down at himself, his bare suntanned chest, a pile of broad, damp leaves covering the fiery ache in his side.

"So. Are they going to eat us alive, or what? Are they marinating me?"

For a moment she looked offended; then she smiled. Not her usual almost-smile that always made him want to coax more out of her, but a wide unstoppable grin he had never seen before.

Jolted by the sheer beauty of her face, he asked, "Finally started to appreciate my jokes, eh?"

"No."

"Then why are you smiling?"

"Because this is the village of my parents."

"*Dios!* You mean we found them?"

"They—or some of the villagers—found us."

"Damn!" He looked at her expectantly. "Well?"

"You'll meet them soon."

"That's not what I was asking. How was it, finding them again?" While he waited for her answer, he felt curiously cheated. He had not realized until now how eagerly he had anticipated seeing the reunion, the joy on Paloma's face, the lifting of the shadows that had hung over her since the first moment he had met her in Seville. At the same time, he felt a sinking sensation. She was home now. He would lose her forever.

"It was like waking from a dream," she explained, forming her words carefully, "to find that it was not a dream at all."

An ache rose in his chest, more painful than the wound in his flesh. He had no parents, only two men who had lied to him, and a woman who had done nothing to rectify the betrayal.

"To find that you made *their* dreams come true." He forced a smile. "I'm glad for you."

"And I'm grateful to you. But . . ." She let her voice trail off, and again he saw the sadness in the depths of her eyes.

"What?" he asked. "Talk to me, Paloma."

Hearing the raspiness in his voice, she gave him the drinking gourd. "So many years have passed. All of us have changed, especially me."

"But you knew that, you were prepared for that."

"I wasn't prepared for the hurt." She shook her head in disgust. "Look at me, Armando. Dressed as a Spanish woman, speaking and thinking and dreaming in Castilian. When I was a child, I had a perfect sense of myself. I knew who I was and where I belonged. Now I don't. The Spaniards have shaken my beliefs, taken my innocence, made me ashamed to go about naked in the way of my clan. How will I live with them again?''

"You're strong, Paloma," he said, angry because the reunion had not had the magic healing power he had anticipated. "If you let yourself be haunted by the past, then you'll never be free." On a surge of strength, he swung his legs over the side of the hammock and sat up, grasping her hands. "It's not enough just to survive. You have to win. You have to push all the bad years out of your life."

"I don't know if I can do that, Armando."

"You will." He squeezed her hands. She gazed at him with an odd look in her eyes. "Now, where the devil are we?"

Her smile held a tinge of irony. "You won't believe it."

"If you say England, I'll know you have a sense of humor."

"We're on Española, in the western hills."

"Española!"

She took a round, flat *batata* cake from a basket and handed it to him. "The storm blew us back here when we were in the Maisi Passage. My clan has been here for years."

He tasted the cake, made of a bright orange tuber fruit, enjoying the nutty flavor. "Why would they settle so close to the Spaniards who hunt them?"

She hesitated, then said, "The conquerors don't know about this settlement. If need be, the clan will mount a resistance against the invaders."

Armando's heart sank. "That's suicide. The natives have no defense against Spanish guns and swords. Besides, you're vastly outnumbered."

"In this settlement, yes." The avid look on her face

troubled him. "But my parents have been in contact with other clans of warriors to the north."

Her naive hope angered him. "Surely you, of all people, know the Spaniards, their greed and their conviction that they're God's elect."

She gripped his hands. "And you will come to know us, Armando. We are a strong people."

Paloma never roamed far from Armando's side during the long days of his recovery. The poisoned wound had weakened him more than he would admit, but only her constant vigilance kept him from leaping out of the hammock.

When he met her parents, he used his most gallant manners, masking his curiosity. With Santiago he was abrasive and surly as ever, a fact that gave Paloma great hope for his recovery.

Santiago seemed hopeful, too, for as they stood together one afternoon watching Armando sleep, he spoke of the future for the first time. "His plantation won't hold much allure for him after this adventure."

Paloma looked at him sharply. "Why not?"

"You've led him on a high adventure, made a hero of him, *preciosa*. He'll not take to the yoke of gentleman planter easily after this." Santiago shook his head. "Pity."

"How can you know that?" she demanded. "And why is it such a pity?"

"Because he's going to get his heart broken." Santiago's smile became distant, and he spoke as if she were not there. "I had a chance—one chance, mind you, a man never gets more than that—to settle down, to build a stable life with the woman I loved. But I threw that chance to the wind for the sake of adventure. And now I regret it."

"The woman," Paloma said shyly. "She was Armando's mother?"

Santiago's eyebrows lifted. "How did you know?"

She suppressed a smile. "You all but turn into a poet at the very mention of her name."

"What else is a gypsy if not a poet?" He sighed. "There's naught to do about it now, but I can help my son. Tell me about this girl he has his heart set on. Is she worth dying for?"

Paloma thought of the girl she had known so briefly. Gabriella Flores had made a vivid impression. Paloma remembered the lovely face, serene as a painted Madonna's, yet piquant with lively humor and intelligence. Most memorable of all was the voice, Gabriella's pure, sweet singing that could captivate a roomful of people, be they princes, prelates, or peasants. And yet her overall impression was one of fragile vulnerability.

With complete honesty, Paloma said, "Yes, she is worth it."

Paloma and Anacaona worked in the *bohía* early one morning, fletching arrows while Armando slept in the hammock. They had left the bandage off, and Paloma could see the healing pink scar in his side below his rib cage.

"He'll be well soon," said Anacaona, following her gaze.

Paloma ran her thumb down the edge of a lime-colored parrot feather. "We never used to spend so much time making arrows."

"When I was your age, we made weapons only for hunting and harpooning. It's all happened so quickly, so inevitably." Anacaona brushed a wiry gray hair from her cheek. "The Spaniards are like the waves. Without number, they never cease, never rest. Wherever we go, they will find us."

"How can we fight them? Can't we learn to live with them?"

"Can a bird learn to live with a fish?"

Paloma glanced again at Armando. He looked beautiful—pale and relaxed, with dark hair spilling over his brow, his muscular chest rising and falling in gentle slumber. She felt a queer tugging sensation somewhere deep inside her. Her fingers grew clumsy, and she dropped the feathers.

When she looked back at her mother, she saw that Anacaona's face was full of sad wisdom. "You love him, don't you?"

Startled, Paloma shook her head. "We've been through many trials together. But I don't love him. I can't."

"Why not? Your father is a Spaniard, yet he became the mate of my heart, practically from the first moment I met him."

"It's best I never think of Armando in that way."

"Best for you? Or for Armando?"

"For us both."

But her mother's insight broke open a secret Paloma had kept buried in her heart, hidden even from herself. Now she knew the truth in all its pain-filled glory.

She wondered when she had started to love him. Had it been that first day in Seville, when he had chased her down, fought Baltasar de León to keep her safe, and taken her to Doña Antonia's?

Or had she started to love him later, after the years of despair and suffering had culminated in her voyage to England? Yes, it was probably the day he had bested Henry Rex and forfeited his future to take her home.

How much more could a woman ask from a man?

As she moved through quiet, sun-gilt days, as she helped her clan gird itself for battle, she embraced the sweet ache of her unfulfilled love. It left no room for food, and she grew thin, ignoring her mother's cajoling. It left no time for sleep, and she became restive and hollow-eyed.

She felt strangely detached from clan matters as her thoughts focused on the man gaining strength under her care. Inevitably, she remembered Gabriella, as beautiful as any Christian's vision of the Holy Mother. For Gabriella, Armando was building a home, building a life. And Paloma had helped him, persuading native people to work with him in the foolish hope of teaching birds to live with fish. All for Gabriella.

Paloma did not begrudge the Spanish beauty her good fortune. Doña Gabriella was born to bring Armando joy. Paloma was born for a purpose she had yet to fathom. She was not right for Armando, nor for any man. The secret that lurked in her past imprisoned her heart forever.

One day, as the clan prepared a feast to invoke the favor of the gods for their enterprise, she went into the *bohía* to find Armando standing, drinking with gusto from a tipped-up *cujete*.

Sunlight streamed through the slats of the hut and gleamed on his bare chest. His brown throat rippled with each swallow. His hair tumbled down his back, and the scar below his rib cage was darkening.

Paloma felt a pulse of awareness deep in her belly. She wondered in amazement at the sensation, welcomed it, for the bonds that had chained her emotions were finally loosening.

"It's good to see you up," she said.

He lowered the gourd abruptly and turned. He grinned, then wiped his mouth with the back of his hand.

"It's good to be up, *chica*. God, I could roar like a lion!" He beckoned with his arm. "Come here, Paloma."

She hesitated, then moved forward to be drawn against him, against his smooth flesh and his fragrance of sweat and fresh pineapple juice. He bent low, brushed a kiss on her brow. Her skin tingled at the feather-light touch.

"That," he said, "is for tending me day and night while I was sick." He kissed her again, pressing his mouth to her temple. "And that is to show you how glad I am that you've found your parents again." Finally he put his finger beneath her chin, tipped her face up to his, and kissed her on the mouth. The old instinct to withdraw never surfaced. She reveled in the silky slide of his lips against hers, in the bracing support of his arms. "And that," he said, smiling down into her astonished face, "is for being everything that you are."

She stepped back, her heart hammering. She moved her lips but could form no words. Then, in a blind panic of passion and hopeless love, she turned and fled.

Armando drew a shaky breath as he watched her go. His knees felt feeble suddenly, but he refused to seek the haven of the hammock. Holding Paloma in his arms gave him strength. Her very nearness was more potent than herbs and medicaments.

He strode to the door in time to see her running across the sandy plaza, her tattered skirt and black hair flying. The sight of her, the memory of her shattered expression after he had kissed her, broke his heart. How fragile she was, the woman who had helped him regain his honor and build a plantation in Santo Domingo. The woman who had become his best friend.

He shook his head. Paloma did not need his kisses. She needed her family, and she had them now. Better he should get himself back to Santo Domingo.

The thought shot an arrow through his heart. He had dreamed of Gabriella in his feverish sleep, had felt sick with missing her. Hurry, he pleaded silently. Hurry.

His gaze stayed on Paloma's form until she disappeared through the gate in the palisades and slipped into the mountain forest.

The night sounds pulsed in tandem with the drumbeats of the musicians at the manioc ceremony. Firelight splashed like golden rain in changing patterns over the crowd. The rich smells of cassava bread, roasting fish, and *barbacoa* mingled with the aroma of flowers and smoke.

Paloma sat unseen in the shadows beyond the plaza, her knees drawn to her chest and her watchful gaze on the scene framed by a fringe of *yaruma* leaves. Armando sat with her parents, a clay platter of fish on the sand in front of him. He ate with a healthy appetite while listening intently to Joseph.

Armando seemed so easy with them, so relaxed. She resented that, for a part of her remained a stranger to her parents, the hidden aching part that had been plundered and violated.

It was appropriate, she decided, that she sat here alone and invisible, watching as if from afar. The secret would always be a wall between her and all people.

"Why don't you join the feast, *preciosa*?"

Startled, she looked up at Santiago. "You're learning to move as quietly as an islander."

He grinned and drew her to her feet. His sturdy rough hand felt oddly comforting. "Do you think it strange that your people celebrate when their certain doom lies on the horizon?"

She shuddered at the darkness in his voice. "They have no choice."

"They?"

She trembled anew, then stilled herself. Being home gave her the strength to speak from the heart. "I'm no longer one of them."

He tugged at her hands. "What foolishness is this? You're clan born. The years you spent as a slave are nothing. Nothing!"

She stared through the leaves at the circle of light. Some of the young men and women were getting up, starting to dance to the music of snail-shell rattles and pipes and maguey drums. "The Spaniards made me ashamed to go naked in the way of my people, made me afraid to sing the songs of the Ancients, to pray to our four brother gods. I am neither Castilian nor Taino, but a miserable Christian-ized slave who cannot live with either!''

"No! God, no!'' A cry of pain tore from his throat, and he reached for her, pulled her close to cradle her head against his chest. "Not you, Paloma. Don't torment your-self.''

She understood his passion. "You were hurt, too. You were made to feel an outsider.''

"Aye.'' He swayed, rocking her from side to side as he spoke. "We're the walking wounded, you and I, Paloma. I too had fears when I was young. My fears nearly de-stroyed me, but then I met Rafael. He seems quiet and meek, but inside he is a lion. He forced me to face my fears, to go back to their source and do battle with them. You must do the same, *preciosa—*''

"Let her go.'' The low, deadly voice intruded like a sword thrust.

Paloma and Santiago broke apart to face Armando, who stood backlit by the bonfire. She could not see his face, but could read his fury in the rigid set of his shoulders.

Santiago swore. "Armando, don't leap to conclu-sions.''

"Just stay away from her! I know you're used to having your way with women, but I never thought you'd stoop to seducing your best friend's daughter.''

"Armando,'' Santiago began again. "If you'd just lis-ten—''

"Listen!'' He gave a bark of laughter. "Oh, I've lis-tened to you. To your lies, your advice, your orders to have me beaten half to death. Why must you defile every-thing I hold dear?''

"Why must you always assume the worst of me?''

Armando laughed. "Do you really need an answer to that?''

Santiago's eyes narrowed to slits. "I suppose not.''

"Why do you stay here anyway?" Armando demanded. "Don't you have business in Santo Domingo?"

"Not anymore, I don't." Santiago's voice lowered. "I've decided to stay with Joseph and the clan."

Paloma saw Armando's back snap as if he had been whipped. "You're staying? Why?"

"They need me," Santiago reported. "When no one else does."

"You think Paloma needs you? No one needs a lying, thieving gyp—"

Santiago's hand struck Armando's face. The violent crack jerked Paloma out of her silence. "Stop it! Stop it, now!"

Hearing the rage in her voice, they turned to face her. She didn't allow herself to think. She grasped the neckline of her blouse and ripped the garment down the middle. "You sicken me, both of you. You fight and curse each other. You speak of me as if I were still a slave, still a piece of property."

She flung the blouse and skirt to the ground along with her smallclothes and kicked the garments away with heart-felt contempt. "I belong to no one. I won't be part of your world anymore!" She stood naked in the darkness. Only maidens went completely uncovered; women who had been mated wore *naguas* around their waists. She was a maiden no more, but she burned to deny what had been done to her, what had been taken from her.

She felt their astonishment as she backed away toward the plaza. "Don't quarrel over me," she said. "Leave me alone!" She turned and ran, swift and silent as a night bird, and burst out into the firelight.

Armando stared, gape-mouthed, as Paloma joined her clan. Santiago was speaking, offering fierce denials, but Armando barely heard.

He walked slowly back to the plaza. The people were

dancing in earnest now, leaping and whirling to the drums
that pulsed like the beating of a heart. Pipes shrilled and
gourds rattled. Shell anklets and bracelets clicked as voices
called to the pagan gods of the night and the wind. Sleek
maidens wearing nothing but flower garlands lifted long
green branches to the sky.

Armando absorbed it all as a vague blur of motion and
sound. He stood rooted at the edge of the plaza, his entire
awareness focused on Paloma.

Naked save for her necklace of shells and feathers, she
joined the dancing. The firelight rippled over her slim
body. Her bare feet pattered rhythmically on the bare earth
while her unbound hair swirled about her face and shoulders and breasts.

Riveted by the sight of her, by the fierce joy on her face,
Armando found it difficult to sift through his emotions. At
first, the unclad island women had been a novelty. He had
been pleasantly shocked and titillated by the brown breasts,
the curling private hair, the curve of a buttock. But the
sight soon became commonplace.

Paloma was different. He could not regard her as other
island women. Her outburst showed him a new side of
her. He realized how torn she was between her clan and
the Spaniards who had stolen her away, baptized her, and
forced her to serve them.

This, then, was her rebellion, the final shaking off of
her bonds, and it was glorious and frightening to watch.
She was graceful and feral. Her round, full breasts capped
by the dark medallions of her nipples swung bare, wearing
only the orange light of the fire. Armando stared at the
triangle of hair nestled between her thighs, and at the muscled contours of her buttocks and legs.

He became aware of his own labored breathing, the heat
in his loins. Shamed by his desire, he tried to look away.
But she captivated him, tugging at an invisible thread that
seemed to connect them. She played on his senses like a

song in motion, fluid and wild, frankly sensuous. He could not swallow past the hot ache in his throat.

As he watched from the edge of the circle of dancers, a youth approached Paloma. Although Armando was ignorant of the meaning of specific gestures, he recognized the look of passion in the young man's eyes.

A lightning bolt of fury struck Armando. Perhaps it was the youth's possessive self-confidence. Perhaps it was the flicker of panic in Paloma's eyes.

The islanders were uninhibited in their mating habits. They loved openly and loyally, and saw no shame in expressing passion. No one thought it strange or sinful that the youth stepped into the shadows and beckoned to Paloma.

Armando held his breath. For no reason he could fathom, he found himself wanting to beg her not to go. He forced himself to stay still and silent. Paloma had to return to her clan. He had gambled his own future to see that she did. She needed to take this step, to find an island mate and make a life with him.

The torn expression on her face broke his heart. She shook her head. The youth scowled and reached for her hand. A cry burst from her. She left the circle of fire as quickly as she had entered it, plunging through the palisade gate and racing toward the stream that trickled down from the heights.

The young man started after her; a single word from Joseph stopped him. Armando knew with chilling certainty that she should not be alone at this moment. He also knew that, if Santiago had seen what he'd seen, Santiago would follow her, find her, then. . . .

Armando left the settlement and ran in the direction Paloma had gone. He found her at the lagoon where the water poured off the mountain into a pool bordered by smooth rocks. She stood submerged to her shoulders, her head thrown back and her eyes closed. A sound of desperation sprang from her throat.

"Paloma."

She turned to face him. "Go away, Armando."

"I want to help you." He stepped down the bank where the cool water lapped at his feet. Feeling awkward, he said, "I'm worried about you. I don't like to see you unhappy."

"Then leave. You have fulfilled your vow to bring me home."

He made a helpless gesture with his arms. "I thought it would be simple. It was stupid of me to believe you would just pick up where you left off. It'll happen, maybe not tonight, but soon you'll feel one with your clan again. Don't expect so much of yourself."

"Leave me," she repeated. "My life is no longer your concern. Already I've caused you to fight with your father."

He listened to the gentle swish of the water. "The fight was not your fault. We always fight. I'm sorry for what happened with Santiago. When I saw you in his arms, I lost my temper."

"Why? Because you hate him, or . . . ?" She looked away, leaving him to wonder what she was thinking.

"Because he makes free with women, seeks only to please himself. I didn't want him to hurt you."

She laughed without humor. "Armando, I have endured hurt beyond anything Santiago could ever do to me."

He stepped farther down the bank, stretched his arms out to her. "Why don't you come out of the water? We could . . . talk." Only then did he remember that she was naked, that facing her in this state would be disconcerting.

She hugged herself protectively. In the silvery moonlight she resembled a mother cradling a babe. "What is there left to talk about, Armando?"

"I don't know." He waded in up to his knees.

Very slowly, she reached out. Their fingers touched; then he gripped her hand and drew her toward the bank. She rose from the water, her body streaked by moonlight and shadows, her face wary and beautiful. She was a pagan goddess, lush and earthy as the thick-tongued orchids that grew wild in the forests. It seemed a sin against nature that, inside, she should be so cold and remote.

She filled his mind completely, driving out all thoughts save those of her: her pain, her loneliness. "Ah, Paloma, I want to kiss you. But the last time I did, you ran away." He pressed his palm to hers, laced their fingers together. "This time, it's up to you. I won't make a move unless you tell me you want it."

"What I want," she whispered, "is to stop being afraid."

He drew her closer and ran his hand up her arm, soft and wet with spring water. "Does this frighten you?"

She nodded. He started to pull away, but she clutched at him. "Help me, Armando. Help me chase away the fear."

He moved so slowly that restraint made him tremble. Long, aching seconds passed as he pulled her closer, felt the brush of her breasts against his chest, felt the sigh of her breath on his cheek. Then he kissed her. She was darkness and mystery, a challenge to the vow he had made to take no woman but his wife.

The promise fell away, dissolved like sugar in the water swirling around their feet. Her lips were soft, her body cool, relaxing against him. She seemed as hungry as he, her mouth pliant beneath his and her hands skimming over his bare shoulders and down his back.

There were reasons, he thought vaguely, that he should not be doing this, but for the life of him he could not remember a single one. He and Paloma seemed locked away from the world, sheltered in the splendor of the fragrant woods with no roof but the star-sprayed heavens.

Paloma's heart took her mind by surprise. She had touched Armando before, had soothed his wounds, but this was different. The impossible was happening. Despite the years of torture and degradation, despite the crimes against her body and her spirit, a new, shining feeling rose through her. She wanted him. Wanted him inside her, embracing her intimately. She wanted to touch and know and feel the passion that others had turned to agony.

"Why is this different?" she breathed against his mouth, barely aware that she spoke aloud.

"Because it's as loving is meant to be. Sharing . . ." He touched his tongue to her lips. "Tenderness, honesty."

She pressed closer, opening her mouth beneath his. She felt his need, tasted the flavor of it on his lips, heard it in his rapid breathing. With an insight born of long friendship, she knew he would not make love to her unless she asked him.

"Will you, Armando?" she whispered, and he understood, rescued her from having to voice the words.

"Yes, Paloma. My God, yes." His hands slid down her back, warming her flesh. "I can't erase the memories, *querida*, but we can make new ones. Now. Tonight." He shuddered.

"Armando? Is something wrong?"

He gave a shaky smile and framed her face with his hands, his thumbs brushing her cheekbones. "No, my darling. Something's right, at long last. I've won your trust."

His words gave her courage. She placed her hands at his waist, her fingers twining in the leather laces of his breeches. He swallowed hard as if in pain, but his hands urged hers on. She helped him shed his clothes and then stood looking at him, all of him, his body lean and muscled, his arousal blatant, yet not in the least threatening. She touched him there, marveled at the ridged, silky flesh and the awed expression on his face.

"God, Paloma . . ." The words seemed torn from him, hoarse with pleasure. "Please, come lie with me. . . ."

The loamy ground still held the warmth of the sun. "Paloma." She loved the sound of her name whispered on the wind. No man had ever spoken her name like that. "Paloma, I don't want to hurt you. If you want me to stop, I will."

She lay very still in the curve of his arm. Then she said: "You won't hurt me, and I don't want you to stop."

He tasted the pulse at her neck and her wrist. Even as the pleasure crested over her, she felt empty, her womb aching in a way that transformed pain into joy.

Armando watched her face, marveling at the changing expressions. At some point, the guarded look had left her eyes; the tightness had left her mouth. She was lovely and mobile now, surrendering the past and offering up hope for the future. He wished he could take away the years of torture, bundle them up and burn them, but those years were a part of her past. Tonight he would become a part of her present and future. He prayed the power of his passion would quiet the torment in her heart.

He loved her slowly, carefully, treating her like a fragile treasure that would shatter at the slightest mishandling. She accepted his caresses with a round-eyed wonder that broke his heart, for he knew she had never experienced tenderness with a man before. He kissed her throat and her breasts, turned her and traced his tongue along the hollow of her back and behind her knees. Stealing glances at her face, he could tell that his actions startled her. And for that he was pleased. He thought that by focusing on her pleasure, he could keep his own rampant urges in check. But he was wrong. When he moved his hand up her thigh and touched her woman's place, when liquid warmth filled his palm and a cry of pleasure broke from her lips, he nearly came out of his skin with the pain of restraint.

He cursed aloud. Perhaps this was his punishment. Retribution for breaking an oath. And yet even as the self-recriminations jabbed at him, he felt her reach out, her touch like a brush of wildfire. His response was immedi-ate, a force blazing out of control until he sheathed himself inside her.

Nothing in his past could have prepared him for the sensation of joining himself with a woman's body. Her heat and wetness, his astonishing surge of pleasure, lifted him out of this world and dropped him into a strange new realm. She moved with him, whispering ancient words that sounded like an incantation. His voice joined hers, creating a savage, primal harmony that rose to the stars.

The joy and wonderment that shone in her eyes lifted him higher, beyond simple pleasure to a place of unearthly contentment. He had wanted to give her memories; instead she had given him her trust, the most fragile and precious gift of all.

The sound of the stream trickled into the long, stunned silence of afterlove. Armando could not shape what he was feeling in words, and so he told her with kisses and caresses, a language of the heart that was more eloquent than speech.

Soon they were loving each other again, and later they slept, the sweet exhaustion wrapping fronds of warmth around them.

But when the feathery light of dawn reached through the forest to touch his face, Armando awakened and grasped the enormity of what he had done. He sat up, saw no sign of Paloma, and groaned with agony.

He had broken his vow. Shattered it to pieces. He had done the one thing he despised Santiago for doing. Fooling himself with lofty ideas of healing, he had taken a woman in the heat of passion—without commitment, without honor, with no thought of the future.

"Oh, God!" His cry echoed across the lagoon. "Oh God, Gabriella!"

CHAPTER 17

Coria del Río, Spain
1510

Five miles from Seville, in a little town shadowed by the convent of Santa Inez, Gabriella emerged from a horse litter. The conveyance had borne her, in tortuous stages, from La Coruña to the heart of Andalucía. She blinked at the brightness of the Spanish sky. How strange the country of her birth seemed after the misty verdure of England. She was used to damp weather and green landscapes, gently rolling hills and cramped, chilly towns. Spain, in contrast, was raw and stark, hot and dry and dusty.

As her eyes adjusted to the light, she watched Will sift a handful of silver coins into the opened palm of the driver. The handsome amount made her wince. Will had paid their passage to Spain, had fed and housed her along the overland route. His unquestioning generosity filled her with affection and gratitude.

She sighed, lifting her thick braid away from her neck and wishing for a breeze. She should have insisted on traveling on foot or by mule, but Will's offer to hire a horse litter had been too tempting. Although the babe in her belly was still not evident, still a secret she kept even from Will, she felt ungainly, exhausted and vaguely ill. And so she had made the long expensive trip in the cubicle of the litter, listening to Will converse with the horsemen as he walked along beside them.

He bade the bearers farewell, then turned a dazzling smile on Gabriella. How could he always be so relentlessly cheerful?

"We've made it," he announced, reaching for her hand and drawing her toward the path that led to the convent. "You'll spend tonight with your mother. How long has it been?"

"Too long," she said, squelching her misgivings. "She left me in England nine years ago. We won't know each other."

He gave her hand a squeeze. "A mother never forgets her child. How could she? You're her flesh and blood. She'll be grandmother to the children you bear Armando."

Hot color stung Gabriella's cheeks. Had Will guessed her secret, then? No, he grinned at her with his usual candid expression of fondness. "My mother is different," she said. "She's always been very . . . detached. Spiritual, Doña Elvira used to say." Even so, Gabriella allowed herself a small hope. Perhaps when she confided her troubles to her mother, Mercedes would understand, would offer advice and help.

"Doña Elvira," Will spat, scowling. "I'd hoped we'd never hear her treacherous name again."

"It's doubtful that you will," Gabriella assured him. "King Henry banished her from England, and King Ferdinand is probably none too happy to have her back in Spain. Perhaps he'll send her to a post in Naples or Turkey. It would serve her—"

The clop of hoofbeats on the rocky road interrupted

her. A man wearing a blue cloak fastened with a silver badge drew rein and dismounted. *"Santa Hermandad,"* he said, lifting the brim of his hat. Before he replaced the broad-brimmed headpiece, Gabriella had a fleeting impression of long unshaven cheeks, thick eyebrows, a beak-like nose. The rider turned in a swirl of self-importance toward Will. "Papers, please."

Gabriella held her breath. This was not the first time the Castilian police had asked to see their traveling papers.

Will reached inside his jerkin and drew out a packet of worn and folded parchment. The official opened the passport and squinted at the script. "William Blythe of London, England."

"That's me, sir." Will caught Gabriella's eye and gave her a broad wink. He had taken the name from the song they had shared long ago. *My bonny, blithe William from over the sea* . . . The new name suited him. Certainly it was much safer than the frankly Jewish Shapiro, or his real name, Chávez of Toledo.

"So you're here to escort"—the official examined the traveling papers—"Doña Gabriella Flores to the convent."

"That's correct, sir."

The official refolded the papers and handed them back. Gabriella tried not to sag with relief. "Well, they'll not offer a bed to travelers today. It's the feast of Santa Inez, and they'll be observing strict silence."

"Santa who—"

Gabriella took hold of Will's elbow and gave it a pinch. "My English companion is unfamiliar with our Spanish holy days."

"Ah, of course," said Will.

"You'll have to find lodgings in town." The official pointed to a plaza dominated by a squat Romanesque church made of sandy brown stone. "There's an inn called the Postulant in the church square." He mounted his horse, tipped his hat once more. "You'll want to settle in before mass."

"Mass," grumbled Will as they walked down the rubbled road toward the inn. "What's this about mass?"

"To celebrate the feast of Santa Inez. Will, we have to go. This is a small town. The police will be watching us."

"They won't find me in a church any more than I'd find a Catholic in a synagogue."

"Hush!" Gabriella bit her lip. "I'm not sure you realize how serious this is. The slightest infraction—even something as small as bathing on Friday or cooking with oil instead of lard—could throw suspicion on you."

He patted her hand. "Believe me, I understand the danger. But mass! I don't know what to do."

"I'll show you," she said.

"Don't forget what I taught you," Gabriella whispered as they stepped into the village church, which was dimly lit by flickering candles. "Do everything I do—Will!"

Startled, he drew his stare from the stained glass window.

"I said, watch me."

How lovely she was, Will thought, her round Madonna face dappled by the jeweled light streaming through the windows, her dress swishing as she crossed the back of the church and stopped at a side aisle. A cream lace mantilla added a hint of exotic mystery to her allure.

He was vaguely aware of the other townsfolk entering the church: black-garbed old women, peasant men in sturdy work clothes, children, their hair slicked back, the girls garbed in white. From the corner of his eye, he spied the official who had checked their papers. The man gave a small nod of his head.

Gabriella stopped and rested her hand on the back of an odd-looking chair with a high back and a low seat. "Here."

He started to take a seat, but she grabbed his wrist. "Genuflect first."

"Genu—what?"

Pressing her lips into an exasperated line, she went down on one knee, touched her forehead, her breast, and each shoulder before kneeling on the strange chair.

Feeling ridiculous, Will mimicked the gesture and knelt beside her. "How was that?"

"You made the sign of the cross backward," she whispered. "I pray no one noticed."

The mass began. Will studied the strange church with its colored windows, painted triptychs, and stone statuary. He was amazed by the ceremony, the acolytes swinging their censers, the chanted Latin invocations, the utter certainty among the faithful that, at the tinkle of a bell, bread and wine were transformed into the body and blood of the Christ.

He watched Gabriella from the corner of his eye, kneeling and standing as directed, mouthing words to unfamiliar prayers.

A creed was sung, and Gabriella joined in with heartfelt sincerity. The sound of her voice transported Will, made him think of places where miracles were born. The Christians were lucky to count her among the faithful. The clear tones of her singing rang through the arched chancel, drawing glances first of startlement, then of awed delight. He could imagine no higher exaltation than this, Gabriella's voice raised in song.

The song ended, and she gave his sleeve a tug to bring him to his knees. The priest fed bits of bread and sips of wine to each person. He reached Will, held out a crumbling piece of bread. "Corpus Christi."

Will tried to swallow past the dryness in his throat. The body of Christ. What savages these Christians were! Cannibals! He felt Gabriella stiffen beside him. For her sake he took bread from a priest's hand and pretended it was

human flesh. For her sake he sipped wine from a silver
chalice and pretended it was the blood of her Savior.

But for his own sake, after the priest moved on, Will
murmured the forbidden Kol Nidre, begging the god of
Abraham to forgive him for practicing Christian ways.

"Will?" she murmured in his ear. "What are you saying?"

"A Hebrew prayer to let God know this is all a pretense."

Her face paled. She began to tremble. He reached down
and took her hand. "Look, don't expect me to change so
quickly," he whispered back. "Even your Lord Jesus
didn't come to the faith until he was thirty."

The next morning they climbed the rocky hill to Santa
Inez. Gabriella leaned heavily on Will. The altitude stole
her breath. She would have to tell him soon that she was
pregnant with the child of Henry VIII of England.

But where could she find the words? Will seemed to see
her as Henry's innocent victim. She had not been able to
bring herself to confess the whole truth—that she had, in
her despair, been a willing lover to the handsome young
king.

He seemed blind to her faults, saw only grace and good-
ness when he looked at her. She found herself worrying
more about the moment of truth with him than the meeting
with a mother who was only an indistinct form in the mists
of memory.

A lay sister met them at the low arched portal of the
convent. Her inquisitive gaze swept over them, focusing
on Gabriella's dusty gown and then Will's blazing red hair.

"We've come to see Doña Mercedes," said Will.

"More visitors for her?" the lay sister asked.

Gabriella cocked her head. "My mother has had other
visitors recently?"

"Yes, in fact—" The lay sister gaped. "So. You're the daughter of Doña Mercedes."

"Yes, sister. Please, may we see her?"

"Of course. This way."

They walked past a fragrant herbiary where the scent of balsam and borage perfumed the air. Their escort brought them to Doña Mercedes. Garbed in a rough brown habit, her face shuttered by a starched wimple, she sat in the chapter house, gazing out an unglazed window at the rippling hills of the Sierra Morena.

Gabriella put her hand on Will's sleeve to draw strength from him. Misgivings poured over her, for her mother seemed even colder, even more distant than Gabriella remembered. She had no idea how to span the gap widened by the years of separation.

She must have made some sound, for Mercedes turned to them, staring without recognition. Gabriella hurried forward, clasped the thin dry hands and dropped to her knees. "Mother, it's me."

The soft hiss of Mercedes' breath punctuated the silence. Her noble face, handsome and dignified beneath the wimple, registered a moment of shock. Gabriella forced herself to look into her mother's eyes, to confront the strange, unsettled regard that had haunted her since childhood.

That look was as difficult to fathom now as it had been in years before. Whom did Mercedes see? Gabriella detected a flash of passion, maternal longing, possibly love. And yet, at the same time, there was an undeniable element that Gabriella had never understood. A cool aloofness. Even as a child Gabriella had respected the distance. With a child's instincts, she had stopped herself from demanding an affection she knew Mercedes could not give.

Gabriella drew back her hands. "You're looking well."

"Thank you." Mercedes glanced at the door where Will stood. Her whole body stiffened, and her eyes went blank.

The reaction seemed as instinctive as a crab's drawing into a shell.

A wave of panic swept Gabriella. Had her mother somehow guessed that Will was a Jew? Gabriella thrust aside the notion. She had never seen her mother in the presence of a man before; surely this was simply evidence of her dislike for all men.

"Meet William Blythe," Gabriella said hastily, and Will bowed. "He's been my escort from England."

"How do you do?" Woodenly, Mercedes gestured at a table. "There's wine in the jar there. Do help yourself."

"No, thank you. I'll wait outside." He closed the door behind him.

Mercedes relaxed her white-knuckled grip on her chair. "I've been expecting you."

Gabriella blinked. "You have? But how could you have known I left England?"

"Doña Elvira Manuel has kept me apprised of your . . . progress. She's back in Spain, you know."

Gabriella shivered. So this was the visitor the lay sister had spoken of. Doña Elvira knew too much. She was back in Spain, dangerous as a spider lurking in the dark. "What did Doña Elvira say?"

"That you tried to steal from your queen. That you travel in the company of a Jew."

Terror iced Gabriella's heart. "She lies! Will is no Jew, only a good man who saved me from false accusations."

Mercedes looked upon her with an unreadable expression. "God is mysterious, but merciful. I'll speak no ill of a man who brought you back to me, back among the faithful. You're here to take your vows at last?"

Gabriella settled back on her heels. The stone floor pressed into her bones. "I can't stay if I'm an outlaw."

"I still wield some influence, thanks to the nobility of my blood and the extent of my inheritance. Were you to stay here as a postulant, you'd not be harmed."

"I know that's what you've always wanted for me, but I don't have the calling," Gabriella said carefully.

Mercedes' mouth pinched at the edges. "Few women do at your age. You'll grow into this life; your faith will deepen."

"No, Mother. You see, I cannot stay here. I—I had plans to marry, but—" Unable to continue, she looked away.

Mercedes' face drained of color. Her cheeks went papery white, almost translucent. The tracery of veins looked blue beneath her skin.

Mercedes made a wheezing sound, then found her voice. "No. You may not marry. Not ever. *Not ever*, do you hear me?"

All hope of maternal compassion died in Gabriella. Her hands dropped to her midsection. Her mother's words held an uncanny portent. The moment she had conceived Henry Tudor's child, she had relinquished all claim on Armando. She could not hold him to his vow now that she carried a bastard, royal or not. Yet a stubborn wish ached inside her. Neither could she relinquish her dreams until she saw him, gazed into his dark, beautiful eyes, and told him the truth.

"I didn't come here to ask your permission," she said, "but to do you the courtesy of informing you of my plans."

"I won't dower you. What sort of husband will have you without a dowry?" Her long-fingered hands came up to clutch her nun's robe to her throat. "No! You'd not do the unthinkable! You'd not marry that Jew!"

"He's a Christian," Gabriella insisted, fighting to keep the desperation from her voice. "And I never planned to marry him. Mother, I know you hold all men in contempt for reasons you have never told me. I've suffered cruelty and torment, but I'm not so quick to judge all men by—"

"Cruelty!" Mercedes' hand grasped Gabriella's arm.

The hard, dry nails bit into her flesh. "What man hurt you?"

To allay her mother's horror, Gabriella gently removed the hand from her arm and said, "I chose my words poorly, Mother. I'm safe now, and what happened in the past is best forgotten."

"I agree completely." With relief, Mercedes rested her chin in her hand. "You're staying. Your companion must leave."

"Mother, there is another reason I can never take vows."

Mercedes gripped the chair arms. She must have heard the mingled shame and fear and wonder in Gabriella's voice. "Go on," she prompted, stiffening as if to brace herself for a blow.

Gabriella stared down at her feet, swallowed hard. She indulged herself in one last foolish hope that her mother would understand, that the baby would bring them together. She said softly, "I am with child."

She looked up to see her mother's hand streaking toward her. The open-palmed blow caught Gabriella full on the cheek. Shock and horror sucked the breath from her lungs. She pitched sideways, saw the floor speeding up to meet her, felt the bruising crush of the flagstones against her brow.

She dragged her gaze to her mother's face, and had another shock. Mercedes' look was naked, raw, as painful to Gabriella as the fiery tingling in her cheek.

Mercedes' look was one of sheer loathing.

"Mother." Gabriella forced herself to speak calmly. "My circumstances are unfortunate, I know, but—"

"Sister Candida, a midwife in town, will help." Mercedes spoke half to herself. She rose and paced the long, stark room. "She'll make a decoction of savin and rue, and if that fails, we can always find that Moorish physick who—"

"Mother." Chilled by Mercedes' tone, Gabriella dragged herself up. "I don't know what you're saying. Savin and rue?"

"Abortifacients," Mercedes snapped. "I was too cowardly to take them myself." Her fury lashed Gabriella. "Would to God that I had."

Shock, horror, and the swift death of a dream took Gabriella in a stranglehold. "Mother, do not wish I had never been born!"

"I wish it with all my heart." The ice-coated remark made Gabriella cringe.

"How can you say that to me? I am flesh of your flesh—"

"More than you know," said Mercedes.

"You dishonor my father, a hero in the crusade against the Moors."

Mercedes loosed a harsh laugh. "Your father was no hero."

"But Roman de Flores was—"

"—a convenient fiction, you stupid little cow. He was merely a means to bleach the taint. I should have realized that the De Montana evil had not died with my father."

"What evil? I don't understand."

"It's time you did, then."

A chill in Gabriella's blood banished the sting of her mother's slap. She rose slowly to her feet, braced her hand on the window ledge. Behind her, a hot wind rustled through an olive grove. "Tell me."

"I paid a scribe to invent Roman de Flores, complete with a personal history and lineage."

"But why?"

"To hide the identity of the man who fathered you."

"Enough of games!" Anger and apprehension pounded in Gabriella's head. She retreated a step, felt a bench pressing into the backs of her knees. *"Who was my father?"*

"Bernal de Montana. He was my father, too."

* * *

Will heard a scream, the crack of a wooden bench hitting the floor. A deep, visceral dread gripped him.

For the past several minutes, he had stood outside the chapter house, unable to hear their voices. He had heard the sound of the slap, which had nearly sent him running in, but he had restrained himself. Now, with Gabriella's scream echoing in his ears, he burst into the room.

Gabriella lay unmoving on the floor. Her mother, with chilling disregard, stood gazing out the window. Spitting an oath, Will gathered Gabriella into his arms, sped out into the cloister, and demanded to be conducted to the infirmary.

There, he placed her on a cot. "She needs help," he said to the anxious nuns gathered in the doorway. "Who—"

"Will, no." Gabriella's voice was thin and pleading. "Just . . . tell them to leave me be."

Something in her shattered expression made him obey. He sat at her side, bathed her brow with a damp cloth soaked in witch hazel, kept the worried sisters at bay. When she slipped into a fitful half-sleep, he stared helplessly at her, his beloved. She had been through such turmoil, had suffered so unfairly.

The red imprint of her mother's hand marked one cheek. And on her forehead, a swelling had started where she had hit her head. Sick with impotent rage, Will squeezed her hand. She had never looked so haggard, her lips bloodless and her hair dull with the dust of the road. And yet he had never loved her more.

He burned to confront Doña Mercedes, but he dared not leave Gabriella to the care of strangers. He pondered the woman they had traveled so far to see. Doña Mercedes was handsome in the cool fashion of the Castilian nobility. She lacked the lavish beauty of Gabriella, lacked her daughter's warm openness. Perhaps, he decided, it was well for both women that they had spent so many years apart.

He lifted her hand, buried his mouth in her palm. She had fallen alarmingly still. "For pity's sake, Gabriella," he whispered, "wake up. Damn it, wake up!"

He inhaled, tasted her flesh, and realized he was kissing her hand as fervently as a lover. Her eyes fluttered open and she made a soft sound of startlement.

Chagrined at being caught with his passions unveiled, Will hastily let go of her hand. "Are you all right?" he asked.

"The stumble didn't hurt me," she said, her voice a curious monotone.

"Gabriella, what happened between you and your mother?"

Tears glazed her eyes. "I can't tell you, Will."

"Damn it!" He grabbed her wrists and regarded her so fiercely that she flinched. "Why not?"

"Because I couldn't bear to have you hate me."

"Hate you?" His control snapped. "God damn it, are you really that blind? Don't you know I'd forgive you anything?"

The pronouncement hung like the weightless dust particles that spun in the shaft of orange sunlight streaming through the window. Gabriella's eyes widened with shock. "No," she whispered after a long silence. "Don't make promises like that, Will. You'll only make matters worse."

He could not imagine what could be worse than the pained confession ripped from him a moment ago. She had wrung the truth from him; now there was nothing for it but to go on.

"Talk to me, Gabriella. I'm not here to judge you."

Shuddering, she drew a deep breath. "My mother lied about the identity of my father. Roman de Flores was but a fiction created by a well-paid scribe."

He smiled with relief. "You expect me to condemn you

for that? Jews make up false lineages all the time to save their skin.''

"Nothing can save me.''

Will tried not to show how her statement frightened him. "You mustn't talk like that. What could be so horrible that you would say such a thing?'' He brushed a stray curl from her brow. "Your mother was never married, was she?''

"No.''

He gave her a smile of encouragement. "Sweetheart, I understand it's a blow to your pride, but it happens to the best of us. Thanks to you, Armando is learning to accept himself again. Given time, you will, too.''

"Were I simply a bastard,'' she said, speaking as if to herself, "I could indeed live with myself.''

"Then what else could it be? I'm your friend, Gabriella.'' Unthinkingly he stroked her cheek. "Nothing is so dire that it could make me turn from you.''

"Oh, no?'' With a sudden, swift movement, she slapped his hand away and braced herself on her elbows. Terror and defiance glittered in her eyes. "Not even the fact that my mother bedded with her own father?''

Will's lungs emptied as if someone had slammed a fist into his stomach.

"Do you hear what I'm saying, Will?'' Gabriella persisted. "I am a child of incest.''

Will's head reeled. He feared he might vomit. He held himself still, absorbing the news, wishing he had heard wrong.

He licked his dry lips. "That is your mother's sin, her burden. You're innocent in this, Gabriella.''

"Don't be naive, Will. Their sin flows in my very blood.''

"No! Damn it, you're a beautiful, talented woman.''

"A tainted woman.'' She drew her knees to her chest and rocked herself slowly, rhythmically, mindlessly. "I wonder why she let him?'' Gabriella mused. ''Or perhaps she didn't. Perhaps he forced her—''

More than the horror of incest, Gabriella's strange behavior scared Will. ''Don't,'' he said, grasping her shoulders and holding her still. ''Don't speculate, don't even think about it. It's all in the past.''

She blinked as if he had awakened her from sleep. ''I know very little about Judaism, but surely Jews, like Christians, have strict laws about incest. The children of such unions are . . . not normal. Traits that are but faint strains in the parents become evil taints in the offspring.''

As a dark moment of doubt descended upon him, Will was appalled by the intensity of his own disgust. He had dared her to test their friendship. And she had. Her revelation had brought him to the brink of an invisible boundary; it defied him to step over the edge. All the laws of nature confirmed her statement and urged him to shrink back. But his heart pushed him forward. Girding himself with his love for her, he took the last step and said, ''Not always,'' he stated. ''Not in you.''

''Particularly in me.'' The pulse in her pale throat fluttered fast. ''You refuse to see the evil in me, Will. I did too, for a while. But the truth is, the lust that drove my father to take his own daughter to bed is a part of me, too.''

''Ah, Gabriella, don't overdramatize this.''

''Don't belittle me, Will! Damn it, open your eyes to the truth! I *liked* fornicating with King Henry!'' she blurted. ''I lived for his visits, for the feel of his body next to mine.''

He fought to keep from clapping his hands over his ears. ''You were innocent. Henry played upon your loneliness. He deprived you of human contact so you would crave his company.''

She sagged back against the pillow. Her raven curls made a black halo around her oval face; she resembled a dark angel. "Think what you wish, Will. In my heart I know I'm right. And if—if you want to take back what you said about forgiving me anything, I'll understand."

"God, no, Gabriella. I meant that from my heart. Your news changes none of my feelings for you."

She looked as if she would never smile again. "Will, did your Uncle David ever teach you the uses of herbs?"

He frowned at the unexpected question. "No. I never showed much interest in his trade. Why do you ask?"

"There's something I need."

"Anything, Gabriella."

"Go into town, find an herbalist. Mother told me about a woman called Sister Candida. I need a decoction of savin and rue. It's for . . . my aching head. Hurry, Will."

He did hurry. In Calle Rubio the herbalist aimed a sharp look at him. "What for?" she demanded.

"For a lady who is ailing. She needs it for headache."

"That's what she told you?"

"Yes."

"She's lying."

He clenched his fists. "How can you know that?"

"Savin and rue do not cure headache. Sir, your young lady is asking for an abortifacient."

Gabriella stared at the shaft of light from the window. The sun's rays streamed over a table that held stacks of folded bandages, pots of unguent, and little brass cups for bloodletting. Black leeches clung to the sides of a clear jar. She winced. Although her injuries were slight, she felt bruised all over, as if she had just fought a battle and lost.

And indeed she was irreparably injured—in her heart and in her soul. First by a king's lust, and finally and most lethally by her mother's sin and betrayal.

Gabriella kept her arms crossed over her stomach and thought about the tiny life there, pulsing and fluttering, innocent of the evil she planned. She could not bring this baby into the world. It was no baby, but a taint, a cancer growing in secret, waiting to destroy.

Her world lay shattered at her feet. She wished she had the courage to take her own life. But a small, stupid part of her snatched at survival like a stubborn flame in the wind. She kept hoping, kept praying. Perhaps Armando would accept her—not as a wife, of course, never that! But she could still make a life in the Indies. He was a man of honor who would surely offer his help to a woman who had nowhere else to go.

She thought of Will, the pain in his eyes, the passion in his voice when he had declared his devotion to her. She supposed she had known the depths of his friendship from the start. But her love for Armando had blinded her to Will's feelings.

Of course, her horrible admission had instantly slain Will's misguided esteem. Despite his assurance to the contrary, she was certain he respected her no more.

She forced herself to ponder the plan. She would abort the child and suffer the sin of it, surely a lesser evil than birthing an unnatural creature like herself. She would make her way to Seville, beg Armando's father to help her flee to the Indies. Beyond that, she could not think. It was too much to abandon her dreams for a new life all at once. Two things were certain, though. She must never marry. She must never give birth to a child.

Sighing, she leaned back against the bedstead. What was taking Will so long? Surely it was a simple thing to buy an herbal remedy. She did not want more time to think. Thinking was dangerous, for her mind conjured images of a small, precious baby in her arms, a tiny trusting hand curled around her finger. She crushed the images with the dark iron of painful knowledge. She was forbidden to have dreams like other women.

Will came slamming into the room, a sack slung over

his arm. The scent of horse sweat clung to him. Gabriella felt a start of surprise when she saw his face. So intent did he look that she felt she was seeing a new person. A decisive, angry man.

"Will? What took you so long?"

He stared at her for a long moment. "Business."

"You must have hired a horse," she said nervously.

He nodded. "I went to Seville."

"Did you get"—she swallowed—"what I requested?"

He set down the bag, took out a small clay bottle, and handed it to her. "Here's your remedy."

With a shaking hand she uncorked the bottle. Her untrained senses could not identify the strong herbal scents. She put the bottle to her lips. Her hand trembled so violently that she had to steady it with the other. She could not look at Will.

Pulling in a deep breath, she tipped up the bottle. Before she could take a sip, she turned her face away. Hot tears rolled down her cheeks.

"Drink it," snapped Will in a cruel, stranger's voice. "It's what you want, isn't it?"

"I . . . can't." She was sobbing openly now. The bottle slipped from her fingers and smashed to the floor. The herbal scent filled the air.

Will's arms went around her shaking shoulders. He cradled her cheek to his chest. Although his voice was soft and tender, he swore vividly. "Damn it. God damn it. I shouldn't have done that. It was cruel."

"What are you talking about, Will?"

"I wanted to see if you'd actually do it. I didn't think you could. I shouldn't have tested you."

"Tested me?"

He nodded, kicking away a broken bit of pottery. "There was nothing in that drink but willow bark and lemon balm."

"You let me think it was savin and rue."

"I'm sorry, Gabriella."

"Don't ever test me like that again."

"Then don't ever lie to me again."

"Oh, Will." She felt a strange sense of relief. Somehow the fact that he knew she carried the king's child eased her burden. "What in God's name am I going to do?"

He drew back. His grin was a bit precarious but genuine, a glimpse of the old Will. "I thought you'd never ask. In Seville, I found Rafael Viscaino. He was more than willing to help." Will began pulling more items out of the bag, handing them to her one by one. "This is your marriage record to one Henrique Real." Her eyes widened, but before she could respond, he handed her another paper. "And here's his death certificate. He drowned, poor soul, after only a few months' marriage."

He touched her damp cheek. "We both hate lies, don't we, Gabriella? But these are small ones and will not hurt anyone."

"Won't they?" she whispered. "I wonder."

"And this"—he unfurled an intimidatingly long document dotted with ink seals—"is an official conduct from the House of Trade, allowing my passage to the Indies."

"I don't understand."

"Foreigners aren't usually allowed to settle in the islands, but Armando's father provided special permission." He gripped her shoulders and smiled down at her. "It's all settled now, Gabriella. We're both going to the Indies."

CHAPTER 18

"Very impressive." Juan Ponce de León stood with Armando in front of the newly expanded house and gazed out at the plantation. The cane fields waved, a restless sea of green that stretched from the hilltop down to the cliffs shadowing the beach. "Very impressive indeed." Juan's hand scratched idly over the scarred and knotted head of his aging deerhound, Bercerillo. "Don Armando has made a success of his enterprise, has he not, Barto?"

Armando glanced at Juan's companion, Bartolome de las Casas, who nodded vigorously. He was a small, compact man with a mulish set to his jaw and an unexpectedly appealing light in his eye. "It's a jewel, a veritable jewel. And without slave labor, I understand. Is that correct, Don Armando?"

"Yes." Since his arrival in Española, Armando had lived in a state of unreality. Here he stood, master of a prosperous sugar plantation with a white-plastered hacienda that was the envy of all Santo Domingo. His *trapiche* had become the model for all growers on Española. His relationship with native laborers had made him the object of curiosity and suspicion.

"You're a man of few words," Las Casas remarked when Armando declined to elaborate.

"True, Barto," said Juan. "Successful men always have secrets to guard. My kinsman, Baltasar, claims his slaves have gotten unruly," said Juan. A native worker balancing a yoke of full calabashes across his shoulders passed by. The deerhound bristled; Juan calmed it with a murmured word. "He blames you."

"I've had no truck with Baltasar since my arrival here."

"But word gets around." Juan planted his booted feet wide and crossed his brawny forearms over his chest. He wore bright red hose and an emerald doublet, vivid colors that looked faintly ridiculous on a man of his years. "His slaves hear that you overfeed your workers, allow them all liberties."

"Baltasar seems to know much of my business," Armando said wryly. He noted the challenge in Juan's stance and hoped to avoid an argument. Reviving the rivalry with Baltasar could cost him his *encomienda*.

Las Casas seemed to sense the tension, for he offered Armando a cigar. Out of politeness Armando accepted it, but only fingered the moist leaf that wrapped the tobacco. *Jouli*, Paloma called it. Santiago was an inveterate smoker, but Armando abstained. Among the natives, only priests smoked tobacco, in their medicine huts. It seemed insulting to smoke for pleasure.

They walked up behind the house, where a broad, fenced area was being built as a stable yard. Juan held Armando back for a moment while Las Casas went ahead. "Keep an eye on Barto. The man's determined to undermine our enterprises. I heard he has appealed to the king and the pope on behalf of the savages. He believes they ought to be treated as our equals. What reasonable man could look upon a savage and see an equal?''

Armando's gaze drifted over the high green fields where islanders labored with placid industry. ''They're not our equals,'' he said, ''but our betters.''

Juan glanced at him sharply. ''You've been in the sun too long, *amigo*.'' He gestured at a woman who had stopped in her laboring to nurse her infant. ''They have no notion of hard work. Bercerillo could teach that one a lesson she'd not soon forget.'' He tugged at the dog's braided leather lead. The hound came to full alert, its muscles bunching in readiness to lunge. ''Would you like a demonstration?''

''Would you like to keep your ballocks attached?'' Armando's hand went to his sword.

Juan's eyes widened; clearly he was not accustomed to being challenged. Then his face relaxed into a wry grin. ''She's your bed slave, eh?''

''What she is,'' said Armando, ''is none of your business.''

''Let's go join Barto. And tell me, is it true you have a Moor working for you?''

''My partner was baptized,'' said Armando.

Juan chuckled richly. His sharp-honed features had once been striking, but lines of strain and cruelty now pulled at his flesh. According to rumor, he was being sued to honor a dowry payment on his daughter, and the fortune he had won by conquering Boriquen, the island he called San Juan, had run dry.

''Demonios!'' He pointed at the new stable yard. In the shade of a purple heart tree squatted three native workers, shaking strings of shells and murmuring in a strange monotone. ''How can you allow idol worship among your workers, Don Armando? It's a disgrace, I tell you. We're here to bring the Indians to the True Faith, not to tolerate their lazy heathen ways.''

"Don Juan," Armando said evenly, "these people have flourished in these islands for years beyond counting. Who are we to force them to change their way of life?"

"We are soldiers of Christ, the son of the one true God, or have you forgotten your vows?"

Armando shrugged. "I'm a planter, not a crusader." He affected a grin of nonchalance. "The Dominicans came here to serve God. The rest of us came to get rich."

Las Casas mopped the sweat from his forehead. "Oh. Well, at least you're honest."

Juan glared at both men. "Those savages ought to be hanged as an example to the others."

"I will not commit murder, Don Juan," said Armando. "Not even in Christ's name. Particularly not in Christ's name."

Juan was a man of capricious temperament. He glared at Armando, his eyes on fire with resentment. Then he threw back his head and laughed. "Have it your way, *padrino*. Far be it from me to tamper with the man who brought the savages of Española to heel and made his mill a model of efficiency."

"So this is how you do it?" Las Casas seemed genuinely interested. "You keep their loyalty by permitting their liberty?"

"Very little of it was my doing," Armando admitted. "In truth, much of the work was done by men like Juan." He watched Ponce de León's skin darken in a flush and knew his barb had found its mark. The conquistadors had destroyed village after village. The displaced islanders were left to choose between death or bondage. Armando took pride in the fact that he was able to offer a third choice: fair keep and safety for fair work. It was not wholly satisfactory to people who had enjoyed freedom and peace for generations, but it was preferable to what the conquerors had offered.

It would never be enough for the rebels who hid in the

mountain village where Paloma now lived with her parents, Armando reminded himself. Despite the moist heat of the day, he shivered with a vague premonition. Anger burned in the people of Anacaona's clan, the deep, concentrated anger of a bull in the *plaza de toros* with its head dropped, ready to charge.

"You have my admiration," said Las Casas, bobbing his head in approval. "Truly, you give me hope that Spaniard and native can live together in harmony."

Juan spat on the ground. "You see the world in shades of pink, Barto. Unfortunately, your inexperience hurts us all. Insisting that Indians live with us as equals is like expecting a beast to do its fucking on its back." He strode down the length of the stable yard, Bercerillo stalking along beside him.

Before he could reach the workers, Armando hurried forward. Instinct told him to knock Juan flat and banish him from the plantation, but he forced himself to be reasonable, prudent. "You must be thirsty from your ride, Don Juan. El Hakim has built a new fountain in the patio. Would you like to see it?"

Juan stopped walking, gave Armando a long, assessing glance, and nodded curtly. In the patio, a servant appeared with bowls of coconut milk chilled by the springs. Juan and Las Casas launched into a debate about whether or not the natives had souls, and if so, whether or not they were worth saving.

Drink in hand, Armando edged toward a stone fence that circled the kitchen garden. Discontent gnawed at him. Here he was, lord of an island paradise. His family lay an ocean away. Santiago stayed on with Joseph's adopted clan. Gabriella was—God willing—on her way to join him.

Even as he put all his sweat and muscle into building a home for Gabriella, his thoughts always strayed to Paloma. Vivid as yesterday, he saw her dancing in the firelight, felt her rage and pain and defiance. Even after months of separation, he remembered the texture of her skin, the taste of her kisses, the desperate, raw passion that had bound them for one wild night.

He had left the next day. Her farewell had been subdued; no emotion had flickered in her eyes. For her sake, he prayed she could live content with her clan. For his own sake, he hoped he would never see her again. She was a danger to his heart.

"We must be tedious company indeed." Juan's comment sliced into Armando's thoughts. "You haven't heard a word I've said."

Armando ran a hand through his hair. It was getting long. Since Paloma had left, he never remembered to barber it. He had forgotten a lot of things since she had left. But never her. "Sorry. What were you saying?"

"I was speaking of my future. I intend to embark on another expedition."

Armando kept his face from betraying him as his thoughts flew to the clan living in the secret settlement. "Are you? Where will you go this time?"

"I've not decided. I might join Velázquez in Cuba—the island's certainly big enough for the two of us. Still, I long for something new, the high thrill of clapping eyes on a land no Christian's ever seen before."

Armando's fears about the hidden village abated. Juan would look to undiscovered lands. He imagined virgin territories penetrated by the sword thrust of invasion. He dreamed of scooping gold by the bucketful from mountain streams, and then returning a hero to retire in a grand stronghold in Extremadura.

"I wish you luck, then," said Armando.

"You could do better than that. You could come with me."

Armando was surprised to feel a tug. There was a seductive danger in the prospect of sailing uncharted waters, coming upon lush new lands, discovering the secrets hidden in the verdant forests. "No, thank you," he said, less forcefully than he had intended. "I have plenty to occupy me right here."

"We'd best be on our way, Don Juan," said Las Casas. "I'm expecting some correspondence from Spain. Let's go see what the new fleet has brought." Wistfulness softened his features. "How things have changed since Colón cut the first wake across the Sea of Darkness. Crossing it now has become as commonplace as fording a river in Andalucía. Will you join us, Don Armando?"

Armando nodded. He saddled a horse and rode with them down the winding road to the main port. As was his habit when meeting a ship, he fought against a sick, pounding hope. Countless times he had made this journey, praying for news from Gabriella, praying to see her beloved face. As the seasons passed without word of her, his hopes subsided to a dull ache in his heart. The months snatched at his few precious memories of her. A distance greater than the Ocean Sea separated them. It was the distance of time, stealing memories and thwarting hope; against his will, she was fading from him like a half-forgotten dream.

He touched the packet of letters in his doublet. He wrote to her incessantly at Queen Catherine's court in England, fanning the embers of their love with words. The lapse with Paloma had only made his writings more fevered, more urgent.

He and his companions gathered with a small crowd in the shade of an ancient ceiba tree. Behind them loomed a new mud and stone wall, the beginnings of a fortification system around Santo Domingo. In front of them, with sails furled and hulls bristling with long ash sweeps, came a fleet of five ships.

These fragile birdlike caravels were their only link with home. No wonder they watched with hungry eyes. Armando settled down to wait. Shipments of salt, wine, can-

dles, and lamp oil were off-loaded. Spontaneous prayers
of thanksgiving erupted when a flock of nuns took their
first unsteady steps on Española.

Armando's vision blurred as he watched the sunlight
striking sparks off the turquoise sea. This place was too
beautiful. An earthly paradise. How could he be feeling
discontent?

All around him, he heard greetings, some of them so
laden with emotion that they sounded like cries of pain.
He saw a haggard woman brave the gangplank, clutching
a little boy's hand. A man ran to them and swept them
into his arms, holding on as if he would never let them
go. A well-dressed young *hidalgo* rushed to his father.
The two shared an embrace that brought heat to Armando's throat. Lies had cheated him of the chance to grow
to manhood under the guidance of a true father.

Bitter, he stood and prepared to seek out a ship's chan-
cellor to carry his letters. He would send one with each
ship. Perhaps this time one would succeed in the long and
convoluted journey to Gabriella.

He started along the wharf. A newly arrived woman caught
his eye, for she seemed more hesitant than the others who
disembarked with her. Even from a distance he could see
that she bore herself with inborn grace. Her slim body was
encased in a simple black dress, her net coif and veil neatly
in place. She had the *delicadeza* of high nobility, yet no
servants hovered around her as they would around a lady of
rank. She stood at the edge of a bulkhead and gazed around
the area, seeming to focus on the crudely ostentatious viceroy's mansion and the squat town church. Lifting a hand, she
drew the veiled coif from her head.

Armando stopped dead in his tracks, momentarily dazzled by the sunlight glinting off her glossy curls, and by
the shock of recognition. Then he was moving—running—
calling her name, brushing past faceless strangers as he
made his way to her.

"Gabriella!"

She turned and spied him. Her smile brought back every bittersweet moment of love he had ever felt for her. She came into his arms. Her feet flew out as he spun her around. Joy felt like a sickness, a fever that made him giddy.

Then he was kissing her, hard and fervently, filling his senses with flavors and scents and textures that were uniquely hers. He had forgotten—or perhaps had never appreciated—how soft and womanly she was, how full her breasts were.

After an endless moment, she pulled back.

"Gabriella!" he shouted. "Christ Jesus, it's a miracle!"

She put her hand on his cheek, threading her fingers into the hair at his temple. Tears misted her eyes, and he detected a difference in her smile. In Southampton, he had left a girl bursting with hopes for the future. Here in Santo Domingo, he encountered a woman whose smile held the rare beauty of contentment. "Yes, it is a miracle. But much has happened. I don't know where to begin. First we'd best find Will—"

"Will?" Armando's eyes widened. "Will Shapiro is here?"

Her smile trembled. "Shh. His name is William Blythe now." Armando nodded; she didn't have to explain further. "He's been with me every moment since . . . I must tell you—"

Amid the milling crowd, Armando spied a bright blaze of red hair. "By God, it's too good to be true!" Breaking away from Gabriella, he raced along the waterfront toward his friend.

Will hurried forward, a bundle clutched protectively to his chest. He looked even taller, lankier, than Armando remembered, his face more careworn. But he grinned broadly, and his expression awakened fond memories in Armando.

Armando grabbed Will's shoulders, loosed a jubilant shout, then kissed him soundly on each cheek.

Will laughed with him, swayed a little. "Have a care, Armando. I still feel the deck of the ship."

"You're here! Here on Española. By God, the two of you have me believing in miracles. You—"

A small cry came from the bundle Will held. Armando froze, then blinked. "Will? What do you have there?"

Will brushed back a corner of the blanket. Gabriella hurried to his side. Armando gaped at a tiny, cherubic face framed by downy golden brown hair.

"It's a baby," said Will.

"I can see that," Armando whispered. "Christ Jesus, you're a papa! Where's your wife?"

Will and Gabriella exchanged a solemn look. Armando's heart sank. The child's mother must have died. Perhaps they were too moved to discuss the tragedy yet.

He kept staring at his friends. A strange buzzing sound started in his ears, the sound of a secret hive suddenly disturbed. Gabriella put her hand on his sleeve, but the gesture only served to heighten his sense of dread. The internal buzzing sound grew louder, a swarm of misgivings and apprehension that crescendoed until Gabriella spoke.

"Armando." Her voice broke; she cleared her throat. "That's Phillip. My son."

They sat alone on the porch, Armando and Gabriella and a clay jug of wine. A brilliant sunset spread gold-feathered rays across the hills that rolled down to the sea. A tropic breeze rustled through the cane fields, awakening the night birds.

Gabriella stood clutching the rail of the veranda, her back turned to him. She looked frail and alone standing there. One part of him longed to reach out, to draw her against him. But another part held back in furious betrayal.

At last she turned, a dusky vision framed by the colors of the sunset. "There is no easy way to tell this."

He nodded, reached for the wine and took a drink straight from the jug. "I'm waiting."

"Please be patient. It's a long story."

He braced himself for a tale of courtly romance, of passions heated by youth and desire. Instead, she told him a horror story.

"The queen sent me on a pilgrimage with a priceless jeweled headdress. She knew her babe would die, for it was born weeks before term, but she hoped the donation would prove her enduring faith. Doña Elvira gave me directions. I know now that she told me to take the wrong road." Gabriella folded her arms across her chest. If anything, motherhood had only enhanced her beauty. Her milk-heavy breasts bulged out over her arms.

"Thanks to Doña Elvira's intrigues, I never completed the pilgrimage. Royal soldiers detained me, arrested me for theft."

"Theft? Didn't you tell them who you were, what your purpose was?"

"Of course. But they had a purpose of their own."

Visions of rape laid siege to Armando's mind. He balled his fists in rage.

Catching the look on his face, Gabriella shook her head. "No, Armando, their purpose was to take me to King Henry. I thought I'd find justice from him. Instead, I found the worst sort of imprisonment. He kept me in a private house on the Thames, in a room with only a single narrow window. I was guarded constantly. I later found out that King Henry let it be known that I had gone back to Spain, to my mother. To keep Doña Elvira from talking, the king banished her back to Spain."

Armando's stomach lurched. "How long were you his—his prisoner?" he forced himself to ask.

"Weeks . . . months. I lost track of the time."

"And he—he visited you, forced himself on you?" The buzzing sound plagued him again. He was coming to know it as the sound of rage.

"He didn't brutalize me, Armando. He simply gave me an impossible choice. I had either to submit to him, or hang for a thief. Had I been more courageous, more honorable, I should have chosen the latter course." She lifted her shoulders. "I must live with the decision I made. I took him to my bed, called him Harry and fancied us the most contented of lovers. I became pregnant with his babe. Thank God Will contrived to free me before the pregnancy was apparent."

The baby cried then, a sharp, insistent appeal that drifted from the bedchamber at the back of the house. To Armando's bitter astonishment, Gabriella's face filled with pure love.

"His hunger cry. Armando, there's more I must tell you. But first . . ." Reaching up, she drew the thong over her head and put it into his hand. "I said I must live with the choices I made. That doesn't mean you have to. I didn't come here expecting you to honor your promise to wed me. When you made that pledge, you were in love with a maiden, not the woman who birthed a royal bastard. I came to tell you the truth, and because I had nowhere else to go."

She closed his fingers around the warm gold of the ring he had won from a merry young man called Harry Tudor.

"Armando, I release you from your promise."

Much later, as he sat on the stoop beside the wine jug, Will came out to join him. He plopped down beside Armando, tipped the bottle and found it empty.

"She told you?"

Armando crossed his hands over his knees and brooded
at the brilliant night sky, a pearly sweep of stars accentu-
ating the black emptiness beyond. ''She explained what
that animal King Henry did to her. She said there's more
to tell, but the baby started screaming. Christ Jesus, what
more can there be, Will?''

''You'll have to hear it from Gabriella.''

''She didn't have a chance to tell me your part in all
this. How did you get her free?''

Will plucked at a vine that grew up the side of the veranda and sniffed the thick leaf. ''I thought she had gone
to Spain; Elvira had me convinced of it. That's why it . . .
her imprisonment went on for so long. Believe me, if I'd
known sooner, I would have taken London apart brick by
brick to find her.''

Armando didn't doubt it for a moment.

''She sent an instrument to me for repair. There was a
note inside. It's lucky I received it when I did, for I was
about to go to Spain.''

''Why the devil would you want to go to—'' Armando
broke off. ''Ah. You were going to find out what became
of her. We've both got it bad, haven't we? We both love
her.''

Will said nothing.

''Damn!'' Armando blew out his breath. ''A royal bastard. What family name did she give the boy, anyway?''

Will stiffened at his derisive tone. ''With your father's
help, I had false papers drawn up showing her marriage
to Henrique Real, who died soon after the marriage.'' Will
crushed the leaf in his fist and flung it away. ''King Henry
paid dearly for his sin, you know. Catherine had a son the
same month Gabriella gave birth to Phillip. The queen's
child lived only a few weeks. But she was breeding again
when last I heard. . . .''

Armando only half listened. He sat and pondered the

enormity of Will's sacrifice. "You gave up your shop. You risked your life by going to Spain."

"He saved my life," Gabriella said softly from the doorway. Will and Armando stood as she stepped outside and settled herself on the stoop. Will started to leave.

"Please stay," she said. "I need you, Will." Tears thickened her voice.

Armando bit the inside of his cheek. He looked at the shadowed fields, the sugar mill quiet for the night. He had built this farm with one aim in mind: to provide a home for Gabriella, a place where they could live in comfort and safety and prosperity. A place where they could raise their children. Now he had nothing; he was cast adrift again without a goal.

"Will told you about our escape, about his special letter of patent from your father?"

"What letter?"

"As a foreigner, I needed special permission to come to the Indies," Will said. "Your father arranged everything, even a *licenciado* who got rid of my Jewish blood with a few strokes of his pen on my purity of blood certificate."

Armando nodded. If only a clever forgery could obliterate the ache in his heart. "That's good."

"Not necessarily, but I had no choice." Will lifted one eyebrow. "You don't hate your father anymore?"

"No. Rafael lied, but he lied because he loves my mother." He pressed the tips of his fingers together and closed his eyes, remembering, drawing parallels in his mind. Like Catalina, Gabriella had birthed a son out of wedlock. Could Armando do as Rafael had done, marry her and claim the child as his own?

Feelings of reluctance and ineptitude rose through him. For the first time, he fully understood the generosity and unconditional love Rafael had shown.

Gabriella seemed remote, very different from the exuberant young girl he had fallen in love with. Her voice, when she spoke, was flat, with none of the sweet music that had captivated him. "I've burdened you with so much news, Armando, yet there's more. It's about my mother . . . and my father."

Will sucked in his breath. "Gabriella, you don't have to—"

"I must, Will. Armando deserves to know the truth." She turned to look him full in the face. "My mother revealed to me for the first time that I am bastard born."

"I'd be a hypocrite to hold that against you," said Armando.

"She became pregnant by her own father," Gabriella said.

Shock stole Armando's breath. He felt like a drowning man, swirling in the dark waters of secrets and betrayal. A cold sweat broke out on his brow. "No."

"Don't blame her," Will said. "It's no fault of hers."

"I know. *I know.*" Armando surged to his feet. "I just . . . just need time to think, to absorb it all. It's all so . . . perplexing."

Gabriella began crying softly. Armando would have gathered her into his arms, but he moved too late. Will was already there, making soothing sounds as he cradled her head to his chest. Armando turned away. Will had guided her through more troubles than most women endured in a lifetime.

He stalked to the stables. Without a destination in mind, he mounted bareback and urged the horse along the steep mountain trail toward the wild interior of the island.

His feeling of betrayal was acute and bitter, but he could direct his rage at no one. The trouble began with King Henry. Golden, laughing Harry Tudor, who had the richest treasury in Christendom and an entire kingdom at his feet. Why did he have to take Gabriella, too? Had he not enough jewels in his crown?

Armando shook with fury. Useless. Useless to rage at a man insulated by the power of his office and a thousand leagues of open water besides.

A sense of futility closed over Armando, as thick and impenetrable as the jungle darkness. He had tried his best to live with honor, and for what? For a woman broken by a king, tainted with incest, and burdened with a bastard son.

Against his will, he found himself brooding about all the times he had checked his own youthful passions, denied himself the fulfillment of sex in order to keep himself pure for his bride. Only once had he violated his vow.

None of this was Gabriella's fault, he reasoned. She was twice a victim, blameless herself. But he could not banish the image of her, lying with Henry Tudor, giving the King of England what should have belonged to Armando alone.

At dawn, he found himself on the outskirts of the secret settlement of Paloma's clan.

"I made a terrible mistake in coming here." Gabriella adjusted the fabric of her blouse. Phillip contentedly sucked his morning meal.

Will tried not to stare. He had seen her nurse the babe countless times. It should be a commonplace event, but each time she nourished the child, it seemed a small, beautiful miracle.

Reining in his sentimental thoughts, he said, "Don't be foolish. It was too dangerous to stay in Spain, impossible to go back to England. Here, we can start anew."

"We have nothing, Will, but our talent for music. From what I saw of Santo Domingo, that will count for precious little."

"Armando's farm is prosperous."

"I won't live off his charity. I can't marry him, not now."

Will's stomach tightened. *Then marry me,* he wanted to say. Instead, he inquired, "You don't love him anymore?"

"No! Yes!" She waved her free hand. "I have no right to his affections, much less his pledge of marriage."

"Shouldn't you give Armando the chance to decide?"

"It wouldn't be fair. If he said he'd marry me, I'd always wonder if he did so simply to honor his vow."

The baby's eyes drifted shut. Rising, Gabriella crossed the room and placed him on a raised pallet. She stared at him fondly as she straightened her blouse and tied the lacings. "Jesus wept, what's to become of my son?"

I'll raise him as my own. Again, he stopped the words before they were spoken. Gabriella had suffered enough cruel shocks. He could guess her response to his absurd offer. What Christian woman in her right mind would allow a secret Jew, a *Marrano,* to raise her son?

She started to pace, thinking aloud. "I could hire myself out as governess or companion. Lord knows I'm experienced enough at that after my years with Catherine of Aragon."

"Why not stay here?" A man strode into the room.

Will and Gabriella swung to face the newcomer. He held up his hand and regarded them gravely. "I am El Hakim."

Will broke into a grin. "It's good to meet you at last. Armando always spoke highly of you."

The tall Moor nodded. "And of both of you. Welcome to *Gema del Mar.*"

"Thank you. Jewel of the Sea?"

"That is what we call this place. What do you think?"

"It's a . . . ." Will gazed out the door at the exotic landscape and groped for words to describe the alien place.

"A new world?" Gabriella suggested.

El Hakim laughed. "It's a very old world. The natives have been here since time uncounted. But it's an adjustment, eh?"

"We were just speaking of adjustments." Will caught his breath. "Paloma!"

Gabriella's hands flew to her cheeks. "We never even asked Armando about her. What's become of her?"

A grin slashed through El Hakim's beard. "Ah. She has found her parents."

Tears filled Gabriella's eyes. "So it ends happily for one of us."

"For us all," El Hakim declared. "Make your home here. Surely you will marry Armando soon, eh? He has waited so long."

"Our plans have changed." Her gaze drifted to the sleeping child.

"You have dishonored yourself, then." The Moor spoke without censure.

"If my son is the reward for dishonor," Gabriella said stoutly, "then I would gladly pay the price."

El Hakim shook his head. Sweat gleamed on his brow. "Infidel women. By Allah, I will never understand them. You should stay. Who says a musician cannot learn to grow sugar?"

"What of appearances?" asked Gabriella. "A woman living alone with three men who are not her relatives is unseemly."

"This is the Indies. Anything is possible here." Darkly he added, "Much is permitted, for good or bad. We have many women. Rosa, a sailor's widow, runs the kitchen." El Hakim counted them off on his fingers. "Flora, a native woman, is married to the overseer, Vasquez. Constanza, María, Sally Johnston—"

"Sally Johnston? An Englishwoman?"

"Aye, she was Sebastian Cabot's woman for a while. I traveled with him for King Ferdinand." El Hakim's face flushed. "Took a dislike to him when he kept a crazy native woman as his love slave. Allah's providence brought me together with Santiago, and I came here." He opened his arms toward the patio, a large square surrounded by cloistered walkways. "This place is like a small town. None will think ill of you, señorita."

Phillip began to whimper. Gabriella picked him up and swayed to and fro in a graceful mother's dance as old as time.

El Hakim turned to Will. "Armando has been seized by the wonders here. This farm is his anchor, but the moorings are loose." He led them outside to show them the mill. The native workers smiled shyly at them. One woman, seeing the way the baby's weight dragged at Gabriella's arms, hurried over with a length of woven cotton. To Gabriella's delight, the woman showed her how to fashion a sling for the baby.

"On the voyage, we heard talk of uprisings," said Gabriella, nodding her thanks to the smiling woman.

El Hakim looked thoughtful. "Those who live among us are resigned. Those who resist us are dead—or will be shortly."

Gabriella shivered. "It's not right."

"According to law, no native may be made a slave unless he is in rebellion. So when the *encomenderos* need slaves, they simply goad a group of islanders into revolt, then seize them. Baltasar de León is said to be a master at torturing a captured boy to the brink of death, then sending him back to his clan so that they make war in order to avenge the injury."

Gabriella's face paled in horror. "Baltasar de León?"

El Hakim nodded. "The very same. But he lives miles from here in the province of Higuey and plans to join his kinsman on some expedition. You needn't worry about him, señorita."

Gabriella watched a pair of bare-chested boys in trousers leading workhorses around the *trapiche*. "These are slaves?"

"They are all freed men. Armando insists on it."

With a lurch of his heart, Will saw her face soften with love and pride. "Armando was ever obsessed with freedom."

"He's like the natives in that." El Hakim scanned the green mountains to the north and west. "Sometimes at night we hear drumbeats . . . It's like a bubbling caldron, soon to boil over."

"El Hakim, what are you saying?"

"That Indios and Spaniards cannot live together. We came to their country, we killed and enslaved them, bribed and flattered them. We will never be brothers." He tugged at his beard. "Armando says the Indians are not as passive as some think."

CHAPTER 19

Armando walked boldly into the center of the settlement where he had once been held captive. A boy tending the fire at the plaza stared in alarm at the blowing horse, then opened his mouth to call for help.

"Don't," Armando said in Arawak. "I come as a friend."

The boy eyed him warily. Armando touched the ground, then raised his hand high. The lad gawked in confusion. Having nearly exhausted his knowledge of Arawak, Armando grinned and spread his arms to show himself defenseless.

The boy muttered something.

Armando scratched his head. "What's that?"

"He wonders," said Paloma, emerging from the largest hut on the plaza, "if perhaps a lizard has crawled up your arm." She now wore the costume of her mother's people with ease. The woven cotton *nagua*, the necklace of shells, the feather anklet looked wholly right on her.

Armando was not prepared for the rush of pleasure he felt upon seeing her. Nor was he prepared for the urge to reach out and draw her against him. He hungered for closeness with her; he remembered vividly the night he had made love to her. Ignoring the urge and feeling his grin widen, he asked, "Why would he wonder that? I gave the customary greeting of your people."

She smiled, too—sunshine warming the darkness that shadowed his heart. "Not exactly." She said something in a placating tone to the boy. He shrugged and went back to tending the fire.

"You're here to see your father?" she inquired.

The thought of Santiago poured salt on Armando's wounded heart. "No. I came to see you, Paloma."

The wind blew her hair in a silky shroud, obscuring her face so that he could not read her expression. "Why?"

Because I miss you. "The farm's not the same without you."

She brushed back her hair, the shells at her waist clicking with the movement. "Trouble with your workers?"

"No. Things are better than ever, but—" He broke off, catching the curious stares of a group of women. They sat in the shade of a tree, grinding manioc root for making cassava bread. Looping the reins of his horse around a wooden stake, Armando said, "Look, could we just go somewhere and talk?"

She nodded, and took a step toward him. As before, her partial nudity shocked him in a highly pleasant way. In shedding her Spanish clothes she had drawn a line, separating herself from the years she had been enslaved among cruel strangers.

Armando reached across the line, took her hands in his. Her arms tensed, but she made no attempt to draw away. In silence they walked past the palisades and wended their way into the forest. They passed a strange totem featuring a catlike creature. A spined lizard darted across the forest floor to hide beneath a broad, thick leaf.

"So my father's still here," Armando snapped.

The jeweled plumage of a jacamar flashed in the trees. "I had not realized Santiago and my father were such fast friends," said Paloma. "They share a past we will never understand fully. My father abhors many Spanish customs, but I think there are things he misses."

Armando tasted the bitterness of resentment in his throat. "He's been here the whole time, living as one of you?"

"Not the whole time. He and my father went overseas to the north. They only just returned."

Suspicion clouded Armando's thoughts. "What were they doing in the north?"

She hesitated. He darted her a look; then she said, "You must let your father tell you that." Her eyes shuttered, and she walked on. The sounds of the jungle rose around them: the whir of hummingbirds, the screeching cries of parrots, the chittering of insects, and the rustle of the wind through the trees.

They came to a place where boulders tumbled around the source of a spring. Armando stood listening to the liquid music pumping from the heart of the earth. Paloma went to the narrow fount of water, cupped her hands, and drank deeply from the spring. Droplets sprayed her hair and shoulders, catching the sunlight, drawing his gaze to her bare breasts. Her movements were so natural and unaffected, her trust in him so complete.

The urge to touch her became a live beast within him, and his only defense was the fast-crumbling shield of his will.

"What is it, Armando? You look . . . strange."

"You're wrong about me," he said harshly.

She turned, shivering as the water showered her. "What?"

"You trust me to come out here alone with you. As if I could hold myself immune from desire. You should know better."

With measured paces, she came toward him. "I brought you here for that very reason, Armando." She ducked her head, peeking at him from between strands of damp hair. "Because I thought—I hoped—you were not immune to desire."

He caught her beneath the chin, lifted her face to his. "Paloma. My God, am I hearing you right?"

Her teeth caught her full lower lip. She nodded.

Disbelief fueled the heat of his yearning. "You mean . . ." He bent his head and touched his lips to hers, savoring the spring water and loving the soft sweetness of her. "You want this?"

She swayed toward him, sliding her hands up his chest and into his hair. Her open-mouthed kiss was a blatant invitation. He drank deeply, forgetting the troubles he had left at *Gema del Mar*, knowing only the long denied passion of the moment.

He lifted his mouth from hers. "Paloma, I didn't know."

She gave a soft, secret smile. "You weren't meant to."

"Is that why you left me that night, why you refused to talk to me except to say good-bye?"

"I thought it best. I can never be part of your world."

Then let me be a part of yours. He nearly spoke aloud, but he stopped himself. On a wave of astonishment, he realized that when he was with Paloma, he felt a completeness that was missing in his life. But he was not free to offer a future to her, not until he settled his situation with Gabriella.

"This will satisfy you?" he demanded. "A stolen moment every year or so—"

She went rigid in his arms. "It's better than lying awake each night, wondering about you, wanting you." She pressed her forehead to his chest, and he felt the fight flow out of her. "I ache," she confessed in a tortured whisper. "Since I learned true intimacy from you, I have ached for you."

The stark honesty of her statement stunned him. He hugged her close, murmuring into her hair. "Ah, Paloma, you should have sent word. I would have come sooner. My love, you'll always be a puzzle to me, yet your heart is as open as a child's."

"In all my years with your people, I never learned to lie," she said. Her gaze drifted to some distant point. "I learned to keep quiet when it was prudent, but I never learned to lie."

She seemed to be floating away from him, her mind pulling back as if she feared being hurt. Desperate to keep her close, he skimmed his hands over her shoulders and breasts until she shuddered and grasped at him. He tasted magic when he kissed her, magic and mystery and a deep, abiding contentment he had glimpsed only once before—in her arms. For a moment, he was utterly convinced that Paloma had for years been his sole reason for living.

Locked in an embrace, they sank to their knees. Armando wrestled free of his clothes; he reached for her again, tentatively, for her sake bridling the searing passion that boiled through his body.

She surged against him, her voice hoarse in his ear. "No. No, I don't want you to hold back. You did the first time, but now I know, Armando. *I know.*" And then, incredibly, she was making love to him, her hands moving over his body, cupping his sex and drawing him toward her. In a distant part of his mind, he wondered briefly if she had been taught these clever, evocative caresses by a Spaniard in the court of the Duke of Albuquerque. Immediately he discounted the notion. These were no whore's tricks, but the heartfelt caresses of a passionate woman. A woman who was no longer afraid.

He felt a pleasure so intense that it had the fine edge of pain. Her touch made him wild, savage, insatiable, and she welcomed that part of him, pressing him back on the damp ground. She leaned down to draw her tongue over his chest, her silky hair dragging across his bare flesh.

He made a sharp, involuntary sound in his throat. "God," he whispered, gathering her against him, lowering his mouth to her breasts, her belly. "God, Paloma . . . Let me . . ."

She let him. Every way he had ever dreamed of touching her, every secret place he had ever imagined kissing. She no longer needed tenderness and restraint. He came to understand the true meaning of taking a woman. His hands and mouth filled themselves with her essence. Her thoughts became his thoughts; her pleasure became his pleasure. Even before he entered her, their spirits were already joined in some inexorable way. They soared, a single star fan-tailed and ascending into eternity, and the moment held the sparkling, ineffable quality of a miracle.

In the afterglow of their love, Armando lay back on the damp, soft ground and drew Paloma against him. He breathed in the sweet musk of their sex. "You are my first woman," he said.

She pulled away, propping her arms on his bare chest while a smile flirted with her mouth. "That was not the act of a novice."

He framed her face with his hands. Lord, a painter would give up a royal commission for a chance to depict such a face. "It's true. I've experienced . . . some aspects of lovemaking, but never what we shared." His voice seemed weighty, so he forced a smile. "You corrupted a virgin, *querida*."

"I heard no protest—either time." She grew pensive, absently rubbing her hand over the ridged muscles of his belly. At even so slight a motion, he grew hard again, but she seemed not to notice as she gazed into his eyes. "Why, Armando? In so many ways, you are a typical Spaniard."

He stopped her roving hand, drew it to his mouth and kissed each finger. It felt right to bare his soul to her. "I never wanted to risk getting a child on a woman for fear that it would be raised as I was raised—loved by sincere but wrong-minded people, lied to—"

"Believe me," she said in a strange, hard voice, "there are worse things than lies that can befall a child."

Her vehemence startled him. "What do you mean?"

She moved away, snatching up her *nagua* and tying it around her waist. "I'm sorry to say this, but I have little sympathy for you. Your mother and Rafael gave you unconditional love. Even Santiago loves you in his fashion."

Armando yanked on his trousers and stuffed his feet into his high red boots. "He loved me a lot better when I thought he was simply my godfather."

Dark fire flashed in her eyes. "Were you so miserable, then, so abused? I wonder why you risk getting a child on *me*."

Her words lashed him with pain, yet at the same time conjured an image of her swollen with his child. No. He could not let himself think about that now. Trying to lighten the moment, he went down on one knee and made a pantomime of offering her his heart from his cupped hands. "For you, *chica*, I would risk the surety of my soul."

His attempt to recapture their intimacy failed, for she turned away. "Your purity would have been a wondrous gift to Gabriella. Why did you not wait for her?"

Gabriella. Christ Jesus, he had nearly forgotten. "She's here," he blurted. "In Santo Domingo."

Paloma whirled around to stare at him, her eyes narrowed in suspicion, her body stiff as if she braced herself for a blow. "Then you'd best tell me why you came here today."

He sat back, planted his elbows on his knees, and drove his hands into his hair. The story poured out of him: Gabriella's captivity, her desperate flight to freedom with Will, even the dark horror of her mother's sin. Armando could hide nothing from Paloma, trusting her with his pain and disillusionment. He spoke from the heart, his voice low with confusion and betrayal. "I can't marry Gabriella now," he finished.

He expected sympathy. Paloma responded with icy rage. "How dare you?" she demanded. "How dare you come here pretending you want me, when all you needed was to soothe your wounded pride?"

"That's not true."

"Isn't it?" She flung his shirt at him. "So Gabriella is not the maiden you dreamed of, but an ordinary woman ill-used by a man. You refuse to marry her because she is not the pure virgin you demand in a wife."

"That's not the reason." He struggled into his shirt. "She's changed—and not just because of the child. I've changed. We're not the same people who fell in love in a music shop in London."

"You enticed her to Española with grand promises. So now that she has made the voyage, you spurn her."

Blistered by guilt, he tugged his shirt over his head. "It's not like that, damn it! Gabriella has already given me back my ring of promise. She has released me."

"Because she's too kind-hearted to do otherwise. Because she looked at your face and saw the disdain and contempt I see."

He halfheartedly laced his shirt. "I don't think she came here expecting to marry me. She and the child need a safe place to live, a place far from King Henry."

"The child, the child," Paloma shouted. "You speak as if it's a head of livestock. You're speaking of an innocent being."

He looked at Paloma's angry face and felt a shame so

deep that his own ire rose. "I don't need your understanding in a matter between me and Gabriella."

"Then why do you come to me now, just hours after learning that she was not your princess in a charmed tower, but a flesh-and-blood woman? If you cared for me—"

"Care for you?" He grabbed her arm, jerked her toward him so swiftly that she stumbled. "You think I don't? Christ Jesus, I challenged the King of England for you. I became an outlaw for you, sailed in the service of a man I despise."

"It was the vow you cared about, not me."

Armando stopped breathing. Could it be so? Could he truly be so shallow that he would use Paloma to prove his honor? Talking to her was like looking in a mirror. He saw himself reflected in an unflattering light. "That's not—" He stopped when he saw her face. Tears. Tears glistened on her cheeks, as out of place as rain on a sunny day.

"Paloma, I've never seen you cry."

She lifted her hand to her cheek and touched the wetness, seeming as startled as Armando.

"I'm going back to the settlement." She struck off into the woods.

He hastened after her, but made no attempt to speak. He could think of nothing to say, for he had much to think about. Honor, love, family, truth and lies. They swirled around him like a poisoned cloud.

In the village, he found himself face to face with his father. His long hair drifting about his shoulders, a shell necklace on his bare chest, Santiago looked as brown and savage as a Carib warrior. He looked from Armando to Paloma. She ducked her head and hurried into her parents' *bohía*. When Armando started after her, Santiago blocked his way.

His midnight gaze seared Armando. "Come here," he said in the clipped imperative of captain general. "Unless you're afraid." Without waiting to see if Armando would follow, he stalked past the palisades and mounted the hill that concealed the village.

Armando didn't hesitate. It was time to confront the man who had sired and forgotten him.

Santiago stood with his brown legs planted wide and his arms akimbo. The lush forest rolled out in deep green waves below the hill. "What did you do to make her cry?"

The fury in his voice touched off Armando's own temper. "That's between Paloma and me."

Santiago's muscular arm shot out and grasped Armando by the front of the shirt. "So help me God, Armando, if you've hurt her, I'll kill you."

Armando wrested himself free. Santiago's eyes widened; he seemed surprised at his son's strength. "You tried killing me once already," Armando said in a low, furious voice. "You won't do it again."

Santiago tossed his head. "I disciplined you for your own good, and to keep order on the ship. Can't you see that, Son?"

"Don't call me Son."

Uttering a sound of frustration, Santiago paced back and forth on the crest of the hill. "You bedded her, didn't you?"

"That's none of your business."

Santiago slammed his fist on a tree trunk. "Damn it, how could you? Why her when we all know she's hurt so easily?"

"That's a good question, *Capitán*. I wonder if you asked yourself the same when you seduced my mother."

His eyes stormy with menace, Santiago took a step forward. Then he seemed to pull himself back. "I was as young and stupid as you," he snapped. "But you've devoted your life to making yourself my superior. You should have shown better judgment. You're guilty of the very faults you despise in me."

"Must be my tainted gypsy blood," Armando said.

Santiago's hand shot out. But unlike earlier times, Armando was ready. His arm came up and deflected the blow. "We're better matched now that I'm no longer a boy."

Santiago raked a hand through his hair. "God damn it, Armando. Why her? Why Paloma? I know willing women are scarce, but surely you could have found one who was not so fragile."

Livid with jealousy, Armando worried that Paloma had confided in Santiago, told him things she would never reveal to Armando. "Unlike you, I don't simply take any woman. And for your information, she was not hurt by my making love to her."

"Oh, and what was that on her face? Tears of joy?"

"We quarreled . . . afterward."

"See that it doesn't happen again."

Armando intended to do just that, but he resented Santiago's imperative tone. "Are you quite finished, *Capitán*?"

Santiago's eyes mirrored the flare of his temper. "No. I didn't call you aside to upbraid you. I—we—need your help."

Armando's first instinct was to refuse, but the repressed urgency in Santiago's tone intrigued him. "To do what?"

"At first the elders of this clan thought they could defend this settlement against the Spaniards, but I've convinced them that it's impossible. Their numbers are too small, their weapons inadequate. So instead of fighting, the clan is going to move."

"Away from Española?"

"Far away. Very far. Not everyone at once. It's safer to move people in small numbers. The migration could take many years, but it's started already."

Armando was not prepared for the sense of loss that tore at him. The idea of never seeing Paloma again left him feeling as hollow as an empty wine flask. "Where?"

"There is a place to the north of here. The elders have known the way for generations. It's no island, but a vast Tierra Firme that the natives call Bimini. It's home to a clan called the Calusas. They're very protective of their territory."

"Then what makes you think they'll welcome this clan?"

"It's already agreed." Squatting in the dust, Santiago used a stick to make a rough sketch. "The Lucayos are here, to the north. Then there's a string of islands sweeping up to the tip of the territory of the Calusas. Joseph, his wife, and I have made the voyage by canoe to meet with the other clan. Little by little, our clan will follow."

"That's crazy."

"No more crazy than staying here, waiting for the *encomenderos* to seize the natives as slaves or infect them with killing diseases."

"Assume they make the voyage safely. What does that get them? A few more years of freedom? New expeditions sail every week. Before long, the conquistadors will find this place."

"I expect so. Here—"

"You're not making sense."

"You're interrupting. Here in the islands, it's impossible to resist the *encomenderos*. The natives are cornered. In a vast land like Bimini, there are innumerable retreat positions."

"Retreat positions? I don't like the sound of that."

Santiago gazed down the hill at the settlement, which was nearly hidden in its green camouflage. "I was on Colón's first voyage. The clan we encountered welcomed us as gods." He spat in disgust. "Those poor souls and thousands of others are now dead. This group will meet the same fate if they don't learn to meet the Spanish threat from a position of strength."

A chill touched Armando's heart. "You're with them. Why?"

"What else am I to do? I can go on with my life as before, plying across the Ocean Sea, bringing more and more colonists, making myself fat and rich as a sea captain." Santiago stared at him for a long moment. "Or I can follow my heart. These people are desperate, Armando."

He could not deny it. Resolve burned past his resentment of Santiago and settled like a glowing coal in the pit of his stomach. "How can I help you?"

The desperate and cold-blooded plan of the islanders preoccupied Armando as he rode back to *Gema del Mar*. He worried about Paloma, he worried about Gabriella, but most of all he worried that his world was coming apart.

Gabriella, his singing angel, had borne the son of Henry VIII. Paloma, his earthy lover, had been disappointed by him one time too many. And Santiago, without apologies, had enlisted his help in this outrageous enterprise.

With his unsettled thoughts as company, he arrived home and found Will and El Hakim deep in discussion, waving their arms and speaking a mixture of Castilian and English with a few Arabic words thrown in. What a contrasting picture they made—pale, flame-haired Will and El Hakim, tanned black by the island sun.

Armando cleared his throat. His friends glanced up. "There you are, Infidel," El Hakim said.

"I'm glad you two met at last. Where's Gabriella?"

"Rosa has taken her walking with the babe. She wanted to see the rest of the place," said Will. His gray eyes darkened to the shade of storm clouds. "You were gone all night, *amigo*."

Armando bridled at the accusing tone. "My betrothed comes with another man's brat in tow. Can you blame me for feeling somewhat . . . chagrined?"

"You speak as if she had a choice. Damn it, Armando—"

"Peace!" El Hakim held up his broad hand. "The two of you bicker like bazaar wives. It does little to solve the problem."

"True." Armando felt the weight of the sleepless night pressing on him. Agitated, he went to his desk and straightened a stack of letters and papers, most of them proprietary documents sent by Rafael. In his haste, he knocked over the freestanding hand mirror, catching it before it shattered on the floor. "But this is between Gabriella and me."

Will made a visible effort to relax his tense shoulders. "El Hakim and I were discussing the farm. I'm impressed."

"I put a lot of work into it." Paloma had, too, he recalled. Moving to the window, he saw his reward: swaying fields ripe with his crops. It was all his now, but for how much longer? If he let himself be swept up in Santiago's plan, how much longer would he be able to give his energy to farming?

"Have you considered powering the *trapiche* with water?" Will asked.

"I . . . Water? No, of course not. The process would be too complex."

"Would it?" El Hakim inserted his finger under his burnoose and scratched his head. "Not to us."

Armando turned from the window to study his friends. Will's craft of instrument-making might lend itself to the mechanical design, and El Hakim—baptized or not—was a Moor. Armando recalled the fabulous fountains and aqueducts of Córdoba and Granada, all the products of Moorish genius. Perhaps between the two of them they could make a workable design.

"Not having to rely on horse power would be a blessing," he said.

"Winning the royal prize would be a blessing. You'd leave Baltasar in the dust," El Hakim suggested slyly.

Armando shook his head. "We haven't got a chance. The prize goes to the plantation that produces the largest yield of sugar. We can't touch Baltasar's numbers."

"Is he a superior grower, then?" asked Will.

"Hardly," said Armando.

"He has more slaves," El Hakim explained. "Hundreds of them. Even some from Mother Africa. His production is high because he feeds them nothing, forces each native to provide tribute in the form of sugarcane."

"His refinery is powered by slaves, too," Armando added. "His workers die by the dozens, and so far he's been able to replace them with ease. But the day might come when he runs out of slaves. It might come sooner than anyone thinks."

"What's that supposed to mean?" Will asked.

Although no one was in sight, Armando lowered his voice. He went to his desk, sat down, and idly turned up the small mirror. He blinked in startlement. For a brief moment he'd had the eerie sensation of staring at Santiago. His hollow-eyed face was taut with rebellion, his beard thick and unkempt.

"Well?" El Hakim prompted.

"The natives have a plan, and they want our help. They intend to migrate to a vast land to the north, which they call Bimini. They've already made alliances with the natives there. It's only a matter of time before Spaniards breach those new shores. When that happens, the clans will ambush the invaders."

Will's jaw dropped. "You mean massacre Spaniards?"

Armando nodded.

"By the boatload?" El Hakim asked.

Armando nodded again and waited for shock and revulsion.

"I like it," said Will.

"I see the gates to Heaven already," said El Hakim.

Armando scowled into the mirror. "These are my countrymen we're talking about."

Will smiled. "*Amigo*, your countrymen murdered my family along with thousands of other Jews. They slaughtered El Hakim's people and stole their kingdom."

El Hakim pressed his palms together. "Don't expect righteous outrage from a Jew and a Moor. I applaud the plan. They must start fighting now, or their race will die."

Armando thought of the natives, crushed by slavery, mutilated by the conquerors with their swords and dogs, sick with diseases hitherto unknown in their culture. In one generation, the Spaniards had shattered their world. Could he turn his back, refuse to watch the extermination of a whole society?

The plan was farfetched and brutal. It was a plan of desperation.

"All right," he said at last, turning his head slightly as he glimpsed something in the mirror. On the side of his neck was a small sucking bruise, sweetly inflicted by Paloma's mouth. An untimely yearning gripped him. With a small, furtive motion he tugged at his shirt to conceal her mark. "I've been trying to talk myself out of this, but we'll help them."

"We need a plan," said El Hakim. "Something to compel the Spaniards to Bimini by the boatload."

"We should appeal to their greed for land and gold," said Will.

"They can gain that by sailing west," Armando reminded him. "We need to invent something with a unique appeal."

El Hakim beetled his brows in concentration. "What is the one thing stronger than a Spaniard's lust for gold?"

"His faith in God?" Armando suggested.

Will snorted and sent Armando a wry glance. "His vanity?"

Armando set aside the mirror. "Bastard."

"No, that could be the key. Here, listen . . ."

"What's that you said?" In the dusty waterfront cantina, Juan Ponce de León lifted his hand to signal for more wine. A native servant came forward and refilled the cups from a large, spouted calabash. Bercerillo, Juan's ever-present deerhound, lifted his lip to bare his yellow fangs at the islander.

Will, Armando, and El Hakim exchanged furtive looks. The Moor only pretended to drink, for his religion forbade imbibing. "Lower your voice, my lord," Armando cautioned. "If too many find out about this wonder, our shares will be diminished."

Juan stroked his beard. His hand trembled slightly as he took a drink. Aye, thought Armando, they had fingered the right man to share their "secret." Having failed to enrich himself with the conquest of Boriquen, Juan was growing desperate for glory. He had two homely daughters to dower and a wife with expensive tastes. Even more important, Juan Ponce de León had the soul of a conquistador—part heathen, part crusader, all man. He had that vital, desperate need to glorify himself with his own deeds, to drape himself in the glittering mantle of his achievements. With the help of his kinsman Baltasar he also had enough capital to finance a major expedition.

"I understand the need for discretion," he said gravely. "This place is being overrun by upstarts and commoners." He slid a glance at Will. "And men of questionable character and background." He then eyed El Hakim.

"Only a true gentleman can be trusted with this information," said Armando. "And only an adventurer as daring as yourself can be relied upon to mount the proper expedition."

Juan drew himself up, passing his hand over his saffron silk neckcloth. "Quite so. But how can we be certain this land is not the product of Indian chicanery? It wouldn't be the first time the savages have misled their masters.''

With a flourish, El Hakim produced a pair of maps on parchment. "This is Cosa's chart."

"Cosa was an intimate of Admiral Colón," Armando said. "He was one of the most respected cartographers of his age."

El Hakim indicated the islands of Española and Cuba. "Look here, to the north."

"Terra incognita," Juan mused.

"And here's Cantino's map, drawn two years later," Will said. "Cantino's charts are so valuable the Portuguese have tried to steal them. You see, again there's a significant land mass to the north."

They talked a while longer, flattering, cajoling, drinking. Juan Ponce de León imbibed their lies like a man who had thirsted too long. His eyes glittered like the treasure conjured by his own imagination.

At the end of an hour, he pushed back from the table and stood. "I shall apply at once for a patent from the king."

"Excellent, my lord." Armando tried to restrain himself from nudging his companions. He sobered his spirits with the thought that, if the expedition ended the way the natives planned, they would be sending Juan Ponce de León to his death.

"Yes. His Majesty will surely grant his indulgence to this new enterprise," Juan enthused. "Think of it, *amigos*. Before long, we shall crown our motherland with her most intriguing ornament yet." He gripped the pommel of his sword. "With the Fountain of Youth!"

CHAPTER 20

Will raced to the top of the rise of land in front of the hacienda. There he stopped, catching his breath and trying to hold back excitement and apprehension.

In the past two years, he reflected, *Gema del Mar* had achieved fame throughout the islands. The water-powered mill he and El Hakim had fashioned had won Armando the royal bounty and deepened the hatred of Baltasar de León. Bartolome de las Casas, now an ordained Jesuit and self-proclaimed champion of the natives, often brought visitors to see the profits that rewarded the virtue of opposing slavery.

Will scrubbed his sleeve across his sweating brow. The odd thing was, Armando seemed to care nothing for the accolades. He had claimed no credit for the innovations, nor for their success. Since throwing in his lot with the natives, he had thought of nothing save the risky and savage enterprise.

Will drew in a breath of air that was heavy and ripe

with the scent of flowers. Finally, with an unsteady hand, he gave in to his pounding sense of anticipation and lifted a brass spyglass to his eye. The lens encircled the towering masts of two ships with sailors perched on the yardarms. Only moments ago, El Hakim had raced up to the hacienda. Juan's fleet had been sighted in the outer harbor; within a few hours, the ships would make port.

It had taken months for Juan Ponce de León to win King Ferdinand's sanction for his voyage. The ambitious explorer had, wisely, omitted any reference to the Fountain of Youth from his patent. Discovering new wonders had become a race among the greedy, a race in which Juan figured himself the champion.

His expedition to Bimini had, at long last, set sail some six months earlier. With his typical ungovernable recklessness, Armando had signed on with the three ships. He had insisted on doing so in order to convince Juan of his sincerity in presenting him with a golden opportunity. Will suspected that Armando's growing restlessness was the true reason.

There weren't supposed to be any survivors, thought Will. The league of natives, led by their gypsy confederate, Santiago, had planned to ambush the invaders and scuttle their ships, sparing only Armando. Something had gone awry, for the fleet was returning and from a distance appeared intact.

Will lowered his spyglass. He had best tell Gabriella.

Like the plantation, the villa had grown with improvements and refinements. The house resembled a sprawling village with lime-washed walls, breezy hallways that opened out to flower-decked patios, arched windows and doorways, and a roof of clay-colored tile manufactured in the new tile works of Santo Domingo.

A gem indeed, Will reflected. The pristine house of a prosperous gentleman. How surprised the haughty lords of the Indies would be if they knew the truth: that *Gema del Mar* was inhabited by a secret Jew, a Moor, an Indian conspirator, and the mother of King Henry VIII's only son.

Secrets, he thought. They were so easy to keep when one lived an ocean away from Europe. Unless . . . He laid waste to the fear before it could form.

Will hastened into the villa, passing beneath the shaded porch and crossing the main patio where a fountain murmured into the late-afternoon quiet. For the sake of propriety, Gabriella kept her own quarters. She was attended by Sara Marquez, a lay sister who was a friend of Fray Bartolome de las Casas.

Will heard Gabriella singing and stopped for a moment to listen. The years had failed to mute the magical quality of her voice. The native residents of *Gema del Mar* believed a spirit inhabited her. With her charm and openness, she had transformed their awe into loyal affection.

Drawn by her soft lullaby, Will stepped soundlessly into the dim outer room of her quarters. He spied her through a doorway hung with strips of rush palm that rustled in the breeze. She sat on an ottoman placed beside the child's cot. Phillip lay sleeping beneath a cotton blanket. At nearly three years of age, he was large and robust, and showed signs of precociousness. He had become the focal point of Gabriella's life.

Will stood watching her, an enchanting picture gilded by sunlight. Eschewing Castilian fashions, she wore a loose white blouse and a lavender skirt. She had long since discarded pattens or slippers; her bare feet peeked from the hem of the skirt. She wore her hair plaited down the back. Curly wisps had come loose to embellish her neck with a silken tracery as delicate and complex as Moorish plasterwork. Her face, in profile, still bore the allure of her youthful beauty, but the lines of her features and the depth in her eyes had been gained through hardship and uncompromising maternal love. She was no longer the ethereal angel who had charmed the English court; she was now a woman of strength and endurance, decidedly earthbound, yet no less appealing for all that.

Will loved her more than ever.

He brushed back the hanging and stepped into the room. Looking up, Gabriella stopped singing. She tucked the coverlet more securely over her son and stood.

Will smiled. "You spoil the lad shamelessly," he whispered. "He'll never go to sleep without your singing."

She led the way out of the room. Her sitting room was small, with native cotton mats on the walls and floor. Bunches of dried flowers hung on strings from the rafters. Gabriella went to a side shelf and lifted a clay jug. "I used to have ambitions to perform in every court in Europe. But when Phillip gives me one last smile before dropping off to sleep, I feel I was born to sing for him, and him alone."

She paused in the act of pouring cups of wine. "Oh, Will, I want life to be easy for him. I never want him to suffer because of who his parents are."

"He won't. We won't—er, you won't let him."

If Gabriella noticed the slip, she gave no sign as she poured wine and handed a cup to Will. "How was work today?"

Her tone sparked a brief fantasy: a wife welcoming her husband home. They would sup together and talk in depth about matters of mutual concern; then they would retire to their bedchamber to—

Stop it. Stop torturing yourself.

"Gabriella, I think you'll want to ride down to the harbor with me. Juan Ponce de León's fleet is back."

She stood very still, but he could hear the swift intake of her breath. "What can it mean?"

"We won't know until we see who survived."

A whirlwind seemed to erupt within her, propelling her through the house as she made her preparations. Within minutes, she emerged with her hair tidied, a shawl draped over her shoulders, riding pattens on her feet, and anticipation dancing with apprehension in her huge, pansylike eyes.

"I'm ready. Sister Sara will look after Phillip." She pulled Will to the yard behind the hacienda. She seemed barely aware of him as he handed her up into the saddle.

Armando Viscaino was a bloody fool, thought Will. Even after all this time, Gabriella still loved him.

Armando felt like a fool. With the adventure passing in a blur of brightly colored memories in his head, he set foot on dry land for the first time in weeks.

He walked over to Juan and his pilot, Pedro de Alaminos, who stood on the steps of the governor's house. The commander of the expedition had been on a sister ship for the return voyage, so this was the first time Armando had seen Juan since the frantic embarkment from the mysterious land they had gone to conquer.

Juan Ponce de León had changed. Six months earlier, armed with a fleet of three ships, a royal charter, and Spanish arrogance, he had sallied forth like a crusader. Now he was thin, pale, unkempt, and angry. A defeated man. He had found no magic fountain; he had seized no cache of gold.

Christ Jesus, but the land! thought Armando. The place they had gone possessed more dense, lush beauty than the Indies, more shadowy promises than Cuba.

But in Juan's eyes, the enterprise had failed.

Armando bowed in deference. "My Lord Captain."

Juan turned away from de Alaminos. "It's not the glorious return we'd hoped for, eh?"

You weren't supposed to return at all. "It was unfortunate indeed. Is the crew of the flagship well?"

"No, we lost four more of the wounded men. Those damned savages poisoned every last arrow and spearhead."

Armando loosened his bright red neckcloth. The garment had been his shield against the fierce and well-organized natives. Santiago, now living among them, had instructed the allies to spare anyone wearing the red scarf. Armando forced himself to ask the crucial question. "Will you be going back?"

Juan tugged at his ill-trimmed beard. "To Pascua Florida? You're mad. Never in all my years have I come upon savages so ruthless, so single-minded in their determination to resist us. That story of the Fountain of Youth is surely a lie."

"Would they fight so doggedly in order to protect a lie?"

The question gave Juan pause; then he turned away, muttering and shaking his head. Armando stood for a moment in the cool shade of the porch. His every instinct told him to find a horse and race off to the settlement in the west. To Paloma.

A notion as ridiculous as it was inevitable. More than two years had passed since she had banished him from her life.

A detail of sailors passed by with a litter. Their burden of a canvas-draped corpse stirred the agony of Armando's torn loyalties. The dead men had families; they'd had dreams and ambitions. Armando had lured them to their deaths.

He walked toward the main plaza, and the sight that greeted him reawakened his sense that he was right. A native woman, naked and lying in the dust, was chained to a stake. One ear had been cut off and her nostrils had been slit. Flies swarmed over her back, which bore the oozing weals of a stout lashing.

Appalled, Armando started toward her. Before he reached her, a passing soldier stopped, felt for a pulse, listened for breathing, then summoned a slave detail to carry off the corpse.

"Welcome home," said a voice tinged with irony.

"Will!" Spinning around, Armando caught his friend in an embrace. Over Will's shoulder he spied Gabriella, who stood watching them, her eyes bright with anticipation.

The familiar taste of guilt flooded his mouth. His promises had lured this woman across the sea. She had, with a grace he did not deserve, released him from his vow. He still felt beholden to her and, though she asked for nothing, he still felt she deserved more than he had given her.

The expedition had provided a temporary escape. While his future was bound up with the native alliance, he had not had to face his guilt. But now he had returned hale and whole.

He broke away from Will and took Gabriella by the shoulders, kissing her on each cheek. "It's good to see you, Gabriella."

"And you, Armando." She trembled slightly in his arms. "I prayed for you."

He affected a grin. "Your prayers must have been answered. I had a safe journey."

"Thank God." She stepped back, looking vibrant as ever, her glossy curls shining in the sun and her face rosy with pleasure. Once, the sight of her had transported him into paroxysms of pleasure. Now he felt only a crushing sense of futility.

"Where's El Hakim?" he asked.

"At the villa," Will replied. "Probably half crazy by now to hear your news."

"Come on." Armando slipped one arm around Gabriella and the other around Will.

As they started across the plaza, Baltasar de León intercepted them. "Well, well. Don't you make a cozy threesome?"

"Stow it, Baltasar," Armando said easily. "You ought to go to your cousin. He needs a shoulder to cry on."

Baltasar planted himself in their path. He looked the perfect conquistador in his velvet doublet shaped like breast armor, silken hose and high boots, a sword slapping his thigh and a glow of arrogance in his eyes. "I want some answers from you."

Armando dropped his arms from Gabriella and Will. "You'll get my fist in your mouth if you don't step aside."

"Easy," Will muttered. "Remember your promise to the governor. One punch could cost you the farm."

Armando found, to his surprise, that the plantation meant nothing to him. Somewhere, sometime, his dreams had changed. He had no interest in wresting a fortune from this conquered land.

He might have abandoned his dreams of *Gema del Mar*, but the plantation had become Will's life. His home. Security. If Armando attacked Baltasar now, Will, Gabriella, and El Hakim would suffer. He forced himself to relax. "I won't give you the satisfaction of stirring up trouble, Baltasar."

"Aye, there's enough trouble, thanks to you." Baltasar aimed a scathing look at the defeated men of the expedition slowly dispersing through the town. "I came here expecting to see my kinsman magically transformed into a young man, his holds sunk to the gunwales with treasure." He lifted one eyebrow. "Isn't that what you promised?"

"I promised nothing."

Baltasar's eyes narrowed. "I invested a fortune in this venture. I might as well have tossed my silver into the sea."

Armando sucked his tongue. "Such a pity. You might be forced to actually work for your living."

"By God, I'll see you brought to your knees," Baltasar warned. "You, and that English pig!"

"Shut your mouth!" Armando ordered.

"Aye, the both of you and"—Baltasar's burning gaze raked over Gabriella—"that whore you share between y—"

A large fist planted itself in the middle of Baltasar's face. He went down without a sound.

Amazed, Armando watched Will shake out his hand.

"Christ Jesus," Armando said. "I had forgotten how quick you are. But you shouldn't have hit him."

Will stepped over Baltasar and headed for the horses. "He gave me no choice."

Armando followed. "You've endured worse slurs before."

"I didn't hit him because of what he said about me." Will tossed the reins to Armando. "I hit him because of what he said about Gabriella."

Outside the palisades of the settlement, Armando dismounted in the jungle. The thick forest canopy gave the darkness a special quality, for the treetops obscured the stars. He could see only the occasional dim flash of a lightning bug.

He paused to whistle in imitation of a motmot bird. An answering whistle confirmed that the agreed-upon signal was still recognized by the natives.

By the time he reached the village, the remaining inhabitants had gathered in the plaza, dark shapes against the blackness of night. There were so few left. Many, out of desperation and blind faith in their mysterious brother gods—and in Santiago—had already migrated to the new country.

Armando's gaze sought Paloma, and when he found her, he closed his mind to all else—the expectant faces, the cautious words of welcome, the flare of the central fire.

He walked directly to her. He did not care that she had refused to speak to him for two years. The tenderness and joy he should have felt upon seeing Gabriella at the harbor flooded him at the sight of Paloma.

Unable to read her shadowed expression, without awaiting her consent, he drew her to him and kissed her long and hard.

"By God, I missed you," he said into her sleek black hair.

She seemed shaken by his greeting, but recovered, tossing her head and extricating herself from his arms. Her eyes, aglow from the firelight, held a guarded look. "Welcome, Armando."

"Come," said Joseph, motioning for the clan to move in front of the *cacique*'s hut, which faced the fire. He seemed unperturbed—and unsurprised—by the way Armando had greeted his daughter. "We've been waiting to hear from you."

Armando settled himself on a cotton mat. Anacaona presided from her sculptured *duho* chair. A clay platter laden with fruit, cakes, and morsels of roasted fish was set before Armando. He drank from a cup of *guayaba* juice and began his recitation.

"It started as we knew it would. Juan Ponce de León excited the Spanish court with his talk of a rich new land."

He paused while Paloma translated for the group.

"Juan obtained a patent and borrowed heavily from investors to outfit the expedition. The fleet cruised northward, and we put in briefly at San Salvador. The place you call Guanahaní."

He glanced at Joseph and Anacaona; she dropped her hand to her husband's shoulder and her eyes hazed with far-off memories. It was the isle of her birth and girlhood, the place where Spaniard and islander had first met and clashed. The beginning of a nightmare of newness, an ugly conquest of a gentle people.

"It's deserted now," said Armando. "We passed the string of islands called the Lucayos and continued northward. The lookout spied a shoreline, and we made a landing. The beauty of the new country was as you said. It took our breath away. It was the feast we call Easter, and so Juan called the place Pascua Florida, claimed it for Spain, and declared himself *cacique*.''

The islanders bristled and muttered at this news; Armando waved a hand to silence them. ''Your allies were ready. They beckoned as if in welcome. The Spaniards expected the usual greeting, as if they were deities from the sky.''

Armando took a deep breath. ''Then the natives attacked.'' He closed his eyes and recalled the screaming painted hordes descending on the astonished Spaniards. ''The battle lasted a few hours. We couldn't get back to the landing boats until nightfall. When we did, Juan decided to explore elsewhere rather than lose more men.''

''Was Santiago there?''

Armando nodded, opening his mind to the astounding memory. With his strong form anointed with body dye, his long hair plaited, and his hands clutching poisoned weapons, Santiago had led the attack. ''He was dressed and painted in the manner of the natives. No one but I recognized him.''

''And did you speak to him?''

''No. It would have been too risky.'' Armando had been relieved. He did not want to face Santiago playing the hero, the champion, the fighter for freedom.

''And so the fleet returned to the islands,'' said Paloma.

''Not immediately. We coasted southward. It was a strange voyage. We had a good strong wind, yet we made very little headway. A piece of wood dropped into the water drifted steadily northward as if borne on a river current.''

Paloma translated this, and several of the islanders nodded. An old man spoke at length.

''He says the people of the cays know of this stream in the sea,'' said Paloma.

''Juan thought it would propel a fleet back to Spain.''

"Excellent," said Joseph. "I hope it propels them all."

"We finally reached the southern tip of the land and came upon more islands. Juan called them Los Martires, for in profile they resemble a line of suffering men. A pity he's such a skilled sailor, for he might have gone aground on those treacherous reefs. We found the west coast of the land. The sea was calm, a dark gray color. We put in at a large bay."

The islanders waited in breath-held expectation.

"It was the same as the first encounter," Armando said. "The natives attacked. Santiago led them there, too, so he must have traveled overland. More people had joined them. They made canoe raids on the ships. The Spaniards gave up almost without a fight, and we returned first to San Juan, then here."

"My God," said Joseph, holding tightly to Anacaona's hand. "Santiago's alliance worked."

"We don't know that yet."

"Juan has a big mouth. Before long, everyone from Havana to San Germán will know it's insane to venture north."

"One man's failure is another man's challenge," Armando said. "What Spaniard would not think he could outdo Juan?"

"Then the battles will go on," Anacaona vowed, speaking for her clan. "They will go on until no Spaniard dares to go near the new homeland."

Armando said nothing. Anacaona was a wise woman of long experience. But she could not know the true nature of the conquerors. Like a terrier after a rat, a Spaniard would not give up the chance to expand the empire and win riches and fame. Besides, Anacaona could not grasp that the Spaniards came in numbers beyond anything she could imagine. Trying to vanquish them one by one was like shooting arrows at the stars. Yet seeing the confidence of his friends gave him pause. He let them revel in the temporary victory. They had outsmarted the conquerors. They deserved to feel pride.

"You have done us a great service, *guahiro*," said Anacaona.

Paloma looked at her mother in surprise. So did Armando. Never had they called him *guahiro*—one of us.

"I'd best get back." Armando grasped Paloma's hand and, before she could protest, drew her away from the firelit circle.

She tried to twist from his grip. "Leave me alone!"

He pulled her against him, closing his eyes as his body welcomed hers. "God, you give me such a sweet pain, Paloma."

"Then take your pain and go. I'm needed here."

"I need you," he said, sliding his arms around her, moving his hands over her bare back. "I've left you alone for too long."

"And I thank you for respecting my wishes."

His fingers caressed her warm flesh, her strong shoulders. "It was a mistake."

He lowered his head to kiss her, but she pulled away. "Our lives have taken different paths. You have your responsibilities in Santo Domingo, and I must go the way of my clan."

Icy fear coiled in his gut. "What do you mean? Damn it, you're not going north to—"

"I'll go when the time is right." When he started to protest, she said hastily, "That time may not come for many more years. My parents won't think of sending me until they're certain the alliance is working."

Armando took small comfort in that. "It's not safe here, either," he said. "Come back to the plantation, Paloma. I know your parents would consent—"

"No." She started walking back. "That's where you belong, not I." She paused, turning slightly, her shape limned by firelight, the breeze lifting the strands of her hair.

His heart called out to her, but he held silent. There was no middle ground. In order to have her, he would have to give up everything he had worked for all his life. He would become an empty, wandering man, a rootless gypsy. Like Santiago.

He rebelled at the notion, numbed himself to the ache inside him, and returned to Santo Domingo.

New expeditions set sail each month. Most men, forewarned by Juan's experience in La Florida, headed west to the long, narrow curve of Tierra Firme. Juan Ponce de León, humiliated by his failure and impoverished by his loss, sought easier prey to the south in the Lesser Antilles. The Caribs had risen against their conquerors, and Juan went to pacify them. He seemed eager to erase the memory of his traumatic defeat at the hands of savages he considered little more than wild animals.

Sebastian Cabot made a brief appearance in Santo Domingo. Swearing that he had reformed his marauding ways, he pursuaded El Hakim to accompany him to Darien, far to the south, where gold lay beneath every rock and flowed in every stream.

Baltasar de León sailed to Spain to repair his lost fortune.

Slave hunters, whose reputations were as questionable as their morals, attempted a few raids on La Florida. Each time, they were driven off by freedom-loving natives whose hatred for the Spaniards seemed to endow them with inhuman strength.

In 1516, King Ferdinand died, and his grandson Charles took the throne. Fray Barto lost no time in paying homage to the nineteen-year-old emperor. His impassioned pleas won the Dominican friar the title of Protector of the Indians.

In 1517, Panfilio de Narvaez mounted an expedition to colonize La Florida. Heavily armed and frighteningly well-organized, the natives came howling out of the dense forests to meet the new invaders. Of the six hundred colonists, soldiers, and priests, only four survived.

In the same year, a ship in the broad gulf of Tierra Firme blew off course. Its pilot, Juan's friend de Alaminos, plotted a course for La Florida in order to take on water. More screaming hordes of natives attacked the shore party, and the ship was barely able to limp into harbor at Havana.

In 1519, Alonso Alvarez de Pineda sought a new western passage around the arc of the great gulf. As with every other attempt to breach the verdant shores of La Florida, he met with fierce and relentless resistance.

In the cantinas of Santo Domingo, seasoned explorers shook their heads in bewilderment. The natives were fighting back. The concept was new and horrifying to men accustomed to instant and unquestioning submission.

The islanders of Anacaona's village were leaving one by one. Armando lived in dread that one day Paloma would be among the passengers in the fleets of giant canoes pointed to the north. But she stayed, living in her parents' *bohía*, aiding runaway slaves and natives who had been driven from their homes.

She treated Armando with cordial reserve. He forced himself to respect her aloofness, for to push her would be to lose her altogether. He always returned home from his visits with a sense of restless frustration. More and more, he found himself watching the ships departing the harbor.

As Armando began looking outward, Will focused his attention on the plantation. Weak from a tropical fever, El Hakim returned from his voyage with Cabot. The bluff adventurer had failed to find the riches he craved. He seemed, El Hakim reported from his divan in the sick-room, to be obsessed with collecting Spanish sea charts for a purpose the Moor did not trust.

The cane fields flourished and the water-powered *ingenio* mill ran smoothly. As more and more luxury goods arrived from Spain, *Gema del Mar* came to resemble a hacienda of Andalucía, with garden patios, glazed windows, a wrought iron gate, even a tiny chapel. It was, Armando realized one afternoon as he was watching the breaking of a new horse, all he had ever dreamed of. The attainment of his ambition. He felt nothing.

Troubled by discontent, he turned to Will, who leaned beside him against the fence. "Tell me something, *amigo*. When a dream is fulfilled, what is there left to hope for?"

Will smiled. "One dream leads to another, doesn't it?"

"Not in my case." Armando swept his arm to encompass the vast reaches of the plantation. "Men have died for less than this. Yet it means nothing to me."

"Because you have no one to share it with."

Armando glanced at him sharply, then hoisted himself up to straddle the fence. The caballeros, two nimble brothers from Cádiz, were trying to wrestle a lunge bridle onto a blaze-faced roan gelding. Across the yard, seven-year-old Phillip perched on the fence, his chin planted in his cupped hand, an expression of concentration on his handsome young face.

"Just what's that supposed to mean?" Armando asked.

"Don't pretend you don't know." Will nodded at the lad, who had climbed down from the fence to greet one of the hands. The worker led a dun-colored pony into the corral. "The boy's old enough now that he wouldn't confuse you as his true father if you were to marry Gabriella."

"Is that what you think is holding me back?"

Will sent him a wry glance. "You claim your confusion about your true father is responsible for all your misery. I assumed you didn't wish the same on Phillip."

"Neither of us wants marriage anymore."

Will whistled softly through his teeth. "Neither of you? Or just you?"

"Damn it, quit preaching to me about Gabriella. She's happy. The boy's happy. Why complicate things?"

"Why, indeed?" Bracing his hand on a fence post, Will vaulted over and crossed the yard to meet Phillip.

"Will! Can you help me ride my new pony?" Phillip asked breathlessly. "Please, Will!"

Chuckling, Will swung the boy into a high-pommeled saddle atop the sleepy-looking pony. "There you go, ca-ballero. *Dios*, but you make a pretty pair."

Phillip sat straight in the saddle. "Let's go, Will. Let's go very fast."

Ambling away from the stable compound, Armando admired Will's ease with the child. Phillip was an energetic, engaging lad, spoiled by servants, clerics, and visitors alike. He was handsome, too—apple cheeked and sandy haired, big and robust for his age. Just like his—

Armando cut off the memory. The boy's heritage was a danger to them all. It must never be spoken of, nor even thought of.

A faint puff of dust above the trees caught his eye. Someone came up the road toward the hacienda. Only a large party could kick up enough dust to be visible at this distance.

Armando hurried down the road, rounding a bend in the hill, then stopping when he heard voices.

"I'd know him anywhere, Your Excellency. That distinctive red hair, his oily Semitic charm. I'm certain he's still here, poisoning good Christians with his evil ways."

Armando had not heard that voice in nearly seven years. Filled with fury and suspicion, he kept to the concealment of the dense undergrowth. Below him, on the serpentine road, he spied Baltasar de León. The haughty gentleman had reined his horse beside a robed cleric on a mule. Behind them, some hundred paces distant, rode a contingent of soldiers.

Armando steeled himself to order Baltasar away. Then a glint of silver caught Armando's eye. The cleric clutched a staff topped with the device of the Inquisition. Armando's blood ran cold as Baltasar's purpose crystallized in his mind. Cutting straight through the trees, he raced to the stable yard and leaped the fence. Phillip's pony shied, but the boy clung stoutly to the pommel of the saddle.

Armando ripped the reins from Will's hand. "Run for your life," he said in a low, urgent voice.

Will frowned. "What—"

"Come on." Armando tossed the reins to a caballero and hauled Will away to the stables, which were dim and close with the smell of hay and horse dung. "It's Baltasar, back from Spain. He's brought an inquisitor and a small army. They've found you out!"

Will's face paled, but he stood his ground. "Then I'll answer the charges."

"Damn it, Will, you can't. I know you." Working with frantic speed, Armando saddled the best horse in the stable. "You won't break under physical torture, but the minute they start reviling the Law of Moses, you'll lose control."

"Then I'll stand and fight."

The sound of milling horses came from the front of the villa. Armando tossed his head in fury. "Fine. You can watch them torture Gabriella and the boy, too."

At that, Will clambered into the saddle of the deep-chested bay. "Where should I go?"

Armando hesitated, gripped by sudden agony. He knew of only one safe place. But by sending Will there, he risked placing Paloma in danger.

In the distance, an iron bell clanged a summons. Baltasar had reached the house. "Go to Anacaona's village," Armando instructed, telling himself that the clan had lived there in secrecy for years, and probably would for many more. "You remember how to get there?"

Will nodded, sawed at the reins, and wheeled his big horse. By the time the soldiers swarmed to the rear of the compound, Armando stood alone with Phillip on his pony. He gave Baltasar an engaging grin. "How nice to see you again."

"Where is he? Where is the *Marrano*?"

Phillip stuck out his chin. "Who are you calling a pig?"

Armando pinched the boy's shoulder in warning. "We keep our pigs in a sty."

"Damn it, you'll tell me where William Blythe went."

"William Blythe?" Armando scratched his chin. "I've not seen him for months. I'm his friend, not his keeper."

Baltasar glared, torn between beating the truth out of Armando and following a fresh trail. "Liar! I'll waste no time on you." He lifted his hand. "Captain Guerrero! Bring the Indian guide and the hounds."

The sight made Armando's confidence falter. It was possible for a man to elude capture in the densely forested mountains to the north. But the sharp-eyed native guide and the chained, snarling dogs evened the odds.

"I've waited seven years for this moment," Baltasar said in a low, deadly voice. "Now we'll see who wins, you bastard."

Hours later, in the deepness of the night, Armando paced the keeping room while Gabriella stared numbly at the small fire burning in the grate.

"Damn! How could Baltasar have found out?" Armando demanded, raking a hand through his long hair. "I thought we were safe."

"No man of Hebrew blood can ever be safe in Spain or her possessions," Gabriella said softly. "We were fools ever to think otherwise."

Armando slapped his hand on the packet of notarized

documents the cleric had produced. "He knew everything—about the family's house in Toledo, Will's uncle David . . . How?"

Gabriella pressed her hands to her mouth. "Jesus wept! It was my mother!"

Armando felt a familiar jolt of distaste. He tried never to think about the sins of Mercedes de Montana and her father . . . her lover. "Your mother?"

Gabriella nodded miserably. "When we went to see her in Spain, she had just been visited by Doña Elvira. Baltasar could have found her with little enough trouble, and she would have been pleased to tell him all she knows. Ah, Jesu, Will!"

The wrenching pain in her voice propelled Armando to her side. He sank to one knee and cupped her shoulders in his hands, bringing his face close to hers. "Never mind, Gabriella. It doesn't matter how Baltasar found out that Will is a Jew. What matters is that he's safe. No one else knows where Anacaona's clan is. When it's safe, they'll send him north."

"But Armando, the dogs!"

"Hush." He swallowed hard, trying to quiet his own inner fears. "Look, if it'll make you feel better, I'll go after him."

"No. They're sure to be watching the villa. You'd risk leading them to Will." She buried her face in his shoulder and wept. Armando's hand came up to stroke her hair. It had been a long time since he had held her.

"If anything happens to Will," she said, her voice muffled against his shirt, "I don't want to live anymore."

Armando pulled back, looking deep into her tear-filled eyes. "Gabriella," he whispered. "You love him, don't you?"

"*Yes,*" she said with fierce conviction.

The numbness of shock spread through Armando. He barely felt the woman in his arms. "But . . . he's a Jew!"

"He's also the man who rescued me from King Henry, braved the Holy Office to go to Spain with me, held my hand through the agony of giving birth to Phillip, and crossed the Ocean Sea with me."

Armando blinked as if a fog had impeded his vision. "Yes," he said at length. "He gave up everything for you. Jew or not, Will has more than earned your love."

"A hundred times over." She dabbed at her eyes.

"Well," said Armando, feeling oddly thankful, as if a burden had been lifted from his shoulders. "Have you told him?"

"That I love him?"

"Yes, goose!"

"I couldn't. What purpose would it serve?"

Armando slapped his forehead. "People who are in love are so foolish. You should have told him, Gabriella."

"It would only have made him feel awkward." She stared steadily into Armando's eyes. "He can't return my love any more than you can."

Stung, he surged to his feet. "What the hell is that supposed to mean?"

"Don't be angry. We loved each other with our whole hearts, once. But we were so young, Armando, with stardust in our eyes and impossible dreams in our hearts. We've both changed."

"Damn it, Gabriella. You've put Will through years of misery, and all because you didn't want him to feel 'awkward.' "

She clutched at his hand. "Armando, what are you saying?"

"That he worships you, goose. He's always loved you."

"No."

"I believe he fell in love with you about five minutes before I did. You seem to have that effect on men. One look at your face, and we're lost. With Will, that was forever."

"Jesus wept!" She paced the room. "He never said a word."

"He didn't want to create an awkward situation," Armando mimicked. "God, what a waste." A thought struck him. "Baltasar's cousin is fitting out another expedition to La Florida, and Baltasar will go with him this time."

"Are you certain?"

Armando nodded. "If servants' gossip is reliable. His boot boy heard him speaking of it. Once he's out of the way, we'll strike a bargain with the Holy Office. The only thing an inquisitor loves more than saving souls is gold. Las Casas will help us, Gabriella. You have to believe that."

A frantic pounding came at the door. Gabriella gasped. Armando drew his sword and rushed across the patio to the main entrance. Armando called out, "Who's there?"

"It's Joseph."

Armando yanked open the stout wooden gate. Into the room walked Joseph, his face bruised and bloodied, his arms burdened with the limp form of Anacaona.

Will lay in total darkness. He wondered where he was and how long he had been there. He pushed his hand along a hay-strewn floor. Inches in front of his face, he felt a plaster wall. A tactile investigation soon revealed that he was in a tiny cell. Probably the San Juan prison, he concluded. Santo Domingo lacked a formal Holy House for heretics, and so the tribunal of the Inquisition kept their prisoners pent along with runaway slaves, pirates, smugglers, and cutthroats.

Flexing his aching limbs, Will pulled himself to a sitting position. The room stank. He was hungry and thirsty. But worse, he had nothing to do but remember.

He tried to build a melody out of the steady dripping sound from a corner of the cell. But memories rushed at him from the darkness. The horse had borne him swiftly away from his pursuers. He had managed to find the way to Anacaona's village. But he must have left a trail, for within hours of his arrival, the soldiers of Christ had made a sneak attack on the settlement.

Will hissed a breath through his clenched teeth. The mounted and armored Spanish had descended like a storm on the islanders, horses tearing through thatched huts, lances and crossbow bolts piercing bare flesh, arms scooping up fleeing natives and carrying them away.

Will had been surrounded, iron-shod hooves raking the air all around him, swords slashing at his chest. He had surrendered immediately in hopes that the conquerors would abandon their attack on the clan.

But their sick, inhuman lust for blood had whipped them into a fury. Will was haunted by images of severed limbs, entrails spilling out of eviscerated carcasses, women and children mown down as mercilessly as grown men. He remembered seeing a few flee down the mountain, and prayed they had escaped.

Horrible as the slaughter had been, Will had no doubt that the natives had died easier deaths than he would. The officials would question him about Catholic ritual and theology, and his answers would betray his ignorance. He would perish in pain-filled glory, a reluctant martyr to his faith.

Ah, Gabriella, he thought. What adventures we've had. His one regret was that he had lacked the courage and the confidence to tell her that he loved her.

His troubled thoughts followed him into sleep. The sound of approaching footsteps roused him some time later. He pulled himself to a sitting position. A key tumbled a lock with a series of metallic clicks. The glow from a hand-held lamp blinded Will for a moment. A robed cleric and his attendant, a youth, stood to one side while a pair of soldiers grasped Will by the arms and dragged him from the cell.

"You don't waste any time," Will muttered.

"Instruct the prisoner to be quiet," the cleric said.

One of the guards backhanded Will across the face. "Hold your tongue, swine," the soldier ordered.

Will poked his tongue at one of his lower teeth and found it loose. He limped in silence along a low-arched corridor. At the end of the tunnel-like passageway, he passed through an unfurnished room and emerged into an office where a lamp lit the lime-washed walls and cast a glow over a plain desk and chair, a crucifix hanging on the wall behind. Christ had been a Jew, Will found himself thinking. Priests and scholars had murdered him. He had died to take away the sins of the world.

No wonder you weep, Jesus of Nazareth, thought Will, gazing at the melancholy plaster face. The very men who claim to adore you have made it their chief business to torture and murder in your name.

The cleric went to the desk, genuflected before the crucifix, then rose. With his back turned, he said, "Leave us."

"But Your Excellency—"

"I said leave us. And take the boy."

The soldiers and the attendant left and closed the door. The cleric turned and dropped the cowl from his head.

Will gasped. "Fray Barto!"

Las Casas heaved a sigh and lowered himself to the chair, making a steeple of his fingers. "Keep your voice down. They think I'm in here exhorting you to repent."

Las Casas' work on behalf of the natives had worn on him, Will observed. The flesh sagged on a face gone thin, and lines of weariness etched his eyes.

"Baltasar de León has produced evidence that you are a Jew, originally a Chávez of Toledo."

Will saw no point in denying it. "Gabriella and Armando know nothing of my past save the lies I told them."

Las Casas brushed his hand over a stack of papers on

the desk. "That will be irrelevant to the Holy Office. They'll be held responsible for harboring a heretic. If indeed it turns out you are a heretic."

"How can it turn out otherwise?" Will asked bitterly.

"We shall make it so." Fray Barto gave him a serene smile. "I like you, William Blythe. You've been an exemplary planter and citizen of Española."

"Why do you want to help me?"

"Don Armando has convinced me that you're blameless. Now, we have six days before the *calificador* comes from Havana to question you. Six days for you to learn your catechism."

"In six days," said Will, "I could learn the catechism backward. But in six hundred years I'd not be able to convince anyone of my sincerity."

"That's unfortunate. Not only for you, but for your friends as well."

Will thought of Armando and El Hakim. Of Gabriella and Phillip. He loved them like family. More than family. He leaned across the desk. "Let's get started, then."

CHAPTER 21

Pierced by arrow wounds, Anacaona lay on a strange low bed in a Spanish house. The haze of approaching death softened the lines of the ceiling rafters. An opening called a window framed a piece of the sky. The light streamed over the stooped shoulders of her mate.

"Joseph." Her voice rasped like the rustle of leaves.

He sank to his knees beside her. His handsome face, normally bright with happiness, now bore the ravages of suffering. A faint, crescent-shaped scar marred one cheekbone, reminding her that he, too, had once been the prey of Spaniards. "You are awake, my golden flower," he whispered.

"Yes, my beloved," she said. The pain in her breast filled her with icy heat. "But my wounds are mortal."

He squeezed his tormented eyes shut.

"What of our daughter?" she asked.

"I saw her leave the village. I think she escaped." Joseph motioned someone to the bed. "Here's Fray Barto."

Las Casas made a hand sign over her. His magic was weak, for she felt no lessening of the pain that wracked her body. "Honored lady," he said, haltingly speaking the Arawak tongue. "This is a great sorrow to me. I have labored much to stay the hands of the conquerors."

"They come like the tide," she whispered. "No man or god can stop them."

"Dearest lady, my most serene Lord, who is called Christ Jesus, is a gentle savior. If you would like his grace, you have only to unburden your troubles to me, and you will be received unto the kingdom of heaven."

"Are there Spaniards in heaven, Fray Barto?"

"Only the good ones."

Her gaze drifted to Joseph. "Even though they be few, I should not like to go where there is a chance of meeting them."

Las Casas's mouth lifted in a melancholy smile. "I understand. God's blessing on you, honored lady." He rose, and melted back into the soft darkness that crept over the room.

Joseph pressed his lips to her hand. "You're so cold."

"But my heart is warm. You have loved me long and well, my Joseph. We have a beautiful daughter who has the strength to keep herself safe from the invaders. Soon I will pass into another world. But I will never be far from you."

His tears warmed her cold flesh. How could she describe to him the visions rising in her? She saw battles fought and kingdoms surrendered. She saw her people dying, yet they died free, as they had been born. How could she tell Joseph the dark, mystic awareness that came to her, as if in a dream, that another lived to mend his heart, one who had kept his memory alive like a flame shielded from the wind?

"The world no longer belongs to my people," she whispered. "But you, my husband, know another way to fight."

His brows descended to a hurt and angry line. "Would you have me flee to La Florida, then?"

"No. That is for the young and strong. For Paloma, perhaps. But you and *guahiro* Barto—you know how to wage a battle with words. Perhaps the new *cacique* of Spain will listen, and extend his protection to my people. For we have earned it with our blood and toil. . . ." Anacaona coughed and her throat tightened, then closed. The pain held her in a relentless and all-encompassing grip.

Unable to draw breath, she favored Joseph with a last look of adoration. Darkness swirled around her, but at its center gleamed a point of light. Her spirit reached toward it. Joseph's words grew faint and indistinct; she felt herself drawing away from him, away from the pain and joy and exhaustion of a life fully lived. A hot white brilliance pulled her inexorably toward a world of whirlwinds and mysteries. She drifted into a realm where her consciousness joined countless others, where she shared the wisdom and wonder of millennia. Into a place of dreams and remembrances.

Into the light.

"Credo in unum, deum in unum. . . ." Lying in the darkness of his cell, Will paused in his recitation. The words Las Casas had drummed into him emptied from his mind like water through a sieve. In their place he found only the Hebrew prayer his heart would never forget. "*Shema Ysrael* . . . the Lord our God, the Lord is one. . . . That won't do," he muttered. "Damn. I'll never fool the *calificador*."

"You must." Fray Barto stepped through the door, bringing a beeswax candle. "Your life depends on it."

"My life is worth nothing if I turn my back on my faith."

Las Casas slapped Will across the face. "Enough of your martyred arrogance! Such matters are not for you to decide."

Will curled his lip in a parody of a smile. "At last your true nature shows itself," he sneered. "You have as little tolerance as those who will come tomorrow to test my faith."

"I have little tolerance for whining and weakness."

"What kind of a Catholic are you that you're not offended by a Jew?"

"To be offended by a Jew is to be offended by the Lord Jesus," Las Casas retorted. "What offends me is your unwillingness to save your own life—a life granted by the grace of God."

"Aren't you worried about my immortal soul?"

"Señor Blythe, I have seen a pagan woman die whose soul was in a higher state of grace than any dying Christian's."

Will's insides chilled with dread. "Who?" he forced himself to ask. "Oh God, not Paloma."

"Anacaona."

Will pounded the earthen floor with his fist. "Damn! it's all my fault! I led them there. Those butchers—"

"—will pay, if not in this life, then the next. You must believe that I am a Christian whose heart is open to truth and closed to twisted dogma. When I defend the Indians and help men like you, I feel the Lord's pleasure."

Will planted his elbows on his knees and took his head in his hands. "You're a better man than I. And we're neither of us accomplished liars. How will I be able to stop myself from proclaiming my true faith to the inquisitors? Who's to stop me from standing up and saying, I am Guillermo Chávez of Toledo. Your brethren raped my mother and sisters, butchered my father and brothers. I spit on your mission. Who's to stop me from flinging the truth at them?"

"Maybe me," said a soft voice from the doorway. "Maybe I can stop you."

Will bolted to his feet. "Gabriella!" Instinct told him to clasp her to him, to lose himself in the fine essence of her. But shame and fear held him back. Shame at his own disgusting, unwashed condition, and fear that she would dare to come here.

She stepped into the room. Candlelight glinted in her glossy curls and shining eyes. "Have you told him, Fray Barto?"

The friar snorted. "The wretch hasn't given me a chance."

"What?" Will demanded. He started to tremble. A horrible death loomed close now. So close. "Tell me."

Las Casas nodded and Gabriella took a step toward Will. "I have asked Fray Barto to marry us."

Will blinked. Surely he had not heard correctly.

Before he could respond, Gabriella rushed on, "Fray Barto agrees that being wed to a Catholic could help your cause."

Marry Gabriella! Suddenly a decade of dreams crystallized into a shining ornament. Marry Gabriella!

"No," he said. "It's too dangerous. If I'm convicted of heresy, I'll not drag you to the stake with me."

"If you're convicted of heresy," she said fiercely, "I would rather die with you than live without you." She grasped his hands and held tight. "Will, I love you."

Her words were a breath of song through his silent heart. "Do you? Truly? You're not just saying that to—"

She kissed him. The softness of her lips nearly sent him to his knees. "I'm only sorry I waited until now to tell you."

A cautious joy broke through his amazement. "But what about Armando?" he forced himself to ask.

"I'll stand as witness," Armando said, joining them in the cramped cell. "And proudly."

* * *

Miracles do happen after all, thought Will. Twenty-four hours before, he had been a mass of filth and despair. Now, bathed and groomed, a free man once again, he sat in the room he would share with Gabriella.

Settling back on a divan woven from reed palm, he savored the night sounds of birds and crickets. From across the patio came the murmur of voices. Armando, Joseph, and Fray Barto had drunk enough wine to sate a small army. It was a time of both mourning and celebration.

They mourned Anacaona, the warrior woman who had been murdered by the very men she had welcomed so many years before; and yet there was a triumph to celebrate. They had cheated the Holy Office of another victim. Will smiled, recalling the incredulous face of the *calificador* when he had recited the catechism perfectly. Jaws had dropped when Fray Barto had, in the coup de grace, introduced Doña Gabriella as Will's lawful wife. She had stepped into the room looking as saintly as a Madonna, her black lace mantilla and onyx rosary beads so indisputably Catholic that it would have been an act of heresy to question her piety.

His wife. After all these years, she was his wife.

The door opened, then shut with a quiet click. The bedside candle flared briefly on the small gust of wind. Will went to greet his wife. Her face soft and solemn, she extended her hands, and he took them in his. "Is Phillip asleep?" he asked.

"Yes, but it took a long while to settle him down. It's not every day a boy gets a father, Will. He's almost as happy about our marriage as I am." She laughed unsteadily and bit her lip. "This is mad, Will. I've known you since I was a girl of sixteen, yet I'm as nervous as if I had only just met you on the church steps."

"It's not mad, beloved. For I feel the same way."

"What shall we do about it?"

He pulled her close, tilted her chin so he could gaze into her eyes. "I have a few ideas that have been stewing in my mind—and other places—for . . . oh, some ten years."

"Ah, Will, do you now?"

Their lips met in their first private lovers' kiss. A feeling of utter contentment rose through Will. No blaze of passion consumed them, but the banked fires of heart-deep commitment bathed them in a heat that held the glow of eternity.

"You taste sweet, Gabriella," he whispered against her lips. He tugged at the ivory satin ribbon of her robe. The gown fell from her shoulders and pooled around her feet. Underneath the garment she wore nothing but a rose-hued blush.

Will's hands trembled as he brought them up to cup her breasts—a mother's breasts that had once nourished a child. He found the thought shockingly erotic. His caress moved over the inward curve of her waist and the outward flare of her hips.

"Oh, God," said Will. "God . . ."

She pressed her palms over his racing heart. "What is it?"

"You. Just . . . you."

A smile lit her face. "Well, what do you think?"

He leaned down to kiss her neck. Her head fell back as her body arched toward him. "I think," he murmured between kisses, "that I'm going to like being married."

She caught his face between her hands and stared deeply into his eyes. "I mean to make certain of that."

He shed his clothes and brought her to the bed. As they eased down on the cottony mattress, he felt a stab of desire so sharp that it hurt. She reached for him, cradling his head to her breasts and skimming her hands down the length of him. She seemed to sense his urgency; perhaps she even shared it, for she stroked his erection, bringing him home with an impatient lift of her hips and locking her legs around him. He moved within her, and all the years of yearning rushed upon him, consumed him all at once. His body convulsed with passion. She cried out as she received him, and he gathered her close, awestruck and panting and indecently happy.

Many long moments later, she braced her hands on his chest and lifted herself to gaze into his eyes. "Will . . ."

His smile was strained. "I'm sorry, beloved. I was too fast, I—"

"Hush." She pressed her finger to his lips. "You were perfect. You have to believe that."

He relaxed, threading his fingers through her silky hair and kissing her. "Never call me perfect, for that would give me no reason to try again. . . ." His hand slipped upward along her leg. "And again. . . ."

"But you seem so practiced, Will." Suspicion shadowed her eyes. "In fact, it gives me to wonder just how you came to be so skilled at bedding a woman."

"I've done so a thousand times"—he held up a hand to stop her protest—"in my dreams, Gabriella. Only in my dreams."

"You exaggerate, surely. I gave you no time to adjust to the idea of loving me."

He laughed without humor. "No time? It's been more than ten years."

"Has it truly? Armando said so, but—"

"Armando! The shameless busybody. He had no business telling you."

"I thought he was lying."

"I said he was a busybody, not a liar." Will sighed. "The man leaves me no pride. He was right. From the first moment I saw you—no, from the first moment I heard you singing in my shop, I loved you."

"Will! But you said nothing!"

He moved to her side, spreading her tangled hair over

the pillow and bracing himself on one elbow. "I told you a thousand times and more, beloved. But not with words."

She caught her breath, then exhaled slowly. "It's true, isn't it? You risked your life to get me out of England. You were at my side when I gave birth to Phillip. You crossed the Ocean Sea for my sake. Mother Mary, but I've been blind. I didn't want to see. I was so ashamed of who I am. . . ."

"It doesn't matter, Gabriella." He leaned down to kiss her, and his hand slipped up to caress her intimately; she was moist and swollen, and his touch made her shiver. The evidence of her desire shot him through with fiery currents of strength, and this time he pleasured his wife slowly, reveling in the fulfillment of a love that had endured so much time, so many trials.

Much later, as a silver filigree of dawn threaded itself over the horizon, they drifted off to sleep. Just before succumbing to the exhaustion of satiation, Gabriella whispered, "Jesu, but I am blessed! From this moment forward nothing will ever keep us apart."

"My God, it's tearing me to pieces." Pacing the spacious kitchen, Armando dragged a hand through his hair, which was already mussed from his sleepless night.

"What's that?" His expression soft with drowsiness, Will ambled into the room. He paused at the table, a heavy, thick-legged piece hewn from native water oak. He selected a pineapple wedge from a bowl and bit into it, closing his eyes as he savored the juice. When he finished chewing, he looked at the others in the room: Las Casas and El Hakim, and finally Armando again. "Well? Speak up, *amigo*. What's tearing you to pieces?"

Half angry, half amused, Armando let his gaze drift over Will, from his tousled red hair to his bare feet. "I'll tell you once you come back to earth, Señor *Amador*."

"Patience, Infidel," El Hakim said. "A newly married man deserves to float for a while."

"It was that good, was it?" Armando teased.

"I'm a gentleman. I'd never tell." Will devoured the rest of the pineapple wedge, smacked his lips, and began to whistle.

"For a gentleman who's determined not to tell," Las Casas said archly, "you're dropping a lot of hints."

Will struggled to wipe the grin off his face. He turned to Armando. "You look terrible."

Armando sagged into a chair and buried his face in his hands. "I feel terrible."

"About Paloma?"

Armando nodded miserably. "Joseph was certain he saw her escape during the raid. But that was a week ago, Will. If she were truly safe, she would have contacted me—or Joseph—by now. She would have found some way to let her father know she's safe. But we've heard nothing. I've searched nearly every square inch of this cursed island. Every time I fall asleep, I dream that she's been wounded, that she lies bleeding, calling my name, but the closer I get, the fainter her voice becomes."

Armando slapped his palms on the table and stood. "What the hell am I going to do?" He moved to the window to gaze out at the southern slopes of the *encomienda*. The cane grew thick as his wrist and twice his height, and all around the borders of the plantation bloomed a necklace of wild, lush color. The sound of the *ingenio* churned across the acres, and it was the song of prosperity, of riches more precious than gold.

Yet Armando had never felt more like a stranger in his own house.

Because his heart lay elsewhere.

Far in the distance, he saw a fleet of ships in the harbor. It had probably made port some time in the night. Santo Domingo was getting as busy as Seville. The thought oppressed him. Somewhere, some way, he had come to crave the savage isolation of the wilderness. He thought of Santiago, off in La Florida living among the rebel natives. And in his heart Armando envied the hard, wild man who had fathered him.

He was about to turn away from the window when a lone figure appeared in the broad front yard. Joseph limped, favoring his injured leg as he crossed the rope bridge suspended over the cascade. No doubt he had gone to visit the site where he had buried Anacaona in the fashion of her people, her corpse gathered into a fetal position and draped in garlands of herbs and shells.

Joseph had only Paloma now, and Armando was beginning to fear, with a sick feeling in his stomach, that she might be lost to them as well.

"I suppose," he said without enthusiasm, "I should go down to the harbor to see what news came in with the fleet."

"No need," El Hakim said, pointing at the rock-strewn path leading up the mountain to the villa. "The most knowledgeable gossip in Christendom is on his way now."

Like a square-rigger under full sail, Sebastian Cabot arrived, borne on a litter manned by four straining natives. Mantled in a robe of parrot feathers, he looked as regal and imposing as an island *cacique*. When he spied Joseph, his mouth opened in a wide grin of greeting.

They spoke briefly, then started for the house.

"Ah, my great and good friends," Cabot boomed across the patio. He settled his bulk upon a stool topped by a woven mat. The stool creaked from his weight. "Such news from the south!"

Armando stood back, listening to Cabot's account of his exploits. As always, he proclaimed himself the hero of the expedition. And as always, Armando felt a sliver of distrust.

"So the new fleet in the harbor is from the Antilles?" he inquired.

"Aye," said Cabot. "But another was sighted coming through the Mona Passage." He aimed a meaningful glance at Las Casas. "It's from Spain. It should make port tomorrow at dawn. I hope your correspondence has borne fruit."

Fray Barto's eyes narrowed in suspicion. "What do you know of my private correspondence?"

Cabot chuckled into his wine mug. "Private correspondence is a contradiction in terms, my friend."

"What of Juan Ponce de León?" El Hakim inquired.

"He and that slimy cousin of his will set sail from Havana any day now."

Armando smiled with dark satisfaction. Perhaps it would be the last he would see of those two.

"A major *entrada* this time," Cabot went on. "Juan fully intends to establish a colony in La Florida. He's carrying horses, clerics, livestock. Soldiers armed to the teeth."

"He must be very confident of success," Will said.

"Aye, that he is. Seems he managed to capture some natives to serve as guides and interpreters."

A twist of apprehension knotted in Armando's gut. He exchanged a glance with Will. His friend's solemn face mirrored his uncertainty. The color in Joseph's face had drained to an unhealthy shade of gray. The vague sense of foreboding Armando had been feeling all morning exploded into full-blown fear. "Where did he manage to snare these natives?" he forced himself to ask.

Cabot stroked his full beard. "Why, right here on Española. Seems he found a band of renegades, incited them to rebellion, and seized a few under the law of the Requisition."

Armando's decision took shape with the speed of a bolt of lightning. He must go to Havana to investigate the guides Juan and Baltasar had snatched from their mountain hideaway. For he knew with ice-cold certainty that Paloma was among them. His heart urged him to flee now, but reason cautioned him to prepare carefully for a confrontation that was sure to alter the course of his life. He had clung too long to the *encomienda*, had denied too long the yearning in his heart. It was time to shake off the bonds, even if it meant following in the path of his father. He sent Joseph a nod that both understood implicitly.

". . . back to England," Cabot was saying.

Armando snapped to attention. "What's that?"

"I'm sailing back to England. It's said Henry of England has a keen interest in maritime matters, that the strings of his fat purse are far looser than those of his stingy father. I'm interested in this Muscovy venture with— Good God above!" Cabot gaped at the arched doorway at the rear of the patio.

At first Armando thought the visitor was struck by Gabriella's extraordinary beauty. Her loveliness shone brighter than usual today: carnation-pink misted her cheeks, her unbound hair tumbled around her shoulders, and she wore the unmistakable look of a woman well loved.

But within seconds, Armando realized the object of Cabot's fascination was not Gabriella, but the big-boned ten-year-old boy at her side. Golden haired and ruddy cheeked, Phillip smiled easy greetings to the men gathered in the patio.

Cabot lumbered to his feet, his face alight with guarded wonder. He looked from Phillip to El Hakim. "It's all true, then," he said in a half-whisper. "Every word you said."

El Hakim laughed nervously. "Don't be fanciful. The fever made me delirious."

"No, by God, the truth is written on the lad's face. It's like looking into a mirror of the past. He's the very image of his"—Cabot paused to quell his excitement—"aye, the very image."

Phillip stepped forward with his easy, inborn grace. "Do I remind you of someone, sir?"

Cabot drew a long breath. Like an iron portcullis slamming home, blankness shuttered his eyes. "No, lad. For a moment I thought . . ." He waved a thick-fingered hand. "I've been too long at sea. And now, my friends, I must be going."

As he headed out of the patio, he paused to clasp hands with Joseph. "Be sure you meet this Spanish fleet at dawn." He winked at Las Casas. "You're certain to be most interested in her cargo."

Will, Armando, and El Hakim stood on the veranda, watching Cabot depart. The soft, steady trade winds soughed through the thatching of dried *bihao* leaves.

"We ought not to let him go," said El Hakim. The Moor's handsome features, strong and hard as polished ebony, were set in a grim mold. "He knows too much."

"And just how do you propose we stop him?" Armando asked.

El Hakim's hand dropped to the hilt of his ever-present scimitar.

"No," said Will. "You're acting crazy."

"It's a crazy world, William Blythe. Like a spider web that wraps the globe. Each thread interconnected with the others."

"How much do you think he knows?" asked Will.

"You saw his face. Phillip is the very image of Henry the Eighth. But even if he didn't resemble his father so strongly, Cabot would know the truth."

"How?" Will demanded.

"I told him." El Hakim lifted his hands as if to shield himself from the anger of his friends. "It happened when we went to the Antilles. I came down with the island fever, was delirious for days. The sickness plagues me still from time to time, but the first weeks were the worst. When I recovered, some of the seamen teased me about my babblings. It seems I told them the story of my life.''

''Including the truth about Phillip,'' said Armando.

''Aye. Including that, Allah forgive me.'' Determination firmed his mouth. ''I could always murder Cabot.''

''We'd rather you didn't,'' Will said. ''I've just gotten out of trouble.''

''Henry's queen has not conceived since the birth of the Princess Mary. Don't you think the King of England would be interested to learn of his son?''

''So what if he is?'' asked Will. ''He's a thousand leagues away. Cabot's a born liar. Do you think Henry Tudor fool enough to give credence to the claim of a man like Cabot?'' Will clasped El Hakim by the shoulders. ''Gabriella and I are safe here at *Gema del Mar*. We'll keep Phillip safe.''

''You speak with the blind faith of an Infidel.''

''I *am* an Infidel now,'' said Will.

El Hakim glanced at Armando. ''You're very quiet.''

''I have a lot on my mind. I'm giving the *encomienda* to you and Will.''

Will laughed in disbelief. ''For God's sake, why?''

''I'm going to join the expedition of Juan Ponce de León.''

The magic of the islands seemed strongest at dawn. As the small party wended its way down from the villa to the harbor, a screeching chorus of bird song and the chittering of monkeys broke the stillness. The dew lay heavy upon thick, broad leaves, and peach-colored sunlight dappled the path. The scents of loam, orchids, and sea mist perfumed the air.

Armando rode in the fore, his gear and weapons clanking with the motion of his horse. If need be, he would take apart Juan's fleet, timber by timber, to find Paloma.

The harbor city was just awakening as they arrived. The church bell in its wooden tower called the faithful to early mass. Brown-robed clerics, with their heads cowled and their hands hidden in their sleeves, scurried across the dusty plaza.

Armando glanced at Will. He seemed unperturbed by the clerics as he guided his horse close to Gabriella's. The influence of Las Casas would keep them safe from further harassment by the Holy Office, Armando assured himself.

Phillip's handsome face, tanned by the strong island sun, drank in the sights of the harbor area. A king's son. Even at this young age, the lad had an unmistakable presence about him.

A small army of Africans labored at the rope walk, twisting hemp into stout cord as thick as a man's wrist. Native laborers plied canoes between the ships in the harbor and the palm-log warehouses. Sailors still stumbling from their first night of revelry on dry land staggered toward the busy port bake-house.

Las Casas and Joseph brought up the rear. The natives in the plaza stopped their work, touched the ground in a gesture of deference to Fray Barto, who had labored so hard to protect them.

Las Casas jerked his head in the direction of the caravels that had just made port. "Joseph and I are going to greet the new arrivals."

Armando and Joseph dismounted. "I should go to Havana with you," said Joseph.

"No, I could be wrong about Paloma. If I am, she'll need you here."

"You think you're right. That's why you're going."

"True." Armando glanced at Joseph's bandaged leg. "But if she's Juan's captive, you'll serve her better by staying here and regaining your health." Armando clasped his hand. "It's good to be starting a new adventure."

The statement drew a smile from Joseph. "You remind

me of someone I once knew, many years ago. If you chance to meet Santiago again, think about forgiving him.''

Armando shook his head. "He cares only for himself."

"For an intelligent man, you're blind where he's concerned, Armando. I've known Santiago for almost thirty years. I've seen him risk his life for complete strangers. He's given up a personal fortune to live with the people of La Florida."

Armando wanted to believe it. He wanted to believe that Santiago was a man of honor. "I'll give him your regards, then."

"Do that."

"Joseph, are you coming?" Las Casas called.

"Aye." Joseph embraced Armando. "My daughter's a lucky woman."

"Thank you for saying so." Armando hesitated, hearing his pulse in his ears, feeling himself on the verge of a great admission. "I do love her." The words came out in a rush. "I have for a very long time. Probably longer than I realize."

Hope and trust lit Joseph's eyes. "Probably so, my friend. Probably so. Find her. Keep her safe."

Armando went to the governor's house. As always, the Viscaino name earned him official sanction in the form of a patent naming him as a participant on Juan Ponce de León's expedition.

When he came out of the office, Will and El Hakim had already paid his passage, placed his few belongings on a pinnace bound for Havana, and were talking with the ship's purser.

Gabriella approached Armando and took his hands in hers. "They say you'll sail on the tide."

He nodded, then eyed her sparkling eyes and the flush of contentment that rouged her cheeks. "You look radiant."

"Still the flatterer," she teased.

"Not this time. You've always been beautiful, Gabriella. But never as lovely as you are today. Here . . ." He fished in the inner pocket, took out the ruby ring he had won from Henry Tudor, and slipped it on her finger. "I want you to keep this for Phillip. Tell him about it some day."

"Thank you." Her eyes misted, and she hugged him close. There had been a time when her embrace threw him into paroxysms of passion. What he felt now was a quiet sense of rightness.

He laced his fingers with hers, and their palms kissed. "Ah, Gabriella, I can't help but wonder if it could have worked for us."

"Perhaps it might have, if you hadn't seen Paloma at King Henry's court, if you hadn't had to help her, if I hadn't been so stupid where Henry Tudor was concerned." She bit her lip. "If I weren't tainted by my mother's—"

"None of that matters," he said. "We grew up, and we grew apart. For your sake and Will's, it's a good thing we did."

"For Paloma's sake as well," she said. "You love her so."

"Yes." Miserable, he plucked at his red neckcloth. "But she's been . . . damaged in ways she will never speak of, not even to one who loves her." He stared out at the horizon, dazzling with the fire of a new day. "She's not like you, Gabriella. You hide nothing, while Paloma guards her heart like a dark secret."

"Don't you dare give up on her, Armando. Not now."

"Of course not."

He embraced Phillip then, savoring the boyish scent of him, the emerging strength of his body. "Take care of your mama," he said, and Phillip nodded solemnly.

The parallels between their lives were impossible to ignore. Armando prayed the boy would react more wisely than he had when he learned the full truth about himself. A shadow passed over his heart. It was dangerous, having a man like Sebastian Cabot privy to such a volatile truth.

Gabriella raised up on tiptoe to kiss his cheek.

"Unhand my wife," Will said, striding over to them. "Don't you know I'm the jealous type?"

With exaggerated fear, Armando stepped back. "The one time I challenged you, you knocked me flat. I won't risk it again."

"A wise choice," said El Hakim, flashing his sly Saracen's grin. "You're growing up, Infidel. It's about time."

"Time to board, too," said Will.

Armando's throat thickened as he opened his arms to embrace his friends. Will and El Hakim had lived with him, suffered with him, shared his triumphs and tragedies for years. He could not imagine life without them, but he could not imagine staying on Española either.

"I should fit right in with the heathens of La Florida," he said. "I've been living with you two heretics for years."

"We're good for your soul," said Will.

"You are." Armando abandoned all pretense of joking. "By God, you are." He embraced his friends one last time. He accepted their good wishes and words of caution. He let their love flow through him like a warm island breeze.

"Good-bye," he said, moving off to the crowded wharf and lifting his hand high, a final salute.

Just as the ship's boat moved off toward the waiting ship, Armando caught sight of Joseph. He was running to meet another boat, this one filled with passengers from Spain. The years seemed to fall away from Joseph and he moved like a young man, spry and full of life. At first Armando was confused; then he saw the reason for the joy that animated his friend.

Joseph stopped at the edge of the dock and extended his

hand. Within moments, he drew her against him: a slim, black-garbed woman wearing a black veil.

Gratitude and disbelief exploded in Armando's mind. So this was what Las Casas' letters had been about. By some miracle, Doña Antonia had survived the raid on her house. By Fray Barto's intervention, she had voyaged across the Ocean Sea to find the love of her youth. Armando was filled first with wonder, then with a warm sense of completeness.

But as he boarded the swift pinnace bound for Havana, he turned his thoughts to the future. To La Florida, to Paloma. What awaited him there? For him, there was no simple solution, no long-lost love to come rushing into his arms.

Armando had nothing but his quest to find Paloma.

CHAPTER 22

Bay of Carlos, La Florida
April 1521

"Is there truly a Fountain of Youth?" Paloma asked the old woman beside her. Dubbed "La Vieja" by the conquerors, the native woman had been captured in the forest swamp and dragged to the makeshift settlement the Spaniards had erected in La Florida.

The woman stared at the soldiers with hate in her eyes. Animal grease coated her face, hair, and body, and mud and sand obscured her features. "There are many wonders here," she said.

"They wish to hear about a magic spring that makes old men young again," Paloma explained in the Calusa dialect. Before the woman could reply, Paloma added, "Take care, mother, how you answer, for your life and those of all your people depend upon caution."

Juan dangled a string of hawk bells in La Vieja's face. "Tell her she can have these if she cooperates."

Sharp as a blade, rebellion knifed through Paloma. "It's a trap," she muttered. "The white-eyes would have you believe they are gods from the sky. They seek to lure you with their cheap trading truck. Do not trust them.''

La Vieja absorbed the words in stony silence. Filled with sympathy, Paloma did not press for an answer. She, too, despised what the colonists had done to this lush plain between the dense cypress groves and mangrove swamps and the broad, sheltered bay. Juan Ponce de León and his followers had plundered the forests to build a picket stockade. They killed game for sport as often as for food; they burned clearings for fields, which they intended to cultivate by the sweat of captured native slaves.

Deep in her soul, she knew the Spaniards had created a disharmony the gods would never forgive. The intruders had upset the totems that had ruled the elements since the beginning of time.

Looking out at the bay, she eyed the kitchen middens in the shallows. Already the offal reeked. Soon it would be worse, for a work detail had just thrown a dead cow onto the heap. From time to time the fin of a circling shark sliced the water beyond the polluted shallows.

''Ask her again,'' said a voice. ''I'm waiting.''

With dull eyes, Paloma stared at her captor, Juan Ponce de León. His men had seized her once before, all those years ago on Cayo Moa. Then, she had been a girl who had dared to hope for deliverance. Now she was a woman whose last hope lay chained in the brig of the flagship anchored out in the bay.

A wind rustled through the palisades built of palmetto logs. Juan glared at Paloma. ''I want your word, you heathen wench. Your word that you'll wrest the truth from La Vieja.''

Paloma tossed her head. The breeze plucked at the skirt and blouse the conquerors had put on her. ''And if I don't?''

''Then your lover dies.''

She fought a reaction. To show emotion now would be

to give Juan even more power over her. A sense of futility seized her. She could promise great rewards to La Vieja. She could tell the silent old woman that the Spaniards meant no harm, that they wished only to live in peace with the natives. And then, if Juan were a man of his word, he would set Armando free.

But Juan Ponce de León was not a man of his word.

No matter how adroitly she followed his orders, he would find no magic water. He would one day kill Armando, and probably her as well.

"I'm waiting," Juan prompted again. Dressed in a crimson doublet and parrot-green hose, he stood with his feet planted wide, the sunlight glinting off his helm. Behind him rose the crude, lean-to that housed his water samples. For the past few days he had sent men out to draw water from streams and pools in the hope that one of them contained the youth-giving elixir.

"Don't keep my good cousin waiting." His handsome face pulled into a sneer, Baltasar swaggered up beside Juan.

His evil presence firmed the decision in Paloma's mind. If she and Armando were to die, then let it be for the sake of freedom. She glared up at Juan. "You promise to set Armando free if I obey you?"

Juan fingered his beard. "Have I not said so?"

"Do you swear on the cross of the Christ god?"

Baltasar drew back his hand to strike her, but Juan pushed him away. "Not now," he muttered. "She's the last interpreter we've got." He sent Paloma a haughty smile. "I so swear."

She lowered her eyes, pretending meek acquiescence.

Juan exhaled in obvious relief. Some of the other captives from Española had been beaten to death during the voyage, or had died of Spanish pestilence. Others had flung themselves overboard, only to be shot while trying to swim to freedom. One woman, raped until she bled between the legs, had seized a Spaniard's dagger and plunged it into her heart.

Paloma had been tempted to commit the ultimate act of rebellion, too. But they had left her alone, needing her language skills more than her body. She shuddered, recalling the terrifying voyage and Armando's foolish attempt to rescue her. A lombard shot from a pinnace had halted the fleet midway between Havana and La Florida. To her shock and joy, Armando had boarded the flagship, planted himself in front of Captain General De León, and demanded a post on the voyage.

With his typical imprudent gallantry, he had expected Juan to honor the patent from the governor.

With his customary lack of scruples, Juan had clapped Armando in irons, thrown him in the brig, and continued the voyage.

So long as Armando was in de León's power, Paloma could not seek escape in suicide. There was another matter, too, that gave her the will to live. It was nothing so honorable as protecting the man she loved. It was the desire for revenge against Baltasar de León.

Years earlier, Juan had taken her freedom, stolen her from her family, and sold her into a life of degradation.

But Baltasar had been party to stealing something even more precious and inviolable than her freedom. He had taken a part of herself. She wanted to live to avenge that horror.

These dark thoughts passed like a storm through her mind, undetected by the conquerors who stood waiting for her reply. She fixed Juan with a bland stare. "What is your will, Master?"

Flanked by Juan and Baltasar, and backed by a column of armored soldiers, Paloma followed La Vieja out of the settlement. The dense forest seemed empty; the presence of the conquerors had hushed the screeching birds and scattered the deer.

The unnatural stillness fooled no one. Paloma sensed, as keenly as if she could see them, the hidden host of warriors.

Not yet, she thought, repeating the words like a litany in her mind. *Not yet.* She and La Vieja had made a plan. Using the lure of the magic fountain, they would lead the Spaniards away from the settlement. Native warriors, watching from concealment, would cut off the path of retreat to the ships anchored in the broad, glistening bay.

When they had gone a hundred paces, La Vieja stopped and pointed to the north. "The pool is one bow-shot away from here."

Paloma translated for the Spaniards. Juan gave the order to advance. Their eyes were hard with excitement as they drew their swords and hacked a path through the undergrowth. Vines and bushes gave way to slender reeds. The soldier in the vanguard gave a shout. Paloma and La Vieja were pushed along to the edge of a green pool. She stood beside the old woman, her bare feet sunk into thick warm mud.

"Is this the water that restores youth?" she asked, translating Juan's demand.

"It is a sacred place," La Vieja replied.

Paloma related the answer. The Spaniards crossed themselves. A few sank to their knees. But Baltasar looked cautious and skeptical. "What can be sacred to a heathen? I think it's a trap. Look at all these footprints."

He stabbed the shaft of his halberd into a heel mark pressed into the loamy earth. Paloma suppressed a grimace. The ancient believer inside her still clung to clan lore. The Old Ones taught that to defile a man's footprint was to pierce his heart.

"This footprint is as fresh as this morning's dung," Baltasar stated. "The place is crawling with savages."

Juan Ponce de León seemed not to hear. He snapped his fingers. His page came trotting over with a large stoneware ewer. With a conquistador's arrogant confidence, Juan scooped water from the pool.

Rather than a fountain of legend, the pond seemed ordinary, brackish water fed by a weak trickle from the deep woods on the opposite side. A thin green scum marbled the unmoving surface.

Juan drank from the ewer, the water splashing down over his cuirass and soaking his beard. He made a face and choked. "Awful stuff," he declared, "but . . ." His eyes glittered. "Sweet Virgin Mary," he whispered, clutching at his throat. "I do believe I feel a change."

His ringing announcement propelled the soldiers into action. "We've found it!" a man cried. "The Fount of Eden!" A score of soldiers fell to their knees at the banks of the pool, sucking greedily at the green water. Others waded in and immersed themselves.

Paloma's mouth went dry. She had seen a stirring in the bushes, a flash of movement behind the huge, twisted knee of a cypress. She and La Vieja exchanged a glance. The old woman's eyes sent a silent message: Time to flee.

She hesitated, thinking of Armando still chained in the ship's hold. "You go, mother," she whispered. "Save yourself."

La Vieja started to edge away. A strong arm with leather gauntlets laced to it shot out and captured her by the hair. "Not so fast, Vieja," snapped Baltasar. His furious tone caught the attention of the soldiers in the pool.

"It's a lie," he screamed, aiming a glare at his kinsman. "Look at you, still gray and grizzled. This water holds no magic, only putrid sewage." While the soldiers muttered in reluctant agreement, Baltasar dragged the old woman to the pool. He thrust her head into the water and held it there, screaming, "You may not get any younger, mother, but by God, I'll see to it that you never get any older!''

La Vieja struggled feebly. Green bubbles streamed up from her submerged head. A lightning bolt of rage streaked through Paloma. She rushed forward. A pair of soldiers grasped her by the arms and held her back. She screamed from the pit of her belly, summoning all the fury and hatred that the years had built in her. Baltasar's insane anger only spent itself when La Vieja went limp. Juan waded out to him and grasped him by the shoulder. ''Have you gone mad? Look, you've killed her.''

Baltasar swore, dragged the body out of the water, and laid La Vieja on her back. The screams in Paloma's throat died, and silence crept like the tide over the watching men. La Vieja lay death-still and astonishingly beautiful. Perhaps, thought Paloma, the beauty had always lain beneath the grease and grime on the woman's face and hair. Perhaps Baltasar's dunking had cleansed her to reveal the loveliness beneath. Or perhaps . . .

Out of the green shadows, out of the heavy, awestruck silence, came a humming sound like a swarm of bees. A mounted Spaniard gave a strangled cry and dropped from his horse. A foot soldier stared in shock at the greenwood arrow protruding from his belly; then he fell like a large tree. A horse screamed and reared, raking the air with its front hooves, an arrow, still quivering, had pierced its neck.

''Ambush!'' Baltasar bellowed.

''Sound a retreat!'' Juan yelled.

The drummer beat frantically; then he fell silent. The deadly rain of arrows thickened.

Even in mortal terror, Paloma felt an acute sense of relief. At last the day of reckoning was upon the Spaniards. In the panic of soldiers and horses, she ducked her head and started deeper into the forest.

Gauntleted fingers sank into her hair. A strong arm

hauled her back. "Not so fast," Baltasar hissed in her ear. His crested morion helmet gave his words a hollow sound. "Bitch! This is your fault! Your lover will pay for your lies."

He held her like a shield in front of him and dragged her back to the settlement while soldiers rushed past, frantically seeking safety. Just at the gate, a painted warrior leaped out. Howling, he drove a spear toward them.

Paloma braced herself for the attack. To die now would be a blessing. At the last instant, another warrior appeared out of the bushes to deflect the black-tipped spear.

The move gave Baltasar time to yank Paloma inside the gate. She caught a glimpse of the warrior as he fled into the woods. He had a swatch of red tied about his head, black hair streaming out behind him, and a circle of gold in one ear.

Santiago.

She had no time to ponder the revelation. In a high fury, Baltasar dragged her across the sandy surface of the plaza. Tiny sharp burrs pierced the soles of her feet. Baltasar hauled her aboard a yawl and ordered a crew of lackeys to row them out to the flagship. Below decks, he shoved her into a room and slammed the bolt home.

Paloma blinked into the dimness. Even as she struggled to regain her breath, she sensed a presence. When at last she found her voice, she said, "Armando?"

He cradled her against his chest. He was on fire with unanswered questions, but he burned, too, with the need to hold her.

In his shipboard prison, he had kept his strength and his sanity by pacing as far as his chains would allow, hoisting himself up and down from a rafter until the sinews in his arms had the tensile strength of iron. With one ankle shackled and bolted to a low beam, he felt like a caged lion, his power coiled tightly and ready to spring at the first whiff of freedom.

But his captors had been vigilant. Armando's only sight of La Florida was a small circle of light glimpsed through a high portal.

"I'm sorry, *chica*," he murmured to Paloma, stroking her hair. "I've failed you."

"It doesn't matter." Her voice was flat. "It will be over soon anyway."

"What happened? An ambush?"

"Yes. I saw only three Spaniards go down. We were still too close to the settlement. We—"

"You?" In fear and anger, he tightened his hold on her, and his heart exulted at the feel of her precious form in his arms.

"Yes. I was forced to interpret for a . . . woman they captured. Baltasar killed her." She shuddered with pain. "I might have been killed, too, but . . ." She drew back. Shadows haunted her thin face. "Santiago saved me."

A host of emotions stormed Armando's soul: relief, resentment, admiration, chagrin. All jumbled by the confusion he always felt with regard to his wild gypsy father.

"So he's still alive." Armando's voice broke.

"Yes. He is a great warrior, but the attack seemed ill planned. The Spaniards will be more vigilant than ever now."

He sighed against her temple. She didn't pull away from him, didn't protest his embrace. Was it only death, he wondered, that made her welcome his comforting arms? Was it the promise of life, no matter how short, that made her cling to him?

"What's the settlement like?" he asked.

"It's fortified. There is an escape route by sea."

He drew a long, slow breath. She, too, needed answers. Painful as it was, he must tell her all.

"My darling," he whispered, "I have news from Española."

She stiffened in his arms. "My mother is dead, isn't she?"

Waves thumped hollowly against the ship's hull and the cables creaked against their moorings, punctuating the silence. At last Armando said, "Yes. Ah Paloma, I'm so sorry."

Her hands curled into fists, tugging at the fabric of his shirt. "She is of the faith of the Old Ones, Armando. To us, death is simply . . . another kind of life." Her voice faltered when she continued. "When I was captured as a child, I used to cry for her. When we were reunited, she told me the Spaniards had ripped out a part of her by taking me away. And now they've taken her."

He pulled her against his shoulder and rested his chin atop her hair. She smelled of wind and water and freedom, the fragrance so welcome after his weeks in this moldering cell.

"Your mother is at peace, Paloma."

"What of my father?"

"Joseph came to *Gema del Mar*. His leg was injured, but he'll recover." Hoping to cheer her, he added, "Listen, *chica*, Fray Barto worked a miracle. He found Doña Antonia and arranged for her to voyage to Santo Domingo."

She stared at him, her eyes pools of wonder in the dimness. "Doña Antonia? Truly?"

"Yes. She will never replace your mother in Joseph's heart, but I think she can heal him, Paloma."

For the first time, a smile glimmered about her mouth, but quickly faded when she asked, "Was Will taken in the raid?"

"Yes, but Fray Barto prepared him well for the questioning, and the ecclesiastical court pardoned him."

She nodded thoughtfully. "It is no small thing, winning a pardon from the Holy Office."

"Will had plenty of help. Not just from Fray Barto, but from his wife."

She gasped. "His wife!"

Armando smiled, remembering the bittersweet day. "Gabriella. She married him on the eve of his trial."

Paloma rubbed her forehead, as though the gesture would help her assimilate all the news.

"They love each other very much," he told her.

"And you're not . . . You don't mind?"

He framed her face with his hands. "My darling, I stood witness for them, and I was happy to do it."

Savoring her surprise, and the gentle pressure of her hands on his shoulders, he went on to tell her about El Hakim and Cabot, confessing his fears about Phillip. When he finished, she took his hand. The high portal turned orange with the gathering of evening. "And what of you, Armando?"

He felt as if he were standing on the edge of a crumbling cliff, much as he had felt the day he had gone to tell her people about the first voyage to La Florida. But that time, he had let pride stand in the way of his decision. "I am changed," he said, tugging at the shackle on his ankle. "There was a time when I thought that to turn my back on the plantation would be to lose myself, to become wandering and rootless like Santiago." Leaning forward, he kissed her hair. "But perhaps to be adrift is my destiny, Paloma. And perhaps it is not such a bad thing."

Her smile gave him a glimpse of the child she had been before the Spaniards, before the English, before her people had been forced from their home. He saw pride and elation, maturity and acceptance and love for him. But at the same time, an immeasurable sadness haunted her eyes. "Juan and Baltasar have used you, Armando, to govern my behavior. But after today . . ." She bit her lip. "I fear I have betrayed you."

"No, Paloma, never—"

Footsteps sounded in the companionway outside the bunk.

Armando stood, fists balled and feet planted, the leg iron grating on his ankle. He had not dared to oppose his jailers before, fearing they would harm Paloma. But now he had her at his side. The tensed energy he had suppressed for weeks would find an outlet at last.

The door swung open to reveal four ax-headed pikes and a pair of pitch torches. Framed by the bearers of the weapons, Baltasar de León gave a haughty toss of his head. "We've come a long way together, eh, *amigo*? Who would have thought, when we were lads in the *Casa de Contratación*, that I would live to see you executed for treason?" He shook his head in mocking wonderment. "And over the same wench who started it all."

Armando felt his insides turn to stone. "Treason? You have no evidence of that."

Baltasar nudged his companions. "Do we need evidence here, alone, in La Florida?" His malevolent gaze darted to Paloma. "As for you, my pretty whore. . . ." Using his teeth, he untied the leather laces of his gauntlets.

Cursing, Armando surged forward. The axes made a descent toward him, and he stopped short of having his chest riven. His chains scraped on the floor. "She's innocent, you bastard!"

Baltasar tossed his head. "She's treacherous and needs to prove her worth . . . again." He dropped his gloves and loosened his breeches.

"No!" Armando screamed, but Baltasar only laughed. His engorged member sprang free and he advanced on Paloma, who had shrunk against the far, curved bulkhead. He flung her down, yanking her skirt to her waist.

Armando nearly maimed himself in an effort to escape; the shackle cut deeply into his ankle. He wasted a futile moment exhorting the guards to stop Baltasar, but behind their iron helms they stayed silent, obviously smug in the belief that Paloma was an animal to be used at man's pleasure.

Armando struggled helplessly as Baltasar knelt with his knees splayed on either side of Paloma. "Look your fill," Baltasar said over his shoulder. "She's as submissive as a bride on her wedding night. She wants me."

To Armando's horror and astonishment, he saw that it was true. Paloma lay unmoving, her face turned to one side, her eyes as blank as stones. How could she accept this degradation? Why didn't she burn with the need to survive? Understanding hammered at him. This was how she had endured during her years of captivity. Silent stillness was her only defense, her temporary escape.

Baltasar reached down to spread her legs. The rage swelled and seethed in Armando's head. It was a madness—hot, unreasoning, wholly bestial. He tried to communicate his fury to Paloma. "Fight him, damn you!" he screamed. "Fight him!"

She blinked. For a moment he thought her withdrawal so complete that she misunderstood. Then her eyes cleared, the sun breaking through banked storm clouds. And burning bright at the heart of her gaze was the same rage Armando felt.

She came to life with a feral snarl and a blur of movement, so swiftly that not even Baltasar saw the attack coming. She used her knee as a battering ram, slamming it into his groin not once, but again and again, pounding at his exposed parts. Even Armando winced as he heard the thin sound of agony that gusted from Baltasar. The men-at-arms moved quickly, but not before Paloma's hammering knee had melted Baltasar to the floor of the cell. The soldiers dragged her to her feet, and she stood glaring

down at her attacker, her eyes burning with hatred and
triumph. Never had she looked so alive to Armando, so
strong.

Baltasar retched, too weak to lift his head out of his
own vomit. One of his companions helped him up. His
face looked like a death mask, and blood smeared his
groin. He had only enough strength to raise his hand at
Paloma. "You . . . filthy, fucking bitch. You'll join your
lover on the scaffold. And you'll never . . . ever . . . learn
the fate of that brat you birthed."

The soldiers helped him out into the companionway,
and the door slammed shut. Paloma stood immobile,
hardly breathing. Rays from the setting sun streamed
through the portal. The rich light limned her tall form and
heightened her wild, pagan beauty. She seemed a statue,
cast in bronze.

"Come here," Armando whispered. His voice seemed
to stir her to life, and she sank to his side. He pulled her
against him, then drew her down to the mat of old sailcloth
that served as his bed. "My God," he said in a shaking
voice. "You fought and won."

"I didn't know I could," she said in amazement. "I
used to wonder if, when he slept, he dreamed of murder
the same way I dreamed of dying." She tucked her head
against his shoulder. He sat listening to the sound of her
breathing and thinking dark thoughts about what Baltasar
had said, and what the dawn would bring.

The scene kept coming back to him—Paloma, lying in
bleak acceptance, Baltasar towering over her. . . . And
then his words, those last, confusing words: *You'll never
. . . ever . . . learn the fate of that brat you birthed.*

The strange statement brought to mind something he
had often heard Paloma cry out in her sleep: *It's mine!
Don't take it away!* Always in Spanish, always ripped from
her like raw silk torn from a body. The nightmare was all
part of the mystery that haunted her.

Suddenly the idea of dying before he knew her secret filled Armando with despair. If his death was to have any meaning at all, he must know the full truth about the woman he loved.

"Paloma. Beloved, please talk to me." He shook her gently.

She brushed the hair from her eyes. "I don't want to talk."

He shook her again, less gently. "Damn it, Paloma, I wish I had a hundred more years to spend with you, but we have only hours, maybe less. Though even if I had ten times that long, I still would never know you."

"What can it matter now, Armando?"

"It does. Paloma, I want to know the answer to something before I die."

She stared at the floor. "I have no answers for you, Armando."

He took her face between his hands and forced her to look at him. "You do, damn it! All these years you've been hiding something from me. I think it's the reason you never let me love you."

Her warm tears rolled over his shaking fingers. He leaned forward to kiss her damp face. The salty taste burned his tongue with bitterness. "Ah, please. Talk to me."

Somehow, his soft plea unleashed a storm. Her tears flowed like a river undammed, hot and copious. She did not weep prettily, but with a raw pain that was older and deeper than the scars on his back. "They—they . . ."

"Who, Paloma?"

"The Duke of Albuquerque and—and Baltasar and . . . others."

"They raped you. My love, I know that. If I could take away your pain, I would."

"They . . . and many others," she continued. "Priests and diplomats. Men from C-Constantinople . . ."

"Hush. It's over now. It's been over for years. They're bastards. They'll rot in hell."

"It's *not* over! I can never be free of what happened." She drew in a shaky breath. Her eyes were windows of heart-deep sorrow. He braced himself for her grief. "Armando, when I was in Naples, I . . . I . . ."

"What? Paloma, please!"

"I had a baby."

So he had guessed correctly. But when she said the words, shock rolled through him in a wave, cresting in a bellow of agony. "Oh my God! Christ Jesus, a baby!" He struggled to control his emotions. He hugged her fiercely. "My poor darling. My God, to carry this burden all these years."

Her shoulders trembled. "I saw its face, all wrinkled and red. It gave a tiny cry and I reached out, I begged them, but Baltasar was there, and a midwife who had dirty, callused hands. . . ." She sobbed out the rest. "I gave my father's silver charm to the midwife, begged her to keep it in trust for the baby so perhaps one day he . . . she . . ."

More sobs wracked her body. Her breath caught sharply, and she turned her gaze to the circle of light in the portal. "I don't even know whether I have a son or a daughter— or if my baby lived."

The complete, cold-blooded cruelty of it raked Armando with steel talons. So this was why she flinched at a man's touch, why she had never been able to open her heart to him.

"You were afraid to love me, weren't you?"

"I was afraid to show it. I have loved you for many years."

Despite the hopelessness of their situation, joy bloomed in Armando's heart. "Ah, *chica*. Such a waste."

"I was afraid to conceive. It was foolish, but I was

haunted by the idea that if I had another baby, I'd lose it, too.''

Shaken to his core, Armando lowered his mouth to hers. He kissed her tenderly, so filled with love and pity that tears ran down his face and mingled with hers. ''I wish I'd known, Paloma. If we survive, we'll find your child.''

''Do you think we could?''

''Anything is possible. I'm not so arrogant as to think I could have healed you. But I love you so much. I have to believe my love would have made a difference.'' A thought struck him. Santiago—his father—was alive. To hell with the rivalry between them. ''Paloma,'' he began, ''maybe we could—''

''My, my, what a tender scene.'' Baltasar de León yanked the door open. He leaned on an oar, using it for a crutch. His ever-present bodyguards loomed behind him. His face was still the color of ash, and he moved with painful slowness, but his eyes glittered with malice. ''A pity to interrupt such moving theatrics, but it's time for you to die.''

Armando's hatred for Baltasar rose like a shooting star, increasing a hundredfold in strength and intensity. This man, blithely announcing their execution, had snatched a newborn babe from an innocent woman's arms.

With a roar like that of the sleek, well-fed lion he had become, Armando lunged. The chains jerked him back, but Baltasar stood close enough to reach. Armando's hands tore at the handsome, sneering face. He would have ripped Baltasar's heart from his chest had not a half dozen guards descended on him.

He felt a tearing sensation in his shoulders, a sharp pain as a gauntleted hand struck his temple. Blackness engulfed him. Sometime later he felt himself being lifted, then landing in a heap in a ship's boat. He was brought ashore, dragged across the compound, and tied by his hands on a rough timber scaffold. He heard Paloma screaming, saw the blur of her midnight hair as she was bound at the opposite side of the scaffold. Their feet rested on fat logs, which would be kicked out from under them by the executioners.

With his voice as biting and cold as a winter storm, Juan Ponce de León snapped out a series of orders. Two sergeants at arms came forward and fitted nooses around the necks of Armando and Paloma. The chaplain muttered a prayer for their souls. The soldiers, alert and heavily armed, gathered round to watch.

Armando cursed at the top of his lungs. "Murderers! You violate the law."

"My word is law," said Juan. He fixed his executioners with a commanding glare. "Ready."

The cold eyes of their captors glared at Armando and Paloma. In the tense pause of silence before the final order was given, Armando became aware of noises beyond the palisade—the rustle and thump of creatures in a foreign land he would never know. He turned his head toward his beloved. She did the same, and their gazes met and caressed across the distance.

"I love you, *chica*. So much."

"I know, Armando. You are in my heart, so you will never be far from me on this . . . journey of ours."

The priest's chanting prayers came to an end. Armando gave one last hopeless, adoring look at Paloma and braced himself for the fall. The sergeant's booted foot pressed on the log.

At the same instant, the stockade fence seemed to move with a life of its own. Some of the pickets separated, then toppled forward. High-pitched yips mingled with the thunder of gunfire. An army of painted warriors poured over the wall and through the gaps. The soldiers scrambled for their weapons.

Armando whipped a glance at Paloma, screaming her

name as he viewed her through a blur of color and movement.

The impact of the native warriors' assault on the palisade had knocked pickets onto the scaffold. Slowly, slowly, the structure toppled. The soft palmetto logs splintered. Paloma was able to free herself from the rough ropes that bound her hands. In seconds she was at Armando's side, yanking with all her might to free him, too, for he was still bound to the one pole that remained standing. She pulled off the noose and set to work on the stout rope securing his wrists.

In a rational part of his mind he understood that there was no time. Already, Juan Ponce de León was shouting orders. Columns of soldiers formed up to battle the attacking natives. Even as Paloma yanked, sobbing, at the ropes, Armando saw three helmed Spaniards racing toward them with pikes extended.

"Paloma, run!" Armando begged.

"No. I won't leave you."

"The way's clear to the harbor. Take one of the canoes—"

"We're going together."

With a chill, he recognized Baltasar among the three soldiers.

"God damn it, Paloma," he screamed. *"Think of the child!"*

Her face drained of color. She planted a swift kiss on his mouth. Her hair flying, she dashed for the waterfront. A pack of howling natives intercepted the three Spaniards.

With no time to savor his relief, Armando gave a jerk on his bonds. The coarse hemp cut into his wrists, but held him fast. Memories bolted like lightning across his mind. He thought of the youth he had been, the carnival trickster, the prodigal son, the island planter, the lover of a woman he would die for.

Not far away, natives and Spaniards fought and killed

and died. The first colony of La Florida resembled a knacker's yard. Spanish and native blood spilled and mingled in the earth. A feeling of helplessness rose through him. He was witnessing the demise of the enterprise in bondage rather than in battle. He swore and strained, even caught himself praying.

Out of the crowd burst Baltasar de León, a steel-tipped pike aimed squarely at Armando's chest.

He redoubled his efforts, yanking until his wrists bled. Still limping from his injury, Baltasar bore down, twenty paces distant, then ten. . . .

A low, strangled cry of hatred, so venomous that not even the clamor of battle could mask it, came to Armando. He imagined the hot pierce of the steel tip, the slam of it into his breastbone and then his heart. He had no time for prayers or pleas. Fighting the bonds was futile now. He planted his feet on the ground and flung up his head.

He heard Baltasar breathing hard behind the helm. He heard the thud of his feet. He saw the lethal tip of the pike driving at his chest. . . .

"Aiiiee!" A blood-stirring cry broke the moment. A painted and feathered shape flung itself in front of Armando.

Baltasar gave a cry of pain, then vanished as other native warriors descended on him. Astonished, Armando found himself staring into a paint-streaked and sweating face.

"Father?" The word slipped from him on a wave of astonishment.

One corner of Santiago's mouth tipped up. "It's good to hear you call me father." He stumbled, put out his hand to steady himself against the upright stake, then slithered to the ground.

Protruding from Santiago's stomach was the gory tip of Baltasar's pike. The steel tip had pierced him from behind, the instant it should have struck Armando.

Rage proved stronger than fear when it came to freeing himself from his bonds. With a bellow of fury, he yanked free. Spongy palmetto wood erupted around him. Momentum sent him stumbling forward. He fell to his knees beside Santiago, who now lay on his side, staved through like a harpooned fish.

"God damn you!" Armando screamed, clumsily gathering Santiago in his arms, smoothing the long hair back from his clammy brow. "God damn you! Why did you do it? Why did you throw yourself in front of me?"

Santiago's mouth twisted in an attempt at wry humor. Flecks of red dotted his lips. "A gypsy never answers questions on his deathbed."

"It was foolish. You've killed yourself."

"To save you. My son."

Armando threw back his head and howled in frustration. "Don't die," he begged, ignoring the sting of tears on his face. "Don't you dare die before I forgive you."

Santiago coughed. "Then you'd best be about it quickly, *hombre*. I think I'm running out of time."

Armando broke down, covered the handsome face with kisses. "Father, I love you. All I did in my life was for you. I thought it was to surpass you, but it was to honor you. You made me strive to be my best. All I ever wanted was to be like you."

"Don't be like me, *hombre*. Be better."

"There is no better man. I should have told you years ago."

"Tell Cat . . . alina. Tell your mother I love her. Always loved her. Always."

"I will. I'll write it in a letter. But I think she knows, Father. She's always known."

The battle had sunk to mindless slaughter by the natives. They went about stripping corpses, chasing terrified Spaniards down to the sea. The air pulsed with a hatred as tangible as the reek of blood and spilled entrails. It was the stink of the natives' fury against men who had come to enslave them; it was the bloody glory of their fight for freedom. Juan Ponce de León was carried past on a litter. A poisoned arrow protruded from his thigh.

"No magic water for that bastard," Santiago said. His voice had become faint and airy. His chest rattled with each breath he took. "Better wear my headdress," he said. "Don't want the Calusas to mistake you for a Spaniard."

With shaking hands, Armando took the red scarf and tied it, pirate fashion, over his head. "God damn it. God damn it, I'll miss you."

"Don't miss me. *Vaya con Dios, hombre.*" Santiago's eyes turned to the sky. The rushing clouds were reflected in the blank stare.

"No, oh, please God. . . ." Armando kissed the still-warm lips of his father. As he reached to close the unseeing eyes, a feminine scream drifted across the water. Armando's head snapped up. Paloma stood in a wildly rocking boat in the shallows of the bay. She was struggling with Baltasar de León.

"Paloma!" Armando shot to his feet. "My God . . ." He snatched up what weapons he could as he raced toward the water. He managed to find only a few broken arrows. A small canoe bobbed in the water. He leaped into it and dug in the oar. The canoe shot into the bay. He fixed his gaze on the struggling pair in the other boat. By now it had drifted past the offal from the settlement, the rank heap topped by the rotting carcass of a cow. Like a cloud of smoke, a swarm of flies hovered over it. In the deeper water beyond the sandbar, the blade-thin, silvery fin of a shark flashed in the dark waters.

Baltasar and Paloma seemed locked in a lovers' embrace. Her fists beat against his armored back. His gauntleted hands encircled her throat.

Armando paddled swiftly to them. With a bellow of soul-deep rage, he leaped aboard the boat. The vessel lurched. Baltasar relinquished his hold on Paloma and spun around to face Armando.

He plunged his dagger forward. Armando almost toppled from the boat. Paloma stumbled, hands outstretched for Baltasar's arm. He knocked her overboard, into the shark-infested waters. She surfaced instantly, arms treading with sure strength.

Armando screamed her name. Baltasar came at him again. His dagger slashing, he backed Armando against the stern. "I've waited a long time for this moment," he said.

The blade arced toward Armando's throat. He felt a hot spurt of blood, watched it spray Baltasar's face. Baltasar cried out, dragged his hard glove across his blood-spattered eyes.

Armando's fists clanged against Baltasar's helm. Armando thrust forward with one of the broken arrows, piercing Baltasar at the jointure between his gorget and breastplate.

"The child," he said between his teeth. "Tell me what you did with Paloma's child."

Baltasar's scream became a hiss. "S . . . s . . . ss . . ."

"Speak up, you bastard," Armando ordered.

"S . . . Sold into slavery," Baltasar ground out. "Mercy . . ." But even as he begged, he brought his hand up. The dagger flashed in the sunlight.

Armando buried the second arrow in Baltasar's neck. He shoved hard. Baltasar toppled backward into the water.

Armando leaned out, extending his hand to Paloma. Streaming seawater, she struggled into the boat and clung to his shoulders.

"You're hurt."

Armando touched his throat. "Not too badly."

"There's so much blood."

"I'll be fine."

They sank together into the boat. Already, the caravels

swarmed with activity as they made ready to leave. A flotilla of war çanoes surrounded them. Cannon fire spattered the sea, and arrows flew into the rigging.

Armando grasped the oars. One of them seemed caught on something. He pulled hard. Paloma screamed.

Like a nightmare, Baltasar burst out of the water, clinging to the oar. He sucked in a breath of air. His face contorted with agony and hatred. Blood streamed from his neck. One arm was a mass of gore, the flesh shredded by sharp, hungry teeth.

Paloma gasped, then placed her bare foot on his breastplate and shoved him back into the water. Within seconds, the frenzied sharks surrounded Baltasar's thrashing form. His screams of agony subsided to gurgles, and finally to silence blanketed by a froth of bloodied foam.

Armando picked up the oars and began rowing.

Evening closed over the abandoned settlement. Armando and Paloma sat in a clearing by the beach. They were drinking *sofki*, mashed corn boiled in water that the natives had given them. It tasted like freedom.

The rise of a sand dune obscured the ruined colony; they could see only threads of smoke drifting from the burned-out huts. A string of horses grazed placidly some distance away, and a stray pig snuffled in the underbrush.

A long row of rocks covered the body of Armando's father.

''I think,'' said Armando, drawing Paloma against his chest, ''the Spaniards have found a land they cannot conquer.''

''For now, at least.''

He glanced at the pile of rubble, the monument to a man who had embraced life with courage and passion, a man who had laughed in the face of death.

Armando's heart ached for Santiago. And yet, with his grief came a sense of peace. Santiago had taught him hard, taught him well. His death had been the best and hardest lesson of all.

Native war drums throbbed in the distance. "They destroyed the first Spanish colony," he said, thinking aloud, "and gained a reputation for savagery. My countrymen will long remember this carnage. Perhaps now, others will be loath to come."

Paloma looked at the receding fleet, black shapes perched on the bloodred horizon. "There are no more of your people here."

"You're here, beloved."

She drew back, and her gaze probed his face. "It's not too late to catch up to them. You could take a canoe."

"No." He kissed her hair, breathing in her fragrance of salt water, wildflowers, and womanly mystery. His certainty grew and swelled inside him. He was a bird . . . like her. "My future is here, Paloma, and I welcome it. Blood and war and pain and joy. And adventure such as no man has ever seen before. A kingdom of gold. It's all out there, waiting for us." She lifted her face to his, and a feeling of tranquility drifted over him. "Just waiting."

BESTSELLERS
FROM TOR

☐ ☐	50570-0	ALL ABOUT WOMEN Andrew M. Greeley	$4.95 Canada $5.95
☐ ☐	58341-8 58342-6	ANGEL FIRE Andrew M. Greeley	$4.95 Canada $5.95
☐ ☐	52725-9 52726-7	BLACK WIND F. Paul Wilson	$4.95 Canada $5.95
☐ ☐	51392-4	LONG RIDE HOME W. Michael Gear	$4.95 Canada $5.95
☐ ☐	50350-3	OKTOBER Stephen Gallagher	$4.95 Canada $5.95
☐ ☐	50857-2	THE RANSOM OF BLACK STEALTH One Dean Ing	$5.95 Canada $6.95
☐ ☐	50088-1	SAND IN THE WIND Kathleen O'Neal Gear	$4.50 Canada $5.50
☐ ☐	51878-0	SANDMAN Linda Crockett	$4.95 Canada $5.95
☐ ☐	50214-0 50215-9	THE SCHOLARS OF NIGHT John M. Ford	$4.95 Canada $5.95
☐ ☐	51826-8	TENDER PREY Julia Grice	$4.95 Canada $5.95
☐ ☐	52188-4	TIME AND CHANCE Alan Brennert	$4.95 Canada $5.95

Buy them at your local bookstore or use this handy coupon:
Clip and mail this page with your order.

Publishers Book and Audio Mailing Service
P.O. Box 120159, Staten Island, NY 10312-0004

Please send me the book(s) I have checked above. I am enclosing $ _____
(please add $1.25 for the first book, and $.25 for each additional book to cover postage and handling.
Send check or money order only—no CODs).

Name _____
Address _____
City _____ State/Zip _____
Please allow six weeks for delivery. Prices subject to change without notice.

BESTSELLERS BY
CAROLE NELSON DOUGLAS

☐ ☐	53596-0	COUNTERPROBE	$3.95 Canada $4.95
☐ ☐	51430-0	GOOD NIGHT, MR. HOLMES *forthcoming*	$4.99 Canada $5.99
☐ ☐	50046-6	HEIR OF RENGARTH Sword and Circlet 2	$4.50 Canada $5.50
☐ ☐	53594-4	KEEPERS OF EDANVANT Sword and Circlet 1	$3.95 Canada $4.95
☐ ☐	53587-1	PROBE	$ 3.50 Canada $ 4.50
☐ ☐	50324-4	SEVEN OF SWORDS Sword and Circlet 3	$4.95 Canada $5.95